PR

'*Ghostbusters* meets *Stranger Things* in Oppel's perceptive supernatural thriller . . . Blending frights, mystery elements, and a tender relationship, the story conjures considerable tension and a deep sense of place as it overlays Canadian history and the paranormal atop a feverish plot'

'A spooktacular story that's surprising. ful'
Kirkus Reviews

'A ghost story like no other . . . masterful storytelling'
Clare Povey, author

'Pacey and thrilling, with one of the best
opening chapters I have ever read'
The Bookseller

'Creepy, cool and disturbing, love it'
Lucas Maxwell, School Librarian of the Year

'This book has everything . . . action, friendship,
innocent first love (boy meets ghost), mystery solving,
sense of place and a spine tingling ghost story!'
View from the Bookshelves blog

'A truly terrifying, clever and brilliantly
written supernatural adventure'
Kevin Cobane, *VIP Reading* blog

GHOSTLIGHT

KENNETH OPPEL

GUPPY BOOKS

GHOSTLIGHT
is a GUPPY BOOK

First published in the UK in 2022 by
Guppy Books,
Bracken Hill,
Cotswold Road,
Oxford OX2 9JG

Text copyright © Firewing Productions Inc.
Map art copyright © 2022 by Fred van Deelen

First published in the US in 2022

978 1 913101 763

1 3 5 7 9 10 8 6 4 2

Papers used by Guppy Books are from well-managed
forests and other responsible sources.

MIX
Paper from
responsible sources
FSC® C171272

GUPPY PUBLISHING LTD Reg. No. 11565833

A CIP catalogue record for this book is available from the British Library.

Typeset by Falcon Oast Graphic Art Ltd
Printed and bound in Great Britain by CPI Books Ltd

For Philippa

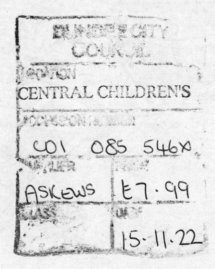

St. Michael's Hospital

N
S

Necropolis

GARDINER EXPY

Centreville Amusement Park

Algonquin Island

Island Café

Ward's Island

Filtration Plant

Lakeshore Avenue

Yuri's Maintenance Shed

TORONTO ISLANDS

1

Rebecca Strand was sixteen the first time she saw her father kill a ghost.

She was woken by a hand on her shoulder, and opened her eyes to Papa's face, flickering in the glow of his lantern. He held out her shawl and said, "Get up. I need your help."

Her first thought was: *At last!*

Immediately she leapt from the warmth of her bed and listened for the weather. No rain lashed against her window. No wind howled. She fastened the woollen shawl around her nightdress.

"Is a ship in trouble?" she asked.

"We need to hurry."

She followed him downstairs and outside. In the calm sky glowed a full moon and stars sharp as gemstones. Not even a hint of mist hovered over the lake. It was hard to imagine a ship foundering on such a night.

Still, boats ran aground on the island's sandy shoals all the time. Jutting from its beaches were the broken ribs of old, wrecked hulls. Many times over the years, her parents had helped drag survivors ashore and into the shelter of their home. But her mother had died of fever two years ago, and last month her older brother, Bernard, had ventured off to Kingston to apprentice as a stonemason. It was just her and her father now, so maybe, finally, she'd have a chance to prove herself.

But as her eyes swept the smooth water, she saw nothing amiss. Her father headed straight for the lighthouse. For a second she wondered if something was wrong with the lamp itself – had it gone out? – but then the beam swung around, cutting its white path through the night.

"Papa? What's wrong?"

At the huge red door of the lighthouse, he turned the iron clasp and entered. Stepping inside, Rebecca shivered. Even though it was summer, cold radiated from the thick stone. Her father was already vaulting up the spiral stairs, and she hurried after him.

The hot, thrilling whiff of lamp oil hit her as she climbed up inside the lamp room. Atop its stout iron column, the blazing beacon turned, sending its beam through the high windows. The Gibraltar Point Lighthouse was the tallest of all the lake lights, rising from the western point of the island that sheltered Toronto's harbour. Across the water were the glimmering lights of the city, home now to almost thirty thousand souls.

Her father hung his lantern from a hook and immediately took up his spyglass. He opened the door and ducked outside onto the narrow catwalk that encircled the lamp room. Rebecca followed.

"I had a warning from the Niagara Light," Papa said, scanning the water to the south.

Rebecca looked across the vast sweep of Lake Ontario. From this height, you might sometimes see the spray rising from the falls. And on clear nights like this, you could often catch the pale flicker of the Niagara Light on the American shore.

"What kind of warning?" She'd never known lighthouses signalled one another; but this was exactly the sort of thing she'd been hoping Papa would teach her one day. Now maybe with her brother Bernard gone—

"Something's coming."

Her skin prickled. The way her father said it, she knew he didn't mean bad weather. Papa lowered his spyglass and turned to her. He was a solemn man by nature, but she had never known him to look so grave.

"Tonight must be the night you learn."

Joy instantly overwhelmed any nervousness. "I'm ready! Papa, I want to know everything!"

She'd been born on this sandy crescent of an island, and her whole life, her father had been keeper of the Gibraltar Point Light. Even though she'd never been permitted to help – that privilege had always gone to Bernard – she was sometimes allowed to watch them tend the lamp. She knew how to replenish the whale oil and trim the wick; she understood the ingenious pulleys and gears that made the beacon revolve. The lighthouse itself felt like a vital gear in her own life. Just as the sun rose each morning, each night the lighthouse beam swept across her curtained window, every two minutes. It was as fine a lullaby and guardian as any child could ask for. For as long as she could remember, she'd wanted to be a keeper.

"You may not thank me," Papa said, "for the things I'm going to tell you."

On the catwalk, she had a powerful premonition that her life was about to change forever.

"You know that I tend the light, to warn ships away from the shoals," her father said, "to guide them into safe harbour. But there's more."

Abruptly, as if he'd heard something, he turned. Following the beacon's beam, he lifted his spyglass to his eye. He did not hold the rail to steady himself, but stood with his legs wide, like a sailor balanced on the prow of a ship, awaiting a storm – or worse.

"What do you see?" Rebecca demanded.

"Quicker than I thought," he muttered. He held the spyglass out to Rebecca. "Look."

Her hands shook as she brought it to her eye.

"Do you see?" he asked.

All she beheld was silvered water, glinting in the moonlight. Then the lighthouse beam picked out something bobbing on the surface. At first Rebecca thought it was a piece of timber washed out from the mill. Her stomach clenched.

"A body!"

Then the lighthouse beam had passed, and all she saw was dark water.

"Where did it go?" She shifted the spyglass to and fro, with no luck.

"Wait for the light to return," said her father.

When the beam swept past once more, the body reappeared. It was facedown in the water. A sodden blouse; long, weed-matted hair. An arm weakly churned the water.

"She's alive!" Rebecca cried, looking away from the spyglass. Her father had already rushed back inside the lamp room. She hurried after him. "Papa, we need to get the boat!"

She didn't understand why he wasn't sounding the alarm, or bolting to the beach. The poor woman had obviously been washed overboard, or her ship had foundered. "Papa?"

From around his neck, he slipped off the tarnished lighthouse pendant he always wore. He inserted it like a key into the sturdy iron column that supported the lamp. Rebecca heard the sound of metal pieces clicking into place. Suddenly the lamp stopped revolving. From the sides of the column two iron handles shot out with a clang. Gripping them, Papa swivelled the beacon, directing the beam as he wished.

"I never knew you could do that!" Rebecca exclaimed.

"Go outside, find her," her father instructed.

Bewildered, she returned to the catwalk. Lifting the spyglass, she found the woman. Maybe Papa wanted to focus more light on her before the rescue. Both the woman's arms were paddling feebly, though her face was still submerged.

"Is the light bright upon her?" Papa called from the lamp room.

"Yes! But she's so weak—"

"Watch now!"

The woman lifted her head clear of the water and revealed her face. All the breath rushed out of Rebecca's body. It was like no face she'd ever beheld, the terrible eyes filled with such malice. The light was bright on the woman's face, and her eyes shut tight, and her tattered hands lifted as if warding off an attack. Holes began to open in her flesh.

"The light's killing her!" Rebecca cried.

"She's already dead," her father replied.

As it disintegrated, the body sank. Rebecca sucked air back into her lungs, then turned to her father, who'd come outside to stand with her. "What was that?"

"A ghost."

He said it like any other word. A chair. A cat. A house. She caught herself shaking her head no, but her brain could not think of any reasonable explanation for what she'd just seen – or hadn't seen.

"I couldn't see it at first," she said, remembering. "Not until the beam passed over it."

"Yes. The brightness of our lamp reveals ghosts."

She stared at the beacon in astonishment. All her life she'd thought it was just a simple lamp – a powerful one, yes, but that was all.

"And it . . . melts them?" she asked.

"Sends them where they are meant to be, be it Heaven or Hell."

Rebecca touched her hand to her chest. "It made me feel like I couldn't breathe."

"Some are terrifying to behold. It's part of their power."

Questions pelted her brain. Through her bewilderment, she felt a sting of indignation. "Mother always said there were no ghosts! You did too!"

"I lied," Papa said, taking the spyglass and scanning the bay. "To keep the secret of our Order."

"*Order?*" Rebecca said.

"We don't have much time." He handed back the spyglass and returned to the lamp room. "She's not the only one."

She hurried after him. "There's more?"

"I'll need your help, Rebecca. My vision is not what it once was."

This, she knew, was true. Despite his spectacles, he squinted, even to see things close at hand. He complained sometimes of headaches.

"You must be my eyes tonight, Rebecca," he told her. "Can I trust you?"

"You can trust me."

"Can you be quick?"

"I have always been quick, Papa."

Her legs were trembling, but she drew strength from her father, tall and steady as the lighthouse itself. If he could withstand the oncoming storm, so could she.

From the base of the beacon's column, her father flipped down a hinged metal plate so that it lay flat against the floor. He stepped onto it and slipped his shoes into two thick leather straps.

"What're you doing now?" Rebecca asked.

She got her answer soon enough. With an upward twitch of Papa's right foot against the strap, the entire lamp column telescoped up, lifting her father with it so his head almost touched the ceiling. With a twitch of Papa's left foot, the column lowered a touch. Using the iron handles, he swivelled the beam to and fro, taking aim with this strange spectral cannon.

"The angle of attack is superior up here," he said.

"Do all lighthouses do this?" Rebecca asked.

"I've made some modifications." He squinted into the night. "Now, go be my eyes!"

She hesitated and startled herself by asking, "Does this mean I get to be keeper?"

"Are you bargaining with me?" he demanded, looking at her sternly but, she thought, also with a new respect.

"If I can do this, will you let me?"

"After tonight, you may not want to. Now go!"

Rebecca ran outside to the catwalk and scanned the water with the spyglass. In the beam's light, a shape suddenly materialized. Her heart clenched.

"There!" she cried, and her father halted the beam. "Back to the south! Yes!"

The light now fully upon it, the ghost raised its terrible head, and Rebecca was certain she could hear a shriek from its fathomless mouth. Under the glare of the lamplight, the ghost flailed and quickly dissolved.

"Gone . . . it's gone!" she said over her shoulder. But her

relief was short-lived. As the beam made another sweep off the point, she gasped at the sight of three bloated shapes, churning the water.

"Near the mouth of the harbour!"

"They're heading for the city," her father barked, aiming the lamp.

Rebecca shuddered at the idea of these things crawling ashore.

"West!" she shouted back to her father, and then, "A little to the southeast," and when that ghost had dissolved, "To the northwest . . . that's the last of them!" She leaned, spent, against the doorway. "Is this what you do every night?"

Her father's eyes crinkled in a quick smile. "Not every night, no."

Rebecca thought of all the people of Toronto, sleeping in their beds, oblivious. Until tonight, she'd been one of them. Blissfully ignorant that the night contained such terrors.

"What do they want?" she asked. "These ghosts."

"They're filled with anger," Papa said, sweeping the light back and forth across the harbour. "Some died with hatred smouldering in their hearts, some are furious they're no longer living. These wish us harm. Keep your eyes on the water, Rebecca. We are not yet finished."

With a shudder, she returned her gaze to the harbour and its entrance. Burned into her mind's eye was the tortured and cruel face of that first ghost she'd spied.

"Are all ghosts so vicious?"

"No. Most are peaceful; some are lonely, and confused. Others have things to set right before they can properly rest. But they're not dangerous."

"But these other ones, you said they can harm us?" Of course she'd heard ghost stories, but she had a feeling they were all about to be proved wrong.

"They are weak for the most part. They can barely shift dust. But over time some become stronger. Maybe they can turn the page of a book, or blow out a candle. Maybe knock a burning ember from an oven, and burn down a city." He squinted. "Where is he?"

"Who?" she demanded. He swung the beam hard, away from the city, out to the open lake.

"Look to the south, Rebecca!"

She ran around the gallery to follow his beam, lifted the spyglass to her eye. "Papa!" she yelled.

It was not a single body, but a monstrosity made of many. Arms and legs jutted crookedly at all angles, and the creature scuttled over the water like a terrible water beetle. It was headed not for the city this time, but the island – and the lighthouse.

"It's coming straight at us!" she cried.

The beam seared a hole in the ghost's carapace, and the creature skittered away.

For the first time in her life, Rebecca heard her father curse. "The others were just a distraction. Be my eyes, Rebecca!"

"To the west!" she cried. "Back two yards!"

But every time she shouted directions, the ghost darted away from the light.

"Angle it down more!" she called out.

"It won't go much lower!"

"It's almost ashore!" Terror welded her feet to the catwalk. With her free hand she clutched the railing, as though bracing for a tidal wave.

As the ghost scrambled onto the beach like a vast human centipede, her father impaled it with the beam.

"It's huge!" Rebecca gasped. Though it had many limbs, it had but one head, with a man's face. His furious corkscrew eyes seemed to suck the very moonlight into them, like water down a bottomless drain. The ghost's many limbs writhed, trying to break free from the light that had spiked it to the sand.

"Is he melting?" her father shouted.

"No!"

"He's too strong. We can't hold him for long!"

Even as he said the words, Rebecca saw the creature slowly ripping itself away from the beam of light.

"He's getting loose! How do we kill him?"

When she glanced back at her father, he was removing a small bundled object from a hidden compartment in the beacon's column. As he unwrapped it, Rebecca's breath snagged. It was a circular lens of beautiful amber glass. Deftly, her father slipped it into a wire frame mounted directly in front of the lamp.

The effect was instant and startling. The beam disappeared, because all the lamp's light was trapped behind the amber lens. Like water behind a dam. The strange lens glowed, brighter and brighter still. When it was almost too intense to behold, an amber beam shot from it, out through the window, down to the beach, where it struck the ghost like a lightning bolt.

In an eruption of fireworks, the vile creature was cut in two. Both halves writhed like overturned beetles as they were cut smaller still by the searing amber beam.

"To the right!" Rebecca directed her father. "There's a little bit trying to get away!"

Melting, the last remains of the ghost disappeared into the sand and water.

"They're gone!" she said, turning to her father.

"Be certain, Rebecca!"

"Yes, yes, there's nothing left!"

Her wobbly legs carried her back into the heat of the lamp room, and she sank to the floor. Numbly she watched as Papa swept the beam back and forth, examining the beach one last time. Then he lowered the beacon to its normal height. He stepped off the metal platform and snapped it back into position against the column. The iron handles were pushed into slots that quickly and creakily concealed themselves. Then, with a cloth, her father removed the mysterious amber lens, steaming, from its wire frame.

"What is that?" she asked.

"It's called a ghostlight." He examined it closely before returning it to its secret compartment. "It's glass, but specially worked to strengthen the beam's power."

"For the really big ghosts?" Rebecca said.

Her father chuckled. "Precisely. Only the Order's master glass-blowers can make them. And they are very rare."

He set the beacon revolving in its usual clockwork fashion: a normal white beam from a normal lamp, sweeping reassuringly over lake and land. Rebecca started shivering so hard that her teeth chattered. All the shock of the last hour came crashing over her at once. She wrapped her arms around herself. Her father sat beside her and she leaned into him, pressing her cheek against his wool jacket with its comforting smell of pipe tobacco.

She inhaled slowly, trying to keep her thoughts from splintering into too many questions. One at a time. "So. You're part of a secret order that destroys ghosts?"

"The Keepers protect the harbours, the cities, the coastlines of the world – and have done so since the Lighthouse of Alexandria."

She pulled back to look at him in amazement. "The Pharos?" she exclaimed. An engraving of that ancient Greek lighthouse hung in her bedroom. "That was over two thousand years ago!"

"We stand guard over the night, to protect the living from the wakeful and wicked dead."

The wakeful and wicked dead. These were words to build a nightmare from. "Do they all come from the sea?" she asked.

"No. They come from anywhere people have died. From a cemetery. A hospital. A palace. We see an abundance upon the sea just because so many people travel by ship." Papa paused. "This is a great deal to hear all at once."

"No, I want to know everything! That last ghost, you called it he."

"He was once a man called Nicholas Viker, and he'd become very strong indeed."

"Why did he have so many limbs?"

"He contained many ghosts. He devoured them to make himself powerful."

Horrified, she looked at her father. "Like a cannibal?"

"Precisely so. He enslaved them inside himself, and stole their vital energy."

"Those poor people!"

"But when the ghostlight struck Viker, did you see how coloured lights exploded from him? Those were the souls he'd consumed, finally released."

"And the ghostlight did that? Freed them?"

"Yes. Before tonight, I had only heard accounts of it."

Rebecca's mind still churned with questions. "Why did Viker come straight for the lighthouse?"

"He wanted to quench our light, the one thing that can stop him. The Order's been watching him for some time, not just because of his strength, but because of his diabolical plan."

"What plan?"

Her father's smile was rare, and all the more wonderful for it. "We'll discuss that another time. Viker's gone now. We have vanquished him, you and I."

Rebecca grinned and felt her body start to relax. "Does this mean I passed the test?"

"It was a mighty test," her father agreed.

She wasted no time pressing her advantage. "So you'll let me be a—"

"I will train you, yes. You will become my apprentice. I hope that is acceptable to my impatient daughter."

She said nothing for a moment, she was so happy. "Thank you, Papa. Do I get one of these?" She pointed at the lighthouse pendant, which he was about to put back around his neck.

He raised a craggy eyebrow at her. "You will get one if and when you become a Keeper."

"I never knew it was a key. May I?"

He let her hold it. Despite its tarnished state, it was beautiful in its simplicity: a tapered rectangular column topped by a beacon of silver flame. Impulsively she slipped it around her neck, just to feel its weight.

"It's the symbol of our Order," Papa said, "and with the key you can—"

Her father skidded away from her across the floor, as though dragged by his ankle. "Papa!"

"He's inside, Rebecca!"

She lunged and gripped her father's arm, but the ghostly force was stronger, and Papa was pulled closer to the gallery door.

As the lamp revolved, its beam suddenly revealed the outline of a crooked creature with arms that looked like they'd been snapped and rejoined to form long, jagged limbs. One of them clutched Papa's ankle. The creature lifted its head, and Rebecca recognized the terrible corkscrew eyes. How had he survived? Then the beam passed, and he disappeared.

"Viker, you fiend!" her father roared. He dug a hand into his pocket, then flung a handful of iron filings at the ghost. With a hiss and the stench of singed hair, the filings somehow coated the terrible creature as he writhed in pain. Papa broke free and scrambled to his feet.

"Rebecca, the key!"

She rushed to her father's side at the beacon. "There!" he told her, pointing at the small keyhole.

Crouching, she inserted the end of the pendant, and turned.

The iron handles snapped out and Papa grabbed them and wheeled the lamp around – but Viker was gone. Before her father could sweep the room, he was snapped off his feet, as if he were no heavier than a puppet. He sailed through the doorway to land hard on the catwalk.

"Strike him, Rebecca!" he croaked.

Rebecca grabbed the handles tightly and swung the lamp until the beam found Viker in the doorway.

"Let go of my father!"

The ghost whirled, ablaze in the lamplight, and his eyes widened, drinking in the light, sucking it down and down – and Rebecca had to drag her gaze away, because she could imagine herself spilling into those eyes and never surfacing.

With a sickening hop, Viker was balanced on the railing like a gargoyle. He was much smaller than he had been – and surely weaker – but still he had the strength to grab Papa's ankle with a freakishly long arm and haul him into the air.

Rebecca aimed the beam right at the ghost's face, but he didn't shield himself with his arms. His mouth curled up in a jagged grin, filling almost his entire face. He swung her father out over the railing.

The normal lamp beam wasn't working fast enough. She needed the ghostlight. Her hands fluttered over the pedestal, searching for the secret panel. Her father must have sensed what she was doing, for he cried out:

"No, Rebecca!"

She ignored him. How else could she save him? Her fingers found the catch and opened the compartment.

"Rebecca, do not let him see it!"

She pulled out the ghostlight. The cloth fell away. In that second, Viker's head turned, and Rebecca felt his entire being locked onto the dazzling piece of amber glass. As she fumbled it into the wire flame, one of Viker's long arms shot toward her with its splintered fingers.

The ghostlight blazed. Its amber beam struck Viker full on, blasting him off the railing, still clutching Rebecca's father. But somehow the ghost, with that long, long arm, and its splintered fingers, still managed to pull the ghostlight loose—

As Viker tumbled through the air, though, the amber lens spun free of his fingers and disappeared into the darkness.

Rebecca burst out onto the gallery. Far below, in the moonlight, she made out her father's broken body.

"Oh," she said. "I'm sorry, I'm sorry!"

The beam from the lamp shone around her as she sobbed against the railing. Too late, she saw the crooked hand that lurked near her foot like some terrible crab. It closed around her ankle. A searing cold crackled through her leg, making her cry out.

Then, with a whiplike motion, the dead hand flung her into the night.

2

"Rebecca Strand's body was found right beside her father's," Gabe told his tour group, "in the exact same spot where you're standing right now."

A girl with a rainbow popsicle took a step to the side and looked at her shoe, like she'd just stepped in dog poop. Her father patted her shoulder reassuringly.

"Some people think they must've slipped off the catwalk," Gabe continued, "maybe when they were doing repairs. But their bodies were too far from the lighthouse – they would've had to be pushed. Or *thrown*. By someone – or some*thing* very strong."

He added that last bit, to make the story scarier.

This was a *ghost* tour, after all. And frankly, it was a little stingy on the ghosts, in Gabe's opinion.

"The mystery was never solved," he went on. "But since that fateful night in 1839, some people say they can see the lamp flickering, and the shadow of Rebecca Strand on the catwalk."

Totally made up, but how could he not say it?

"So you're saying it's haunted?" asked a young boy, his eyes narrowed suspiciously.

"Absolutely."

Gabe checked over his small audience. It was the last tour of the day. There was a mom and dad with Popsicle Girl and a toddler in a stroller. There was the suspicious kid with his texting mom, who needed more sunscreen on her pale arms. And there was a girl with wavy shoulder-length hair, about Gabe's age, who'd been listening intently through the whole thing. She had black-rimmed glasses that made her look studious. She hadn't said peep, but he felt like she was mentally taking notes.

When Gabe had applied for a summer job at Island Amusements, he'd been hoping to do rides. The Ferris wheel or the Scrambler or the bumper cars. But Karl, the manager, had seen a different future for him. The Island Ghost Tour was new this year, and Karl had decided Gabe was the person to do it. Gabe partly blamed his mother. He hadn't wanted to put his history prize on his résumé. But Mom said to include it, because it was an achievement.

So now, he gave the Ghost Tour.

His best friend, Yuri, got to work in the maintenance shed and take care of the bumper cars and other rides, while Gabe tramped around the island in the blazing sun, reciting the lame script they gave him – with some improvements of his own to keep him from slipping into a coma.

"So we get to go inside, right?" the boy asked angrily.

"Chut-neeeeeey," the texting mom said mildly, without looking up. "Was that the politest way to ask?"

"This is so boring!" the boy hissed, like no one could hear.

"You certainly do get to go inside," Gabe said.

Over the summer he'd had lots of time to practice his pleasant expression, which came in especially handy when there were little brats called Chutney around.

"Why did they build it so far back from the water?" the dad asked him.

"Oh, they didn't. It used to be right on the lakefront, but over two hundred years, the sandbars built up, so now it's actually a hundred metres from the shore."

You couldn't even see the beach through the trees anymore. The Gibraltar Point Lighthouse stood tall in its little clearing. Even after all his visits, Gabe had to admit it was a fine-looking thing.

"So how high is it?" the dad asked.

It was always the dads who wanted to know the stats.

"Twenty-five metres – about eighty feet," Gabe added, in case anyone on the tour was American.

"Not even that tall," Chutney sneered.

"Maybe not," Gabe said, "but—"

"There's way taller ones. I've seen them."

"Chut-neeeey," his other mom said in a singsong voice. "Do you want to lose Smarties points?"

The kid's shoulders sagged and Gabe almost, *almost,* felt sorry for him. The kid's hair was plastered to his face. It was hot, and he'd been dragged around for over an hour, when he'd rather be on the log flume ride. Frankly, *Gabe* would rather be on the log ride.

"I don't even like Smarties," the kid muttered.

"Well," said Gabe. "Believe it or not, in 1808 when the Gibraltar

Point Lighthouse was built, it was the tallest building in Toronto – and stayed that way for the next fifty years. And it was a good thing, too, because the harbour was notoriously hard to get into safely. The entrance was really narrow and shallow. They had to dredge it out all the time, because ships kept running aground. In the old days there were wrecks everywhere."

"Is that what they're digging up over there?" the dad asked.

Gabe nodded. "Just down on Blockhouse Bay, yeah. Some workers found old ship beams when they were digging, and now a team of archaeologists from U of T is excavating."

"Do they know what the ship is?"

"Not yet," said Gabe. From time to time he ran into one of the archaeologists at the Island Cafe, and he'd ask her how the dig was going. He said, "Likely the ship was caught in a storm and wrecked, with all hands lost."

He didn't know if this was true, but it felt right to throw it in. *All hands lost.* He liked old nautical sayings. He liked old things in general. History was his favourite subject, and he honestly did like learning about the history of the island, and giving the tours – as long as he could make little things up, to keep it interesting.

Right now, mostly what he was thinking about was the hamburger he was going to eat after work. He'd only had time for a slice of pizza for lunch, and the breakfast panini he'd made for himself seemed like a long time ago. It had been exceptional, though, with avocado, and cremini mushrooms, and goat's milk Brie, and bacon – cooked just right, not too bendy, not too brittle.

"So let's go inside," Gabe said, "and I can tell you about the haunting of the Gibraltar Point Lighthouse."

From his pocket he removed the heavy key, unlocked the tall red door and pulled it wide. Cold air tumbled over him. Sighing gratefully, he stepped inside. It was always cool in here, no matter how hot and humid it got outside.

"Mind your step," he said, flipping on the light switch and inviting everyone into the small space. He backed up to the steep staircase. Inside the lighthouse, he always felt like he'd left the world behind. The windowless walls were so thick that all outside sounds disappeared the moment you crossed the threshold. No birds, no planes landing at the Island Airport, or kids yelling from their bikes, or outboard engines from Blockhouse Bay. Even the air felt different. Older somehow. The group became more attentive.

"Huh. No signal in here," the texting mom said, looking up.

"The walls are a metre thick," Gabe told her.

"I wouldn't live here," Popsicle Girl whispered to her dad.

The girl with glasses laughed. She had a nice tinkly laugh that made Gabe think of wind chimes.

"Well, the keeper didn't actually live inside," Gabe said. "They had a house right next door. It was demolished ages ago."

"So what's so haunted about this place?" Chutney asked challengingly. "It doesn't look haunted to me."

"After Rebecca Strand and her father died," Gabe began, "there were many other keepers. Over the years, some of them reported hearing footsteps on the stairs in the middle of the night. Some thought it could only be the ghost of Keeper Strand – or Rebecca Strand – coming back to tend the lamp. Even now, some people claim that if you listen very carefully, you can hear those footsteps."

No one said anything, and he knew they were all holding their breaths, listening.

As if cooperating, something somewhere in the lighthouse creaked.

"Oooooh," said Chutney's mom, smiling at her son, but there was concern furrowing her forehead. Maybe this was too scary, Gabe thought.

"Then there's the fourth step," he added.

"What about it?" asked the boy too loudly.

Gabe turned to face the spiral stairs. "One of the keepers claimed that if you put your hands on the fourth step, you felt a weird tingle. Right . . . here!"

This was Gabe's favourite part, when he got to smack his hands down on the stone.

Chutney said, "You're making this up!"

He was, actually.

"I want to try," the boy said, looking fiercely at his mom.

"OK, sweetie, you go right ahead."

"Sure," Gabe said, "right here."

He'd read somewhere that if you told someone to concentrate on any part of their body, they often reported a kind of tingling. He made way for Chutney, who had to stretch to reach the fourth step.

"I don't feel anything," he said, frowning.

"That's OK. Not everyone can feel it."

The mom chuckled, and Chutney glared at her. "'Cause it's not real!"

"I've never felt it either," Gabe said reassuringly. He didn't want the kid to have a meltdown. "Maybe we just don't have good ghost sense."

"I do, though!" the kid said sullenly, and then his eyes widened and he gave a little gasp. "I feel something!"

Gabe felt an icy creeping down his neck.

"It's like electricity in my fingers!"

"Really?" Gabe asked.

"It's moving up my arms!"

Then Chutney snuck a sidelong glance at him, smirked, and walked away.

"You believed me!" he crowed. A few people chuckled, and Gabe wondered if they'd been taken in too. He couldn't believe he'd been fooled so easily.

"Do we get to go all the way up?" Chutney asked.

"Unfortunately, no, it's off-limits."

"Lame," grumbled Chutney.

"Chutney," said his mom, "let's remember to use our nice words."

"Who took over from Keeper Strand?" the teenage girl asked him, speaking for the first time.

"Mr Debenham. He was keeper for twenty-five years, and then his wife took over for another thirteen. And then their son took over for another twenty or so. It seems being a lighthouse keeper sort of runs in families."

"Thanks," the girl said.

"And that, ladies and gentlemen," Gabe said, rattling off his script, "concludes our Island Ghost Tour. Thanks so much for joining me, and please enjoy the rest of your day on the island. Don't forget that your tickets get you a ten percent discount at Centreville Amusement Park. It's open until eight o'clock!"

"Yay! It's OVER!" Chutney hollered, and bolted outside.

His mother pressed a ten-dollar tip into Gabe's hand and murmured "Thank you" before leaving.

As he was locking the red door, a voice behind him said, "I've been on a lot of ghost tours, but yours was right up there."

He turned to see the girl in the serious glasses. "Oh, thanks."

He wondered if she was one of those people who wanted to tell him about her own ghost experiences. It happened sometimes, and always made him feel awkward.

"I especially liked the parts you made up," she added.

His eyes widened. "Sorry?"

"Your face changes. Your eyes kind of flick to the side, and you get a crease in your forehead."

He blushed. He wasn't used to people studying him so closely, and he wasn't sure he liked it.

"The haunted step. That was good."

He cast a worried look around and lowered his voice. "I just throw in a couple things, to spice it up." What if she complained to Karl?

"Don't worry," she said, "your secret's safe with me. My name's Callie. I write a ghost blog. Here."

She handed him a business card. It was very slick, with the name of her blog, *Ghostly,* written white on black. Her name, Callie Ferreira, was printed underneath with a web address.

"How many followers do you have?" he asked.

"Five, including my parents," she said with a small grin. "I'm just getting started. I have a target of ten thousand followers by the end of the summer."

"Ambitious," Gabe said.

"Delusional, really. Anyway, I'm doing a piece on lighthouses and wanted to ask you some questions."

His heart sank. "Honestly, I'm just a guide. You should talk to someone from the historical assoc—"

"I'd rather talk to the person who actually does the tours."

"Yeah, but wouldn't you rather, you know, talk to someone who—"

"*Believes* in ghosts?"

He nodded.

"You don't?"

Behind her head, two dragonflies hovered against the blue of the sky.

"Not really."

"Nothing after death, huh?"

"When you go, you just go."

For a second he thought he was going to cry, but he caught

himself and did a pretend cough. It happened like that sometimes: a sudden spasm of sadness out of nowhere.

"It's kind of funny," she said. "A guy who does ghost tours who doesn't believe in ghosts."

He shrugged. "It's just a summer job. I wanted to do rides, but—"

She tilted her chin at the lighthouse. "So you've never seen or felt anything weird in there?"

He shook his head. "Honestly, I don't spend that much time inside. Just that little bit at the end."

"You ever been up to the lamp room?"

"Once. My first day when the parks people showed me around. So, I guess you believe in ghosts and all that?"

"I didn't at first." She chewed on her lower lip. "I liked the way ghost stories drag you into the past, and other people's lives. My dad's family is from Goa, and my dadi – that's my paternal grandma – she told some great ghost stories."

Gabe nodded. He'd heard of Goa but was too embarrassed to ask where it was. Callie saved him the trouble.

"It's a state on the west coast of India. It used to be a Portuguese colony until 1961, when India took it back."

Gabe got the sense she'd explained this many times in her life.

"Cool," he said.

"Anyway, I guess I started the blog just to write down some of those stories: Three Kings Church, Borim Bridge, Igorchem Bandh – that's a stretch of road behind Our Lady of Snows Church in

Raia. You should check them out. Ghost stories are kind of like history class, only better. It's sort of like time travel."

Time travel. He'd never thought of it that way. He realized he liked talking to her. And he didn't feel quite as nervous as he usually did when he talked to a pretty girl. Normally he got distracted by her hair and eyes and forgot what he was supposed to be saying; he'd feel like his arms were attached all wrong to his body, and his hair was stupid.

"But then I started reading up on *this* place," Callie said, "and what happened to the Strands. I have a special interest in them. Any chance you could take me up to the top?"

"I'd get in trouble."

"I think there might be clues up there."

"After almost two hundred years?"

"It wouldn't take long. Just a few minutes? Who's going to know?"

A group of people wandered into the clearing to take selfies in front of the lighthouse.

"Sorry," he told her, because she looked truly disappointed.

"OK," she said. "I'll ask you again tomorrow. Will you be here tomorrow?"

"Yeah, but—"

"I think there's a big story here," she said.

"Which is?"

"Well, you said it yourself. They never solved the mystery. Rebecca Strand and her father died right here under very suspicious circumstances."

"Oh, come on, they fell!"

"A seasoned lighthouse keeper just fell from his own lighthouse? And his daughter? No."

A cloud passed across the sun, and he noticed that her eyes had green flecks in them.

"See you tomorrow," she said. "You have my card if you have any questions." She began walking away but looked back over her shoulder. "I think Keeper Strand and his daughter were murdered. And I'm going to find out who, or *what*, did it."

Gabe found Yuri in the maintenance shed. It was at the far end of the amusement park, tucked behind the bumper cars. The shed was lined with cluttered shelves of spare parts, and things covered in grease, and things that looked more like junk than anything useful. Hanging on the back wall among vintage license plates was an old Coca-Cola clock. It said 6:30, but Yuri was still hunched over one of the workbenches, doing something to the underside of a bumper car.

"Burgers at the Island Cafe?" Gabe asked him.

"Almost finished," said Yuri.

Gabe leaned in to watch his friend expertly bolt something together. He envied the talent in Yuri's fingers, which seemed to instinctively understand machines, how their parts fit together. At school Yuri was an ace at physics and robotics and there didn't seem to be anything he couldn't build. His father was an engineer, and Yuri had told Gabe that he'd grown up playing with tools and circuit boards instead of building blocks.

"This is fixed, but really, they do not maintain these cars as they should," Yuri said disapprovingly. Yuri had moved from Russia when he was twelve and still spoke English with a strong accent and a kind of formality that Gabe liked. Yuri hardly ever used contractions, and sounded like a gentleman from another century.

Which was perfect, since Gabe was the kid who actually looked forward to school trips involving museums and pioneer villages. But unlike pioneers, he would not have been able to build his own log cabin or windmill. "Wish I could make stuff like you," he told his friend.

Yuri wiped his hands on a rag. "You could, if you were not so brutal with machines. Always thumping and smacking."

"I'm not!" Gabe objected.

"I have seen you *shake* your phone when it is too slow."

"It takes forever to load!"

"Shaking will not make it faster. This is not how such a machine works. Machines are like flowers. You need to caress them."

"What does that part do?" Gabe asked, pointing underneath the bumper car.

"Please do not touch—" Yuri said, at the exact moment something clinked to the floor.

"Was that me?" Gabe asked, wincing.

"It is OK," said Yuri, dragging his hand through his hair so it spiked up. "I will fix it later. Let's get hamburgers."

"All I did was touch it!"

"I know. That is the problem."

Gabe snorted. But his friend was right: he hated machines, and machines hated him right back. Once at school he bought a Coke from the vending machine, and all the drinks fell into the tray; everyone waiting behind him cheered and got free drinks. But after that, the machine stopped working altogether, and people still blamed him.

He and Yuri grabbed their bikes and headed out through the main street of the amusement park. They weaved their way around families with little kids clutching ice creams or helium balloons or stuffed animals. Some kids were ecstatic, some whined because their ice creams were too drippy, and others bawled because their balloon was the wrong superhero, or had slipped from their hand and was now floating above the amusement park.

"I am wasted in this job," Yuri said as they cycled over the canal and past the fountain. "My potential is unrealized."

"You're sixteen!" Gabe told him.

"Mozart composed his first symphony at eight. What have I done? Greased the axles of bumper cars."

Gabe had heard Yuri talk like this before. "Yuri, it's just a summer job!"

"I have a fire in me to create something amazing. I offered to make the roller coaster faster, but this idea was not popular with Karl."

"Well, these rides are mostly for younger kids," Gabe reminded him.

Yuri lifted his shoulders and made a sound that Gabe had never quite deciphered. It seemed to mean a lot of things. *This is disappointing,* or *I am weary,* or *The world is a crazy place but what can you do?*

"I could design a brand-new ride for them if they let me."

"One day you absolutely will," Gabe assured him as they made their way along the wide avenue that led to Ward's Island.

Even though everyone called it the island, it was really fifteen separate islands, many of them man-made, separated by canals and connected with bridges. People actually lived on two of the islands, Algonquin and Ward's, on narrow, tree-lined streets with intriguing houses of all shapes and sizes. Gabe liked them all: the freshly painted ones with welcoming verandas, and the rickety ones that were little more than crooked shacks.

Gabe steered around a sunburned family in a big quadricycle, heading back to the rental place. The father was telling one of his kids to quit horsing around and do some pedalling.

The Island Cafe was right beside the community centre and the lawn bowling club. With its view of the yacht club and ferry dock, it was a popular restaurant for visitors, but also a favourite hangout for locals. The place was always bustling.

The patio was already pretty full tonight, but Gabe liked sitting up at the long outdoor bar anyway. He loved this place: the food was delicious, he got a discount because he worked on the island, and the waiters never got snooty about serving teenagers.

"What's it going to be tonight, gentlemen?" asked Jeff.

Gabe ordered the vegan Schooner Burger with extra mushrooms, blue cheese, and a side of sweet potato fries.

"Why can you never have just a regular hamburger?" Yuri asked.

"This *is* my regular hamburger. What you ordered, that was a pitiful little burger."

Yuri made his sound and said, "I am content with my pitiful little hamburger."

Gabe didn't know how he would've survived the last year without Yuri. Not only was he his best friend, but Yuri was pretty much the only person he felt normal around. Yuri never asked him the usual questions, so Gabe didn't need to reply with the usual lies.

Are you fine?

I'm fine.

Do you want to talk?

No thanks.

It's OK if you feel rotten. Grief is a very—

Honestly, I'm good.

With Yuri, he just talked about regular things like schoolwork and girls and gaming and food. It was relaxing.

"Here you go, guys," said Jeff, setting their meals in front of them. "Enjoy."

"Oh-h-h-h yeah," Gabe said, taking an eager bite of his burger. Some mushrooms tumbled out.

From the patio, a piping voice said: "Hey, it's the ghost guy!" Gabe swivelled to see the bratty kid from his tour, pointing him out to his mom. "Look, he's eating a hamburger!" The mother smiled apologetically and shushed her son.

"You know this child?" Yuri asked Gabe.

"That's Chutney." Gabe gave a little wave.

Yuri chewed thoughtfully. "Chutney is something you put on food, yes?" With a grin he added, "And it is also the only thing you do not have in your hamburger."

"He was on my last tour. Along with a ghost blogger."

"A ghost blogger?"

"She's doing a story on the haunted lighthouse." Callie Ferreira had been wisping through his thoughts since work ended. "Hey, do you believe in ghosts?"

Yuri's pale eyebrows lifted with interest. "There is an explanation for this. I saw a very good show. They say ghosts are caused by certain sounds."

"I don't get it."

"Certain frequencies, like maybe a vibrating pipe in your house, or faulty wiring – they can cause visual hallucinations."

"So you just *think* you've seen a ghost?"

"Yes, maybe a little shimmer in the corner of your eye. Something like that. This is why people think old houses in particular are haunted. They make lots of noises."

"Wow, I'd never heard that," Gabe said. "That's an excellent theory."

He was surprised to feel just the tiniest bit disappointed.

"You want to do bumper cars?" Yuri asked.

The amusement park closed at eight, and it was a tradition that the summer staff rode the bumper cars after closing on Thursdays. They finished their meals and cycled back.

"Do not take that green one," Yuri told him as they walked into the stockade. "It is rubbish."

Gabe and Yuri made a good team, and proceeded to mash and batter as many of the other summer students as possible.

"I think we won," Yuri said after they emerged, sweaty and triumphant.

They said goodbye to their coworkers and headed off to the Centre Island ferry dock, swooping to and fro along the broad empty paths. It began to drizzle, but Gabe didn't mind. The day had been hot and humid. The very last of the visitors were heading home. Near the dock, Gabe saw a big extended family with grandmothers and uncles and aunts, pulling wagons filled with coolers and lawn chairs – and he thought of his mom. Just the two of them now.

"The ferry is not here for another twenty minutes," Yuri said, checking his wristwatch. "We can catch the Hanlan's Point if you like."

Gabe nodded. The Hanlan's Point ferry dock was on the far west end of the island, and Gabe loved riding his bike along that stretch of road. As night came on, it was practically empty. You could really zoom.

They took off. They passed the island school and the old yellow bus that had been parked forever outside the Artscape studios. Across the road was the chain link fence that enclosed the island water treatment plant.

"I always think that place looks like a secret medical facility where they experiment on mutant children," Gabe said to Yuri.

"Such an imagination you have," Yuri said, and then pointed up ahead: "You left a light on."

They were close enough to the Gibraltar Point Lighthouse that, through the trees, Gabe saw a flicker from the lamp room. For a weird second he thought the actual beacon was lit, as it hadn't been for over half a century. Then he realized it was just a regular overhead bulb.

"Wasn't me," he murmured. "I wasn't even up there."

"Is it on a timer?"

"Nope." He would've noticed before.

"There is maybe a switch on the main floor," Yuri suggested reasonably.

"That bratty little Chutney probably flicked it on. I'd better go check."

"You'll miss the ferry."

"I'll get the next one." He might get in trouble if he left the light on all night. "You go ahead."

"You sure?"

"Yeah, go on." Yuri had a longer bike ride home than him.

"See you tomorrow," Yuri said, and pedalled off.

Gabe turned onto the dirt track leading to the lighthouse. When he looked up at the lamp room, a shadow flitted behind the windows. Probably just a reflection off the glass.

The rain came harder. Off in the distance he heard a rumble of thunder.

He hopped off his bike and tilted it against the lighthouse. He couldn't shake the feeling that he'd seen a girl-shaped shadow. And his first thought was Callie, the ghost blogger. Had she somehow gotten inside? She'd seemed pretty determined.

At the red door he tested the handle. Locked. So. There couldn't be anyone inside. It was a fact, but it didn't exactly make him feel better. From his pocket he dragged out the key and opened the door. Turning on his phone flashlight – he tried to tap the button lightly, like Yuri taught him – he stepped inside. He left the door open.

Cold radiated from the thick stone. He found the light switch for the entranceway and flicked on the single overhead bulb. The sound of the rain seemed suddenly a long way away. There was only one other switch in the room, and that one turned on the light for the stairs.

Which meant that whatever switch controlled the lamp room, it was *up there.*

He called out, "Hello?"

It was stupid, when he knew there couldn't be anyone inside. It was also stupid, because now came a sudden, terrible fear that someone *might* answer back.

No one did.

Of course no one did.

"Come on, Gabe," he muttered to himself. "Just get it done."

He started up the stairs and couldn't help glancing at the haunted fourth step. *You made that up,* he reminded himself. Built against the hexagonal stone walls, the stairs wound their way up to the storeroom. It was mostly empty now except for a few crates. Old wood, dust, and the smell of the whale oil that fuelled the lamp long ago.

From here, a set of steep steps – more ladder then stairs – led up to the lamp room. The hatch was closed. Teeth clenched, he climbed up and pushed it open. The hinges made a terrible, high-pitched creak that lifted the hair on his neck.

He stuck his head into the lamp room, grateful there was already a light on. He climbed the rest of the way. Rain pattered against the roof. The only problem with having a light on was the ghostly reflection of himself in each of the wraparound windows. A lanky kid with a pale face, big startled eyes, and a mop of curly hair that needed a trim. It felt like there were lots of people in the room with him.

Or maybe just one other person.

Where did *that* thought come from? The room was small, nowhere to hide. In the middle, a tarpaulin had been draped over the tall beacon. The metal floor was really dusty. He could see his shoeprints, and no one else's. Which meant no one else had been up here for a while.

Which also meant that no one could have turned on the light. He looked around for the switch. Where the heck was it?

The bulb buzzed and flickered. What would Yuri say? Bad wiring. He'd mention it to Karl in the morning.

From outside on the catwalk came the loud *drip drip drip* of rainwater overflowing from a blocked gutter. Across the harbour, the city looked like a distant mirage, veiled by mist. Finally he found the light switch. He walked over, then realized he didn't want to turn it off. He made sure his phone flashlight was still on, so he wouldn't be plunged into total darkness.

Drip

    drip

       drip

went the rain outside as he reached for the switch, and then:

Drip

    silence

       silence

As if someone was standing right underneath the drip, stopping it from hitting the walkway.

Quickly Gabe turned – and electricity surged through him when he saw the tensed body of his own reflection. He shook his head and let out a big breath. Outside on the catwalk the rain went *drip drip drip.*

He flipped off the light switch. The buzzing ceased. With his flashlight he started to guide himself backward down the steep steps. When his head was level with the metal floor, his eyes snagged on a handprint in the dust. He'd probably put his hand there when he came up, but . . .

His heart made a gulping beat. Was that handprint even the same size as his? It looked too small. His hand hovered over it, then touched it.

The metal floor felt winter cold, so cold he was afraid his

hand might freeze to it. He pulled away. But in the split second before he did, he saw a face. A girl's face, gazing urgently into his. Then it was gone, and Gabe backed down the stairs so quickly he nearly fell.

Outside the lighthouse, it was all he could do to lock the door, his hands were shaking so hard. He vaulted onto his bike, not glancing back until the lighthouse was hidden by trees.

3

"Was she attractive?" Yuri asked him over the phone.

"What?" Gabe exclaimed as he paced the living room, towelling his hair dry after the bike ride home. "What has that got to do with anything?"

"Nothing," Yuri admitted. "I was just trying to make you laugh. To lighten the mood. So you saw this girl; then what happened?"

"She disappeared, and I just got out!"

"She was a hallucination," his friend said. "We talked about this. These things are triggered by sound, remember?"

"OK, right," said Gabe. This was exactly what he wanted to hear. This was why he'd called Yuri.

"You said there was rain clattering on a metal roof, yes? And thunder, and buzzing! The buzzing of the light, which is probably faulty wiring, and a disgrace – and possibly a fire hazard—"

"Sure, I buy all that," Gabe interrupted. "But that handprint in the dust?"

Gabe's mom was working an overnight emergency shift at St. Mike's so it was just him – and Charlie the budgie, whistling cheerily from his cage. Gabe was glad of any company. He paused before the balcony doors. Their condo on Queen's Quay was five floors up and overlooked the harbour. The island was just a low shadow now, but his eyes strayed to the rough location of the lighthouse. He half expected to see a light flicker.

"That handprint was probably your own," Yuri said.

"No. It was definitely smaller."

He checked his hand to make sure. His fingertips still felt tingly, like he'd just come inside on a very cold winter day.

"Hmm. Let's say you are correct," Yuri said. "Then I would say—"

In the background, Gabe heard Yuri's little brother, Leonid, holler something.

"Yes," said Yuri, "I will do Legos with you in just a moment." Coming back to Gabe, he said, "This little handprint, it probably belonged to someone who was in the room earlier. You said they were doing work."

"True. But wouldn't I have noticed it when I came up?"

"More likely you simply stepped over it."

It was a reassuring thought. And, yes, the most likely explanation.

"*Legos!*" wailed Leonid.

Yuri shouted something fiery in Russian.

"Speak English!" Leonid complained.

"I said, there will not *be* any Legos if you keep up this hullabaloo!"

Gabe couldn't help smiling. *Hullabaloo.* Definitely a word Yuri must have been taught back in Russia. No one used it anymore.

"I apologize for this little barbarian," Yuri said.

Gabe only wished that his own brother were here, instead of off at university in Montreal. It didn't seem like so long ago the two of them had played Lego.

Gabe would've liked to be over at Yuri's right now. The Baranovs lived in an apartment building that had lots of other Russian families. Wafting through the hallways were the sound of Russian television and the smell of beets and cabbage. He liked Yuri's noisy family, the way their sentences were sprinkled with Russian words. Yuri's mother had much better English than his father; and Leonid, who'd been only five when he came over, spoke English all the time, and got impatient and angry when everyone else spoke Russian.

"OK, thanks," Gabe said. "I don't feel so freaked out any more."

"See you tomorrow," said Yuri. "Have a good evening, my friend."

Gabe had always liked the way Yuri signed off, formal but warm. And he liked being called "my friend".

He migrated to the kitchen. The burger seemed like a long time ago and he felt like a grilled sandwich. He always got hungry this time of night. He started by sautéing some onions and red peppers. In the fridge he found the eggs and some of that smoked Gouda he liked.

From the living room, Charlie chattered nonsense to himself. They'd had the budgie forever, but Gabe still caught himself mistaking the bird for the radio. Charlie was an amazing mimic, and spoke so quickly that you had to listen carefully to pull out phrases like "Do you want a drink?" or "Charlie-Charlie-Charlie" or "Hello, sweetie."

Gabe made some space in his frying pan and cracked in an egg. He'd leave the yolk just a little bit runny. He assembled all his ingredients on whole wheat bread and pressed the sandwich in the panini grill.

"Love-you-plenty!" trilled the budgie. "Love-you-plenty!"

Gabe caught himself wincing. That was one of the many phrases his father had taught Charlie. It was Dad who'd bought the bird – then left it behind, just like the rest of them, when he moved out.

"Charlie-come-out, out-out-out," tweeted the budgie.

"Why not," Gabe said, walking into the living room, taking a bite of his delicious sandwich. He was glad he'd added the Gouda.

He opened the cage, and the small green bird flitted into the room, landing briefly on a chair, then the sofa, before settling on his head.

"How you doing, Charlie bird?"

"Hello sweetbird-sweetbird-sweetbird."

Charlie was noisier than usual tonight, and Gabe figured he must be lonely too. As he ate, Gabe pulled out his phone and sent his big brother a funny message, and they texted for a few minutes before Andrew said he had to run. His brother was good at running off to other things. Gabe couldn't exactly blame him. There were plenty of times he wished he were somewhere else too.

"What d'you think of this place, Charlie?" he asked.

The bird hopped onto his shoulder but made no reply. The condo still didn't feel like home to Gabe. It was fun living downtown near the water, and everything was shiny and new, and he had a nice room with its own bathroom. It was a great condo; it just wasn't their *home*, which got sold after the divorce last year.

And even though the condo was filled with their old furniture and decorations – as much as they could fit, anyway – the place felt strange and empty with only him and Mom living here. She'd made sure to get a three-bedroom so Andrew would still have a room of his own, but he didn't visit that often. And even less after Dad died in January.

"Back-to-the-cagebacktothecageCharliesweetbird."

"OK, Charlie, bedtime for you, sir."

He put his finger out for Charlie and walked the budgie across the room. Charlie hopped inside his cage, dinged his bell, then looked at Gabe with his head tilted expectantly.

"HellohellohelloGabriel."

Gabe grunted. "Hey, you've never said my name before." It was a bit odd, but not surprising. Charlie sponged up words.

"GabrielGabrielGabrielweclaspedhands."

We clasped hands. Startled, he looked down at his hand, remembering that icy tingle in the lighthouse.

"GabrielGabrielpleaselistenGabriel—"

Please listen, Gabriel.

Heart pounding, he grabbed the cloth cover and yanked it down over the cage. Instantly Charlie fell silent. Gabe stepped back.

"OK. Go to sleep, Charlie."

He walked around the living room, turning on more lights. Charlie said a lot of crazy things, simple as that. Gabe opened the balcony door and stepped out. After the air conditioning, the heat enclosed him like a wool overcoat. A streetcar rattled past. It had stopped raining. Across the street, a busker played guitar in the quayside music garden. A pair of bicycles swished by, their tyres sounding sticky on the wet tarmac. The ceaseless sounds of the city comforted him. He went back inside. The birdcage was silent.

When his phone buzzed he pulled it out gratefully, hoping it was Andrew or Yuri, but there was only an empty text bubble. *No Caller ID*. He tapped the screen – maybe too hard, or maybe it had gotten wet in the rain, because a second empty bubble appeared, then a third and a fourth. He'd busted his phone. Yuri was right: all he had to do was touch a machine and he broke it.

A new text bubble appeared, and inside it was a single:

i

Followed, after a moment, by another bubble:

a

Then more quickly:

m

r

eb

Every time his phone pinged, Gabe felt like it was giving him a little electric shock.

ecc

astr

and

Nothing more. His heart went *bang bang bang*. It was just broken phone garbage, he told himself. But he scrolled back to the top of the messages. As he read the letters aloud, he realized they actually spelled something.

"No," he said. "This is a joke."

Angrily the phone pinged:

iamrebecca

strand

Could it be Yuri? He didn't know how his friend was doing this, or why, because Yuri hated practical jokes, and wouldn't be so cruel.

Pleas

elistento

me

"You are not Rebecca Strand!" Gabe shouted at his phone.

Speak with

me I beg you

Gabe threw his phone to the floor. It kept buzzing, but luckily it had landed facedown, so he couldn't see the text bubbles stacking up. After a moment it fell silent, which was somehow even creepier.

He jumped up; he'd take a walk around the block. Halfway to the door, his right hand felt icy cold, and when he glanced down, he saw another hand holding his.

A smaller hand.

His eyes pedalled up a lacy cotton sleeve to a shoulder covered in a woollen shawl. He swallowed and lifted his eyes higher still.

Before him stood a girl with dark hair and large greeny-grey eyes: the same urgent face he'd seen in the lighthouse. This time she spoke: "Are you able to see and hear me—"

He yanked his hand free and she evaporated. He bolted for the front door. But again, an icy chill clamped his fingers, and the girl reappeared, blocking his way.

"So you *can* see me, yes?" she asked.

He bellowed.

"Please don't be alarmed!" she cried.

"I'm alarmed!" he yelled.

"I'm sorry. That's why I tried the bird first—"

"That was terrifying!"

"—and then the machine." She pointed to his phone on the floor. "I learned by watching you, but you refused to answer, so I had to clasp with you."

Clasp. He looked at the hand gripping his and realized he couldn't feel its pressure at all. All he felt was the cold.

Desperately the girl said, "Please don't pull free again!"

Which was exactly what he meant to do, but her look was so beseeching that he faltered.

"I think this is the only way for you to see and hear me," she said.

In a split second his thoughts forked into many questions. Nightmare? No, he knew what a nightmare felt like, and he could always pull himself out when things got too rough. Hallucination? Two in one night was surely too much of a coincidence. Insanity? (He'd come back to that one later.) The final possibility was that this was really happening, and he was talking to a ghost. Right now, this felt like the truth.

"You're really Rebecca Strand?"

"I am indeed."

Her voice carried a trace of a British accent. Gabe had never seen a picture of Rebecca Strand – he doubted any existed. She'd died before photography was commonplace; and only wealthy people got their portraits painted. The girl before him wasn't flickery black-and-white, but full-colour. She looked as real as anything else in the room – not that a girl dressed in an old-fashioned nightgown, knitted shawl and boots was exactly something he saw every day – in fact, she somehow looked *more* real. Everything else around her appeared strangely washed out, as if all the colour had seeped into the girl so vividly before him.

She was his age, a few inches shorter, with a frank oval face, long hair hanging messily around her shoulders and eyes that, with the help of thick eyebrows, could telegraph any emotion. Especially urgency. She had a very pretty mouth, though her teeth weren't the straightest. Or the whitest. And, to be honest, she looked a little crazed.

"What year is this?" she demanded.

When he told her she murmured in astonishment, "So very long. I might have slumbered forever if you hadn't woken me!"

"Woken you? Me? How?"

"I heard you speaking my name over and over."

With a sinking heart, he realized she was right. He'd given hundreds of tours over the past weeks, and during each one, he said her name multiple times. Thanks to his job, he was personally responsible for waking up a ghost.

"I didn't mean to," he said, worried she might get angry. In stories ghosts often got angry. "I'm sorry about that. Could you just . . . um, go *back* to sleep?"

Her eyes flashed with annoyance. "I have no desire to go back to sleep! I've already lost too much time. I need your help!"

He inhaled sharply. "Nah," he said, trying hard to stay calm. "No you don't."

She looked taken aback. "I certainly do!"

"I think you've got everything totally under control," he babbled, slowly taking a few steps back; she moved with him, gripping his hand. "You can handle it. You seem like a very . . . capable ghost."

"There are things that are impossible for me to do alone!"

"Oh, there's *way* better people!" He had no idea what kind of help she needed; he just didn't want to be involved. "You know, people with special training. And a driver's licence. I'm just a kid."

"You're the only person to say my name in over a century, Gabriel."

He startled at the sound of his full name. She must've heard him introduce himself on the tour. How long had she been watching and listening?

"You know my story," she said.

"Not really! Honestly, I just make stuff up for the tourists!"

She frowned. "So you don't know what happened to me and my father?"

"Just that you were found dead together."

"We were murdered!"

An idea suddenly came to him, from a ghost story he remembered. In a calm, soothing voice, he said, "Please tell me what happened to you, Rebecca Strand. Tell me your story so you can rest in peace, and return to your slumber, and go . . . wherever you need to go, or whatever—"

"Don't be ridiculous," she snapped. "You need to help me save my father!"

Her father. Who was already dead. He gave a little shiver as he glanced down at the ghostly hand that gripped his. He wanted that hand gone. He wanted *her* gone altogether. He could pull away again, but she might just grab him again. She didn't seem like a ghost who gave up easily.

"Look, I'm very sorry for your loss," he said, wincing at the clichéd expression, "but I really have nothing to do with all this. Could you please leave me alone?"

"But we clasped!"

"You keep saying that! So what?"

"In the lighthouse, you accepted my invitation!"

He stared at her in incomprehension. "I didn't get any invitation!"

"In the dust on the floor, I wrote 'Clasp with me' and put out my hand."

"I didn't see any writing!"

"The letters were very faint," she admitted. More defiantly, she said, "It took a lot of energy to move all that dust! And then you went and smudged the letters!"

"You tricked me!"

"Simply so we could talk!"

With a shiver, Gabe had a terrible thought. "Hang on, this isn't some kind of supernatural contract where we're welded together forever, is it?"

"No! At least I don't think so." She sighed in frustration. "Just because I'm a ghost doesn't mean I'm an expert about them. I died before my father could tell me much. All I've figured out is that when I clasp with a living person, they can see and hear me."

Gabe released his breath. "So, can we just . . . *un*clasp now? For good?"

Her eyes narrowed. "Perhaps I was wrong about you."

"How?"

"I thought you were kind. But you obviously have no idea what it's like to lose a father."

"Yeah, I do, actually," he said, anger flaring inside him. "People die all the time, all right? It's too bad, but there's nothing special about it. I'm not making it everyone else's problem!" His voice was actually shaking. "Anyway, I'm done talking to you. Do not touch me. Do not text me. Do not do weird things to the bird!"

"But you said you wanted to hear my story, Gabriel."

He wished he hadn't said that. And it wasn't fair that she kept using his name, like they were friends. She looked suddenly so forlorn that he felt mean. Was he mean? No, he was being completely reasonable. He forced himself to keep going.

"Just go back to the lighthouse. Good luck and everything. This is goodbye."

He pulled free and jammed both hands into his pocket. Everything in the room snapped back into crisp, colourful focus. Rebecca Strand was gone – or rather, she was invisible, which was more unsettling in a way. He hadn't been afraid when she was right in front of him, talking.

He looked warily at the birdcage.

Silent.

He looked at his phone on the floor.

Silent.

He nudged it with his foot, then picked it up. On the screen was the stack of her earlier text bubbles filled with the word *please*. Now he felt even meaner.

He also felt incredibly tired, like he'd just finished a long run. He gave a shiver and massaged the cold hand she'd been holding. In his room he turned on all the lights and sat down on the edge of his bed. He hoped that Rebecca Strand was floating back across the harbour to the lighthouse. But how could he know for sure? If she was still here, she was certainly keeping quiet, just like he'd asked.

"I don't know if you're here, but would you mind giving me a little privacy?"

His words hung in the room. He wondered if maybe he preferred being able to see her.

"Just don't appear and scare the crap out of me, OK? That would be a really rotten thing to do."

She must be gone. What was the point of her hanging around? She didn't seem like a mean or vengeful person. Just desperate and lonely. He wondered if he was the first person she'd talked to since she'd died.

"OK, I'm going to change now, so I hope you're not looking at me because that would be creepy."

In the end, he kept his underwear on and got under the covers.

He didn't want to turn out the lights, so he dragged his laptop over and played a game of *LeagueQuest*. He got crushed, because he kept looking away from the screen to make sure his room was empty. On the floor beside his trousers he saw the business card Callie Ferreira had given him.

"Hey," he said, "if you're still here, and I hope you're not, there's someone who'd probably love to hear your story. Maybe you could clasp with her. Her contact info's on that card there, if you want it. So, yeah."

After another game of *LeagueQuest,* he watched a cooking show where they made a Death Star out of bacon. And then, amazingly, he felt his eyelids getting heavy. He hadn't thought it was possible to fall asleep after seeing a ghost, but it turned out it was.

Across the harbour, the island slept too.

In the amusement park, the concession stands were shuttered. The swan boats bobbed against the dock. The Ferris wheel creaked a little in the light wind. On Algonquin and Ward's Island, the windows of the cozy houses and cottages were dark. The beaches were empty. The doused embers of a bonfire clicked and steamed; the teens who'd lit it had long ago headed home with their damp towels and empty bottles. Over the water carried the haunting call of a loon.

A hundred metres from shore, on the lake's bottom, among groves of weed, rock, and the remnants of old, wrecked ships, Nicholas Viker slumbered fitfully, one eye open.

Overhead, through the rippled surface, he saw the full moon. He'd languished down here for so long, it was hard to know how many years had passed. Sometimes he saw the sun, and it seemed never to move; other times it streaked like a comet, crossing the sky again and again.

He was such a tiny thing now. After being massacred by the ghostlight long ago, he'd been so weakened it had been all he could do to scuttle into the lake like some pathetic crab.

And that had proved a most terrible mistake.

The lake had once been a rich source of food. The dead would flutter down from wrecked ships or furtive burials - and he'd feed upon their bewildered ghosts. But those times were long gone. Year after year, a hunger grew within him, the likes of which he'd never known when alive. A huge aching chasm, expanding within his wracked and ruined being.

To stay powerful, to do the things he did, he needed to feed on the dead. Constantly. But now he was too weak to come ashore to new hunting grounds, too weak even to drag himself around the lake bottom. He was fixed like a barnacle, waiting for something to come within reach. It took all his strength just to keep his single eye open.

And right now he had that eye fixed on something very interesting.

For many years, in the warmer months, a man had come here to swim. He came at all hours, during the day and sleepless nights, and he would pass directly overhead before returning to shore.

Here he came now. He was quite old by this time, and Viker could hear his heartbeat through the water. That thing he envied most of all. That thing he would never have again. Blood pulsing through his veins.

But listen! The man's heartbeat, once so steady, had a warble to it. If Viker could have moved, if he had been stronger like in the old days, he might have reached a long arm up and touched the man's chest and stopped his stuttering heart altogether. But on this night, this glorious night, the man's heart stopped all on its own.

With terrible appetite, Viker watched as the man began to sink.

Closer to the bottom, the man's ghost slipped free of his body, and saw Viker. "Good evening," said Viker. "Lovely night for a swim."

"Why are you down here?" asked the man's confused ghost.

"The same reason you are, my friend."

"I should be getting back. I have another length to do."

"Dear me," said Viker, "it seems you're having a touch of trouble."

"Yes," said the ghost dolefully. "Just a bit tired."

"Come closer, and I can help," said Viker.

"That's awfully kind of you," said the ghost. "I don't know what's wrong with me."

"Just a little closer," Viker encouraged him, "that's it."

Using the last of his strength, Viker closed his hand around the ghost's neck.

"Could you let go, please," the man asked politely. "That's a bit tight."

In reply Viker opened his mouth awfully wide and devoured the ghost headfirst. Down he went, now lively as a snared eel, but Viker shut his mouth and clamped down. He felt all the man's thrashing fear pass into him, and with it, his vital energy.

That was better.

So much better.

Slowly he turned himself toward the shore, and began a feeble crab-like shuffle. With luck he'd have enough energy to make it to land. And there, he could find more ghosts to feed upon. He would make himself strong again

And then he would make things happen.

4

Gabe woke to the smell of toast and coffee, and was surprised by how refreshed he felt. Eight o'clock sunlight slanted through his blinds. For a moment, the events of last night seemed impossible, maybe a vivid dream. But when he glanced at his phone he saw the stack of Rebecca Strand's messages. He checked the room, wondering if she was still here – it didn't *feel* like anyone was there, but what did he know? – then pulled on his clothes.

At the dining table Mom was reading the newspaper and drinking coffee. Charlie flitted around merrily, and landed briefly on Gabe before fluttering off to Mom's head.

"Love-love-love-you-plenty!" the budgie chirped.

"How was your shift?" Gabe asked.

"No one died."

An old joke. Mom smiled, but he saw the smudges of tired-ness under her crinkled eyes. He wondered how easy it was to go to sleep after an emergency shift. He didn't know how she did it: figuring out what was wrong with all those sick people, and the best way to help them, and not having much time to do it.

"How about a superduper omelet?" he asked her.

Her smile widened. "I would *love* one of your superduper omelets, thank you."

Gabe went to the kitchen and got to work, chopping up some onions, mushrooms, and tomatoes.

"How was the island yesterday?" she asked.

"Oh, fine. Yuri and I grabbed dinner and did bumper cars with everyone." *And then I came home and Charlie was possessed by a ghost that followed me home, and then the ghost and I had a nice long chat.*

He started to sauté the vegetables. "Hey, I've got a question for you."

"Shoot."

"If someone told you they'd seen a ghost, would you believe them?"

Through the archway, he saw her look up from her newspaper.

"Is this a someone I know well?"

"Sure. Like a good friend, or say another doctor."

He cracked the eggs into a bowl and whisked.

"And what exactly did this someone see?" Mom asked.

"Oh, I don't know. A ghost who just pops up out of nowhere, dressed from a long time ago."

"Does the ghost talk to them?"

"Um, maybe, sure," Gabe said, melting some butter in a bigger frying pan, then starting the eggs cooking.

"What does the ghost say?"

She'd put her newspaper down. Gabe saw the change in the way she was looking at him. More professional. More concerned.

Gabe shrugged, glad he had an excuse to break her gaze. He

spooned the sautéed vegetables on top of the cooking omelet, then grated some cheese to melt.

"Oh, I don't know," he said. "A bunch of us were talking about ghosts last night, and someone said they'd seen one."

"Is this someone *you* by any chance?"

"No! I just wondered what would make *you* believe in ghosts."

"Well, I'd certainly want to rule out any neurological cause first."

"Oh, for sure," Gabe agreed.

He wanted to drop it now. This was a mistake. There was no way he could tell her. Mom saw patients who sometimes told her very, very strange things, and she sent them to psychiatrists. If he told her about last night, she would worry. Mom's job was hard, and he didn't want to make her life any harder. She was strong; she hadn't fallen apart when Dad left, or when he died. And Gabe could be strong too. He'd keep this to himself.

The omelet folded over perfectly. He divided it in half and sliced an orange to put on the side of their plates.

"Looks delicious," she said as he placed hers in front of her. She took a first bite and made an appreciative grunt. "You definitely inherited your father's culinary talents."

Gabe grunted. Dad had been a chef at a high-end Mediterranean restaurant. It was still weird to hear Mom talk about him, especially when she said something nice. Gabe wasn't sure how to talk about Dad, or even how to *think* about him.

"It's OK to miss him, you know," Mom said.

"Do you?"

"It's different for me, but yes, of course."

Dad had fallen in love with another person and left. But he didn't just leave Mom. Gabe felt like he'd left him and Andrew, too. Since then, Dad hadn't been very interested in seeing them. In fact, he'd disappeared entirely for six months with Pauline, his new partner. There were a few calls and, when he returned to town, some lunches, but they were miserable. Somehow he and Dad had nothing to talk about. Dad usually brought Pauline along, and the two of them just talked about the latest restaurants they'd been to, and the new place they were renovating, and their trip to Southeast Asia. Gabe felt like he'd been downgraded, from son to pal.

And then, in January, Dad had died crossing the street. The driver of the SUV said he'd just walked out into traffic, looking at his phone. Probably texting the new love of his life. It was a really stupid way to die.

"I should get going," Gabe said, taking his dishes to the machine.

"Have a great day, sweetheart." She stood to wrap her arms around him, and held him longer than usual. He dutifully dropped his head so she could kiss the top of it. Then he was off.

His first ghost tour of the day was a wipeout.

His timing was off, and his mind and eyes kept straying to the lighthouse. He was so frazzled he could barely make stuff up. When he finally reached the lighthouse and took his group inside, his skin prickled in anticipation of Rebecca Strand's cold grip. His phone never buzzed, but it felt *hot* in his pocket. He imagined her angry. Or sad. Sad was even worse.

However, it seemed like she was being very polite, or had lost interest in him. Or had never existed at all. Which was a complicated thing to wish for, because it meant last night was a hallucination and he would probably need a brain scan.

He and Yuri were on different lunch breaks today, so they wouldn't get to talk until after work. Gabe didn't want to tell his story over text. It was too much, and anyway he wanted to see Yuri's face, so he could tell if his friend thought he'd lost his mind.

He did feel a little off-balance. Learning that ghosts were real, that there was a kind of life after death, was a mighty shift in his world view. But as the day went on, with the sun bright on his face, the smell of suntan lotion from passing cyclists, the happy shouts from the log ride – with all that, last night started to feel less and less real.

When he finished his final tour of the day, he locked the lighthouse door and gave a jump when he turned to find Callie Ferreira in the clearing.

"You look like you've seen a ghost," she said with a smile.

He made himself laugh. "I didn't hear you, that's all. Do you live nearby or something?"

"No, but I work just over there." She pointed to the distant summit of the CN Tower, jutting above the tree line.

"Cool. What d'you do?"

"Same as you. Tour guide. Would you like to know how much the tower weighs?"

"No, but I do have a question for you."

"Really?" She looked pleased. "Shoot."

"Does everyone become a ghost when they die?"

"No. I mean, there's all sorts of theories. The most common is that it's only people who were very angry or sad or confused when they died."

"Unfinished business on Earth," Gabe said.

"Right."

His first thought was not about Rebecca Strand but, to his surprise, his own father. What was in Dad's heart when he'd died? And if Dad was a ghost, why hadn't he tried to talk to Gabe? He'd had over six months now. He'd never so much as dinged Charlie's bell, or buzzed Gabe's phone or moved a speck of *dust*. Maybe Dad wasn't a ghost. Or maybe he just couldn't be bothered to get in touch with Gabe, dead or alive.

"Why do you ask?" Callie inquired. "Something spooky happen to you?"

"Anything spooky happen to *you*?"

He couldn't help wondering if Rebecca Strand had maybe gotten in touch with Callie last night.

"Nothing," she replied, "unless you count my sister's new boyfriend. He came over for dinner last night, and he was not a hit. Listen, I didn't explain myself very well yesterday. There's a bunch of stuff I should've told you."

"Are you going to ask to see the lamp room again?"

"Yes. But this time I'm going to convince you."

He laughed again, this time for real. "Are you hungry?" he asked impulsively. "Because it's taco night at the Island Cafe and it's really good and I get a discount."

"Oh," she said, "well . . ."

Maybe she thought he'd just asked her on a date.

"I mean, I'm meeting my friend Yuri, so you could—"

She seemed even more hesitant.

"Maybe tacos aren't your thing," he suggested dejectedly.

"You sure your friend wants to hear a bunch of ghost stuff?" She lowered her voice. "I mean, some of this stuff's pretty—"

"Unbelievable?" This was exactly why he wanted Callie at dinner. He planned to tell Yuri what had happened to him last night, and he wanted some backup. Someone who might actually believe what he said.

"Actually I was going to say *confidential*," Callie said. "I've done a lot of research, and I wouldn't want anyone stealing my stuff. I want to be a reporter and this is a pretty unique story. Is Yuri trustworthy?"

"I'd trust him with my life," Gabe answered.

"That is a very solemn reply," she said.

"He's that kind of guy."

"OK, if you're sure," Callie said.

"Awesome," said Gabe in relief. "Let's go."

"Is that *imperial* tons or *metric* tons?" Yuri asked Callie after she'd told him how much the CN tower weighed.

"Imperial," she said, swallowing a mouthful of her fish taco. "It's a nice even number that way. In metric it's 117,910 tons. It just takes longer to say."

"True," said Yuri, "but this is Canada so we should use metric."

"I totally agree," she said. "You want to guess how much concrete it took to make it?"

"Oh my goodness, yes!" Delighted, Yuri grabbed at his hair and had a good long think. "I am going to say fifty thousand cubic metres."

"Close! Just over forty thousand."

Yuri sat back in his chair, shaking his head in admiration. "She has so much information!" he said happily to Gabe.

Gabe was glad that they'd hit it off right away. Seated around a slightly tippy table on the Island Cafe patio, the two of them had been eagerly trading statistics for the last few minutes.

The sun was starting to drop toward Hanlan's Point. Gabe smelled basil from the community herb garden next to the patio.

"You guys should really come up to the tower," Callie said. "I can give you a VIP tour. Maybe even get you on the EdgeWalk."

Gabe squeezed more lime juice onto his taco. "What's the EdgeWalk?"

"It's at the top of the LookOut Level. They suit you up in a safety harness and let you walk outside onto the ledge that goes all the way around the tower. No railing. It's insane."

"Is that where they mounted their new spotlight?" Yuri asked.

Gabe glanced over at the CN Tower and saw a beam of intense light aimed straight up into the sky.

"Yep. It's a xenon lamp. The Luxor Hotel in Las Vegas used to be the brightest spotlight in the world – but ours is just a teeeeeny bit brighter."

Gabe cleared his throat, thinking it was time they got down to business. "So," he said to Yuri, "Callie knows a lot about another tower, too. The Gibraltar Point Lighthouse."

"Ah, yes." Yuri raised his eyebrow at Callie. "When I heard you were a ghost blogger I was a bit worried you were maybe . . ." He decided not to put a name to it.

"I understand," Callie said. "But don't you ever wonder why there are so many ghost stories around lighthouses? It's like they practically attract ghosts. You know, like a candle attracts moths."

"Perhaps this is because lighthouses are often in the middle of nowhere, and it is very foggy and lonely, and people convince themselves they see things that are not there."

"That's true," said Callie. "Some of the time."

Gabe caught Yuri glancing his way, and his expression said *Uh-oh*.

"But I wonder if there's a different reason," Callie said. She looked around and leaned in, making the table tilt a little. "What if ghosts are real? And lighthouse keepers can see them in the lamp beams. And keepers use the beams to destroy evil ghosts."

Gabe forced himself to chew carefully so he didn't choke on his coleslaw.

"OK," he said. "Wow, that is strangely specific . . ."

Calmly Yuri dabbed his greasy mouth with a napkin and asked, "I am curious about why you think this?"

"I'm glad you asked." From her backpack, Callie pulled out a tablet. As she lightly brushed and tapped at the screen, Yuri nodded approvingly; Gabe rolled his eyes. When she'd found what she wanted, she slid the tablet across the table. On the screen was an image of an old newspaper. "This is a story from the *Globe,* October twenty-second, 1839, about the lighthouse keeper who replaced Mr Strand."

"Michael Debenham," Gabe said.

"So, about three months after he started, he ends up in court."

Gabe didn't see where any of this was going, but he asked, "What did he do?"

"Debenham didn't do anything. He was pressing charges against a man called Mr Serge Delacroix, from Montreal. According to Debenham, he caught Delacroix in the lighthouse one night, tampering with the lamp."

"Tampering?" Gabe asked, more interested.

"It's pretty great stuff," Callie said. "I found the actual court transcripts. Hang on a sec."

"How did you know where to find all this?" Gabe asked enviously as she swiped her screen and another old document appeared.

"Student librarian, four years running," she said. "I know my way around a database. OK, here it is." She cleared her throat and read:

Under sworn oath, Mr Debenham testified as follows: "When I asked Mr Delacroix what his business was, he began to spout outlandish nonsense. He asked if I had ever seen *the dead* in the *beam of my lamp*?

"I told him no, I had never seen any such thing. He told me I must have done. I insisted I had not! Mr Delacroix told me I must be the most *blockheaded and unobservant* man in Creation. I took offence and threatened to box his ears.

"Mr Delacroix proceeded to tell me that I must join an *ancient order of lighthouse keepers,* whose duty was to protect the living from *the wakeful and wicked dead.*

"I asked him if he was a member of such an Order and he produced a pendant *in the shape of a lighthouse* and showed it to me. He said the city was not safe if I neglected my duties. He claimed that Keeper Strand had fallen victim to *malicious ghostly fiends.*

"Further, Delacroix insisted that my lamp needed *a special lens* – and he produced *a coloured piece of glass* – and tried to show me how to *affix it to my beacon* so I might obliterate these wicked ghouls.

"Mr Delacroix raved of ghosts and ghasts and all manner of occult and unchristian things, until I called out to a passing guard from the Blockhouse, who apprehended this lunatic Frenchman."

Callie stopped reading. Gabe noticed that her cheeks glowed and her eyes shone. "It's a lot of fun to read aloud." She looked like she'd scored a huge victory. "So what do you guys think of *that?*"

"Delacroix sounds unhinged," Yuri remarked into his water glass.

"What happened to him?" Gabe asked.

"The judge ordered him to leave the city at once, or get locked up in the lunatic asylum. That's what they used to call CAMH. But I think this Serge Delacroix knew *exactly* what he was talking about. I think there really was an order of keepers who fought ghosts."

"Why?" Gabe asked. Listening to her all this time, he'd wondered when he should mention last night, but he'd been completely swept up in her story.

From around her neck Callie pulled out a pendant on a chain, and held it out to them. A tarnished silver lighthouse with a beacon of flame.

"Just like the one Serge Delacroix had," she said.

"That is a charming piece of jewellery," Yuri said, "but it doesn't prove anything."

Callie said, "Rebecca Strand was wearing this when she died."

The Ward's Island ferry tooted before pulling away from the dock. At the bar, a couple laughed. A boy on a bike shouted for someone to wait up.

"How can you know that?" Gabe asked in a whisper.

"Because I'm related to her."

In astonishment Gabe looked at Yuri, then back to Callie. "You said your family was from Goa!"

"My *father's* family. Listen. Rebecca Strand had a brother, Bernard, who married and had lots of children. And *those* children had lots of children! And after almost two hundred years, my father marries one of those Strands! So here I am, part of the family!"

Gabe shook his head. "Incredible."

"And the pendant?" asked Yuri.

"Bernard kept it. And it got handed down through the generations. My mom's mother gave it to me last year, along with the story of the Gibraltar Point Lighthouse. And I thought my Goan relatives had good ghost stories! I don't think the Strands like talking about it, though. It's complicated for them."

"Why?" Yuri asked.

"There's so many theories about how they died, but one of them is that Keeper Strand went insane and killed his own daughter, and then himself."

"They told me not to mention that one on the tour," Gabe said. "It's too awful. Especially for little kids."

"But it might be true," Yuri said gently.

"I don't believe that," said Callie. "And I want to prove it."

"You can," Gabe blurted out. "I've met her. Rebecca Strand. I talked to her last night."

5

"You told her to go away?" Callie exclaimed, the moment Gabe had finished his story.

"Of course I did!"

"Go *away*?"

"It was terrifying!"

"Rebecca Strand was about to tell you how she died, and solve a mystery two centuries old—"

"OK, yes, I get it—"

"—and unveil a secret world of the supernatural, and you just got rid of her?"

"Hey," Gabe said defensively, "it's not like I didn't feel mean about it. But come on, you would've done the same! Yuri, wouldn't you have done the same?"

He looked over at his friend for support. Yuri had been holding the same piece of taco, halfway to his mouth, which was a little bit open, the whole time Gabe had been telling his story.

Slowly Yuri asked, "Your *budgie* was actually speaking?"

"Yes!"

"That bird is a very unusual creature," Yuri said. "I have never liked it."

"Yuri, focus! Did you even hear the rest of my story?"

"How is it possible that a ghost could *text*?" he asked.

"I think I can explain that," said Callie. "I've read that ghosts have a small electromagnetic field, so I don't see why they couldn't touch the keys of a phone – or even send wireless messages, which, after all, are just little streams of electromagnetic radiation, right? Make sense?"

"Look," Gabe said, "all I know is she can *do* it, OK?"

Yuri stared straight ahead. "I am still processing."

"OK, you just take a little vacation," Gabe said.

Across the harbour, the glass office towers and condos were ablaze with the setting sun. The CN Tower's spotlight sent a perfect white line into the darkening sky.

"Gabe, you need to go back to the lighthouse," Callie told him, "and talk to her, right now!"

"No I don't!"

She glared; he glared back. High in a tree a squirrel ate something noisily. A bit of nut hit the table.

"If *you* don't talk to her," Callie said, "I will! I'll go clasp with her."

Gabe was surprised by how much he didn't like this idea.

"Who says she'll even *want* to clasp with you?"

He said it mostly to annoy her, but realized he suddenly felt possessive about Rebecca Strand. She'd invited him. *Chosen* him; that had to mean something.

"At least I'll listen to her!" Callie retorted. "And I'm *related* to her, after all!"

"Fine! I'll talk to her!"

It wasn't like he hadn't considered it already – many times. He'd felt cruel yanking his hand away, cutting her off.

"I would very much like to meet this ghost," Yuri said finally.

Gabe looked over in surprise. "Seriously?"

The whole time he'd been talking, he'd worried what Yuri was thinking. His friend was very rational, and it was one of the things Gabe liked about him, but it was also the thing most likely to make Yuri think he was having a nervous breakdown.

"If it's real I would like to understand it," Yuri said.

"OK, great," said Gabe with relief.

"I still have many doubts, I must admit."

"Fair enough." Gabe finished his glass of water. "So, back to the lighthouse?"

Callie nodded. "Ghosts usually hang around the place they died."

They paid the bill and headed off to Gibraltar Point. Callie didn't have a bike with her, so Yuri gave her a lift, pedalling standing up while she sat on the seat.

By the time they reached the lighthouse, Gabe was feeling a lot more nervous. He was starting to remember Rebecca's icy grip, the hair-raising shock of seeing her appear while everything else around him dimmed. Like he was leaving the real world behind and entering the world of the dead. He unlocked the lighthouse and went inside. The cold was abrupt.

"Make sure the door's closed all the way," he told Yuri before flicking the light switch. He didn't want anyone passing to see them. Last thing he needed was to get fired.

"No cell signal," Yuri said, checking his phone.

"Nope. But I don't think that'll be a problem for her." Gabe took out his own phone. He released a deep breath, deciding how to begin. "Rebecca Strand, I'd like to talk to you." Quickly he added, "But there's got to be rules. You can't just grab my hand suddenly. You'll give me a heart attack. Just send me a message first on my phone." He waggled it. "On this thing, like you did last night. You can only clasp with me if I say. OK?"

Silence. Had he sounded too bossy?

"So, just message me." He waited for his phone to vibrate, then looked up at Yuri and Callie. "I think she's ticked off at me."

"Maybe she's upstairs," Callie suggested.

Gabe sniffed. "You just want to see the lamp room."

"True. Still, she might be up there."

Gabe led the way up the spiral stairs. Last night in his panic, he'd left the hatch to the lamp room open. A square of twilight. With two other people in tow, he felt braver climbing up this time.

He poked his head through the opening in the metal floor and peered around before going the rest of the way. Yuri and Callie followed.

"Don't turn on the light," said Gabe. "If anyone notices they'll think someone's broken in."

The view from the lamp room was commanding. He saw the island end to end. To the south, across the lake, were the lights of coastal towns and cities. And to the north was the sprawling ziggurat of Toronto's skyline.

Gabe pulled his attention back inside. Yuri gingerly lifted off the tarpaulin and revealed the Gibraltar beacon – or what was left of it. A sturdy iron column rose from the floor. At waist height it widened into a circular turntable. In the centre was a socket without a lightbulb. Surrounding one half of the turntable was a curved wall of ribbed glass.

"This is a Fresnel lens," Yuri said, touching it. "To focus the light into a single beam."

"Did you just happen to know that?" Gabe asked.

Genuinely surprised, Yuri said, "Doesn't everyone?"

"I did," said Callie.

Gabe sighed. The only reason *he* knew was because of his notes for the ghost tour. He felt like he'd better get in there with some facts of his own.

"In the old days, it was just a lamp that burned sperm whale oil. There was a mirrored reflector that revolved around it." He looked mischievously at Yuri. "Aren't you going to ask what powered it?"

Yuri grinned good-naturedly. "Please tell me."

Trying not to look too smug, Gabe said, "Clockwork! The gears were turned by a weighted cable; it slowly unwound over twelve hours, down the inside of the lighthouse, then you had to wind it up again. It went electric in the early 1900s."

"Thank you, Gabe, this is very good information."

"There's not even a lightbulb in there now," Callie remarked.

Gabe looked around the room, wondering if Rebecca Strand was here. How would he know? Once, in High Park, a small bird had flown past his head, very close. He'd not *seen* the bird, just felt the quick gust of air from its wings – and an overwhelming sense of *presence*. He had that same feeling now.

"Rebecca?"

Nothing. She was definitely in the room, probably sulking. If she kept up the silent treatment, Yuri was never going to believe in ghosts.

"Maybe apologize to her," Callie whispered.

"Are you serious?"

Gabe wasn't sure he had anything to apologize for, but it was worth a try. "Rebecca Strand, I'm sorry I didn't talk to you last night." He steeled himself and stretched out his hand. "Will you please clasp with me?"

Immediately an icy band tightened around his fingers. It was different this time. The cold was almost painful, crackling up his fingers into his arm. His vision frosted over; Yuri and Callie all but disappeared.

What *was* very clear was the hand that gripped his. It was a very large hand, attached to a crooked, bone-thin arm that zigzagged to a wizened body. The ghost was the size of child, yet its oversized head was that of a man's, with a heavy brow, and eyes that blazed with darkness.

Gabe tasted metal, like he had a ball of aluminum foil in his mouth. The ghost was hunched near the lamp like a gargoyle. A voice emanated from its ragged hole of a mouth:

"Open it!"

With a yelp of horror Gabe ripped his hand free, staggering backward. The room snapped back into focus.

"What?" Callie demanded. "What did you see?"

"*Not* Rebecca!"

Callie threw something. Black sand? Gabe heard it patter to the floor. But some of it hung suspended in the air, sparking – and forming the shape of the grotesque creature he'd just glimpsed.

The ghost writhed, trying to shake off the smoking sand without success. It leapt on top of the beacon, tensed, then sprang right through the window into the night. Rivulets of sand drizzled down the inside of the glass.

"I think it's gone," Gabe panted, peering out. He felt suddenly hot and cold all over, and squatted to catch his breath.

"Are you all right, my friend?" Yuri asked, putting a hand on his shoulder.

"You saw it, right? That thing?"

His friend nodded. "Its shape anyway. What was it?"

"A man, but his body was really small. And his eyes drank the light."

Just describing it made his skin crawl. He'd *touched* that thing.

"This does not sound like a happy ghost," Yuri remarked, then asked Callie, "What did you throw at it?"

"Iron filings. Ghosts have a slight magnetic charge. The filings stick to them."

"And hurt them," Gabe said, massaging his icy hand. "It was actually smoking."

"Do you always carry iron filings with you?" Yuri asked with genuine curiosity.

"When I think there might be ghosts nearby, yes! Iron's supposed to be the only thing ghosts can't pass through. And the filings let you see them for a sec." She paused, out of breath. "Wow. That was my first ghost."

"Likewise," said Yuri.

"Second for me," Gabe said, feeling a little proud of himself. "I was OK with Rebecca Strand, but this thing was next-level scary."

"Did it say anything?" Callie asked.

Gabe could still hear the echo of that terrible voice. "*Open it.* It was bent over the beacon, like it was looking for something."

"Huh," murmured Callie, aiming her phone light at the lamp. "Whereabouts was it looking?"

Gabe moved closer. "Yeah, it was just around—"

His hand went icy again and he hollered. Crouched beside him was Rebecca Strand. She shone while everything else in the room dimmed. Yuri's faraway voice called out his name; hazily Gabe saw Cali plunge her hand into her backpack and come out with another fist of iron filings, ready to throw.

"I'm OK!" Gabe shouted. Even his own voice sounded muted. "It's Rebecca Strand!"

Rebecca's look was intent. "Gabriel, did you see him?"

"That freaky dude? Yeah, I saw him! *He grabbed my hand!*"

"When I saw him approaching, I fled!"

"I don't blame you! Who is he?"

"His name is Nicholas Viker. He killed me – and consumed my father."

6

"Are you ready to hear my story now, Gabriel?" Rebecca asked him.

He took a breath. "Yes, I'm ready."

He knew that he was standing in the lamp room of the Gibraltar Point Lighthouse, and that Callie and Yuri were beside him, but when Rebecca Strand began her story, she spoke so vividly that he felt transported to a different time. She conjured that terrible night, all those years ago, when she saw her first ghosts churning their way across the harbour. Gabe pictured them, hideously dissolving under the lighthouse beam. He shuddered as Nicholas Viker scuttled ashore onto the beach.

"He was much bigger and more powerful then," Rebecca told him. "Swollen with the ghosts he'd devoured. My father said he'd enslaved them, stealing their energy, using their legs to move him, fusing their arms with his."

Then she described the amazing ghostlight, and how its amber beam had blasted Viker, cutting him in two – and with a firework blaze releasing the ghosts he'd eaten. And yet the fiend had survived, and slunk inside the lamp room.

"It was entirely my fault," Rebecca said miserably.

"How?"

"I was supposed to be my father's eyes that night! And I told him we'd destroyed Viker on the beach, every last bit of him! I ought to have been more vigilant!"

Her distress was so intense he instantly wanted to make her feel better. "You were doing your best."

She shook her head angrily. "We weren't ready when Viker got inside."

And she described the struggle in the lamp room, how Viker had seized her father and dangled him over the railing.

"Then I failed my father a second time," Rebecca said. "Even though he told me not to, I put the ghostlight back in the lamp."

Gabe didn't understand. "You needed to, to save his life!"

"But Viker *wanted* the ghostlight. The way his eyes went to it!"

"Why?"

"It's the only thing that can destroy him."

"And you blasted him, right?" Gabe asked.

"Yes, but he took my father with him as he fell – and snatched the ghostlight." Her eyes drifted to the night beyond the windows. "Viker lost his grip on it, though. It sailed out of his hand. And then he turned on me."

After Viker had hurled her from the lighthouse, it took her some time to die. And in that fluttery state between life and death, she saw her father's ghost emerge, bewildered, from his dead body. Helplessly she'd watched as Viker dragged himself from the shadows. He was much smaller now, severely wounded. But he had just enough strength to dislocate his jaws like a python and devour Keeper Strand: first the legs, then his torso, and lastly his gasping head.

"It was like watching my father drown," Rebecca said. "Drowning inside that monstrous creature."

Gabe was silent a moment. He didn't think he'd ever heard anything so terrible. "But *you* didn't get eaten."

"No. I think because I was still alive, and by then Viker was too weak to harm anyone living."

So she'd watched as Viker slowly dragged himself away like a reptile that had gorged on an animal twice its size. Carrying her father trapped within him, Viker disappeared into the dark lake.

"Then I died," she said, wincing, "and I think there must have been a long time when I was terribly confused. As though I were trapped in a feverish dream. I wandered about the island, trying to talk to people, but they all ignored me. All the while I clung to the hope that I would wake. But finally I realized I was truly dead – and that I am stuck here. I don't think I can move on until I save my father. And to do that, I need the ghostlight."

"You think if you blast Viker, you'll free your father?"

"Yes, that's the only way! I saw it done on the beach that night, remember? We freed many of the other ghosts he'd devoured."

"Did you ever search for the ghostlight? After Viker threw it?" Gabe asked her.

"Ghostlight?" Callie exclaimed, sounding a long way away. "What's a ghostlight?"

"Of course I searched for it!" Rebecca replied, as if he were dim-witted. "And I found it!"

"That's great!"

"But then I lost it."

"Oh," said Gabe, feeling bewildered. "So—"

"Never mind about that one," Rebecca said. "There might be another one inside the lamp's secret compartment!"

"Gabe, we can only hear your side of the conversation!" Yuri said in frustration.

Callie pushed in: "Hang on, is the ghostlight the lens that Serge Delacroix tried to give to Debenham?"

"Who's Serge Delacroix?" Rebecca demanded.

"Yes," Gabe said to Callie, and then to Rebecca, "He was a Keeper from Montreal who—"

Rebecca's eyes were bright with excitement. "And he brought a ghostlight for the lamp?"

"Well, Debenham didn't want it, but—"

"—he might have left it behind! Or a later Keeper may have acquired one!"

Gabe nodded eagerly. "Can't you just take a peek inside the secret compartment?"

"I've tried. I can't see or pass through it. It hurts even to touch."

He remembered what Callie had said about ghosts and iron. Then he also remembered Viker, hunched over the lamp. "That's why he told me *Open it*! He's looking for it too!"

"You didn't open it for him, did you?"

"Of course not! I don't even know where it is!"

"Gabe, you are driving us bananas!" said Yuri.

Rebecca touched the base of her throat. "You'll need the key to open the compartment. It was around my neck when I died, but—"

Gabe's overloaded brain finally made the connection: "We have it! We have your key!"

"What key?" Callie almost shrieked.

It was an effort for Gabe to pull his attention away from the bright face of Rebecca Strand to the dim figures of his two friends and the washed-out world they inhabited.

"Your lighthouse pendant!" he told Callie.

Callie pulled it from her pocket. "This is a *key*?"

Rebecca's eyes filled with amazement, then narrowed with indignation. "How is it possible this girl has my father's key?"

"She wants to know how you got it," Gabe told Callie.

Nervously Callie asked, "Is she angry?"

"Nah," Gabe replied, but he couldn't quite fathom Rebecca's expression. Indignation, certainly. But also suspicion, and maybe jealousy? "Callie, you want to tell her the story?"

"Oh, OK," Callie began uncertainly. "Hi, Rebecca." Her gaze darted about the lamp room. "Sorry, where should I look?"

"Just to my left," Gabe told her.

"Got it. Would it be easier if we clasped?" Callie asked hopefully.

Gabe could see how eager she was; she'd spent a lot of time reading about ghosts, but she'd never seen one face to face, and talked to one.

"Tell her no thank you," Rebecca said, and Gabe was surprised by a pulse of pleasure. For whatever reason it seemed that she wanted to clasp only with him.

"She wants to talk through me," Gabe said.

Callie's shoulders fell a little. "All right." She cleared her throat and introduced herself, then launched into how she'd inherited the key.

As Rebecca listened, her annoyance slowly disappeared, and a wistful smile appeared on her lips. "I'm glad my brother had a family. And please do tell Callie that I'm delighted to know I have a niece."

He relayed this to Callie.

"And I am very happy to have a ghost aunt. A *great*–ghost aunt. With five *greats* in front."

"She needn't have stressed how very old I am," Rebecca said crisply. "Now, could you please tell my *little* niece that we're going to need that key to bring the lamp back to life." Kneeling beside the iron column, careful not to touch it, she pointed. "Gabriel, put your finger there."

With his free hand, he did as she said. "Slide it to the right."

A piece of metal slid aside, revealing a tiny hexagonal hole. He heard Callie's gasp of surprise. "I never would've found that," she murmured. "So, the key goes in bottom first, right?" Gabe watched as she pushed it into the column.

"Tell her to turn it to the left," Rebecca said.

"It's stiff," Callie said. "I'm not sure it's moving . . . oh, there!"

Gabe heard the click. It was a very promising click.

"Should something be happening?" Yuri asked after a moment.

"It's been many years," Rebecca said, biting her lower lip. "Perhaps give it a whack."

"Are you serious?" Gabe asked.

"I don't see how it can hurt. I always whack things when they're stuck."

"Me too!" he said happily, then turned to Yuri. "She wants me to give it a whack!"

"Oh, no," his friend murmured. "Another machine hater."

Gabe smacked the iron column hard enough to make his palm sting. From deep inside came the laboured sound of springs and gears, then silence, followed by a worrisome clanking.

"I think I broke it," Gabe said over his shoulder.

"Such a surprise," Yuri quipped.

With a bang that made everyone jump, including Rebecca, two corroded iron handles snapped out from the sides of the column.

"Here we go!" Rebecca said happily.

"You could turn the beacon to aim at ghosts!" Gabe told his friends, remembering how Rebecca had described it to him. "And the whole column went up and down when you stood here." He pointed to the base, where a panel now creakily opened to reveal a metal platform. He pulled it down with a squeal of rusty hinges. The leather straps were extremely frayed. "You can slide your feet into these and—"

"Is this the secret compartment?" Callie interrupted, pointing higher up the column to another hexagonal hole that hadn't been visible seconds before.

"Yes!" Rebecca said.

Callie slid the key in and turned. With the faintest of clicks, the door swung open. Before the others could aim their flashlight beams inside, Rebecca leaned in for a look. When she pulled back, she was frowning in disappointment.

"Empty," Yuri corroborated.

"So Serge Delacroix didn't leave it in there," Callie said.

"Or any other Keeper," said Gabe.

In a forlorn voice, Rebecca said, "I wonder how long the Gibraltar Point Lighthouse has been without a ghostlight? It's a frightful thought, the city being so unprotected."

Gabe frowned. "It's still standing, bigger than ever. It's not like terrible things have happened or anything."

"Haven't they?" she asked darkly.

He felt an unpleasant tingling in his neck. "Hang on, are you saying that every bad thing that happens is because—"

"Not *all* of them, no."

But some of them. *The wakeful and wicked dead.* He'd never forget that vivid phrase. He wondered about all the things ghosts might be able to do. A small spark to start a house fire? A whisper in the ear to distract a driver? A pinch of an IV tube to stop medicine during an operation—

Callie interrupted his thoughts. "Gabe, now would be a good time for the rest of us to hear everything Rebecca's told you."

*

It was a lot to tell.

"I knew the Strands' deaths were suspicious," said Callie afterward. "But I never thought it would be *this* terrible."

"A ghost that *eats* other ghosts," Yuri murmured.

"Well, you've got yourself one heck of a story," Gabe said to Callie, rubbing the pins and needles from his cold hand. Rebecca had released her clasp on him and gone outside to the catwalk, saying she'd keep watch, in case Viker returned. Gabe got the feeling she was also trying to give the three of them some privacy, though maybe she could still hear them through the glass windows. "Now you know exactly what happened that night. You've solved the mystery."

Callie looked almost ashamed. "I feel like a jerk. I was hoping I'd get some great story and that'd be the end of it. But this isn't a story anymore. It's something that really happened – that's *still* happening – and we need to do something about it."

"You're suggesting—" Yuri began.

"That we help her, obviously! Her father's trapped inside a cannibal ghost! Can you even imagine what that must be like?"

Yuri puffed out his cheeks thoughtfully, then exhaled. "I am a practical person and do not have a very good imagination. But I think it might be like a terrible darkness, churning with other tormented ghosts. Confusion. Wailing voices. Perhaps you would have terrible flashes through the eyes of Viker himself. You might be forced to helplessly watch him consume other ghosts. He might even use your own limbs to chase down and crush his victims, and—"

"OK, that's good," said Callie, looking a bit queasy.

"Rebecca's trapped too," Gabe pointed out. "I mean, she can't go on to the next place until she frees her dad." He admired her devotion to her father, but felt a stab of sadness, because his feelings toward his own father were far from noble. If it were his father in there, what would he do? He darted away from that question and said, "Callie's right, we need to help. Both of them."

"This is an extremely dangerous ghost," Yuri cautioned. "He throws people off lighthouses."

Gabe's skin crawled as he looked at the spot where he'd touched Viker. "He's smaller now. Still freakin' scary, but weaker."

"But how long before he gets stronger?"

"That's why we need to find the ghostlight right away," Gabe said.

"You mean the one Viker snatched that night?" Callie asked.

Gabe nodded. "Rebecca said she found it, then lost it. So we need to find it, get it back in the lamp and blast Viker to pieces and free Rebecca's father."

"That was quite a forceful speech, my friend," said Yuri. "But it will be a big job. Maybe an *impossible* job. Almost two hundred years have passed! It could be anywhere. Buried deep in land or water."

"Rebecca," Gabe said. "Can you tell us what happened to it?"

Cold fingers slipped between his, and Rebecca was suddenly beside him.

"After I died," she began, "after I realized I was a ghost, I went searching. I found the ghostlight in the Lighthouse Pond. It was more of a marsh in those days. The ghostlight was just a few inches underwater, half covered by mud. Of course I had no strength to move it, so I tried to tell Debenham, the new lighthouse keeper. Back then I was too weak to even write him a message in dust. I tried to clasp with him, but he shook me off easily, thinking me a devil. I tried a few other people, but none of them wanted to clasp either."

Gabe didn't exactly blame them, but said nothing.

"In the end, it was a little girl who came to my aid," Rebecca continued. "She was a patient at the Island Convalescent Home for Children, poor thing. She couldn't have been more than four years old. She was walking by the marsh one day, and I managed to blow a dandelion puff past her, and set it down on the water, right above the ghostlight. At that moment a bit of sunlight struck it, and it sparkled. She saw it and fished it out."

"What happened then?" Gabe asked, not sure how a little girl could help out.

"The most astonishing thing," Rebecca said. "As she held it up to her eye and peered through it, she could see me. And not just see me, but *hear* me when I said hello."

"Was she afraid?"

"Startled, certainly, but mostly very curious. We had a little conversation. Her name was Charity Bowles and she had consumption, and her mama had promised to bring her a new doll on her next visit. I asked her to take the ghostlight to the lighthouse keeper, so he could see and hear me."

"And?" Gabe recalled Debenham's violent reaction when Serge Delacroix had shown him a ghostlight – and couldn't imagine this would go well.

"We never got the chance," Rebecca said. "Charity's nurse found her and scolded her for wandering off. When Charity showed her the ghostlight, the nurse took it, and checked her forehead for fever, and said she was tired of her tales. Charity asked for the ghostlight back, but the nurse said it wasn't hers to keep."

"That's rotten," said Gabe. "So the nurse kept it."

"Not for long. A few days later, a Mr Boulton and his wife were visiting the convalescent home. They'd donated money and wanted a tour. Boulton saw the ghostlight on a shelf and thought it very pretty. He offered the nurse a handsome price for it. And that was the last I saw of the ghostlight. Boulton took it back across the harbour to the city."

"You didn't follow him?"

"I couldn't."

"You crossed the harbour with me, though."

"Perhaps because you'd clasped with me, and somehow that clasp gave me the strength."

Gabe liked the idea that he could give her strength. "OK, let me tell the others all this," he said, and Rebecca released his hand.

"Boulton," said Callie, after Gabe had filled them in. "That name's familiar."

"To me, too," Gabe said, but still couldn't quite place it.

"It's not much of a lead, "Yuri said. "Knowing who had it over a hundred years ago."

"It's a start at least," Gabe said.

"I'll do some digging around," Callie said, checking the time on her phone, "but right now I really need to get home."

Gabe looked around the lamp room. "Rebecca, what if Viker comes back?"

His phone vibrated:

I can hide.

He hated the idea of Viker skulking around the island, looking for more ghostly prey. Before he could think better of it, he blurted out, "Do you want to stay at my house?"

He caught the surprised look Callie and Yuri shared, and immediately regretted his invitation. Did it seem weird? He hardly knew her, after all. But she'd already been in his house—*without* an invitation.

Only if you're quite certain it's no inconvenience.

"No, it's fine. My mom's doing another overnight shift, anyway."

Then, yes. Thank you very much.

"You're welcome," he said.

"She is a faster texter than you," Yuri remarked.

"Very funny. Let's put the lamp back the way it was," Gabe said, "and get out of here."

7

Gabe was usually ready for a snack when he got home late from the island, but tonight his legs were wobbly with hunger. He slapped together a panini and started wolfing it down at the counter. After a few bites he looked apologetically around the kitchen and said,

"Sorry. I'd offer you something, but—"

On the counter, his phone lit up:

Describe it to me, please.

"Oh, OK. It's a panini."

Panini?

"Italian for grilled sandwich. I usually like the bread crispier, but I was really hungry. The goat milk Brie is nice and runny and has a bit more kick than regular Brie. Maybe that's the goat. And I threw in some avocado—"

Was that the green fruit?

"Yeah. They don't grow up here, so maybe you never had one. We get ours from California or Mexico. The flesh is rich and creamy and it tastes" – he couldn't find the right words and started to laugh – "I really have no idea how to describe avocado."

You're doing a fine job.

"Oh, and I also added some sliced cherry tomatoes—"

Tomatoes! What I would give for a tomato in my mouth!

"I like the cherry ones because the skin is really firm and they kind of burst, and you get the tangy flavor all through your mouth. I sometimes like to add fried mushrooms, but—"

Stop now! You are making me miss food too much!

"OK, sorry."

I miss eating.

A pause.

I miss everything.

Those few words contained a multitude of feeling. Gabe could not imagine what it must be like to be her. To see but be invisible. To hear, but be unheard. She could watch him eating, but never taste. He assumed Rebecca couldn't smell or touch, either.

Worst of all, there was no happy ending: she would never come back to life and taste an onion ring, smell fresh-mown grass, hug her father. At best, she'd get to *see* her dad, and then . . . what exactly?

"What happens afterward," he asked, "if . . . *when* we free your dad? Where do you go? Heaven . . ."

He trailed off. Heaven, Hell, Purgatory? A place no one had even imagined?

All I know is there is another place where I will go.

"Not the same place as Viker, right?"

I sincerely hope not, no.

He hastily finished his sandwich and began returning things to the fridge. Before he could close the door, he felt a cold hand clasp his. He gave a jolt as his vision frosted and Rebecca was suddenly beside him.

"Too sudden?" she asked apologetically.

"I'm still getting used to it."

"Is this your icebox?"

"We call it a fridge, and it doesn't use ice. It's, um, some kind of gas coolant. Inside coils, I think?" He was embarrassed by how little he knew about such an everyday machine. "Yuri could tell you if you—"

"What's this?" She pointed at a thin red bottle.

"Sriracha sauce."

"I've never heard of such a thing."

"Did you guys have ketchup?"

"Catsup? Yes. A sauce made from tomatoes and anchovies."

"*Anchovies*? Wow, well, they don't put fish in it anymore. Anyway, Sriracha's a kind of chili sauce. It's hot. Like ketchup but for grown-ups."

"And this?"

"Mango chutney."

She frowned. "Wasn't there a boy called Chutney?"

Gabe gave a laugh. "On the tour, yes. But this is a condiment used for curries. Did you ever have curry?"

"Never."

"It's from India, a bit spicy; or a *lot* spicy. I love it."

Fascinated, she wanted explanations or descriptions of everything. What was pitta bread? What did soy sauce taste like? She had been responsible for making all the meals after her own mother died, and his kitchen seemed especially interesting to her.

"Is that your oven?" she asked. "Show me, please."

She led him across the room. She wasn't actually pulling him, but he thought it was polite to keep up with her so their hands stayed clasped.

"Does it use wood or coal?" she asked.

"Electricity. Did you guys use electricity?" He didn't think most households had electricity until the twentieth century, and he couldn't remember when it was first discovered. "I mean, that's what powers a lot of things now. The lights, inside and outside. Those big red streetcars we passed on the way here."

"The very small room that lifted us up here?"

"Elevator, yep, that too."

"Remarkable! How does electricity work?"

He cleared his throat. "Well, it's the flow of electrons."

"Where do they come from?"

"They're just hanging around," he said, nodding. "You've just got to, um, get them going."

"How?"

"Magnets? Maybe?"

She frowned. "You don't seem very certain."

With a sigh he said, "I'm really bad with machines."

Her face softened. "But very clever with food."

After her tour of the kitchen – Gabe thought he'd done an OK job explaining the microwave – she seemed curious to explore the living room.

"How're you doing, Charlie bird?" he asked the budgie.

"Loveyouplenty," said the bird, "loveyouplenty!" and then let loose with a string of excited nonsense. Gabe wondered if the budgie sensed their invisible visitor – the same one, after all, who'd hijacked his voice.

Rebecca headed straight for a framed photograph.

"Is this your mother?"

"Yeah. She's an emergency doctor at St. Mike's. And that's my big brother, Andrew. He's at university in Montreal."

She looked at the picture a long time, and reminded Gabe of someone turning their face to the sun after a long winter. He was aware of her cold hand around his, but even more aware of their closeness. It was like their hands made a circuit so they could communicate properly. He felt somewhat awkward that she was dressed only in boots, a nightdress and shawl. But he supposed changing wardrobe wasn't an option for her.

Turning to him, she asked, "How long ago did your father die?"

How did she know? he wondered, then remembered he'd told her when they'd first met.

"January. But he was kind of gone, even before then."

"How so?"

"He left my mom, us, about a year earlier. He moved in with another woman." He checked to see if she was shocked. "People didn't do stuff like that in your day, right? Or not as much anyway."

"Oh, there has always been abandonment."

Abandonment. It wasn't a word people used today when they talked about divorce.

"That's exactly how I felt after Dad moved out. Abandoned."

He dropped onto the sofa, breaking his clasp with Rebecca for a moment before she took his hand once more. For the better part of the year, he'd avoided talking about his father. Not with Mom or his brother, not even with Yuri. Now he was sitting side by side on the sofa with a ghost, telling her stuff he'd shared with no one else.

"You never saw him again?" Rebecca asked.

"No, I saw him, but it was just no good. I almost wished I hadn't seen him."

After a moment, Rebecca said, "When I was fourteen, my mother died. She'd always preferred my brother, and she was a stern woman by nature, but I would have given anything to see her again. As for my father . . ." She faltered, and Gabe sensed she was overwhelmed by feeling; all she said was "I never had the chance to say goodbye to him."

"Now I feel like a jerk," he said, "whining about my tiny little problem."

"It's not little. Neither of my parents left of their own choice. I can imagine it was painful to see your father afterward."

"With my dad . . . ," he began, and faltered. He felt like he was searching through a bunch of word magnets, trying to assemble his own thoughts. "He never talked about *us*. You know, the way we were when we were younger. Things we did as a family. It was like his memory had been wiped. Or like he'd just retired from being my father."

"Perhaps he was wracked with guilt."

Gabe snorted. "He did *not* seem guilty, believe me. He was living the life of Riley!"

A small crease appeared in her forehead. "Who is Riley?"

"Oh, sorry, it's just an—"

"Was he the other woman's husband?"

"No—"

"And your father stole his life!"

"There is no Riley! It's just an expression. It's pretty old-fashioned so I thought you'd maybe . . . anyway, it just means he's having a wonderful time."

"How could your father be having a wonderful time after *hurling* such a huge part of his life *overboard?*"

Her forceful image left Gabe speechless for a moment. "Well, he managed it."

"Hm. I wonder," Rebecca murmured.

"Anyway, it happens all the time," he said, not wanting to sound like a baby. "Not a big deal. And he's gone now, so . . ."

"I hope he's at peace, Gabriel."

Just days ago, such a thought would never have occurred to him. *At peace?* His father was dead. Gone. All that remained of him were other people's memories – as lousy as some of those were. But now Gabe knew differently: maybe his father still lingered restlessly on Earth.

"You think he might be stuck here, like you?" he asked. "If people die when they're confused or angry, aren't they supposed to turn into ghosts? Getting hit by a car would be pretty confusing."

"He may be a ghost, then."

Bitterly, Gabe said, "Well, if he is, he sure hasn't tried to talk to me."

Or maybe he'd already gone someplace where he was very, very unhappy. Gabe's stab of sadness was quickly blunted by anger. He shrugged.

"If he's unhappy, he deserves it. I don't care."

Rebecca said, "I don't believe that. After you woke me, I could have clasped with anyone. But I chose you. I was watching when you first met Callie. You two spoke about ghosts, and there were tears in your eyes. Just for a moment. So I suspected someone had been lost to you, and quite recently."

He studied the carpet, embarrassed that she'd seen him almost cry.

"And I could tell you were a kind person," she added. "Which is why it was very unkind of me to say you weren't, when we first met."

"That's OK." Gabe knew he was blushing and hoped she couldn't tell. Probably she could tell. She seemed very observant.

"I have a temper," she confessed.

"Hey, I'd have a temper too, if I'd been dead for so long. What did you do? All those years?"

"After I saw the Boultons take the ghostlight off the island, I think I lost hope. I was overcome with exhaustion. I must have slept for a long time."

"Where?"

"In my old bedroom at first, but eventually I moved to the lighthouse itself. Time passed so erratically, I was never sure how long I'd slumbered. It seemed every time I looked out over the harbour, things were different. Ferries with great paddle wheels, then larger metal ships that spewed black smoke. The city grew. How high the buildings became! Finally I woke with you saying my name."

He shivered and glanced at her fingers folded around his. She must have followed his gaze because she asked, a bit sadly, "Does my touch make you cold?"

"I'm probably just tired," he said, not wanting to hurt her feelings. "Can you feel anything when you touch me?"

"I feel warmth." She inhaled. "It spreads through my hand and up my arm. It's a little bit like . . . being alive again. As though some of your life comes into me."

He looked at their enfolded hands and felt himself flush again. Energy flowing from him to her. He was like some kind of supernatural battery. But did the batteries run down?

As if reading his thoughts, she said, "If it's unpleasant, I can clasp with you less—"

"No, it's OK," he said quickly. "I don't mind."

On the coffee table his phone lit up with a message from Callie: **Found some good stuff. Turn on your laptop.**

Gabe opened his laptop on the coffee table and clicked the link Callie had sent him. After a few seconds, she appeared on the screen, looking excited. She was sitting up in her bed in Spider-Man pajamas, wearing headphones. On her night table, Gabe glimpsed a bottle of some blue energy drink. Behind her bed was a poster of huge cresting waves that looked like dragons' heads.

"Hi," Gabe said. "So what did you—?"

Callie squinted. "Gabe, I can't see or hear you! Gabe?"

"Oh." He looked at his screen for things to click.

"You need to turn your camera and mic on," Callie said a bit sarcastically.

"Yeah, yeah, I know," he muttered. At least Yuri wasn't here to see this.

"It's the button that looks like a *camera*," Callie added. "And there's another one that looks like a *microphone*? Gabe?"

He found both, clicked, and saw himself appear on-screen. A third box now opened up to reveal Yuri, yawning, in the lower half of the bunk beds he shared with Leonid. He patted down his spiked-up hair.

"Sorry, guys," said Callie, "but I couldn't sleep, so I started digging. I think you'll want to see this stuff. Gabe, is Rebecca with you?"

"Yep," he said, and she appeared beside him as she clasped his hand.

Callie squinted. "Weird. Is she on your right side?"

"How'd you know?" Gabe asked, surprised.

"It's like a shimmer. Do you see it, Yuri?"

"I do. It's a pixel glitch. I am thinking perhaps she produces a small electromagnetic charge."

"What's an electromagnetic charge?" Rebecca asked, looking slightly alarmed.

"It's nothing," Gabe told her. "I have no idea."

The upside-down head of Leonid dropped down into Yuri's frame. "Hey, what's going on?"

"Nothing," Yuri told his younger brother. "Leo, go to sleep."

"You woke me up! Hi, Gabe! Look, I lost a tooth!" Leonid grimaced to show a gap in his smile. "There was so much blood! Who's the girl? Is that your girlfriend, Yuri?"

"No. Go look at your comics."

"She's pretty!"

"Comics!" Yuri reached up a hand and pushed his brother's head out of view. "I hope one day to have a room of my own."

"He's cute," Callie said, and Gabe thought she looked pleased. "He looks like a mini you."

Yuri cleared his throat. "So, Callie, what did you find?"

"All right, check this out."

An old oil painting filled the screen. A pale man in a fancy red uniform was swooning on the ground like he was having a really bad day. Gathered around him was a group of grief-stricken soldiers. In the background a battlefield simmered under tumultuous grey cloud.

"I've seen this painting!" Gabe said. "It's *The Death of General Wolfe*, right?"

"Remind me, please, who Wolfe was?" Yuri asked. Coming from Russia when he was twelve, Yuri hadn't studied much Canadian history.

"He was the British commander," Gabe and Rebecca said at the exact same moment, then laughed together. It occurred to him that, for her, this stuff was much more recent history. Since his friends couldn't hear Rebecca, Gabe carried on: "England was fighting France for control of North America. Wolfe defeated the French outside Quebec City in 1760."

"Seventeen fifty-nine," Rebecca corrected. "The Battle of the Plains of Abraham."

Gabe nodded, impressed. "I'd forgotten its name."

"Aren't you going to tell Callie and Yuri?" asked Rebecca.

"Oh, sure. Guys, Rebecca wanted me to tell you it was called the Battle of the Plains of Abraham. And it was actually in 1759."

"Pretty awesome name for a battle," Callie said.

"Yeah," said Gabe. "Wolfe won the battle but died."

In the painting, a shaft of sunlight made Wolfe's body glow angelically.

"When I die," said Yuri, "I would like a picture of myself like this. But why are you showing us this?"

"Because Viker's in it! This was the first image that popped up when I searched his name."

Callie drew a green circle around one of the soldiers. "That's him! Captain Nicholas Viker!"

Gabe couldn't see his whole body, but saw enough to know he was tall and powerfully built, with a craggy brow and dark hair beneath his hat.

"His hand is out of proportion," Yuri remarked. "I think maybe the artist was not so good."

"No, it's correct," Rebecca said solemnly. "He has an abnormally large hand. Tell them."

Gabe felt a chill, remembering that he'd clasped with that terrible hand. "Rebecca says Viker's hand is actually like that. I noticed it too, in the lamp room."

"Weird. So this was 1759," Callie said. "Viker was only twenty. Then I found him again in 1776."

Another painting filled the screen. A man stood tall in a boat while a ton of people paddled it across an icy river.

"Hang on, is that George Washington?" Gabe exclaimed.

"Yep. *Washington Crossing the Delaware*," Callie said. "The American War of Independence."

Leonid's upside-down head popped back into view. "That boat would sink! It's way too full!"

"Excuse me a moment," Yuri said, then got up to wrestle Leonid into bed, making various Russian threats.

"You guys are too noisy!" Gabe heard Leonid complain.

"I will whisper," Yuri said. When he returned to his computer, he was wearing headphones.

"He's a riot," Callie said. "So, guess who else is in this picture?"

"No way." Excitedly Gabe clicked to make the picture bigger, but he must have done something wrong because it disappeared altogether. In a panic he clicked more things.

"Gabe, what are you up to?" Yuri asked.

He couldn't see Callie but heard her say, "Gabe, you've turned your camera off again. And scrambled up the entire screen."

"Oh, geez." Beside him, Rebecca pointed to a button. "I believe it's that one, Gabriel."

He sighed. "A ghost is helping me with the computer." But she was right, and when he clicked, his friends could see him again. "Sorry about that. Where's the painting gone?"

Callie made it reappear. "Don't touch anything, OK? So our guy Viker is here!" She circled an officer helping to hold the enormous American flag.

Gabe studied the man, uncertain, until he saw the vast hand that gripped the flagstaff. "Viker was very good at having his portrait painted," Yuri said.

"So by now he's thirty-seven years old," Callie said.

"I don't understand," said Rebecca. "Before, Viker was fighting for the British. Now he's fighting *against* them, for the Americans."

Gabe had wondered the same thing, and asked Callie.

"I'm not sure Viker cared which side he was fighting on," she replied, "as long as he was fighting. In what I read, he was described as 'insatiable in battle.'"

"Insatiable?" said Yuri. "I don't know the meaning of this word."

"Impossible to satisfy," Rebecca said, then looked at Gabe expectantly. "Aren't you going to pass it on?"

"It means always hungry, always eating," Callie told Yuri. "Or in this case: killing."

Rebecca looked peeved. "You need to be quicker. I had the answer first."

"You're kind of bossy," Gabe told her.

"I want to be part of the conversation! You need to be my voice!"

"OK, sorry!"

"Are you guys all right over there?" Yuri asked.

"Fine," said Gabe.

"I found one last record of Viker," Callie said. "In 1812."

"No way," said Gabe. "He'd be way too old. He would've been . . ."

"Seventy-three, yes. But still raring to go in the War of 1812."

"This was the one when the Americans invaded Canada, yes?" asked Yuri. Gabe nodded. "And torched Toronto."

"It was still called York then," said Rebecca.

Gabe looked at her warily. "Did you want me to tell them that?"

"Yes, please."

Whispering, he said, "I just feel like I'm interrupting all the time."

"Go ahead."

Gabe sighed. "Hey, Rebecca wanted me to tell you that the city wasn't called Toronto yet. It was called York."

Good-naturedly, Yuri said, "I like a ghost with good information."

Gabe was glad he had some information of his own to add. "And after the Americans burned down our city, we went down to Washington and burned down the White House."

"This is all very entertaining," said Yuri. "Is there another picture?"

"So which side was Viker fighting on this time?" Gabe asked Callie.

"Canadian side – well, the British side technically, since Canada was still a colony – and he served with General Brock at the Battle of Queenston Heights."

"Where is that?" Yuri asked.

"Near Niagara Falls," Gabe said. "Hour and a half from Toronto."

"So get this," Callie continued, "the night before the big battle, Viker disappears. Next morning he's spotted in *American* uniform, fighting against the British!"

"He's a traitor!" Gabe said.

"I found an account by one of Brock's soldiers," Callie said. "And apparently Viker fought like a demon that day. Do you guys mind if I read it?"

"Please do," Yuri said. "You read very well."

"Thanks, Yuri!" She cleared her throat:

In such a frenzy was Viker that even his fellow soldiers feared him. His rifle was never silent, always ablaze. He felled one man after another on the field of war. When General Brock was killed during a charge, many a man swore the shot came from the muzzle of Viker's traitorous firearm.

This was something Gabe had *never* heard in any history class. "*Viker* killed General Brock?"

"It's just one account," said Callie.

"So what happened next?" asked Yuri.

"Brock's soldiers killed him. Sort of."

"Sort of?"

"Viker kept getting shot, then would get back up and keep fighting. They said it took a lot of musket balls before he stopped getting up."

Yuri dragged at his hair. It was pretty spiky by this point. "But he did die?"

Callie nodded. "Battle of Queenston Heights. Thirteenth of October, 1812. That was the end of him."

"Sadly, it was not," Rebecca said. "Twenty-seven years later, his ghost killed my father and me."

Gabe promptly relayed her remarks to the others.

"Why, though?" Callie asked. "Rebecca, do you have any idea what made Viker like this?"

"My father said he had some terrible plan. But he died before he could tell me more."

"Well, thank you, everyone, for this lovely bedtime story," said Yuri. "I am sure I will have sweet dreams tonight."

"I'm not done yet," said Callie.

"Tremendous."

"I also started digging into the guy Rebecca told us about. The one who bought the ghostlight from the nurse. I knew his name was familiar. D'Arcy Boulton! He was a wealthy merchant and he owned—"

"The Grange!" Gabe said, kicking himself that he hadn't remembered sooner. "It's one of the oldest houses in the city!"

"I ought to have remembered that as well," Rebecca confessed.

"Is that the one in the park behind the art gallery?" asked Yuri.

"It's actually connected to it," Callie said. "Look familiar?"

Filling the screen now was a tinted photo of a handsome red-brick house. Ivy grew thickly around tall latticed windows. On one side was a domed greenhouse, bright dabs of flowers visible beyond the glass.

Gabe had walked past this building many times without ever properly looking. He wasn't sure it still had a greenhouse, but the rest was the same, including the stone porch with grand columns. The front door had a pretty semicircular fanlight above it. A pinched-looking woman holding a baby stood on the porch with several children.

"Is that Mrs Boulton?" Yuri asked.

"No," said Rebecca. "It must be a governess."

"So this was Boulton's home when he took the ghostlight?" Yuri asked.

"Absolutely. He had the house built in 1817," Callie said. "He lived there till he died in 1846, and the house stayed in the family till it became the art gallery in 1913."

"What would a wealthy man do with the ghostlight?" Yuri mused.

"It's too big for jewellery," said Callie.

Rebecca stared hard at the photograph. "I wish I could go closer to the door."

"You can," Gabe said, and asked Callie to zoom in.

"Is it possible to go closer still?" Rebecca asked intently.

"The resolution won't be great," Callie said as the photo became grainier.

Rebecca's hand seemed to get even colder, or maybe it was just Gabe's own excitement making him shiver.

"There!" Rebecca said, pointing. "Do you see it, Gabriel?"

He dipped his head so close to hers they seemed to overlap for a moment, sending a strange flutter through his body that made his heart skip a beat.

"Look at the fanlight," she told him.

Gabe squinted at the blurry window above the front door. The glass was divided into panes to look like golden rays coming from a small setting sun at the bottom of the window. Gabe's breath snagged. The sun itself was a beautiful circle of amber glass.

"Yes," he said. "I see it. It's the ghostlight."

Viker slunk across the island, his body wracked with pain from the iron filings flung at him by that dreadful girl. There was a time when iron filings would have been no more harmful to his ghostly body than raindrops. But this time they'd half blinded him, sapped the strength from his already feeble limbs. It appalled him to be so weak and lowly, sniffling about like a shrew.

He had once been mighty.

Alive, he had defeated armies around the world, striding like a titan over battlefields, charging on horseback, fearlessly taking lives. No other soldier equalled him.

And yet he had always served others: General Wolfe, General Washington, General Brock. Always an underling. Never a general. And so he'd fought on, driven all the harder by his envy, until the day he was killed.

His rage was boundless. His dream denied. His envy unvented.

But that day on the battlefield he discovered he could still kill.

Hundreds of ghosts stumbled about, confused, grieving, and he fed upon them. Over time he had grown strong enough to kill the living — until he was decimated by the Gibraltar Point Lighthouse.

But he would be mighty again, mightier than ever — as soon as he destroyed the ghostlight.

How different this island was now. Fields that used to be marsh. Canals between islands that did not use to exist. Streets and houses on the eastern shore.

And across the harbour! The city was a towering galaxy of coloured lights. Even at this late hour, it had the perpetual hum of a great engine. The thought of all the souls over there, living and dead, amplified his hunger. He would cross this harbour soon enough.

For now, he doubted he had the strength to defeat any but the feeblest ghosts. He spied one leaning on an oar and gazing across the harbour with a watchful eye, and decided to stay away. The same went for a furious-looking fellow in a kilt, who paced back and forth in a field, a pistol in his hand.

Fortunately, there were slumbering ghosts. Some had made themselves small as cocooned insects, clinging to branches. Tiny morsels they were, but enough to keep him going. In the hollow of a tree Viker found another ghost, curled like a hibernating squirrel — and ate it.

His pain eased. With pleasure he noted that he had grown a little taller and his limbs had thickened.

The night stretched toward dawn. He spied the ghost of a small girl, wading on the shore. He crept up behind her, unhinging his mouth. But there was something so intent in the way she peered into the water, he hesitated. He put his jaws back together, tried to smooth the grotesque arrangement of his limbs. In his most soothing voice he asked:

"What is it you're looking for, child?"

Without turning she said, "Oh, just trying to find another one."

"Another what?"

Still bent over the water, she replied, "The prettiest jewel," and went on to describe its round, bevelled shape and amber colour.

If Nicholas Viker had had a heart, it would have skipped a beat. "It does sound lovely indeed. Shall I look with you?"

"That would be very kind, sir." For the first time she beheld him. "You are very odd-looking."

"I know. But it's hardly polite to mention, is it?"

"Please excuse me." She gave a determined nod. "I will mind my manners. Nurse always says I must."

"This amber jewel, you've found one like it before?"

"In the pond by the lighthouse!"

"And whatever became of it?"

At this the girl angrily stamped her foot, and told him the whole story.

"Thank you, my dear."

Viker devoured her. As sometimes happened when he consumed another ghost, her thoughts and memories flashed through him. The girl's name was Charity Bowles and she'd died of consumption while in the hospital, waiting for her mama to visit with a new doll.

8

Grange Park had once been the private grounds of the Boulton family; now it was bustling with parents pushing strollers, and kids roaming over play structures and shouting in the splash pool.

Under a tree, a man slept surrounded by bulging plastic bags. A group of art students sprawled on the grass and mocked a big outdoor sculpture that, to Gabe, looked like a giant dinosaur bone. It was Saturday morning, and by chance he and Callie and Yuri all had the day off. The air smelled like wet dog.

They made their way across the park toward the Grange House. Rising behind its old redbrick walls was the modern blue glass of the art gallery. Historic and new side by side. Sort of like how Rebecca Strand was walking, invisibly, alongside him right now. She'd stayed at his place a second night.

"I still think this is a long shot," said Yuri. "Are we really sure it was the ghostlight in that old photo?"

"That's why we're here," Callie said. "To find out."

"The photo was hand-tinted," Yuri said. "Not very accurate."

In Gabe's pocket his phone buzzed with a message from Rebecca. **It was the ghostlight. I'm certain.**

He showed her text to the others.

"Still," said Yuri, "it was a long time ago. People redecorate."

"You're being pretty negative," Callie told him.

"Apologies."

Gabe thought his friend looked weary, and he'd been unusually quiet all morning. "You OK, Yuri?"

His friend made one of his shrugging sounds. "Last night my parents had one of their big discussions."

Gabe knew about these. In Russia, Yuri's mom had been a well-known journalist, and she'd wanted to come to Canada because there was more freedom of the press and it was safer for her family. But Yuri's dad was an engineer, and he wasn't allowed to work here until he got recertified. Which was turning out to be more complicated than anyone thought. So he was working as a draftsman, which was insulting, and didn't make much money. Yuri's mom worked for a small Russian-language newspaper, and her salary was modest too.

"What's going on?" Gabe asked.

"My father is fed up. He is saying if he doesn't get certified by the end of the year, we will return to Russia."

Gabe stopped dead in his tracks. "You can't!"

"It will not be up to me, my friend."

"I'm sorry, Yuri," Callie said. "That stinks." They all started talking about it, asking questions and making suggestions and trying to figure out what they could do – which was nothing much.

"It sounds like it just takes a super long time for all the forms to get processed," Gabe said, trying to stay positive.

"True, but they also say his English is still not good. He is taking lessons, but . . . it is very difficult for him."

Gabe shredded a twig he'd picked up. He couldn't lose his best friend.

"We will see," said Yuri. "For now, let's take a look at this window."

With a sigh, Gabe walked up the stone steps to the porch. Before him was the big front door, and above it, the beautiful fanlight. Unchanged after all these years except . . . it no longer contained a beautiful amber disk. In its place was a regular piece of clear glass. Gabe felt even more dejected. His phone buzzed.

They must have removed it!

"If it was ever there," Yuri remarked.

Callie said, "Looks like I didn't need to bring my glass cutter."

"You brought a glass cutter?" Yuri asked, impressed.

"Are you crazy?" Gabe said. "In broad daylight?"

"It doesn't hurt to be prepared. People are pretty unobservant. Anyway, you think they would've just given it to us? 'Oh, sure, let's just pop it out for you! There you go!'"

Another vibration of his phone:

Callie is right. We need to get the ghostlight. Whatever the cost.

"I like the way this girl thinks," Callie said. "We are definitely related."

Yuri said, "I'd rather not end up in jail."

"Maybe they know something about it inside," Callie said. She tried the front door, but it was locked. She knocked. Just as they

118

were about to turn away, the door was opened by an annoyed waiter.

"You can't get to the gallery this way," he said. "This is the members' lounge. You have to go through the main entrance on Dundas."

"Oh, sorry," Callie said, with the brightest smile Gabe had ever seen. "We're just doing a summer school project on the Grange House and wondered if we could look inside?"

"You'll have to ask in the gallery."

Behind the waiter, Gabe spotted a woman coming down a curving staircase, looking at them curiously.

"Can I help?" she asked, letting herself through the velvet cordon at the bottom of the stairs.

Tersely the waiter said, "They want to know about the house."

"We do tours at the end of every month," she told them kindly.

Callie's face fell. "Oh, that'll be too late. Our project's due this week. We just had some questions about the windows and decorations, and that wonderful fanlight in particular."

Callie's enthusiasm brightened the woman's face. Gabe figured she was probably pretty delighted when anyone was interested in an old window, especially kids. He wondered how delighted she'd be if she saw Callie's glass cutter.

"Come on in," the woman said, "I've got a few minutes."

"Thanks very much," said Gabe, stepping inside the cool entry hall. To either side were large, beautiful rooms with sofas and tables and chairs where people, mostly older women, were eating lunch, or simply chatting with each other over a glass of wine. That lobster roll looked good.

On the walls of the entry hall hung several old portraits. The men all looked smug, like they were super proud of their dogs, or how tight their vests were. The women wore enormous skirts that made them look pregnant, and embarrassing bonnets. Little ringlets of hair were plastered to their foreheads. Gabe tried to imagine Rebecca dressed like this, and couldn't.

"Are you a curator here?" Callie asked the woman.

"A guide. I've given tours for quite a number of years. This is one of my favourite houses in the city. So tell me about your project."

Callie froze momentarily, but Yuri chimed right in, "We are supposed to compare a building from the old days with how it looks now."

"Interesting," said the guide.

"We found this archival photo of the Grange House," Callie said, smoothly pulling out her tablet and showing the tour guide. "And we noticed that the fanlight had this very cool stained glass in it."

"Ah, yes," the guide said with a pleased smile. "You're very observant. A long time ago, there did used to be a piece of amber glass there, quite unusual. There's actually a good story about it."

"Really?" said Gabe.

She began telling them about D'Arcy Boulton. Gabe already knew some of it, but he tried to keep his impatience leashed; Callie smiled and nodded.

"Now, Boulton's wife, Sarah Anne, kept a diary, like many ladies of her time. And it turns out she *hated* that coloured glass in the fanlight."

"Why?" Gabe asked. "Did she think it was ugly?"

"She thought it was haunted."

Gabe cut a sidelong glance at Callie.

"On several occasions, she was convinced that when a full moon shone through it, she saw a ghost on the staircase."

Gabe noticed how patches of sunlight were scattered across the staircase right now. He could easily imagine the ghostlight sending its amber beam inside, revealing the dead.

"Did she say who the ghost was?" Callie asked.

"The governess. The Boultons had eight children, and some of them fell ill during a cholera outbreak. The governess died while tending them."

"Was she the woman in our photo?" Gabe asked.

"Very likely. In her diary, Sarah Anne wrote that she was angry with her husband, who thought she was imagining things. She claimed he wouldn't notice a moose in the same room as him!" She gave a neighing laugh, and Gabe chuckled politely. "So after he died, Sarah Anne hired a glazier to remove the coloured glass."

Overtop each other Gabe and Callie asked, "Where did it go?"

"That detail was not included in Mrs Boulton's diary, alas."

"Maybe it ended up in the attic or basement," Callie suggested.

"If Mrs Boulton was frightened by it," said Yuri, "wouldn't she want it out of her house?"

"Or destroyed altogether," the guide agreed.

Gabe inhaled sharply at the thought of a hammer shattering the ghostlight. A brutal end to their quest, and Rebecca's hopes.

"We still have ghost sightings from time to time," the tour guide said. "Some people claim to have seen a woman on the staircase. Always good to have a ghost story up your sleeve, isn't it? And now I'm afraid I have to go. I hope I've been some help."

"You absolutely have, thank you," said Callie.

The tour guide said goodbye and walked through a hallway into the art gallery. Gabe felt his hand tingle with cold. As his vision frosted, Rebecca appeared beside him, her expressive eyebrows angled urgently. "We need to go upstairs!"

"Why?"

"What do you mean *why*?" he heard Callie ask, as if from a great distance.

"Sorry," he whispered, "I'm talking to Rebecca."

As usual during their clasp, the real world had dimmed; Callie and Yuri had become smudges.

"If the governess is still here," Rebecca said, "she'd likely be upstairs in the servants' quarters."

"But we're not allowed," Gabe mumbled, nodding at the velvet cordon across the stairwell.

"It's a rope, Gabriel, not a spiked gate!"

"Fine!" he whispered. If there was such a thing as a rule-abiding ghost, she was definitely not one of them. To his living friends he said, "She wants to go upstairs. To talk to another ghost."

"Awesome, let's do it," said Callie, and unclipped the cordon.

Gabe checked to make sure the waiter wasn't looking, then followed with Yuri, who refastened the cordon. Dashing upstairs, hand in hand with Rebecca, he held his breath – as if that would make him any quieter. Luckily the carpeted steps didn't creak.

"This way," Rebecca said, and pointed down the hallway to a door that was ajar. Through it he spied another staircase.

"There's an attic," he told the others.

Rebecca urged him up the narrow steps to a landing with a sloped ceiling and a circular window overlooking the park. The air conditioning didn't work very well up here. Heat pricked Gabe's chest. On either side of the landing was a closed door.

"Will I be able to see the ghost too?" Gabe asked her.

"I don't know. Perhaps. Since we're clasped."

"Which door?" Gabe asked.

Rebecca tilted her head like a bird listening for worms, then pointed to the door on the left. He turned the knob and entered. The room was filled with file boxes and all the stuff people didn't want to deal with. Broken printers and ugly chairs and things they'd throw out later.

When he heard Rebecca gasp, he followed her gaze across the room. Sprawled on the floor, a tall woman was fending off another ghost that squatted atop her like a gargoyle, an oversized hand pinning her down.

"Viker!" Gabe gasped, and he heard the name echoed in alarm by Callie and Yuri.

The ghost of Nicholas Viker turned. A hideous tongue lolled from jaws that were open so wide they seemed dislocated.

"Get off her!" Rebecca cried.

Viker obliged. He hopped off the governess, his tongue snapping back into his mouth. When he stood tall, Gabe saw he'd grown since last time. His arms and legs had too many joints, and his flesh bulged strangely, like there were things inside trying to get out. Viker's face was more defined now, more like the man in the portraits he'd seen. But beneath his brutal brow, darkness still spiralled within his eye sockets. Gabe tried not to look into them.

"Good day to you, sir!" Viker exclaimed in a jagged voice, striding toward Gabe like a boneless speed walker. "I believe we've already met."

"Stay away from us!" Gabe shouted.

"Where is he?" Callie cried, and wildly threw some iron filings, which missed the ghost.

"Hide!" Gabe told Rebecca. How could he protect her against this thing? "Go!"

"Don't let go of me!" she pleaded, clinging tight to his hand.

"And I certainly remember you, my charming girl," Viker said to Rebecca.

Gabe stepped in front of her. Abruptly the ghost pulled up short, like an animal confronted with fire. He snorted. He stamped. Each time he tried to lunge at Rebecca, Gabe blocked him. He realized the ghost was afraid of him. Was it his size? His living heat? Whatever it was, as long as he clasped hands with Rebecca, she, too, was safe.

"What a pleasure it was to fling you and your father from the lighthouse," Viker said. "I regret I couldn't consume you, too. He was a goodly morsel to be sure. Lots of sinew and salt to him."

"Release him, you vile thing!" Rebecca cried.

Laughter echoed inside his gaping mouth. "Impossible. Could you surrender up your heart? Your lungs? The meat on your bones? What I have consumed is now part of me."

He made another lunge at Rebecca. Instinctively, Gabe punched him in the face. His fist passed right through, and Viker clasped it with his oversized hand. Cold blazed up Gabe's arm. He yanked his hand free easily, but Viker clutched at him again and again, smiling with his corkscrew eyes.

"Stop it!" Gabe shouted.

"Gabe, what's going on?" he heard Yuri shout. "Are you hurt?"

In alarm, Gabe realized Rebecca had stepped out from behind him. She faced Viker in fury. Her teeth were grinding; then her jaws parted and he thought he glimpsed swirling darkness inside.

"Rebecca?" He was almost frightened of her.

With a cry, she lunged at Viker and struck him square in the chest with the flat of her hand. The other ghost flew back and landed on the floor like a limp puppet. Rebecca advanced toward him, and Gabe hurried after her so their clasp wouldn't be broken. Viker scrambled to his feet and fled, disappearing through a wall.

"He's gone!" Gabe told Callie and Yuri. "It's OK. Viker's gone!"

He turned to Rebecca, who looked normal again, but bewildered.

"What happened?" he asked. "You clobbered him!"

"I felt such rage; I wanted to destroy him. *Consume* him."

"It's all right," Gabe reassured her, though he was still shaken by the change he'd witnessed in her. The vortex inside her mouth.

"I would have been as bad as him! Don't you see?"

Her face was guilt-stricken. "No, you were just angry! You weren't thinking straight."

This seemed to calm her, and her eyes moved across the room to the thin woman, now standing.

"Thank you," said the ghost, "for saving me from that demonic creature."

Gabe watched as she and Rebecca introduced themselves, quite formally. The ghost's name was Miriam Haddon, and she was indeed the governess from the old photograph. Her mouth was small and round, with lips that were very red for such pale skin. She had the long, scholarly face of a librarian, and bony knuckles that looked chafed from cold and maybe too much washing. The pinched quality of her face and the worry lines in her forehead looked permanent.

"Hey, Gabe and Rebecca," came Callie's faint voice, off to his right. "It would be super nice if we knew what was going on!"

"Sorry," Gabe said, "we're just talking to the governess right now."

With a touching eagerness, Miriam slowly stepped closer to Rebecca. "It has been so long since I've spoken to someone."

"We're trying to find something that was once in this house," Rebecca said. "An amber glass that—"

Miriam recoiled. "*He* asked just the same thing!"

"Viker? How can that be?" Rebecca looked anxiously at Gabe.

His heart thumped. Why had Viker suspected the ghostlight might be here?

"What did you tell him?" Rebecca asked Miriam urgently.

The lines in the governess's forehead deepened, and she clutched at her raw hands. Abruptly she asked, "Do you bring news of the children?"

Children? Then Gabe realized she must mean the Boulton children, and his heart went out to her. All these years later she was still worrying about them.

"I don't," said Rebecca. "I'm so sorry. But please, if you could tell us about—"

"The two of them had such fevers." It seemed impossible for the governess to bend her thoughts elsewhere. "Then I fell ill, and" – she frowned, confused – "when I came to myself again, no one would tell me if they were well. No one tells me anything."

Gabe exchanged a quick look with Rebecca. Did the governess even understand that she herself was dead?

"What were their names?" Gabe asked. "The two children who got sick?"

"Susannah and Charles. Are you certain you have no news of them?"

Gabe turned to the smudgy shape of Callie and quietly asked, "Can you do a search for Susannah and Charles Boulton?"

"On it," she said, pulling out her tablet.

"I barely left their sides," Miriam said. "I could not have loved them more had they been my own."

Gabe remembered something Mom had said to him and Andrew after Dad left: "I still have you two." And how worried he'd felt, thinking he and his brother were all that stood between his mom and sadness. It felt like a lot. It felt like too much responsibility.

"Susannah died," Callie said, looking up from her tablet. "But Charles survived. He married and had six children."

Gabe watched Miriam for her reaction.

"Oh, poor Susannah. She was always frail." Yet the lines in her forehead relaxed a little. "That is happy news, though, about Charles. Six children of his own!"

Maybe the worst thing for her, Gabe thought, had been not knowing all these long years. Now, even though some of the news was sad, she at least *knew*.

"Thank you." Her face didn't seem as pinched anymore, and was quite lovely. "I think I will take some fresh air now."

"Before you go," Rebecca said, "do you remember that piece of amber glass in the fanlight?"

Miriam inhaled, as if she could think clearly again. Gabe waited tensely.

"Yes," she said at last. "I do remember it now. Mrs Boulton had it chiselled out."

"Is it still in the house?" Gabe asked.

Miriam shook her head. "Mrs Boulton gave it to one of the servants to dispose of." Her eyebrows lifted. "But, do you know, I saw the servant remove it from the rubbish bin that same night. Shortly after that, he left the household."

"His name, do you remember his name?" Rebecca asked.

Miriam walked to the window and stared out longingly. "What a beautiful day for a walk."

"Miriam, his name, please," Rebecca prompted impatiently.

"What was it now? Ah! Edward Shaw."

Worriedly, Gabe asked, "Did you give his name to the man who attacked you?"

"No! I couldn't remember then," Miriam replied, "and if I had, I wouldn't have told it to that fiend."

"Thank you," said Rebecca. "Thank you so much."

Gabe felt a gust move through the stifling attic. The faded curtains at the closed window rustled, and Miriam Haddon seemed to undulate with them. As he watched, her body became a million dancing dust motes and disappeared through the window.

"She's gone," Rebecca said wistfully. "She had no reason to remain."

Gabe thought about Rebecca's unfinished business. She'd stayed in this world since 1839, slumbering for most of it, yes, but also waiting to find the ghostlight and free her father. And if he understood things correctly, she wouldn't be able to move on, to evaporate and disappear like the governess, until these things had happened. She was a prisoner.

"I should tell the others what happened," he said to Rebecca.

She nodded and released his hand. The room snapped back into sharp focus.

"Hey, guys," he said to his friends, "sorry about that."

"Ah," said Yuri wryly, "you are back just in time."

"For what?" Gabe said, then heard the footsteps coming up the stairs. His shoulders sagged.

"Surprised it took them this long," Callie said to Gabe. "You did a lot of shouting."

The footsteps were almost at the landing now.

"I hope you have another good story ready," Yuri told Callie. "We are about to get in trouble."

It wasn't so bad. Luckily, it was the nice tour guide who discovered them – along with a security guard, who was not nearly as friendly. But Callie apologized and smiled a lot, and explained how important their summer school project was, and how they'd just really wanted to see the bones of the house, and especially the attic, since it hadn't been updated. The security guard chewed them out, and threatened to call their parents, and Callie and Gabe apologized some more, and Yuri dragged his hair into spikier spikes. In the end the three of them were warned never to do this again, and told to leave.

"They just let us go!" said Yuri happily as they crossed the park.

"Well, they were hardly going to throw us in jail," Callie told him. "Especially with you looking like a deranged porcupine."

Yuri patted down his hair. "Not everyone is a calm criminal mastermind like you."

"Criminal mastermind!"

"You spun a lot of stories to get us inside that house. I hesitate to use the word *lies*—"

"Hey, that's called persistence," Callie said. "If you want to be an investigative journalist, you do what you need to."

"And in Russia," said Yuri, "sometimes journalists get arrested. Which is why my family left."

"OK, fine, but what about you? When the tour guide asked what our project was and I blanked, you were right in there. We're partners in crime."

Yuri made his shrugging sound but looked pleased.

Callie turned to Gabe. "OK, let's hear it. Everything that happened up there. Hey, you look kind of pale."

Gabe *felt* pale – and winded, too, as if he'd finished a sprint. "I just need to sit in the sun for a second." He plonked down in a bright patch of grass and rubbed his hands – the one that had clasped with Rebecca, and the other, which Viker had clutched.

"I'll go get us some iced coffees and snacks," Yuri said. "I think you need a little pick-me-up. You like those almond croissants, yes?"

"Anything's good, thanks, Yuri," said Gabe, and handed his friend some cash before he headed off to the café at the park's edge.

"He's a good friend," Callie said, putting on a pair of stylish sunglasses.

"The best." Gabe lay back on the grass with his hands clasped behind his head, hungrily drinking in the heat. A cardinal flashed red from a branch. "Don't worry, I'll tell you everything when he gets back."

"It's just so frustrating! Waiting on the sidelines while you get to go all spectral with the ghosts!"

"You might not like it."

"Maybe I would! Just to experience it."

"It's pretty freaky. And sometimes it's terrifying. And clasping with Rebecca—" He knew she was listening, of course, and didn't want to hurt her feelings. "It can tire you out if it's a long clasp."

His phone vibrated.

I am sorry, Gabriel.

"It's not your fault," he said. "It's the only way."

"Maybe I could clasp with you sometimes, Rebecca," Callie began, "just to give Gabe—"

"No, it's OK," Gabe said at the exact same moment his phone buzzed:

It is best not to break the clasp.

"Is this some kind of ghost rule?" Callie asked suspiciously.

"I guess so, yep." Gabe wondered if he was blushing. He'd been startled by how quickly he'd nixed Callie's request, and was pleased Rebecca had done the same.

"Well, I need to know this kind of stuff," Callie said, "if I'm going to write about it, so . . ."

Yuri returned with coffees and snacks for everyone. Gabe propped himself up on his elbows and devoured his croissant. Then, sipping his drink, he told his friends what had happened upstairs, with Rebecca interjecting regularly by text. She was very happy to correct him and add things he'd forgotten.

"I can't believe you actually punched Viker!" Yuri said to Rebecca afterward.

Gabe noticed that she hadn't described how her jaws had widened like a furious animal. Likely she was ashamed and didn't want to frighten Yuri and Callie. So Gabe decided he wouldn't say anything either.

He finished his coffee. "When she clasps with me, it makes her stronger. Stronger than Viker!"

Only for now. The more he feeds, the stronger he will become.

"That was too big a coincidence, Viker being there," Yuri said. "How would he know the ghostlight might be in the Grange House?"

Callie shook her head. "Hardly anyone knew about it. Charity Bowles. The nurses at the Island Convalescent Home. I guess there's other ghosts that might've known—"

"Could he have overheard us talking last night?" Gabe asked.

It was terrible to imagine Viker's ghost slinking unseen around, spying. And where was he right now? As if sensing his worry, Rebecca said:

I never saw him last night. And he is nowhere nearby at the moment.

"Well, however he found out, I don't like it," Gabe said. "It means he's definitely looking for the ghostlight."

"We're in a race, then," said Callie.

"More like a collision course," Yuri added uneasily.

Callie said, "Luckily we've got a very good lead now. Edward Shaw."

Yuri huffed. "Is it? A *good* lead? A man who took this thing almost two hundred years ago? That is a lot of years for it to go missing again."

"You have a better idea, Yuri?"

"It's a good lead, guys," Gabe said, wanting to head off an argument. "But maybe we should try as many angles as we can. We know there's at least one more ghostlight, right?"

Callie's eyes lit up. "Serge Delacroix from Montreal! He didn't leave it here, so he must've taken it away with him. He had to be a Keeper, too, right?"

"Rebecca, did your father ever mention him? Gabe asked.

She frowned. "He may have, but I can't remember any details."

"There's got to be lots of lighthouses around Montreal and the St. Lawrence," Gabe said.

"And how do we get to them?" Yuri asked. "This would take a lot of time. And explaining to our parents."

"True," said Callie, wilting a bit. "Unless . . . Rebecca, could *you* go and visit some of these lighthouses?"

Before Gabe could object, his phone buzzed with her reply.

Yes, of course.

"We can make a map," Callie said, "and you can do a little sleuthing."

Gabe didn't like the idea of Rebecca going off by herself. The world had changed so much since her time. What if she got lost? What if she encountered a more powerful ghost? A mean one?

"I have another idea," Yuri said. "If I understand things correctly, in the old days, regular lighthouse beams were enough to kill most ghosts. Is this right, Rebecca?"

Yes.

"OK. So I have done a little research. The typical intensity of a lighthouse lamp in the 1840s was around one hundred fifty candlepower. Nowadays there are lightbulbs with much more power."

"How much power exactly?" Callie asked.

"Maybe seventeen hundred candlepower."

"Whoa!" she exclaimed. "That's over ten times more powerful!"

Gabe said, "We could make our own lighthouse beam!"

"And then we'd be able to see ghosts!" Callie said to Yuri.

"And kill them," Yuri added gravely.

Gabe's phone vibrated:

My father could not harm Viker with regular light.

"No, but he was much stronger back then," Gabe said. "You saw how weak he is now. You punched him!"

Only because I was borrowing your strength.

"So we should be trying to destroy Viker *right now*," Yuri said, "while he's still weak, instead of chasing after this other ghostlight."

Gabe had to admit, it made a lot of sense. And it would mean that Rebecca wouldn't have to go off to Montreal alone.

"So could we put one of these new bulbs in the lighthouse and give it a try?"

Yuri made his shrugging noise. "We could do that, sure. But why limit ourselves to the lighthouse?" He grinned. "When we can go *mobile*."

"You mean like a flashlight?" Callie asked.

"More like a powerful searchlight. With some modifications."

"You could really do this?" Callie asked, impressed.

"Yuri can make anything," Gabe told her proudly.

His phone buzzed.

Your new light may well be stronger. And perhaps it might *destroy* Viker. But the only light I saw that *freed* the ghosts trapped inside him was the ghostlight.

Troubled, Gabe looked at Yuri. His friend dragged a hand through his hair. "That may just have been a question of the light's power . . ."

Or it might be something unique that only the ghostlight can achieve.

"We don't know, is the truth," Callie said reasonably. "So my vote's we try every angle. Rebecca tracks down Serge Delacroix's ghostlight in Montreal; Yuri, you rig up a light for us; and Gabe, you and me will find out everything we can about Mr Edward Shaw."

9

Gabe headed home from the Grange House, with Rebecca Strand invisibly hitching a ride on his bike – and suddenly took a detour. He knew where he was going but tried not to think about it, as if he could keep it a secret from himself a little bit longer.

When he was almost at the intersection, he stopped pedalling and coasted. Impatient cyclists pulled around him in the bike lane.

He took a big breath. For a long time, he'd avoided this place. It wasn't hard. He had no reason to go to this part of town. If he ever realized he was getting close, he went a different way. Still, for the past six months, this meeting of streets had pulsed in his mind like a GPS dot.

Gabe dismounted and pulled his bike onto the sidewalk. Just twenty steps would take him to the corner. More than once, he'd Street Viewed it on his phone, his avatar slowly turning north, east, south, west, looking at all the freeze-framed people who had no idea what had happened here that January day, the cars all motionless. Harmless.

In his pocket his phone vibrated.

Is this where your father died, Gabriel?

How had she known? Maybe just the way he was standing, staring.

"If you and I clasp," he asked, "will I be able to see him? Like I saw the governess?"

If your father is still here, yes.

Was he? Maybe Dad had wandered off somewhere, or been spirited off the Earth to the next place.

"And he'd be able to see me, right?"

Yes.

He often wondered if, in that fatal moment, his father had even looked up from his phone to see the car hit him. Or whether it was simply a quick blunt blow that had bundled him into nothingness.

Never knew what hit him.

He died instantly.

It was painless.

Who knew what Dad had been thinking about in that final moment? All Gabe knew was what Dad *hadn't* been thinking about. Which was him.

Tell me when you feel ready.

He locked his bike to a ring. Now that he was so close, he felt himself pulling back. Once he clasped with Rebecca, the spectral world would become visible to him and he might see his father. When Dad had moved out of their house, Gabe had thought: *Is this the last time we will all be in the same room together?*

"I'm ready," he said, and felt Rebecca take his hand. She appeared at his side and he immediately felt a little stronger. She stood bright and clear while, around her, the day dimmed, the people and traffic faded. The entire city was put on mute. He saw the smudgy shapes of the living crossing the street.

In the very middle stood a man, clearer than the others.

It felt like falling off your bike: hitting the pavement didn't hurt at first, but when the pain came soon after, it came in a big aching blow. Gabe wasn't prepared for the sorrow. It knotted in the back of his throat, made his nose and eyes tingle.

Dad was staring down at the phone clutched in his hand. He looked bewildered, like someone who'd just woken up in an unfamiliar room.

Gabe hated himself for his tears. Dad didn't deserve tears.

Rooted to the spot, his father seemed so utterly alone. Unable even to leave the place where he'd been killed.

Gabe's head was loud with sadness and anger. The yearning to go closer was almost overwhelming. He knew he should clasp hands with his dad, but still he felt frozen. He took some deep breaths, reminded himself of the world all around. A taxi honked. A passing couple argued about how much they'd just paid for parking.

Gabe waited for the crosswalk light, then stepped out into the street with Rebecca. Near his father, he stopped. Even though he knew he had less than a minute before the light changed, he could only stare.

Not once had his father looked up from his phone. There was grey in his beard. Gabe had caught him dyeing it once in the bathroom. His clothes were achingly familiar. Gabe had never thought about what he was wearing the day he died. Dad in his Dad clothes.

Gabe stood, dimly aware of people walking through his father. Quietly he said, "Dad?"

His father didn't look up.

Someone jostled him.

More urgently Gabe said, "Dad!" He waved a hand. His father's eyes lifted and looked at him – or right through him. It was impossible to know where his eyes were focused. He glanced up at the crosswalk sign; it was counting down from twelve now.

"He is still very confused, Gabriel," Rebecca said quietly at his side.

He tried something different. "Michael Argus Vasilakis," he said, using his father's full name.

At this, his father's face turned slightly, as if sensing a breeze.

"It's me, Dad. Gabe. Gabriel."

The furrow in his father's forehead deepened.

"Dad, it's me!"

His father looked right at him now, no mistaking it, but there was not even a flicker of recognition in his eyes. Gabe felt his sadness curdle into anger. Typical. His dad had completely forgotten him.

A car horn blasted, and Gabe looked over with a gulp. The grille of an SUV snorted heat against his face. The giant vehicle blared again, and he saw the driver pounding on the steering wheel, his mouth big and mean.

Gabe darted back to the sidewalk. With another long honk, the SUV roared past.

Heart racing, he turned back to the street. His father was no longer looking in his direction; he'd gone back to staring stupidly at his phone. Another car swept through him, and he didn't even notice. Gabe had wanted so badly to talk to him. To shout at him. To say terrible things: *You didn't have to leave me, too! You made things so much worse. You broke my heart.*

Yet he would have forgiven his father everything. But Dad wasn't even paying attention.

"Let's go," he said to Rebecca.

"Gabriel, give him some time—"

He pulled free of her clasp, and she flickered out of sight.

"He can have all the time he wants," Gabe muttered. "He's just not getting any more of mine."

For the rest of the day he felt like a wounded animal that just wanted to slink into a dark cave.

But Mom was off work and had decided to be Supermom and focus all her attention on him. And the one thing he wanted to tell her (*Hey, I just saw Dad's ghost getting run over in the middle of the road*) he absolutely could not tell her.

Over the delicious dinner she made, she lobbed questions at him. How was his job going ("Your tour sounds amazing; I'm really going to try to get over and see it soon"), what was Yuri up to and how was Yuri's father making out ("Ridiculous that the government isn't certifying him more quickly; it makes me so angry!"), and had he made any new friends at the amusement park ("You seem to be texting a lot! Tell me more about Callie!"). She even wanted to know what his favourite video game was at the moment, and her eyes glazed over only slightly when he explained it.

After helping with the dishes, he retreated to his room, where he promptly fell spread-eagled on the bed. His phone buzzed.

Your mother seems very interested in your life.

"Sometimes I think she tries to do the work of two parents."

My own mother was never so curious about my opinions or interests.

Even without hearing Rebecca's voice, he could tell she felt wistful. Trying to cheer her up, he said:

"That's just the way things were back then. Parents barely noticed their kids. Anyway, your mother probably taught you all sorts of things, like" – he cast his mind back to his last pioneer village visit – "coring apples and carding wool and needlepoint and—"

scrubbing floors and making soap and emptying bedpans and wringing out laundry. Drudgery! I liked the things my father taught me better.

"What was he like, your dad?" Gabe asked. From the little Rebecca had told him, he had an impression of a strong, capable man.

Can we clasp?

"Sure," Gabe said eagerly, then felt awkward that he was sprawled on his bed. Quickly he sat up, back against the headboard, and shifted to make room. Her cold fingers entwined with his, the real world dimmed, and there she was, bright beside him.

"He was a big man, and the house often seemed too small for him. He'd knock things over, a whole tea set once – a wedding present from his aunt." She giggled. "He told me later he'd never liked it. My mother got exasperated with him sometimes. But you always felt safer when he entered a room."

Gabe watched her eyes as she spoke.

"He took his job as Keeper very seriously, but he liked his fun, too. In winter he was the one to teach me to skate on the harbour. In summer to swim, and row and sail. The quickest way to tie a bowline. He liked ice sailing, which terrified all of us. He read a lot, Charles Dickens and Victor Hugo were favourites. He played the fiddle badly. He sometimes drank too much with the soldiers stationed on the island. Especially after Mother died. But even when Bernard left for Kingston and it was just him and me, the house didn't seem too lonely. We'd read to each other sometimes in the evenings."

Gabe thought of what it had been like since his own brother had left for Montreal. There were definitely times he'd felt lonely. Reading aloud with someone sounded kind of nice.

"My mother had hoped one day I'd marry an officer from the garrison," Rebecca continued. "But I always got the sense my father had something else in mind for me – even if he never admitted it. He knew my wish was to become a Keeper. And he granted it that night."

The same night her entire future ended, Gabe thought. His phone pinged with a message from Callie.

"She's got a lighthouse map for you," he told Rebecca, and dragged his laptop over. When he opened Callie's attachment, an annotated map of Quebec filled the screen.

"These must have been built after my death," Rebecca said, pointing to several lighthouses around Montreal, "but *these* three . . . I remember their names."

"Any idea which one Serge Delacroix might have been Keeper at?"

She shook her head. "I'll just have to visit all three."

There was a good distance between them.

"How fast can you move?" he asked.

"I've never tested myself; I know that I do tire easily – or used to before we started clasping."

Gabe grinned. "That's why I'm charging you up right now."

"I appreciate it. But I would definitely be faster in one of your trains or buses."

They studied maps and timetables to plan her route. Rebecca asked if she could try the computer – bwas he being too slow? – and her free hand glided confidently over the keyboard. Menus and windows fluttered open and closed.

"It's kind of depressing that you're already better at computers than me," he said.

"I'm sure that's not so. I was practising last night while you slept. I hope you don't mind. It's an extraordinary machine. It's like a wonderful Chinese spice cabinet with endless drawers."

"I could probably break a spice cabinet, too."

Together they put a plan together for her. "You sure you can remember all this?" he asked.

"I have a good memory."

"I bet people's memories were better back then, because you didn't have computers doing it all for you. But if you do forget something, you might be able to sneak onto someone's phone or laptop, right?"

"True."

"And text me. Just grab a random person's phone. Just once a day," he added when she looked at him curiously. "So we know you're OK."

"I will be quite safe, but yes, I will try to write."

"You sure you want to do this?"

"I must do this."

"You remember how to get to Union Station?"

"Yes."

He yawned. "Your train leaves at six-fifty-five tomorrow morning. You should probably get some . . ." He stopped himself. "Do you even sleep anymore?"

"I'd like to, but I'm afraid I'd sleep too long."

He felt his own eyes drifting closed and sat up straighter. "I'd wake you up," he said.

"And how would you do that?"

"Same way I did before. Saying your name over and over again."

She smiled at him. "I think you're the one who needs some sleep. Your eyes want to shut."

"Pretty tired," he admitted.

"I'll let go of your hand. I don't want to make you cold."

"No, I want you to be as strong as possible for your trip," he murmured, letting his eyes stay shut. "In case . . . you run into trouble. Let's just clasp a little longer . . ."

10

The atrium of the Fisher Rare Book Library reminded Gabe of the Death Star's central core. Walls of books soared up around him on all sides, their spines glowing in the electronic light.

"Are we even allowed in here?" he whispered to Callie.

From the outside, the University of Toronto's main library definitely looked like something Darth Vader had designed in his spare time. It was a fortress of grey concrete, with slitlike windows, walls that sometimes met at sharp angles, and a skinny tower shaped like a periscope that was probably an energy ray designed to obliterate planets.

Gabe hadn't even been able to locate the door until Callie led him up a broad staircase to a barren courtyard. Inside the rare-book library, Gabe had half expected to see stormtroopers and droids, but the only other people in sight were other humans who Gabe assumed were university students or professors.

"My mom teaches here," Callie told him, "so I've got a library card. Anyway, it's also open to the public; we just have to register at the desk."

It was Monday morning, and they both had the day off, unlike Yuri. All their schedules were different and it was difficult lining them up. But Callie wouldn't have another day off till Friday, and she didn't want to wait to track down Edward Shaw.

After checking in, he followed Callie through the turnstile and toward the elevators.

"So what's your mom teach?" he asked.

"Dentistry. My dad's a dentist, too. They met at university and were overwhelmed by their passion for flossing. I have really excellent teeth. Look." She gave an exaggerated smile.

"I don't think I've ever seen such excellent teeth," Gabe admitted.

"My grandfather and uncle are dentists too. Oh, and my cousin's studying orthodontics. Guess what they want me to study?"

"You're kidding."

"You can never have too many dentists, Gabe. Not as far as my family's concerned."

They stepped inside an elevator and Callie pushed the button for the sixth floor.

"But you want to be a journalist, right?"

"Some kind of writer anyway. You can imagine the arguments at the dinner table. They don't think it's a reliable way to make a living."

"Well, it's not like they're going to force you to be a dentist, right?"

"No. I mean, there are other things they'd be happy with. But in our last argument, my dad said he wouldn't pay for university if I did journalism."

"Maybe he was just upset."

"Hope so. Anyway, maybe I can change their minds if I win this contest."

"What's the contest?"

"It's a student writing competition. Three categories: fiction, nonfiction, and memoir. There's a pretty big cash prize. And your story gets published in *Pulse* magazine. I was thinking maybe I'd enter something about this whole thing. When it's all over."

Gabe couldn't help smiling. "What category would you enter?"

"That's a very good question."

The elevator doors opened, and Callie breezed out along the high mezzanine, past shelves of glowing books.

"You sure know your way around this place," Gabe said, hurrying to keep up with her. She led them away from the central atrium, deeper into the stacks.

"I thought I'd be able to find more about Edward Shaw online," she said. "But all I got was a list of articles from old newspapers that haven't been digitized yet. Mostly the *Globe.* Luckily, they've still got actual copies here."

Off to their right, shelves stretched on and on until they disappeared in gloom. Gabe wondered why it had to be so dark. Maybe it was better for preserving the books. He supposed it was also energy-efficient, since not a lot of people seemed to be up here. So far he'd only seen one other person, scurrying along, clutching an enormous tome like he was stealing it. Maybe he was.

"Have you heard anything from Rebecca?" Callie asked.

"Just a text yesterday to let me know she's OK."

It was strange, being without her. It had only been a few days, but he'd already gotten used to having her around. He liked the way she talked; the words she chose. They weren't everyday words. And even in her texts, she always wrote in complete sentences, with punctuation and everything.

Most of the time she was invisible, but he liked to think he could sense her nearby presence – the fluttery feeling that, at any moment, fingers would graze his own and suddenly she'd be beside him, the brightest thing in the room.

"Here we go," said Callie, and pressed a button at the end of a bookshelf. With a whirring noise, two long rows of metal shelves parted and created an aisle they could walk down.

"Cool," said Gabe. "I guess you fit in a lot more books this way."

As they started down, it was dark, but after a moment overhead lights flickered on. Gabe looked at the rows of tall black volumes, roman numerals tooled into the spines.

"OK," Callie said, checking a list on her tablet, "this is the first." She pulled out a book and dumped it in Gabe's waiting hands. "Look for April eighth, page two. The headline should read 'Ferryman Joins Harbour Fleet.' I'm going to check out this one." She walked a few steps along and pulled out another volume.

Gabe opened the dusty tome and blinked at the columns of tiny text. Sitting, he slumped against the shelves, holding the newspaper pages close to his face. The light was hardly ideal. He turned carefully through the brittle pages to the right date. Luckily, the headlines were in larger print. Underneath was a grainy photo. A skinny man stood proudly at the end of a wharf. Alongside was docked a very strange boat. In the centre of the deck were three horses on a treadmill that was connected to a paddle wheel at the ship's stern. On the ship's boxy side was stenciled EDWARD SHAW FERRY CO.

"He started his own ferry company," Gabe told Callie, skimming the tiny text. "He took people over to the island on a horse-powered paddleboat. He had just the one boat. The reporter isn't very polite. He said it stank. I guess it would get pretty stinky with the horses pooping on the deck all the time. Summer especially."

From some twilight area of the library, an invisible voice said, "Shhhh."

"Still," he said more quietly, "even a stinky horse ferry can't have been cheap. Pretty good for a guy who used to be a servant."

"And a year and a half later," Callie said, eyes darting over her own newspaper article, "what do you think happens to our guy Shaw?"

"He goes bust?"

"Look."

He scooted closer to Callie. Her hair smelled nice, and weirdly it made him miss Rebecca, whose hair he'd never get to smell.

Callie pointed to the smeary newspaper photograph. The Toronto harbour was busy with dozens of small steam vessels, and almost every one of them had EDWARD SHAW FERRY CO. painted on its hull.

"That was fast!" said Gabe. "Where'd he get all the money?"

"Let's find out." She checked the list on her tablet "Next article! Come on!"

At the end of another aisle she pressed the button. As Gabe watched the shelves part, he felt a cold tingle of excitement across the back of his neck. He was on a treasure hunt.

Callie's fingers bumped along the spines of more tall black tomes. Then she dragged one out. They dropped to the floor and opened it across their laps.

"Should've brought a magnifying glass," she murmured, turning pages. "OK, here we go . . ."

"So this is three years later, right?" Gabe said.

"Yep." She turned one last page, and her finger swished to the headline: YORKVILLE'S NEWEST TENANT

Gabe knew that, for over a century, Yorkville had been home to some of the city's richest families. His eyes went straight to the photograph of an imposing mansion with a steeply angled copper roof and arched windows. Standing proudly before it was Edward Shaw, wearing his new wealth in extra weight and fancier, stiffer clothing. In his right hand, he held a gleaming pocket watch connected to his vest by a chain . . .

"That is one freaking big house!" Callie said. "How many rooms would you say—"

"That's not a watch in his hand."

"You sure?" Callie asked him.

He leaned back so she could take a closer look.

She sucked in a breath. "It's the ghostlight."

Gooseflesh prickled across Gabe's bare arms. Even in an old black-and-white photo he could make out the telltale bevelled surface of the lens. Shaw had mounted it like a pendant, so he could keep it on a chain.

"Why would he carry it on his body all the time?" asked Callie.

"He doesn't want to lose it. It's valuable."

"But *how?*"

Gabe chewed at his lip. "Shaw's a servant. He has next to no money. He steals the ghostlight, or takes it from the trash, whatever. Next he buys a boat. Where's the money come from? Then he buys *all* the boats. Now he has a mansion. It's got to have something to do with the ghostlight, right? What does it do for him?"

The overhead lights blinked out, and his heart thumped in his throat.

"So annoying," said Callie. "They're on a timer."

Crazily she waved her arms over her head. With a fizz, the lights came back on.

Gabe's pulse slowed, but he looked around uneasily. The gloom of the stacks was starting to creep him out.

"Last article," Callie said. "This way."

She led the way to yet another pair of sealed bookshelves. Gabe pressed the button.

"Open sesame," he said as the shelves parted.

The volume they were searching for was halfway down the aisle. Callie leaned it against an empty shelf and hurriedly turned pages. She came to a stop at August 10, 1909. The front-page headline read: HANLAN HOTEL BURNS TO GROUND.

"Is this the same one you talk about on your tour?" Callie asked.

Gabe nodded. The first time he'd seen photographs of the hotel, he could barely believe anything so grand had ever been built on the island. It was a palatial four-storey building with verandas and balconies and turrets. Nearby they'd also constructed a baseball stadium, a carousel and amusement park, a summer opera house – all lost in the fire.

"But why's Edward Shaw in this story?" he asked.

"I'm reading . . . ," Callie said, her eyes skittering across the page.

The lights went out again. This time they didn't come back, even after Gabe waved his hand around. With a metal squeak the shelf they were leaning the book on moved – and kept moving. In alarm he realized that both sides of the aisle were closing.

"Hey!" he shouted into the darkness. "We're still in here!" The other shelves hadn't closed this quickly, had they?

"Come on!" Callie told him. "Run!"

Gabe looked at the shrinking light at the end of their aisle and knew they wouldn't make it. "Up!" he shouted.

Pushing and kicking away books to make room for his hands and feet, he jumped onto the shelves and clambered up them like a ladder. He scrambled onto the top, lay flat and reached down for Callie: "Hurry!"

The narrow canyon of books was closing fast, and she was trying to climb holding their big volume.

"Just drop it!" he yelled.

"Take it!" She thrust it toward him, then lost her grip. The book fell, but at least she had both hands free now. She hauled herself up and into the clear, seconds before the aisle snapped completely shut.

Panting, they lay side by side.

"People are always talking about how libraries saved their lives," Callie said with a giggle. "They never tell you they can also *kill*."

"You think this was just an accident," whispered Gabe, his skin crawling.

Callie's eyes darted. "Viker? You think he followed us here?"

"If he did trail us to the Grange House, why not here?"

Maybe that prickly chill he'd felt earlier wasn't mere excitement; maybe it was Viker, melding with the shadows of the book stacks, reading over his shoulder? If Rebecca had been here, she could've warned them.

At any second, Gabe expected the searingly cold clamp of Viker's hand; the terrible flash of that hideous face near his own.

"He can't hurt us," Gabe said, trying to sound reassuring; hoping he was right. "He's not that strong."

"Come on, let's see if we can get that book back."

Gabe was eager to get out of the library *now*, but he supposed Callie was right. That unfinished newspaper article might hold a vital clue about Edward Shaw – and the location of the ghostlight.

They slid along the top of the shelves to the end. Just as they dropped down to the floor, a cardiganed librarian hurried into view.

"Are you all right?" she exclaimed.

"The shelves started closing while we were inside!" Callie said.

"I am so sorry! Maintenance was in just last week and they said they'd fixed the problem. You're sure you're all right? You didn't lose anything inside?"

"Just the book we were looking at. We weren't done."

"Well," said the librarian, pushing the button to no effect, "it'll likely be a while before we can get this looked at. If you leave the details, I can contact you when we retrieve the material."

Callie cast a despairing look at Gabe, but there was nothing they could do about it right now. Personally, he was very happy to leave the murky realms of the stacks and get outside. Even the drenching August heat was welcome.

"Maybe it wasn't even Viker," Callie said. "Could he really do something like that?"

"If Rebecca can work my laptop, why can't Viker trigger an electric switch?"

"We really need that book."

"We'll get it."

"In the meantime . . ." Callie dug into her satchel and pulled out a small Ziploc bag. "Here, take this."

"Iron filings?"

"Just in case," she told him.

11

"This is what I have been saying," Yuri told Gabe in the maintenance shed the next day. "This is why we need a mobile lamp. Then you would've seen Viker coming in the library."

"If it even was him," Gabe pointed out.

"Sure, but if it was, you could've blasted him."

"Hey, I would've loved that, believe me."

He hadn't slept well. Even with Callie's bag of iron filings under his pillow, he kept waking up in a sweat. Turning on his light, he'd look around his bedroom, wondering if Viker had followed him home and was standing in the shadows. Today he felt wiped—and worried, because Rebecca still wasn't back. All through his tours, he'd been hoping his phone would vibrate with a message—or, even better, that she'd suddenly clasp hands with him. At least he was finished for the day and could now hang out with Yuri.

"So, any progress on this new lamp of yours?" Gabe asked.

"Oh, much more than ideas." Yuri went to his locker, reached inside and lifted out a machine that resembled an electric leaf blower with a smidge of bazooka. He placed it on the workbench.

"Whoa!" Gabe exclaimed. "How did you do this so quickly?"

"This is merely a prototype," Yuri said modestly.

"Explain this to me."

With a small flourish Yuri said, "What we have here is a portable halogen spotlight, two million candlepower—"

"Two million?"

"Yes. We have come a long way since the Gibraltar Point Lighthouse. The battery makes it bulkier than I would like, but it's an OK start. Attached to the light is a two-foot measure of metal rod with a series of lenses I added inside, to focus the beam. That coupling is temporary; do not look at it; I am ashamed. On the barrel I have mounted sights, so we can aim properly. Underneath, here and here, two handles for a steady grip."

Gabe shook his head in admiration.

"I've also added a power dial, here. At low, I'm hoping it will be just enough to reveal ghosts without harming them. I am assuming Ms. Strand is not the only nice ghost out there, yes?"

"Good thinking," Gabe agreed. He hated the idea of Rebecca getting hurt accidentally.

"But," said Yuri, his eyebrows shooting up enthusiastically, "crank it up to full power, and then we are really cooking! If the Gibraltar Point Light could shred ghosts, this lamp should incinerate them!"

Gabe desperately wanted to hold it. After his encounter with Viker in the Grange House – and possibly the library – he wanted to be able to fight back. Even if this lamp couldn't destroy Viker, surely it would hurt him enough to drive him away.

"Can I hold it?" he asked.

"Aren't you going to ask me how long it can hold a charge?"

Gabe grinned. "How long can it hold a charge?"

"Continuous use with full power? Fifteen minutes, tops. I know, pathetic. I will figure out some way of improving on this."

"Awesome. Hey, do you think I can hold—"

"So, to preserve battery power, you need to squeeze the trigger to release the light. At whatever intensity you've selected on the power dial. Low, medium, high. Keep squeezing, the light keeps coming. Release, it goes dark. So you don't use up all the power too fast."

"That's really smart," Gabe agreed, nodding. "So can I ho—"

"Also, a more powerful battery would make it too heavy."

Gabe and Yuri regarded each other silently a moment.

"You really don't want me to hold it, do you?" Gabe said.

Yuri sighed. "If you hold it, you must promise to be gentle and not break it."

"I never mean to break things!"

"Yes, but you have a history of, well, rough treatment. OK." With some reluctance, Yuri lifted the machine and offered it to his friend. "Are you ready? I am giving it to you now."

Gabe gripped the handles. The back end was surprisingly heavy, and he adjusted his stance.

"I'll add a strap for extra stability," Yuri suggested. "You can also rest it on your shoulder."

"Like a missile launcher," Gabe said, hefting it up and looking along the sights.

Yuri gingerly pushed the end of the barrel away from him so it pointed at the far wall. "Please never aim this at a person. Or look directly into the beam."

"Got it."

Gabe set the power dial to low and squeezed the trigger. A small circle of light painted itself vividly on the bricks.

"Increase the power now," said Yuri.

Slowly Gabe dialled it up. He heard the buzz of the battery and felt the growing heat of the lamp against his cheek. Within seconds the white circle was almost too bright to look at. "I'm worried I'll burn a hole in the wall" he said, dialing down and releasing the trigger. "Yuri, you're a genius. This is awesome!"

"It's merely a glorified flashlight," Yuri said modestly.

"Oh, come on!" said Gabe. "And we can't call this thing a flashlight. We need something with a bit more oomph. A bit more poetry!"

"You have a suggestion, Mr Shakespeare?"

"How about . . . beam blaster?"

Yuri gave one of his shrugs.

"Light thrower?"

Yuri made an ambiguous sound.

"OK, OK. Light launcher!"

Yuri looked thoughtful.

"Come on!" said Gabe. "You love it!"

"That one is good, yes."

"Let's grab some food," said Gabe happily, "and then test it out when it gets dark."

"You think we can find a ghost so easily?" Yuri asked.

"Leave that to me," Gabe said. "I give the ghost tour, remember?"

After sunset, the light launcher jutting out of Yuri's backpack, the two of them biked to the west end of the island where it would be less crowded. On the way they passed a few families heading to the ferry dock, and a field where four teenagers threw a Frisbee in the deepening twilight. But by the time they passed the filtration plant, it was pretty deserted. Cicadas buzzed from high in the trees.

"Callie's not joining us?" Yuri asked. Something about the way he asked made Gabe think his interest in her was more than just friendly.

"It's her sister's birthday tonight."

"That is a shame," Yuri said. "She would want to see the light launcher in action."

"I'm sure she'll be very impressed."

Yuri gave him a glance. "Oh, you think I am interested in her *that* way. No, no, no."

"Right."

With stoical resignation, Yuri said: "Gabriel, we are not the kind of boys who have girlfriends."

"What does that mean?" Gabe demanded. "Why not?"

"Let us be honest. We are oddballs. I am a bit odd-looking—"

"What? No you're not—"

"I have a strong Russian accent which I am in no hurry to get rid of—"

"I think it's cool—"

"And really, I am most interested in machinery. Not many people share my interests. I must accept it."

"I don't believe you," Gabe said. "You like Callie. And she gets you. You guys were geeking out over the CN Tower together."

"As for you," Yuri went on, "you are shy, and feel more comfortable cooking, and being around books and old things. You look at girls like they are beautiful alien creatures."

"I do not!"

"It's true. I have seen it many times. Whenever a girl comes over to talk to you, you make the face of an astronaut seeing a beautiful alien."

"I don't even know what that looks like."

To demonstrate, Yuri made his eyes widen and go glassy, like his brain had frozen inside his space helmet.

"Please tell me you're not serious."

Yuri did his all-purpose shrug, which, in this case, meant yes he was, sadly, serious.

"That's terrible," said Gabe. "I've got to work on that."

"Although," said Yuri, "you seem to get along pretty well with Rebecca Strand."

"Ha ha," said Gabe, but felt heat creeping into his cheeks. "She's almost two hundred years old."

"The perfect match for you! You love old things."

"She's also dead."

"So, an unusual girlfriend. Or should I say *ghoul*friend?"

"Nice," Gabe said, laughing.

"On the subject of ghosts," Yuri said, "I was wondering something as I worked on the light launcher. Today our lights are so much more powerful. Streetlamps, car headlights, even a regular lightbulb. So why aren't we seeing ghosts all the time?"

"Maybe we are," Gabe said, thinking about something Rebecca had told him. "But we just don't notice. I mean, say you're walking down the street. Even at night, there's lots of people and cars and buses, and traffic lights. Are you really going to notice a ghost that flickers into view for a split second? Your brain would just think it was something normal."

"Maybe so," said Yuri, "but here comes another question. Why don't these ghosts get melted by all the powerful lights?"

"That is a very good question." Gabe thought about it as he pedalled along. Past the filtration plant, past the high fence of the archaeological site where they were excavating the shipwreck. "OK, how about this. Ghosts would avoid the light, right? If it harmed them, they'd just skip away. The way Rebecca described it, you had to train the lighthouse lamp on them for a certain amount of time."

Yuri nodded. "So maybe it's a question of intensity and time. This is a good theory."

"Let's test it," Gabe said, dismounting.

They walked their bikes through the trees into a small clearing that jutted into a big pond called Hanlan's Bay. The night was cooling and a layer of mist hovered over the water. In the middle of the pond, the hump of a tiny island blocked their view of the filtration plant on the other side.

"Why this place?" Yuri asked, pulling out his light launcher.

Gabe was slightly disappointed that his friend would be the first to try it out. But it was only fair; this was Yuri's invention. "People from the city used to fight duels here," he said.

"You mean, 'Take ten paces, turn, and shoot'?"

"Yeah. It was illegal even back then, so they did it out here where no one would see. I figure there might be some casualties hanging around."

Yuri looked around uneasily. "How many ghosts do you figure are on this island?"

Gabe slapped a mosquito off his neck. "People have been using this place for thousands of years, way before Europeans came. I read that Indigenous people hunted and camped here. Anyone who died here with unfinished business could still be hanging around."

"So, potentially, a lot of ghosts," said Yuri, aiming the light launcher at the ground. "Let's start on the lowest setting."

He squeezed the trigger and lit up a circle of grass. Slowly he moved the beam across the clearing. A small shape darted out of the light.

"Squirrel," said Gabe.

"Yes, squirrel," agreed Yuri.

As he swept the beam across the bushes along the water's edge, Gabe caught a silver glimmer.

"Go back a bit," he whispered.

Deep within the branches was something that looked like a giant chrysalis. It took a moment for Gabe to realize it was a person, curled up very tight and small in a deep sleep. It glittered as if coated in frost, which made it hard to tell its age or size, or even whether it was wearing clothing. It flinched as the light remained on it.

"Don't wake it," Gabe said.

Yuri let the lamp go dark. "Was that a hibernating ghost?"

"I guess Rebecca was like that, for a long time," Gabe said. With a pang, he imagined her slumbering, alone and defenseless, on the island. He hoped she was OK now, travelling by herself. The last "I'm fine" text he had from her was late yesterday night.

Yuri sent a beam of light darting across the pond. Gliding soundlessly through the beam was a canoe that had not been there a second before. "Did you see that?" Yuri whispered, and angled the beam after the boat.

Gabe inhaled sharply. In the stern of a wooden canoe sat a man, working his paddle to bring the boat to a standstill. Up front stood a second man with a spear, peering intently at the water. From the canoe's bow jutted a long pole with a basket at the end. Within the basket burned a small fire.

"There's more of them," Yuri whispered.

Farther away, at the very fringes of their beam, Gabe saw the misty outlines of several other canoes, each with a torch at its bow, each carrying two people.

"What are the torches for?" Yuri asked.

"I think they bring the fish to the surface."

The man in the closest boat plunged his spear into the water and pulled it back with a fish impaled on the tip. When he turned to flick it into the canoe, he noticed the light launcher's beam. Lifting a hand to shield his eyes, he stared straight at Gabe. There was no alarm or malice in his face. He said something to the other man, who dug his paddle into the water with a soft plash. The canoe scudded out of the light's beam and disappeared.

Yuri killed the light and turned to Gabe, his eyes wide with wonder.

"These are my first ghosts," he said, sitting down. "Real *sightings*, I mean. It's quite something."

"He looked at me like *I* was the one out of place," Gabe murmured.

"Did they seem like the dangerous kind to you?"

"Not at all. And they looked normal. I mean, they didn't have corkscrew eyes and freaky long arms like Viker. I felt almost guilty, disturbing them."

"So we've got many different kinds of ghosts," Yuri said, like he wanted to break down a complex problem. "Sleepers, like the one in the bushes. Confused ones, like Miriam Haddon, who aren't entirely sure they're dead, but need to learn something before they can move on. Nice ones like Rebecca who *know* they're dead and know exactly what they need to do. And dangerous ones like Viker, who want to eat other ghosts and get as strong as possible."

"These fishermen didn't seem dangerous or confused," Gabe said. "They seemed content."

"So why are they still here?"

"No idea. We can ask Callie, or Rebecca when she gets back."

"Well," said Yuri, "we know the light launcher can show us ghosts without hurting them. But we also need to *destroy* a ghost to make sure it works properly."

After seeing the fishermen, Gabe realized killing one might be harder than he'd thought. "Let's find a really bad one," he said. "Over there maybe."

Yuri slowly moved his beam of light across the clearing.

"Kindly git that light outta me eyes!" a man shouted in a thick Scottish accent.

Gabe jumped, and Yuri's finger must have slipped off the trigger because the light launcher went dark. The ghost instantly disappeared.

"We can *hear* them, too!" Gabe whispered. For some reason he hadn't counted on this. "Do it again."

Yuri aimed his beam low. Gabe saw mud-spattered boots, then, as Yuri moved the light higher, a pair of hairy legs in argyle knee stockings. Next a red-and-black kilt, and above that, a burly body in vest, jacket and black tie. Finally, Yuri's beam revealed a ruddy face with bristling ginger sideburns and angry eyes.

"There ye go agin!" the ghost shouted, shielding his eyes. "Douse that light, laddie!"

Yuri moved the beam off so the ghost was illuminated only at its very fringes. This seemed to work, for the ghost dropped his hand, but looked no less angry. For the first time, Gabe noticed he held an old-fashioned pistol.

"Ye nearly blinded me, ye little spittoon!"

"Spittoon?" Yuri whispered to Gabe.

"A bowl people used to spit into."

"And where's Mr Buchan, I ask ye?" the ghost demanded. "Where has that festerin' little pustule gone?"

"Is *pustule* another rude word?" Yuri asked.

"Yes. A zit. Full of pus."

"Ye kin go tell Buchan," the furious ghost said, "that he can't hide from me forever! He's been *challenged* to a duel and I'll not *rest* till I see his brains *splattered* upon the earth."

"Look at his chest," Yuri whispered to Gabe. There was a singed hole in his vest, right through his heart.

"I think," Gabe said quietly, "our guy lost the duel."

Clearly, this angry duellist didn't realize he was dead. Maybe if Gabe told him the truth, he'd be able to move on.

He cleared his throat. "Sir, you've been shot."

The ghost squinted. "Don't talk *nonsense*, laddie! No one's ever beaten Malcolm Macbeth MacCready in a duel! Buchan'll find *that* out soon enough. Unless the coward sent *ye* to fight for him?"

"What? No!"

"Come on then, ye little prat, ye can count out ten paces, can't ye?"

"Sir," said Gabe. "I know this is hard to understand, but you were shot by Buchan and—"

"What a lot of cheek!" Malcolm Macbeth MacCready took a threatening step forward.

Gabe stepped back. "There is a *hole* in your *heart*! You are *dead*!"

"*Ye*, sir, will fight with me, I challenge ye! Take yer pistol this moment, ye steaming heap of yak dung!"

"No wonder someone shot him," said Yuri. "Shall I increase the power and—"

Despite himself, Gabe felt pity for the obnoxious ghost.

"I'm *counting*!" MacCready said, starting his paces. "One! Two! Three . . ."

"He can't hurt us," Gabe said. "Let's just leave him."

"You sure?" asked Yuri. "He's very unpleasant."

"Six . . . seven . . ."

"Let him go," Gabe told his friend.

Yuri reached for the power dial. "Gabe, we need to test this machine!"

"Nine! I'm coming for ye, laddie!" cried Malcolm Macbeth MacCready. "Ten!"

Yuri switched off the light, and the ghost vanished.

Gabe stood with his friend in silence for a moment.

"I couldn't do it," Yuri said. "Why couldn't I do it?"

"He was a jerk, but I'm not sure he qualifies as the wicked and wakeful dead. Also, he did use some pretty fun words."

A grin spread across Yuri's face. "Steaming heap of yak dung! Who says such a thing?"

"Me, from now on!"

Yuri sighed and patted his light launcher. "We still need to test it out properly."

"We will. Let's just wait for a bad ghost."

"We can't wait too long, if we want to destroy Viker before he gets stronger."

"Tomorrow," Gabe said. "It's late, and I need to get home."

Yuri wanted to store the light launcher in his work locker – "I can just imagine what my little brother would do with this at home" – so they returned together to the deserted amusement park. The concessions and games were shuttered for the night, as was the antique carousel. A breeze whistled through the spokes of the Ferris wheel. The gondola cars swayed gently from their overhead track. As they passed the log flume ride, Gabe dipped his hand into the still water and splashed it on his brow.

"Someone forgot to close up the bumper cars," Yuri said.

Up ahead, Gabe saw all the multicoloured bulbs blazing merrily in the ceiling above the track. The bumper cars had been parked at the back, except for a single red one out in the very middle of the track. Gabe looked around to see if anyone was coming to put the ride to bed, but saw no one.

"Sloppy," Yuri murmured, and hopped over the railing. As he walked toward the lone car, it made a buzzing noise. A spark flashed underneath. "I had this one in the shed just yesterday. It was fine. These kids are so rough."

"They're bumper cars, Yuri. They take a beating."

Gabe leaned against the railing as his friend set down the light launcher and ducked to take a look underneath the car. Sparking, it nudged against him.

"Shouldn't you shut it off first?" Gabe asked. "Don't get electrocuted or anything."

Yuri looked back at him in amusement. "That's impossi—"

The car knocked him hard enough to make him stumble.

The hairs stood up on Gabe's arms. "Yuri. Get the light launcher."

It was already in his friend's hands. Yuri aimed at the bumper car and squeezed the trigger. Nothing there. In a slow circle he swept the beam around the entire stockade.

At the very back, near the control panel, stood a man who had not been there a second before. He was taller, altogether bigger, than the last time Gabe had seen him, but his face was unmistakable.

"It's Viker! Blast him!"

Yuri dialled up the power but Viker leapt away from the beam. Yuri slammed it back onto him and tracked him, even as he ran. Viker's left arm melted off his shoulder – and then he jumped and disappeared.

"Where'd he go?" Yuri muttered, making quick sweeps all around.

With a crackle of electricity, the red bumper car rammed Yuri and sent him sprawling. The light launcher flew from his hands and went spinning across the track.

Gabe jumped the railing and ran to help his friend.

"Get it!" Yuri shouted to him.

At the far end of the track, all the other bumper cars leapt forward and came screaming toward Gabe. Before he could reach the light launcher, a yellow car ploughed into the path of another car. He heard Yuri call out a warning, then was slammed backwards onto the hood of the car that had rear-ended him. He clung tight, then realized it was hurtling itself toward the stockade wall. Seconds before it collided, he threw himself off, rolled and got up fast.

Across the track, Yuri was desperately swerving and jumping over cars, trying to reach his battered light launcher.

"Leave it!" Gabe hollered at his friend. "Get off the track!"

The light launcher spun toward Yuri and he made a final grab for it. Two cars collided head-on, mashing the light launcher – and Yuri's right hand. When the cars veered off, Yuri's invention was nothing but scattered debris. And he was cradling his bloody hand.

Even so, Yuri bent to try to pick up some of the mangled pieces, not noticing that every single car on the track had angled itself toward him. Gabe ran over and grabbed his friend by the arm, hauled him to the railing and shoved him over before vaulting clear himself.

Immediately, the bumper cars stopped. The overhead track lights blinked off, and the only noise was the cicadas in the hot night air.

12

"Good news, no broken bones," Gabe's mother told Yuri after they'd taken an X-ray of his hand.

"Oh, that's great," Gabe said. He was relieved and also pretty surprised, because Yuri's hand looked terrible. Right after the accident, there'd been blood all over it. Using the first aid kit in the maintenance shed, he'd helped clean and disinfect the cuts and bandage them, but by the time they got back to the city and reached the hospital, Yuri's whole hand was pretty swollen, and he said his wrist hurt a lot. Luckily, Gabe's mom was on shift, so they hadn't spent too long in the waiting room, with Yuri holding an ice pack against his wrist.

In the curtained cubicle of the emergency department, Gabe's mom said, "Your wrist, though, is pretty badly sprained."

"I don't need a cast, do I?" Yuri asked worriedly.

"No, but I'm going to give you a compression bandage. It'll help reduce the swelling."

Gabe watched his mother show Yuri how to wrap the bandage around his wrist. It wasn't often he'd seen his mom in action in the ER. Dr. Helen Dunne. She'd kept her own name when she married. Right now, Gabe felt a bit in awe of her. With her white coat and stethoscope and clipboard, she seemed ferociously competent.

"How's that feel?" she asked Yuri.

Gabe knew his mom had a soft spot for Yuri. He was one of those kids that grown-ups liked, on account of his old-fashioned manners.

"It feels good," Yuri said, "and I'm glad it doesn't cover my fingers."

"But I don't want you using that hand for forty-eight hours, Yuri," she said.

"Are you sure that's absolutely—" he began worriedly.

"Necessary, yes," she said firmly. "You're going to need to take a couple days off work."

"It's not so bad," he said, then winced as he waggled his fingers and flexed his wrist.

"I'll write you a note." She told him to keep his arm elevated and gave him directions on how to ice his wrist.

"Thank you very much, Dr Dunne."

"You didn't ride your bikes here, did you?"

Gabe said, "We left them locked up on the island."

"Good. I'll send you guys home in a cab." She handed Yuri a couple of sheets of paper. "There's a prescription for some painkillers, only if you need them. Tom at the nursing station can give you a voucher for the cab."

"Thanks, Mom," Gabe said.

She turned a stern eye on him. "You don't look too hot yourself."

"Just tired."

"I hope you guys weren't goofing around, doing something dangerous?"

Just hunting ghosts, Mom.

"The ride went crazy." That was not a lie, at least.

He was surprised when she gave him a quick hug, and was puzzled by the sadness in her eyes. He got the sense he wanted to tell him something else, but all she said was "I should get going. Yuri, follow up with your family doctor if it's not improving. And Gabe, I shouldn't be much later than twelve-thirty. Try to be asleep."

In the taxi Yuri said, "Your mom's pretty awesome."

"Yeah, she's good. I think she's worried about me."

"Maybe she should be," Yuri said after a moment. "We are keeping a lot of secrets." He looked at his hand. "This is not so bad, but next time it could be worse."

"Well, you didn't have to jam your hand between two bumper cars. That was crazy."

"Thank you for your sympathy," Yuri said stiffly.

Gabe felt like a jerk. "Look, I'm sorry about what happened to your light launcher."

"Those parts were not cheap," Yuri said.

"I can chip in," Gabe said. "And I'm sure Callie will too."

Yuri made his shrugging sound. "The bigger problem is, I can't start work on a new one until I have both hands. Which means no way of fighting Viker."

"But it works!" Gabe said, trying to cheer him up. "Did you see the way it melted his arm?"

"It was a trap," Yuri said. "He lured us onto the track so he could smash the light launcher. We were idiots. How long before he's strong enough to smash us?"

"We'll stop him before then."

"This is your place," said Yuri.

Surprised, Gabe saw that they'd already reached his building. The cab pulled over. "I'll call you tomorrow. Hope you feel better."

Yuri just nodded without looking at him, and Gabe slammed the door and watched the taxi drive off, taking his friend home.

He rode up in the elevator with a pizza delivery guy and could tell it had roasted red peppers on it, but he was too dejected to feel hungry. His best friend had got his hand busted up, he was keeping secrets from his mom, he missed Rebecca, and Yuri was right: things were only going to get more dangerous, the stronger Viker got.

He crinkled the iron filings in his pocket. He'd completely forgotten them in the panic of the bumper cars. What a bonehead.

Inside his apartment, he turned on the lights and Charlie greeted him with an arpeggio of cheery whistles, then: "Hello-hello-hello-there-you-are!"

He narrowed his eyes, the hairs lifting on the back of his neck. In his pocket, his fingers parted the seal of the bag of iron filings.

"Hello-hello-hello-Gabriel-I've-returned!"

"Rebecca?" he said uncertainly, and then jolted when his phone buzzed.

Of course it's me!

"You're not supposed to do that to the bird!" he said, but he was far too happy to be annoyed.

I'm sorry. I forgot! Shall I write you my news, or shall we clasp?

Eagerly he reached out his hand. The cold entwining of fingers, and his vision frosted. There she was, smiling, before him. She'd only been gone two nights and days, but he felt ridiculously happy to see her. She looked weary. He didn't remember her cheekbones standing out so much; her shoulders drooped; she seemed *less* somehow.

"Are you OK? Did anything happen?"

"No." She closed her eyes for a moment. "That feels better." She tightened her grip on his hand, though he couldn't feel the pressure, of course. But he realized she was drawing energy from him – with greater urgency than usual. It felt almost greedy. He couldn't suppress a big shiver.

"I'm sorry," she said. "Is it too much?"

Her face was already looking fuller. "No, it's OK, I'm fine." But he was glad to drop down into the sofa.

"You'll tell me if it's too much. I can always send text messages."

"It's no fun, waiting."

"I've become quite speedy."

The truth was, he'd missed her voice. And being able to look at her. And he was glad she was getting stronger. "So tell me everything about your trip."

"Do you know," she said, "I'd never been beyond the Scarborough Bluffs, my whole life. It was very exciting, seeing other places. Especially Montreal! At first I was rather startled by the brightness and noise of it all. But I so enjoyed its vitality . . ."

She trailed off, and Gabe thought she looked wistful, and maybe a bit bitter.

"But the three lighthouses were all in remote locations, and I think those places have changed very little since my time. They had no keepers any longer, and the lights were run automatically by clockwork. I searched each one of them for ghostlights, unsuccessfully. But in one, I did find a logbook. It took a lot of time and energy, but I managed to turn the pages and discover that Serge Delacroix had been keeper there."

Gabe sat up straighter. This sounded promising.

"But, strangely, the log dated the end of his service at August 1839."

Gabe frowned and thought back to the newspaper article Callie had showed them. "Wasn't that the same month he came to Toronto? When he tried to give the ghostlight to Debenham?"

"Yes. And he was ordered to leave the city. I assumed he returned to Quebec and resumed his duties as keeper. But clearly he never did."

"Maybe he quit?"

"That would be most unusual. In my day, keepers usually remained with a lighthouse their entire lives."

"He might've died." Gabe didn't like to think about the ways in which he might have died. Back then, there were a ton of ways. They didn't have to involve anything supernatural, anything with black-hole eyes or too many arms and legs. But he couldn't help wondering.

"I tried my best, Gabriel," she said, "but I could find no further information about Delacroix, or any sign of ghostlights. I peered in every cupboard, and under every floorboard, pushed myself into every nook and cranny. Whatever happened to their ghostlights, I don't know. My trip was a failure. I'm sorry."

"No, you did a great job," Gabe said. "I'm really glad you're back."

"Me as well. The farther I went, and the longer I was away, the weaker I felt. I needed your clasp."

He was pretty sure he was blushing. It was a novel experience, being told someone needed something from him. She hadn't said "I need *you*"—but it was pretty close. It was like she was snuggled up against him, warming her cold feet on him.

"Now," she said, "tell me everything that happened here." He told her about his trip to the library with Callie, and the squishing stacks, and then what had happened earlier tonight on the islands with the light launcher and bumper cars.

"Poor Yuri!" she exclaimed. "Will he regain the full use of his hand?"

Gabe couldn't help smiling at her outdated expression. "Yes, absolutely. My mom said in a few days. I think Yuri's way more upset about losing the light launcher. And that he won't be able to make another one for a while."

Rebecca looked concerned. "Not too long, I hope."

His phone buzzed and he saw a message from Callie, asking him to join a video call.

"I'll tell her we can talk tomorrow," he said to Rebecca. "I'm pretty beat and so are you."

"No, don't. She might have interesting news."

So he got his laptop and logged in. Callie's energetic face appeared on-screen. "Gabe, I still can't see you!"

Rebecca pointed him to the right buttons. Obediently he clicked.

"How was your sister's birthday?" he asked.

Callie frowned like she'd already forgotten. "Oh, fine. Hey, is Rebecca there? I see a shimmer beside you."

"She just got back, yeah."

"Rebecca, welcome back! I missed you! Did you find anything?" Callie listened to the news Gabe relayed to her, then sighed and said:

"Aw, man, that's too bad. It would've been great to find another ghostlight. But listen, don't give up hope, I think I've got a new lead. Where's Yuri, anyway? I texted but haven't heard back."

Gabe told her about their evening on the island, and as he described what had happened to Yuri in the bumper cars, she looked stricken.

"He's OK, though, right?" she asked with a catch in her voice.

"My mom said his hand'll be absolutely fine."

Gabe knew Callie wouldn't like what he was going to say next, but he went ahead anyway.

"I was thinking maybe we should slow this down. Rethink things."

"What do you mean?" Callie and Rebecca asked in unison, sounding equally surprised, and indignant.

"Guys, Yuri's hand got mashed. His light launcher got mashed.

And we have no way of fighting Viker right now. I think we might want to, you know, think about bringing some *adults* onto our team."

"No one's going to believe us!" Callie said.

"How about your grandmother who told you all those ghost stories—"

"I don't know if she actually believes—"

"Gabriel, we don't have any time to lose," Rebecca said.

"—and even if she did, she's like eighty years old! And who would you tell? Your mom? She'd worry you were hallucinating!"

"How about parapsychologists," Gabe said, "don't they believe in—"

"Even if they believed us, it would all take so long—"

"Listen to me!" Rebecca shouted at Gabriel. "Every day we wait, Viker gets stronger. Tell Callie."

Gabe told Callie.

"Darn right!" Callie exclaimed. "If Viker keeps getting stronger, people might get *really* hurt. And we *can* fight Viker right now! Even if Yuri can't build a new light launcher – awesome name, by the way – we can just slap a superduper bulb in the Gibraltar Point Light and—"

"Gabriel," Rebecca said over Callie, looking hurt, "how can you falter now, when my father's still trapped inside that monster? You said you'd help me!"

"I want to, it's just—"

" – and I've got a new lead—" Callie was saying.

181

" – Callie has a new lead!" Rebecca echoed eagerly.

Gabe sagged deeper into the sofa. He realized he didn't have a chance against these two. Callie would argue until he was exhausted, and Rebecca was literally sucking his life-force out of him. "OK," he said weakly.

"I got hold of the rest of that newspaper article!" Callie reported. "About the fire at the Hanlan Hotel. Ready for this?"

"Oh, I'm ready," said Gabe.

"Edward Shaw was *there* that night. He *died* in that fire."

Gabe sat up, his weariness forgotten. "No way!"

"Yep. And I got thinking. Shaw carried the ghostlight with him everywhere, right? Chained to him."

It only took Gabe a second to catch up. "It was with him the night he died!"

"Exactly!"

"OK, but who knows what happened to it afterward? Where it ended up?"

"But if Shaw died there," Callie said with a grin, "his ghost might still be there."

Rebecca nodded. "So let's go and ask Mr Shaw ourselves."

13

At ten-thirty the next morning, Gabe was the only person who got off the ferry at Hanlan's Point. Rain streamed from the edges of his umbrella. Out over the lake, thunder rumbled.

Gabe had always liked a good storm, and today the weather had worked in his favour. Karl, his manager, had messaged him that they weren't opening the park till the thunderstorm warnings were lifted. Callie still had to work at the CN Tower, and Yuri was off work altogether because of his hand, so Gabe was all alone.

But not really. Rebecca was with him. He would have liked the company of his two *living* friends but was also glad it was just him and Rebecca. *A date.* The word popped into his head, and he quickly squashed it. Weird.

The road from the dock was deserted, except for a small group of people hurrying for the ferry. As they drew closer, Gabe recognized the archaeologist he sometimes saw from the ship-wreck dig.

"Too wet to work today?" Gabe asked her.

"Oh, hi," she said, dipping her head to see under her umbrella. "Yes! We just finished putting tarps over everything."

"Found anything good yet? Treasure chest maybe?"

"Ha! I'll be happy if we find out the ship's name. You're not giving tours in this soaker, are you?"

He shook his head. "Day off."

"Well, stay dry," she said. The ferry gave a warning toot and she hurried off. Gabe watched the boat disappear into the fog. He could no longer see the CN Tower, or the skyline: the entire city had disappeared.

He might have pedalled back in time.

Which was exactly what he was trying to do. "You seeing anyone?" he asked Rebecca. "Anyone dead, I mean?"

A text bubble inflated on his screen.

Not yet.

Gabe had always thought of Hanlan Point as the lonely part of the island, far from the bustle of the amusement park and the neighborhoods on the eastern shore. But back in the day, the Hanlan Hotel had been a centre of the city's social scene. He always brought people here on his tour but had never known exactly where the grand hotel had stood. There was no sign to mark it, which was crazy. The Olympic rower Ned Hanlan got a historic plaque near the ferry dock. Babe Ruth got one, too, because he'd hit the first home run of his professional career in 1914, at the island's rebuilt baseball stadium. But the Hanlan Hotel went unremembered.

"What if Edward Shaw's sleeping?" he asked, thinking of those long chrysalis-like slumbers ghosts sometimes made during their afterlives.

Call out his name. Wake him like you woke me.

He looked around to make sure he was alone. "Edward," he hummed quietly. "Ed-ward Shaw-aw."

Oh, louder than that, Gabriel!

"Edward! Edward Shaw! Ed! Eddie! Ed buddy!"

He felt ridiculous, shouting out a dead man's name. His voice went swooping like a bat into the fog, through the trees, over the rippled water of Blockhouse Bay. Trying to wake up a ghost – if he was even around to be woken.

There is someone up ahead.

Gabe opened his hand and felt Rebecca take it. He gave a little shiver, as much from excitement as the coldness of her clasp. The misty world around him became even mistier, and he and Rebecca seemed the only vital things in it.

Up ahead, near a shuttered burger shack, a man stepped out of a vending machine. He gave a mighty stretch, then wiped his hands over his eyes. Gabe wondered just how long he'd spent inside.

The fellow was from another century, that much was obvious from his clothing. But there was no way this was Edward Shaw. For one thing, he wasn't old enough; for another, he did not have the look of a wealthy man. A sailor maybe, though not an officer. He wore a flat-topped hat, a neckerchief, a threadbare baggy shirt and trousers. He had no shoes, and his feet were yellow with calluses. Gabe wondered if he'd died at sea and washed ashore to his new ghostly life.

The man looked forlornly at the rows of drinks inside the vending machine. His chafed fingers slipped right through the glass but of course could not grip the cool cans.

"Vexing," Gabe heard him say. "Most vexing."

The voice was clear, though somehow out of tune.

Hand in hand with Rebecca, Gabe walked closer.

"Good evening, sir," she said.

Surprised, the man turned. His lips and sparse teeth were blue, as if permanently wine-stained. Below his eyes, his skin hung in loose pouches. His entire face looked at risk of slipping off altogether.

Please, thought Gabe, *don't let his face slip off.*

"Tommy Flynn at your service," the ghost said, after Rebecca had introduced herself. His pouchy eyes settled on Gabe so intently it was almost frightening. "And who might you be, young sir?"

"Gabriel."

"How do you do, Gabriel? I see you two have clasped. Regular sweethearts, aren't you? How very touching."

He winked lewdly, but Gabe caught genuine yearning in his face.

"Would you be so kind as to tell me the year?" Flynn inquired. "I was taking a little nap and I do tend to oversleep."

"We are looking for a Mr Edward Shaw," Rebecca said after giving him the date. "Do you know this gentleman, or his whereabouts?"

Tommy Flynn's face became sly. "Ah. It just so happens that I am very well acquainted with that gentleman. You might say we were business partners."

"How did you come to know him?" Rebecca asked.

"Well, he approached *me,* didn't he? He *saw* me. First living person who'd ever paid me notice."

Gabe frowned. "So you were already dead?"

"Oh, a good many years."

"But how did Shaw see you?" Gabe asked, though he already had a suspicion.

"That wondrous lens of his, that he kept chained about him, even in his sleep. When he looked through it, he could *see* me. And not just that, he could *hear* me. We had a good chat. He found me most excellent company, and most useful."

"How were you useful?" asked Gabe.

The ghost's head pulled back, as if he was offended by the question. "How, you ask? I'm observant. I notice things. Lost things. Hidden things. A few banknotes in the pages of a book. A gold ring under the floorboards. A strongbox with silver coins buried in a hole in the ground. Maybe I've watched a banker at his vault, and know the combination. Well. You can see how these things might be useful if I were to whisper them to the living."

So *this* was how Edward Shaw had made his fortune. Using a ghost as a spy and accomplice, he'd become a very successful treasure hunter – and thief.

"We became inseparable, Mr Shaw and me. He was me dearest friend, closer to me than any brother."

"So do you know where he is now?" Gabe asked. "He died here."

"You don't need to tell me!" cried Tommy Flynn. "I saw the whole thing."

Gabe cut a glance at Rebecca and saw that she could barely suppress her excitement. Calmly she asked, "Will you please tell us what happened?"

"Well, it brings a tear to me eye every time I think of it."

Gabe had a hard time imaging those sly eyes shedding too many tears. "We know he died in the fire," he prompted.

"No, no. The fire came later. It was his birthday, and quite a party it was. You can't imagine it." He waved his hand dramatically, like he could conjure the grand hotel. "Candles twinkling from every veranda, a string quartet playing in the ballroom, and all the finest in Toronto here to raise a glass to Edward Shaw. But not all the guests were friends, if you take me meaning."

"He had enemies?" Gabe asked.

"Not the living so much as the dead. There were some ghosts who'd been useful to him, told him valuable things, and they felt he'd treated them shabbily. That he'd made promises he didn't keep."

"What kind of promises?"

"Oh, a view of mountains, a reunion with a loved one, a quick passage to Heaven."

"And could Mr Shaw deliver such promises?" Rebecca asked.

Tommy Flynn's sly face took on a sorrowful look. "Afraid not, miss. And I did tell Mr Shaw, I did say to him, 'Sir,' I said, 'it is not kind, this trickery, for it's quite easy to fool a ghost, isn't it, we're so desperate, you see, for little treats.'"

Little treats. Gabe couldn't help wondering what Mr Shaw might have promised Tommy Flynn.

"That's dreadful," Rebecca said. "So Mr Shaw just took their secrets, and their money, and never gave them anything in return. No wonder he had enemies."

"Indeed." Tommy Flynn licked his blue lips with a quick blue tongue. "He broke promises, so in the end they broke *him*."

Gabe winced. "What do you—"

"Oh, I tried to calm them down," Flynn said dolefully. "But they were quite unmoved. Some people do bear a grudge. One little bit of mischief led to another."

Fear prickled across Gabe's arms. "What did they do?"

"Well, over the years my Mr Shaw had clasped with many ghosts," Tommy Flynn said, "so he could speak with them, you see. So that night, at the Hanlan Hotel, the night of his great birthday party, they all clasped him back. At the *same* time."

Gabe fought back a shudder. He remembered the icy clutch of Viker's terrible hand.

"The clasp of a single ghost, so I'm told, is an icy tingle, yes?" Tommy Flynn's eyes settled on Gabe. "Like this fine young lady holding your hand right now. Pins and needles, sir, am I right?"

Gabe nodded.

"But you take thirty angry ghosts, sir—"

"Thirty!"

"Oh, at least! And they put their hands on you, that's an altogether different proposition. You have those thirty cold hands tight around your wrists and arms and shoulders, and that's a fearsome cold grip. One thing leads to another and they drain a body! Well, it's quite a thing to watch." Tommy Flynn seemed to have forgotten that Edward Shaw was his dearest friend, closer than a brother, and he told the story with considerable relish.

"Oh, it drains the life right from a body! I tried to stop them, I truly did. But what is one ghost against thirty! I feared for myself, they were in such a lather. They drained poor Edward Shaw's life away till his heart stopped dead."

Gabe couldn't help looking down at Rebecca's hand in his. He imagined a little bit of his life draining away. Like his phone's power bar shrinking one percent at a time.

It's just one hand, one ghost, he told himself.

"And even afterward, the ghosts were bent on mischief, so they tipped over every lamp and candle in the hotel. The place went up like kindling. But Mr Shaw was already quite dead. My poor Mr Shaw," Tommy Flynn murmured.

"Is he nearby?" Rebecca asked.

"Oh, he's long gone," said Tommy Flynn with an evasive flick of his eyes. "He didn't linger."

Inwardly Gabe sagged. Another lead lost.

"But *you* are left behind," observed Rebecca.

Tommy Flynn gave a little burp. "Well, I'm a survivor, ain't I? Wily old Tommy, he's got a way of coming out on top."

You can't even use a vending machine, Gabe thought.

"Did you see where the ghostli— Shaw's special lens went?" Rebecca asked.

"He died with it chained to him. An unusual and valuable thing, ain't it?" He turned back to the vending machine. "I'm awfully thirsty. Wouldn't I like to slake me thirst, just this once!"

"Sorry," Gabe said. "We can't help you with that."

"Oh, I know, I know. I'll never know the true feeling of ale going down me throat. But there's other things I crave. We could help each other, I think, sir." Once more he turned an avid gaze on Gabe. It was hunger and thirst and avarice combined. "If you were willing, that is."

Uneasily Gabe asked, "How?"

"I could help you, just like I helped Mr Shaw. Would you like that, young sir? Become a wealthy man, have everything you desire. And in return, because fair's fair, you could help *me*."

Again, Gabe asked, "How?"

Tommy Flynn shuffled a little closer. "I haven't clasped with a living person since Edward Shaw. And he was generous that way. He shared his energy and heat with me. I miss having a living person of me own, you see." He reached out a hand toward Gabe. "Would you care to clasp with me, young sir? So I can feel some warmth and the pulse of a beating heart. Just for a brief moment."

"Don't, Gabriel," Rebecca said.

"Oh, greedy, greedy!" said the ghost. "Keeping him all to yourself, is it? I'd watch her, young sir! Watch this one! She'll *want* things from you. She might bleed *you* dry if you're not careful."

Gabe couldn't stop himself from glancing at Rebecca, and was relieved by the genuine look of shock on her face. Still, the ghost's words had planted a seed of doubt. He knew she wanted something from him – she'd been very clear about that – but was there something more ominous behind her clasp?

"Tommy Flynn, do you know where the lens is?" Rebecca demanded crossly.

The ghost turned his back on them. "Don't see why I should tell you anything, since you're so unfriendly."

"If you tell us," Gabe said, "I'll clasp with you."

He regretted the words the moment he spoke them, for Tommy Flynn wheeled around with a terrible eagerness.

"Is that a promise?"

"Yes," Gabe forced himself to say.

"Oh, I would cherish that! I wouldn't be a nuisance to you, sir. Just the once."

"Gabriel—" Rebecca began.

"I'll do it," said Gabe, "to find the lens."

"Very good, excellent news indeed!" Tommy Flynn said. "Well then, let me tell you this. The lens was still chained to Mr Shaw's vest when they carried him from the burning hotel. And that was the last I ever saw of him. But the lens was buried with him. The instructions were in his last will and testament. It was to be a decoration for the family crypt."

"And where's that?"

"I imagine it's in the Necropolis. That's where all the best families were buried."

Gabe looked at Rebecca, barely able to contain his excitement. The Necropolis was in Cabbagetown, right next to Riverdale Farm.

"Thank you, Tommy Flynn," he said.

"Now what about our little clasp?" the ghost said.

Gabe felt his skin crawl. But he'd promised.

"You need to offer me your hand," the ghost reminded him primly.

Gabe extended his free hand. Like a cobra striking, Tommy Flynn clasped his wrist.

"Ah, yes, that's the stuff!" cried Tommy Flynn.

Gabe shuddered. A taste like blood filled his mouth.

"My goodness, yes!" warbled Flynn. Gabe could imagine the rank smell of Tommy Flynn's breath. The ghost's eyes emptied of all light and became sinkholes; his mouth cratered into darkness. Gabe felt bolted to the ground with fear.

"Just like old times!" Flynn wailed.

"That's enough!" Rebecca shouted at the ghost. "Gabriel, pull your hand away! You're much stronger than him."

Gabe pulled free. Instantly Tommy Flynn's face returned to normal, and he slumped like a disappointed schoolboy. Gabe rubbed his wrist to return feeling to the spot. It tingled painfully.

"Ah, I thank you, kind sir," said Tommy Flynn. "Truly, you don't know the good turn you did me. If there's ever anything else I can do for you, do not hesitate to ask old Tommy Flynn. If you find that lens, we can have many an interesting conversation, and I can help you, lad, mark me words. You come back when you've found it, and I'll make you a rich man!"

As if from another time zone, Gabe heard the ferry approaching and turned to the dock. He kept his hand clasped with Rebecca, perhaps from habit, perhaps for a little bit of comfort, too. Glancing back, he caught a last glimpse of Tommy Flynn peering mournfully at the drinks inside the vending machine, forever out of reach.

After the ferry had left the dock, Tommy Flynn still stood before the vending machine, lost in his own memories. A can rolled from its slot and thudded to the bottom. Flynn's amazement doubled as the flap lifted and the can floated out and hovered in the air before his eyes. With a hiss, the can's lid snapped open.

Only then did he see the skinny fingers that gripped the can.

Before he could turn to see the owner of these fingers, the can moved to his face and tilted. Excitedly, Flynn opened wide and the liquid flowed into his gaping mouth. And though he could neither feel nor taste the beverage, he *imagined* he could. He gurgled and gasped with pleasure until the last of the drink was pooled at his feet.

"Oh," he said, "oh, that was wonderful! Thank you!"

And finally he turned to behold a powerful man in the tatters of a military uniform. His eyes were shadowed beneath a craggy brow. He appeared to be missing an arm. His other had a vast hand out of all proportion.

"I am very pleased to make your acquaintance, sir," Nicholas Viker said.

Despite his polite greeting, Viker was in a foul mood. Two days ago, he'd followed the boy and girl to a hideous library. They'd been most useful, finding newspapers and unwittingly turning to the correct pages for him. He was a faster reader than either, and so learned before them that Edward Shaw had died here on the island with the ghostlight.

Armed with this information, he'd triggered the shelves to crush them. Returning to the island, he'd searched in vain for Edward Shaw. Most ghosts had fled at the sight of him; the few he'd caught had told him nothing useful, and he'd feasted on them. Just as he was about to resume his search, however, he'd spotted Rebecca Strand and Gabriel (uncrushed, alas!) parting company with this blue-lipped ghost.

"Tommy Flynn at your service," Flynn said. "I have not seen you here before, have I, sir?"

"Tell me everything that you told the boy and girl," Viker commanded.

"Well, sir," said Flynn slyly, "that was a confidential conver—"

Viker parted his jaws. From within came a faint wail of torment from one of the ghosts he'd recently devoured.

Tommy Flynn recoiled in horror. "I'd be pleased to tell you!" he cried, and Viker had to slow him down as he tripped and tumbled over his words.

"And where is it now, that special lens of Shaw's?" Viker demanded.

"I have a suspicion that the moment I tell you, you will eat me. So I am reluctant to say."

"Then I will devour you nonetheless," said Viker, seizing Flynn with his massive hand and ratcheting his jaws wider.

Flynn winced, but his voice was steady: "But then you will be no farther ahead in acquiring your prize!"

Viker considered him. This little parasite was wilier than he'd thought. "You are unwise to bargain with me."

"Not bargaining, sir; simply offering me services. I can be very useful, you see. Indispensable. I can see how much you want that amber lens. It's got special value for me, too, sir. Many fond memories. Might I ask what you mean to use it for?"

"That is my business," snarled Viker. He couldn't believe the boldness of this little barnacle, but he did respect it. This was no meek and confused ghost. Perhaps he might indeed be useful.

"May I make a suggestion, sir?" Flynn asked.

Viker grunted, and Flynn pressed on.

"That girl, and that living boy - let *them* find the special lens first."

"Why?"

"I've already told them where it is, sir, but it's in a very difficult place for the likes of us. We're not strong enough to extract it."

"Not strong enough?" It enraged Viker to be reminded of his weakness. The urge to devour Flynn was almost overwhelming.

"Oh, I can see you're powerful," Flynn said, patting the air with his hands to calm him. "You took a can from that machine, and kindly offered me a drink - thank you again, by the way. And I can see you've fed on other ghosts." He winced. "They do tend to bulge out from time to time, if you don't mind me saying. But are you strong enough to split stone? Forgive me, sir, but you're not. Not yet."

With disgust, Viker knew Flynn was right. "But that living boy, Gabriel," Flynn said, "that strapping young lad, he can do it! He can free the amber lens! Let him do our work for us. Watch and wait. Meanwhile you can feed and get stronger, and we can follow these young ones, and when we—"

"*We?*" Viker said. "That lens is mine alone, Flynn."

"Absolutely it is, sir. But you'll need help keeping an eye on our young friends. You can't be everywhere at once, now, can you? I've *clasped* with the boy, sir."

"As have I."

"Then we'll make a fine pair! We've both felt his pulse, and that'll help us track him. They don't realize it, sir. And when the time is right, you can *take* the ghostlight. Take it in your hand. And that's how you'll get it, sir!"

With grudging admiration, Viker realized that Flynn had still not told him where the ghostlight was. He looked at the blue-lipped man more carefully. There was a slight crookedness to his shape, as if he were trying to conceal something behind his back.

"You, too, have fed upon ghosts," Viker said.

Flynn bowed his head modestly. "Well, sir, I cannot tell a lie. But just the once."

"And who was that?"

"Someone very dear to me, who might have treated me better."

"So you, too, have tasted the power we can have over the dead. But power over the living is within our reach as well."

Viker saw the curiosity and hunger spark in Flynn's eyes. He could use that hunger. He would need to be wary of it, too. But how pleasant to have a lieutenant, someone to serve under him.

"Now, Mr Viker, please banish any more thought of eating me. I will be a dutiful and loyal servant."

"We have an agreement, then," Viker said, and clasped hands with the blue-lipped ghost. "That special lens is called a ghostlight. It can destroy us, but I will show you how it can also make us rulers over a new world of the dead. And the living."

14

The Necropolis was one of the city's oldest cemeteries, its paths meandering around moss-covered monuments and faded gravestones. Gabe kept his flashlight beam low. He wasn't sure if there would be a security guard.

"Is this grave robbing?" he whispered.

"It's not like we're digging anyone up!" Callie whispered back.

"But we do have a chisel and hammer," Yuri added.

Gabe's phone vibrated and he pulled it out to see Rebecca's message.

Edward Shaw was the thief, not us. And before him, D'Arcy Boulton.

It was Friday night, and the first time all four of them had been together for a while. Maybe normal teenagers were hanging out on beaches, or watching movies, but Gabe didn't care. He was happy to be surrounded by his friends, even if he was in a shadowy graveyard, planning to chip the ghostlight out of a family crypt.

"Rebecca's right," Callie said. "The ghostlight belongs to the Gibraltar Point Lighthouse."

And the Order.

"Exactly," Callie agreed. "Just taking back what's ours."

Yuri gave her an amused look. "You are speaking as a member of the Order now?"

"I'm related to Keeper Strand, so yeah."

Ahead of them, something with a humped back scuttled across the path on all fours, and Gabe's body went electric. He chased after it with his flashlight.

"Just a racoon," said Yuri in relief. He still wore his compression bandage, but the swelling had gone way down, and he'd told Gabe it didn't hurt very much any more. He was planning on going back to work tomorrow.

"Rebecca," he asked, "is this place crawling with ghosts?"

Not as many as you might think.

"Seems odd," Yuri remarked.

"Ghosts usually stay where they die," Callie reminded him.

"Has anyone actually ever died *in* a cemetery?" Gabe wondered.

"Maybe they got buried alive," Callie suggested.

"Thank you for that horrible image," Yuri said.

"Also," she said, "there were people here *way* before this grave-yard was built. Or Toronto even existed."

"Good point," said Gabe, startled by the vast span of time over which people must have died on this patch of land. Before Europeans ever set foot here, there were Indigenous nations. He remembered the names from his school's land acknowledgment: the Mississauga of the Credit, the Anishnabeg, the Chippewa, the Haudenosaunee and the Wendat peoples.

Callie said, "I think Shaw's around here somewhere." On her

tablet she checked an online directory of gravestones. "I'm guessing it's a fancy one."

"Like that?" Gabe played his flashlight beam on a large stone structure built into the side of an ivy-covered hill. Roman columns flanked two arched doorways. There were carvings and decorations and medallions everywhere. At the corners of the crypt were statues of people kneeling in prayer. A tall stone cross rose from the peaked roof.

"This is bigger than my bedroom," Yuri remarked.

Above the doorway, chiselled in stone, was the name Shaw. In the triangular pediment above it was carved an ornate wreath.

"This place could fit a lot of Shaws," said Yuri.

Gabe's phone trembled.

Inside the wreath!

Gabe angled his beam up. The centre of the complicated twist of ivy and leaves was exactly the size of the ghostlight. Except that the ghostlight wasn't there. Where it might have been, the stone looked scraped and chipped.

He didn't know how many more disappointments he could endure.

"Someone beat us to it!"

"But when was it done?" Callie wondered. "Recently, or a long time ago?"

"I am no stonemason," said Yuri, "but looking at the spot, I see some moss growing. So I'm thinking it was done a while ago. This treasure hunt is never-ending."

"Rebecca," Gabe said quietly. "Is there anyone here? Anyone who might've seen what happened?"

There is a gentleman watching us.

He inhaled sharply at her cold clasp. Ice crystals crept across his vision. Yuri and Callie dimmed; the crypt and gravestones faded. Across the graveyard, Gabe saw a ghost smartly dressed in suit and hat, leaning jauntily against a tombstone.

"Let us know if you need help," Callie said firmly. "I've got extra iron filings."

The ghost was an older man with a high forehead, white hair, and sideburns that swooped all the way down to his chin without quite joining in the middle. It looked weird to Gabe, but he supposed it had been fashionable at the time.

"Is he safe to talk to?" Gabe whispered to Rebecca.

"I believe so."

As they drew closer, the ghost's eyes were quick and bright and regarded them with the utmost curiosity.

"I don't believe I've seen either of you here before," he said.

"No, sir," replied Rebecca.

"Your names, if I might ask?"

"My friend is Gabriel Vasilakis, and I am Rebecca Strand. My father was Matthew Strand and—"

"The Keeper at Gibraltar Point, of course! You and he were found dead at the base of the lighthouse. If I'm not mistaken, the year was 1839."

"Your memory is excellent," Rebecca said.

"You and I are roughly the same vintage, Miss Strand. I was twenty then. I'm delighted to make your acquaintance now!"

"You haven't told us your name," Gabe said. After his encounter with Tommy Flynn, he was a bit wary of ghosts, even if they didn't have corkscrew eyes and jaws that dislocated.

"Forgive me," said the dapper ghost, and nodded at the tombstone beside him. "Here I am."

"George Brown," Gabe read, then looked back at the ghost in surprise. "*The* George Brown?"

"Well, there are many of us. It's a common enough name."

"I did a project on you!" Unlike some of his fellow students, Gabe did not think Canadian history was boring. "You founded the *Globe* newspaper!"

"Guilty as charged."

"This is George Brown," Gabe told his living friends excitedly. "He's one of the—"

"Fathers of Confederation," he heard Callie say, and caught her glancing at her tablet, which he thought was cheating. "He helped put Canada together."

"What he did," said another voice, "was help make a confederation of white men from among the European settlers."

In surprise, Gabe saw a second ghost approach. Unlike Brown, he was clean-shaven, and his face was scarred with pockmarks. Beneath a flat, wide-brimmed hat, he kept his black hair at shoulder length. Around his double-breasted jacket was tied a red sash. Gabe noticed he wore moccasins rather than shoes.

"But you certainly didn't consult me," this ghost told Brown. "The Mississauga of the Credit had little or no voice shaping this country, or our way of life afterward. None of the Indigenous peoples did."

"Ah," said George Brown, "may I introduce my dear friend Joseph Halfday."

"We were not always friends," Halfday added wryly. "It took us the better part of a century."

"One of the true joys of death," Brown said, "is that we have ample time to learn and reconsider our opinions."

"There were many spirited conversations," Halfday agreed. "But in the end I believe we reached an understanding."

"What he means to say is that I was wrong," Brown said, amused.

Halfday grinned. "I was being polite, but yes."

Gabe shared a glance with Rebecca. It was pretty obvious these two had been sparring partners for a long time, but at least they were friendly and respectful ones now.

Joseph Halfday turned his full attention to Gabe and Rebecca. "Hello to you both – and to your other living friends."

"*Aanii*," Rebecca said in greeting.

Joseph Halfday looked pleased. "You speak some Anishinaabemowin."

"I learned a little from the Mississauga who camped and hunted on the island. They were always friendly with my family. I remember children would sometimes come to the house and trade fish for our milk."

"I know the island well," Halfday said. "I often fished there."

"They still fish there!" Gabe exclaimed. "Yuri and I saw them at night, using torches."

"Yes. Some spirits have found their paradise there, and can remain. Unlike when they were alive, and displaced by settlers."

"Those settlers included me, I am ashamed to say," Brown said. He turned his fiery gaze on Gabe. "And what is the current generation doing about it?"

"We learn about it in school now," said Gabe, feeling defensive. "Colonialism, broken treaties, the residential schools—"

"Not enough! From what I've observed, there is still a great deal to be done!"

"It is a start," Joseph Halfday said, placing a calming hand on his friend's shoulder.

"Which may be why we're still both here," Brown said, patting his whiskers down. "Much more work to be done. My theory is that I am a newspaperman to the bitter end. And the best stories are still here on Earth. Which is why I make a point of being here at the Necropolis. You might have thought I was just being swell-headed, perching on my own grave. But many of us ghosts come back to visit. And the dead are so much more willing to share stories than the living. Why, I could tell you—"

It seemed like George Brown was winding up for a very long gab, and Gabe didn't want to appear rude and interrupt him. Luckily, Callie did the job for him:

"Are you guys going to ask him about the Shaw crypt, or what?"

205

There was nothing wrong with George Brown's hearing. "Ah! The Shaw crypt. Yes, I saw you having a good look."

"We think there may have been a coloured stone set into the wreath," Rebecca told him.

"Indeed there was. Grave robbers took it."

"You saw it happen?" said Gabe.

"We both did, do you remember?" Brown asked Halfday. "Not more than twenty years ago, wouldn't you say, Joseph? It was quite brazen. In the dead of night, not even a slip of a moon, two people came, cloaked in black clothes and hoods. One of them had tools and seemed to know what he was about. It didn't take long. A few strikes of a chisel and then the jewel was passed to the other person. Some money changed hands, and they left in separate automobiles."

"I don't suppose you overheard their names," Gabe asked.

"I did not. Which was why I followed them."

"Wow! Really?"

"Of course! I wasn't about to let a story like this get away from me! I hitched a ride in the thief's automobile. After a while the hood came down and I discovered it was a woman. Her lodgings were in a rather damp basement. Absolutely crammed with books of a supernatural nature. She took the lens out and held it to her eye. And then – this was most curious – she looked about the room and saw me! I was as startled as she was. She gave a cry and put the lens away."

"Who was she?" Rebecca asked.

"I took note of her licence plate and ambled down to police

headquarters," said Brown. "A newspaperman never truly dies, my friends. After observing the officers at their work, I taught myself how to use their computers."

"Aren't they interesting!" Rebecca said enthusiastically.

"Wonderful things!" Brown agreed. "I found I had the energy to tap out the thief's license plate number, and discovered her name was Gillian Shaw. After a bit more sleuthing, I learned she is the great-granddaughter of Edward Shaw himself."

"Gillian Shaw," Callie said, sliding her tablet over for Gabe and Yuri to see. "She's got her own website."

They were sitting side by side at the window counter of the Boxcar Cafe in Cabbagetown. Yuri and Callie had ordered iced drinks, but Gabe, despite the heat, cradled a big decaf latte. After clasping with Rebecca for so long, his hands and body needed warming up.

The website's home page featured a woman's face lit from below, making it skull-like in the surrounding darkness. There was no text, and Gabe's eyes skittered around, trying to find something to click. He started randomly tapping at the screen.

"Please do not touch the tablet," Yuri said. "Let Callie do it."

"You're afraid I'll break it?"

"Yes. It's a very nice piece of equipment."

Gabe took a sip from his mug. "Fine, you do it."

Gently Yuri touched a nearly invisible icon and a new page opened. There was another picture of Gillian Shaw, dressed like a Victorian gentleman: trousers, black jacket, a shirt with a high starched collar. Clipped to her vest was a chain, the end of which disappeared into a pocket.

"'Ms. Gillian Shaw,'" Yuri read aloud, "'is one of the world's foremost supernaturalists.' Is that a real word?"

Callie pushed closer so all three of their heads were smushed together. "Says she does séances at historic sites all over the world."

Another photo faded up on-screen: Gillian Shaw seated at the head of a large table. Before her hung strings of coloured beads. Fixed on one of the strands, at face level, was a familiar amber lens.

"There! Look! She must use the ghostlight to talk to ghosts," Gabe said. "Just like her great-grandfather!"

"Does it say where she lives?" Callie asked.

Yuri scrolled, and Gabe's heart sank when he read the last line of Gillian Shaw's bio: "'Originally from Toronto, Ms. Shaw now makes her home in a haunted villa outside Florence.'"

Gabe slumped back in his chair. "Italy. That's just great."

"Can we please, *please,* finally give up on this idea of finding the ghostlight," Yuri said. "Our best hope is to build another light launcher."

"Hold on," said Callie, "she travels, remember?"

She opened a new page headed "Tour Dates." Gabe looked at the long list of cities. Shaw had already visited half of Europe, with almost all of her shows marked "Sold Out."

"She's in Florence right now. After that Rome, New York—"

"—then Toronto!" said Callie, scrolling down a smidge. "Next week!"

Gabe's phone vibrated on the counter.

I must see her! She must return the ghostlight to me.

"As if she'll just give it to you," Gabe said. "She robbed a grave for it! This is how she makes all her money. She's talking to ghosts and who knows what kind of arrangements she makes with them, but there's no way she'll give it to you!"

Which is why we will have to steal it.

"Is this girl awesome, or what?" said Callie admiringly. "I'm with you, Aunt Rebecca!"

"There're still some tickets available," Gabe said.

"You are actually proposing we go to a séance?" Yuri asked. "And steal the ghostlight, right there?"

"Whoa!" said Callie. "The tickets are super expensive!"

Yuri actually jerked back in his chair. "That's the price for *one*?"

That is a vast fortune!

Gabe could practically see the worry lines on Rebecca's forehead. "Maybe in 1830," he said, "but not anymore. Still, it's a ton of money."

"We could split it three ways," suggested Callie. "How much do you guys have saved up?"

Gabe glanced worriedly at Yuri, who was silent. Gabe knew that money was sometimes tight at his house.

"Or," Callie said, picking up on the awkwardness, "Gabe, maybe just you and me—"

"Listen," interrupted Yuri, "we have a big decision to make. With this kind of money, we could build *three* new light launchers. Which I think is the *smart* thing to do. Or we could buy a ticket to a séance. Which I think is the *insane* thing to do."

Gabe's phone buzzed angrily.

The ghostlight will be right before us. We will never have a better opportunity!

"But Rebecca," Yuri persisted, "with three powerful light launchers, don't you think that—"

The phone nearly rattled itself off the counter.

And what if your normal light *destroys* Viker, but seals my father *inside* him for all eternity?

Gabe shared a horrified glance with Callie. He'd never thought of such a thing.

"That is a terrifying idea, I agree," Yuri murmured.

The ghostlight is the *only* light that we absolutely know will free my father.

Yuri exhaled and rummaged around in his hair until it resembled a mountain peak.

"So it seems," he said, "that we are left with one option. Which is basically a bank heist." He took a long sip of his iced drink and peered out the steamy window. "And this requires planning." Decisively he smacked his palms against the counter. "So let's plan."

Gabe looked at him in surprise. "You sure you're OK with this?"

"Stealing? No. But you are my friends and it seems we have made a decision."

It's not stealing. We are merely reclaiming what belongs to the Order.

Yuri made his shrugging sound. "OK, sure, but it's going to look like stealing, and I don't want to go to jail."

No, I would not want to see you hang for this.

"Hang?" Gabe exclaimed. "Rebecca, they don't *hang* people for stealing anymore."

They don't?

"No. It's more . . . merciful now. You'd just go to jail, maybe."

But surely hanged later?

"No! There is no hanging!"

"Let's focus on the heist," Callie said.

Gabe tried to organize his thoughts. "The ghostlight's probably going to be right in front of Gillian Shaw. So we need to cause a ruckus – some kind of scene."

"Right," Yuri agreed. "A distraction."

"And then snatch the ghostlight in all the confusion," Callie finished.

"So what's the distraction?" Yuri asked.

Gabe thought a moment, then laughed. "Well, we do have a real ghost."

I will put on a show.

"It'll have to be quite a show. Gillian Shaw's used to seeing ghosts by now. You'll need to be scary."

I can be scary.

"How scary?"

I will spread fear like a terrible fog. I will raise the hair from people's necks until they howl like wolves. I can make them crumple themselves into balls. I can bring the night and the nightmare both.

Gabe's throat felt dry. He'd spent a lot of time with Rebecca

Strand and mostly knew her as a gentle presence – a bit intense sometimes, and yes, stubborn and bossy, and there was that moment when it looked like her jaws might dislocate. But *overall*, pleasant. It was disturbing to imagine her morphed into something horrific.

"You can really do all that?"

Wait and see.

"OK," said Callie, "so Rebecca creates a panic, and people will be running around and wailing and *swooning* or whatever, and we snip the ghostlight off that string and get out fast."

"What could be simpler?" Yuri said. "Now, since we can only afford one ticket, who gets to go?"

Gabe could tell that Callie wanted to go. She'd been thinking and writing about ghosts for a while, and this was, after all, a story with a strong family connection.

She looked at him with a rueful smile. "No question. You and Rebecca are a team. It's you guys."

Yuri nodded approvingly. "Two for the price of one."

Gabe knew that Rebecca was essential. They'd need to be able to communicate during the séance.

Thank you, all, so much. I will try to think of some way to repay you.

"No need," Gabe said.

"We're family," said Callie. She pulled out a credit card. "My parents said this was only for emergencies, and I figure this counts. So, let's get ourselves a ticket to a séance."

15

After all the frantic sleuthing and searching of the past week, it felt strange having nothing to do. Or nothing *supernatural* to do. In some ways, Gabe was relieved to return to his normal routine, but he realized he missed the excitement of the treasure hunt. He'd liked delving into the city's past, exploring libraries, historic houses and cemeteries; seeing and talking to ghosts. And he also missed seeing more of Yuri and Callie. There were still four more days until the séance.

But the break turned out to be good timing, overall. Mom had been doing more day shifts at the hospital, so she was home evenings, and it would have only gotten harder for Gabe to explain why he was out late yet *again*.

And he liked having Rebecca stay with him. Even though she was invisible, the condo felt much less lonely. They spent a lot of time talking. Sometimes they clasped in his bedroom and he had to whisper. Mostly they messaged on his phone. Yesterday they'd had a conversation using only emojis. They'd spent the better part of an hour sending each other tiny filing cabinets, and pumpkins, and the weirdest symbols they could find until they were both laughing helplessly.

Gabe was pretty sure Mom thought he had a girlfriend. And Rebecca wasn't making it any easier.

"Who keeps texting you?" Mom asked one night, after his phone vibrated for the tenth time while they were watching a movie.

"Don't know," he said, sliding the phone under his bum.

"Callie, by any chance?" she asked playfully.

"Mom, I told you, Callie's just a friend."

"I'm bored!" Rebecca said, clasping his hand and appearing on the sofa between him and his mom. "This movie is idiotic!"

"Could we pause it for a sec?" Gabe said to his mom. "I need to go to the bathroom."

"Take your time," Mom said in amusement.

"I'm sorry I clasped with you suddenly," Rebecca said as they walked hand in hand to the bathroom. "But you weren't answering my texts!"

He locked the door, turned on the tap and whispered, "I can't answer your texts all the time, especially when my mom's around."

"I have no one else to talk to!"

"I know, but—"

"I haven't had anyone to talk to in almost two hundred years!"

"Rebecca, I'd rather to talk to you than anyone else in the world. I could talk to you for hours."

"Truly?" she said, her eyes softening.

"Yes! But I have to spend time with my mom sometimes."

"You're right, of course."

"I worry she gets lonely."

"Is that why she watches those absurd movies?"

"Romantic comedies? Yeah."

"They all end in the same manner."

Gabe sighed. "I know."

"You're a very good son. I will try to be more self-sufficient." Anxiously she asked, "What day of the week is this again?"

He told her. "Only four more days till the séance. Don't worry, we won't miss it."

The next day, he went to work with Rebecca as usual. He liked knowing she was there, invisibly, beside him – the only ghost tour with its own ghost! – even though she had an annoying habit of texting him to correct his historical facts.

Today, by good luck, his lunch break coincided with Yuri's, and Callie had the day off, so they'd arranged a picnic lunch. On the big field near the Ward's Island ferry dock, they found a shady patch. It was the first time they'd been back together in person since the night of the Necropolis, and Gabe felt celebratory. He'd even made spanakopita the night before so he'd have leftovers to bring today.

"This is amazing," said Callie, eating her second piece.

With a tentative nibble, Yuri asked, "What is in this?"

"Spinach and feta cheese," Gabe told him. "You like it?"

Callie said, "It's a traditional Greek dish, right? They're a tiny bit like the veggie samosas my dadi makes, but I like how light and flaky your pastry is."

"It is very good," Yuri decided, taking a larger bite.

"Thanks, guys. I was worried I overcooked it."

He loved it when people liked his food.

"I wish I could taste it," Rebecca said, clasped with him, cross-legged on the grass.

"Me too." He was amazed that, even on a sunny day, Rebecca could still be the brightest thing around.

"Yuri's sad," she said.

Gabe had noticed too. From the moment his friend arrived, he'd seemed preoccupied. Part of it might have been his sprained wrist, which had turned out to be more stubborn than expected. It was only yesterday he'd been able to turn a screwdriver without pain. But Gabe sensed it was more than that, though he didn't want to push.

They all talked for a while about the upcoming séance, and the best plan of attack once they got the ghostlight. Rebecca had been incredibly impatient over the past few days, and her anxiety was obvious by how often she interrupted with questions and comments – which, as usual, all had to be made through Gabe.

"I'm sorry," she said. "The waiting is agony. I can't stop worrying that every day Viker is getting stronger and stronger."

"No doubt he is," Yuri replied testily. "Which is why I said it was much better to use our money to make light launchers. But no one else agreed with me. We could have had a powerful weapon to destroy Viker right now, but instead we wait. And wait some more. All for a stupid bit of coloured glass."

For an uncomfortable moment, no one said a word. Two dogs barked at the edge of the field. Callie swallowed a bite of spanakopita.

"I am sorry," said Yuri, "I am bad company."

He started to get up but Gabe said, "No, Yuri, wait. What's going on?"

Yuri looked out at the city. "My father was given notice yesterday."

"Oh, Yuri, I'm really sorry," said Callie.

Gabe said, "He can get another job, right—"

"He says he does not *want* another job like this." Yuri was tearing out little bits of grass. "He wants to go back to Russia where he can work as a proper engineer. And so my mother is angry with him because she thinks he *wanted* to get fired." Yuri ripped up more grass. "And Leo does not want to go back, and my mother says it is not safe to go back, and my father says maybe he will go back *alone*." He clawed up an entire clump of grass and threw it as far as he could. "And so everyone is yelling and crying and it is chaos in my house."

Gabe had never seen his friend so upset. He wanted to give him a hug, but they'd never done that before and he wasn't sure how Yuri would take it.

"Your dad's not going to—" Gabe began.

"I need to walk," Yuri said abruptly, and stalked off.

Gabe was about to go after him when Callie said, "I'll go."

It was probably best, Gabe thought. Girls were always better at knowing what to say.

"Poor Yuri," said Rebecca. "Would his father really leave them?"

"He's probably just really upset," Gabe murmured, "but it's a crappy thing to say. Why would he do that to his family? To Yuri?"

He felt a flare of anger. "You know what, let his dad go, I don't care, as long as he doesn't take Yuri with him." He realized his heart was pounding and he had to take a couple of breaths to slow it down.

"Gabriel, are you all right?"

"Yeah. I just suddenly thought of all the terrible things I wanted to say to my own dad."

"I think you might also have some good things to say to him."

"Doubt it."

Rebecca's hand moved across his phone, and suddenly a photograph appeared on the screen.

"I came across this yesterday," she said.

He thought he'd deleted that photo; how she'd found it he didn't know. He held it closer. Dad was in the bustling kitchen of Monterosso's, just after he'd been appointed executive chef. He wore his white coat and had his arms around Gabe and Andrew. Gabe must have been about nine. He was looking up at Dad and smiling.

"Never have I seen a look of such admiration," Rebecca said.

Gabe was silent, then shrugged. "He was a really good chef."

She waited patiently.

"He didn't cook Greek or Italian much at home – he wanted a change. He ate all over the place, really simple things sometimes. A burger, omelettes, panini. That's the kind of stuff he taught me first."

He saw Yuri and Callie sitting closer to the water. Yuri had his hands in his hair, mussing it, but he was talking, and Gabe thought that was probably a good thing.

"Did you often cook together?" Rebecca asked him.

"Sometimes, yeah. It was a lot of fun. And we'd watch cooking shows and laugh about how insane some of the challenges were, or how mean the chefs were. Once, for a school project, I said I wanted to make the world's largest cupcake—"

"What's a cupcake?"

"Oh, right, it's just a really small frosted cake that you can hold in one hand."

"If it became too large to hold in your hand, would it still be a *cup*cake?"

"That's a good point, but yes, you can have a giant cupcake—"

"Would it not simply be a *cake*?"

"Can I just finish my story?"

"Of course. I'm sorry."

"So Dad said I should go for it, and we could use the big oven at his restaurant. We calculated how much flour and stuff we'd need and went shopping for the ingredients, and mixed up a ton of batter. We poured it into this enormous mould we rigged up. And then the whole thing just collapsed in the oven. It made a huge mess, and we had to clean it all up. But even that part was fun. He could make things fun. After Yuri, I guess he was my best friend."

What he'd just told her was more than he'd told anyone else.

"Those are good memories," she said. "I'm certain there are more."

There were. Including one from when he was eight and the whole family was eating out one summer night on the patio of their favourite Italian place. They'd ordered the same things as always. When it got dark the strings of lights came on, and Gabe felt excited and happy to be up so late, and safe, too, in the warm glow of the light around their table. Mom and Dad slowly finished their bottle of wine, and Gabe and his brother got to order as many fizzy drinks as they wanted, and play cards on the table. And then Mom and Dad joined in their card game, and Dad had looked around at everyone and said, "I love you plenty," and Gabe remembered not wanting the evening to end. There was nothing spectacular about it, maybe, but it was a memory his brain often brought back to him.

"Anyway," he said, scratching at a mosquito bite. "What's the point listing off all the good stuff?"

"Because those stories are important," she told him. "And it's not too late to tell him. We could go see him again, Gabriel."

Dad, standing in the middle of the crosswalk. Dad, looking right through him.

"No, he's forgotten everything," Gabe said, feeling suddenly very tired. "Including me. My next tour's in ten minutes. We should go."

After Gabe and his friends left the field, a small girl was playing with a pile of rocks she'd found on the beach. They'd looked prettier when they were wet, but she still liked them. Her mom had told her they weren't taking them all home, so she had to decide which ones to leave behind.

She looked over her shoulder at a dog barking at the edge of the field. She was worried it was barking at her. It was on a leash, and the owner was trying to shush it.

When she looked back at her rocks she saw her littlest one lift off the ground and hover for a few seconds before drifting back down. She blinked and looked around to see if anyone else had seen. But her mother was over at the swings, pushing her brother.

"Mom!" she called. "Look!"

But Mom didn't hear because there was a yappy little dog nearby, also barking in the girl's direction.

She put the little rock in her pocket. It was one of her favourites, and she didn't want anything else weird happening to it. But then she noticed a bigger, boxier rock start to tremble on the grass. Very slowly it lifted, just an inch or so, before falling fast, as if dropped.

"Mom!"

A third dog was barking at her now, a really big one, tied up to the bike rack and nearly strangling itself.

The girl wanted to go back to her mother. She started scooping up more of her rocks. As she reached for a lovely disk-shaped one, it vibrated, and she pulled back her hand. She didn't know it, but that rock was roughly the shape and weight of the ghostlight.

She couldn't help imagining that an invisible hand was trying to lift it, but the rock was just a touch too heavy. She felt a bit sorry for the hand.

"Almost!" she said. "Good trying!"

After a few seconds, the rock stopped vibrating. Seconds later, the dogs all at once stopped barking, and the girl's mother came to say, "That's a great set of rocks, now it's time to catch the ferry home."

16

On the evening of the séance, Gabe dressed in the jacket and dress shirt he'd worn for his summer job interview, because on the ticket it said "formal attire." Which, for him, also included a slim pair of wire cutters in one breast pocket and a bag of iron filings in the other.

"This is crazy," he whispered to himself – and to Rebecca. Knowing that she'd be with him every step of the way made him feel better.

As he headed out, his mother said: "You look nice."

Gabe had his explanation ready, but then frowned. Mom was definitely more dressed up than usual.

"So do you."

They regarded each other in amusement.

Mom said, "I'm meeting a colleague for dinner."

"So it's not a *date* or anything."

"It's a *little* bit of a date, I suppose."

He could tell she was watching for his reaction, and she seemed a bit nervous. With a start he realized he still thought of Mom and Dad fused together. It was definitely strange to think of Mom on a date. Also, frankly, it was weird thinking of old people dating, period. Not that his mother was *old* old, but did people her age even care about that kind of stuff any more?

He noticed she was wearing a necklace she hadn't worn in a long time. "It's great, Mom," he said with a bit of an effort. "I hope you have a good time."

And before she could ask him any more questions, he slipped out the front door.

On Queen's Quay he hopped aboard the Spadina streetcar. As he sat down Rebecca clasped with him and said: "Your mother is beautiful."

He nodded. "Thanks, yeah."

He wasn't worried about people thinking he was talking to himself; everyone wore earbuds nowadays, so you never knew who was talking on the phone, or to themselves – or frankly, to a ghost.

As if trying to comfort him, Rebecca said, "It's very common for widows to remarry."

"*Widow!*" The word made him think of someone with a steel-grey bun sitting in a creaky rocking chair. Which was absolutely not his mother. But technically she *was* a widow. "She's just having dinner with—"

"Likely the gentleman was recently widowed himself."

"I have no idea—"

"I imagine he'll propose tonight."

"What?"

"Life is short, Gabriel."

"People live a lot longer now!" But with a pang, he realized that for Rebecca life *had* been terribly, cruelly short. She said:

"And surely your mother is eager for companionship."

Gabe remembered what Mom had said once to him and Andrew: "I still have you two." But Andrew was already gone, and one day he would be too, and then what?

"Well, courtship takes a little longer these days," he told Rebecca. "This is our stop."

In the front hall of Campbell House, Gabe felt underdressed. Most of the women were in evening gowns. The men wore full suit and tie, and some of them had even donned period costume with top hats and canes and pocket watches on fobs. Gabe was the youngest person here by at least twenty-five years. A few of the other guests gave him puzzled looks; one woman smiled at him like an affectionate aunt.

"Is this your first séance?" she inquired.

"Yes."

"I hope you have a steady heart. They can be quite intense."

If only she knew the things he'd already seen.

"I think I'll be OK," he told her.

He didn't feel OK. His stomach felt empty and too full at the same time. All day he'd been running through all the things that needed to happen, and that might go wrong. There was a lot riding on the next few hours, and Gabe felt the pressure building in his head like a storm cloud.

Campbell House was a beautiful redbrick Georgian mansion and one of the city's most historic homes – built pretty much the same year Rebecca had been born, as it turned out. Gabe hoped this was a good omen. The Toronto Historical Association gave tours of the house, but mostly it was rented out for private events, like parties and weddings.

And tonight, a séance.

The front hall was pretty full now, and when the chandeliers dimmed, everyone looked up the grand staircase. A woman had stopped halfway down. Gabe recognized Gillian Shaw's face from the website. She wore a charcoal-grey suit with a red vest. Her greying hair formed a mane around her face.

"Ladies and gentlemen, welcome."

Gabe was surprised by the spontaneous applause from the guests in the hallway. Gillian Shaw must have been a real celebrity in the supernatural world.

"Thank you, you're very kind. Please, join me upstairs."

Gabe mounted the staircase with the others and entered what must have been the ballroom. Heavy velvet curtains were drawn against the night. The only light glowed from candles and oil lamps. The room smelled of wood and polish, and that slightly sweetish odour that old buildings accrued over decades and centuries.

In the centre of the room was a huge oval table, laid with a red cloth. A fabric canopy hung overhead. From its outer edges hung beaded strings that enclosed the table without hiding it. As he drew closer, Gabe saw that the beads on the strings were interspersed with glass decorations.

All of which were the same colour and size as the ghostlight.

"Please find your place," said Gillian Shaw.

Gabe parted the beads and stepped through. Eighteen antique chairs were arranged around the table with a name card at each place. The guests milled around, finding their spots. Gabe was midway down the table. In the centre was an elaborate candelabra that held twenty candles. Smaller oil lamps were positioned down the length of the table. With a dramatic bang, an attendant closed the ballroom's double doors.

Gabe's stomach felt sick. They'd paid an insane amount of money for this ticket, and if he came away empty-handed, it was all wasted. He still wasn't sure he was ready to become a thief – and how was he even supposed to know what to steal? Right now, dangling all around him were hundreds of things that *might* be the ghostlight.

"This house has many ghosts," Shaw said quietly, walking around the table, "and some of you have brought your own. You may be unaware of the ghosts who travel with you. Or you may feel their weight upon you like a lead vest."

Gabe thought of Rebecca, Viker, his own father.

At the middle of the table, Gillian Shaw reached through the beaded strings with a long candle snuffer and extinguished the flames of the candelabra one by one.

"For the conjuring of spirits," she said, "it is best that the room

be dimmed. Spirits are timid and weak, and best seen in shadow."
One of the candles seemed to snuff itself out, and Gillian raised
an eyebrow at the guests. "It seems someone else is eager for us to
begin." There were some mild titters. But already the atmosphere
in the room was thickening.

"I'll remind you to turn your phones off, please," said Gillian
Shaw, slowly orbiting the table. "No photographs are to be taken."

Gabe turned off his ringer but left his phone on vibrate so
Rebecca could reach him. He wondered if there were other ghosts
already here in this old house, or travelling with these guests. Some
of them might have been thrill-seekers, just hoping for a good
story, but he figured most had lost someone important to them.

"We are here to encounter and speak with the dead," Gillian
Shaw said. "Things might be revealed that will shock and surprise
you. Things of a personal nature may be revealed to me. Whatever
I learn from the dead, I can speak aloud to you, or pass on to you
privately by paper. The choice is always yours."

Darkness seemed to congeal around the table. The only light
now came from the oil lamps, their wicks turned very low. The
chiselled faces of the others guests hovered in darkness.

At last Gillian Shaw took her seat at the head of the table. Gabe
noticed that, unlike the guests, she sat outside the strings of beads.
Before her were three evenly spaced strings, and fixed to each of
them, at eye level, was an amber disk.

Gabe's heart thumped. One of them had to be the ghostlight! But
which one? Rebecca had described the ghostlight to him, and he'd

glimpsed it in grainy photos, but in this shadowy light, these three disks looked awfully similar.

Rebecca would be able to tell him. He looked at the strings on which they were fixed. Definitely wire, and not too thick. The plan was still the same:

Distraction.

Blackout.

Rebecca leading him to the ghostlight.

Quick snip.

Ghostlight in his pocket.

And out.

The pale underside of the fabric canopy flickered with the light from the oil lamps. Everything beyond the glittering strings of beads was darkness.

"You will notice the empty chair opposite me," said Gillian Shaw. "That chair is reserved for any guests that might come to our table. We must be welcoming hosts. Are we in agreement?"

Murmured yeses from around the table.

"I have no authority over these beings; they come and go as they wish."

"They said the same thing when we went whale-watching," the man to Gabe's left whispered grumpily to his wife. "Didn't see a darn thing. And that was cheaper."

"I promise you," said Gillian Shaw, "that none of you will leave here with the same opinions you brought with you."

Gabe rubbed his sweaty hands on his trouser legs.

"I will warn you," said Shaw, "that when I commune, I sometimes sit and sometimes stand. I sway. Sometimes my eyes will be closed, sometimes open. Sometimes I might shout. Please do not be alarmed. There is never any danger – as long as you observe the rules and do as I ask. Now. Open your minds."

There were some big exhalations and shifting in chairs. Some nearby strings of beads clinked and chimed together. Gabe noticed that most people focused their gaze on the table. He let his rove.

"Is there someone here who has lost a spouse recently?" asked Gillian Shaw.

Tentatively a woman put up her hand.

"There is a man here called Arthur," said the supernaturalist.

A small cry emerged from the woman's throat. "Yes, that's him!"

"He has come with you; he is very devoted to you. Please, Arthur, sit down with us."

Gabe's eyes, like everyone else's, locked onto the empty chair at the end of the table. A small sigh seemed to escape from its fabric, like someone had just taken their seat. Or was he imagining it?

"Can you describe him?" asked the woman. "Can you see him?"

Gabe looked at Gillian Shaw, and saw her sway. He was pretty certain that she was staring through the amber lens not on the middle string, but the one to the right. *That* one must be the ghostlight.

In a few short sentences Gillian Shaw described the man. The woman was soon in tears, nodding and saying, "Yes, that's him, that's definitely Arthur."

"There is something he wants to tell you," Gillian Shaw said.

"He is greatly disturbed. Would you like me to speak his words aloud or write them down?"

"Write them down, please," said the woman.

Gillian stared straight ahead, then with her right hand quickly scribbled a note. She folded the paper and asked that it be passed down. When the lady opened it, her eyes darted across the lines. She began to cry harder, with such force that her shoulders jerked.

After a moment, Gillian asked, "Is there a return message you would like me to send him?"

"Yes. There is. Tell him I already knew. And I forgive him." She turned to the empty chair. In a broken voice, she said, "I forgive you, my darling. I do."

Gabe held himself stiffly, worried that he might start to cry himself. There was such anguish, but also so much love in the woman's voice; she'd *wanted* to forgive her husband – and he'd come tonight because he needed to be forgiven. He thought of his father, standing alone on that street.

"He is leaving now," said Gillian Shaw, gazing straight ahead through the ghostlight. "He is going. And he is calm now. He is peaceful."

Gabe turned back to the widow, and she, too, seemed calmer, drawing in a big smooth breath. There was a sad, but relieved, smile on her face. She apologized to everyone and pulled a tissue from her sleeve and dabbed her eyes so that a little bit of mascara spotted. Gabe's heart went out to her because the same thing happened to Mom sometimes.

He'd come thinking Gillian Shaw was just a hustler, using the ghostlight to make money. But maybe she actually helped people. Still, the ghostlight didn't belong to her. It belonged to the Gibraltar Point Lighthouse. He needed to keep reminding himself that, or he wouldn't be able to pull this off.

"Someone else has joined us," Gillian Shaw said abruptly, turning her head to and fro. "Someone who perhaps is not yet comfortable in our room."

Had she spotted Rebecca already? It seemed a bit early for her to start her big show. Beneath Gabe's hands, the tablecloth jerked a few inches, as if someone had tugged it from the other side.

He guessed it was showtime after all.

Several guests cried out in surprise. Gabe looked at Gillian Shaw, who held her hands aloft.

"It was not me, my friends." As if to confirm this, the tablecloth gave another tug, from a different direction. "Please, friend, sit in the chair we have provided you."

Instead, one of the lamps on the table was snuffed out. Gabe had to stop himself from smiling. Rebecca was putting on a good show; he knew it would get even better yet.

"This spirit has restless mischief in it," said Gillian Shaw.

"Is it my sister?" someone asked. "Tall, with blond hair?"

"Sounds like my father," another guest quipped.

"They are moving too quickly for me to see," Gillian said. "Please, friend, let us speak with you."

Across the table from Gabe, all the strings of beads swayed in the same direction, as if an invisible hand had brushed them. More oil lamps guttered and went out. At the end of the table something thudded.

"Dear God!" the woman beside him gasped.

The empty chair jerked, as if something heavy had just taken a seat. Gabe turned to Gillian Shaw. Just by her startled expression, he knew the supernaturalist was seeing something frightening. What was Rebecca doing? Making herself terrible to behold? He remembered her jaws, the darkness swirling inside.

"You are among friends," Gillian told the empty chair. "Please reveal yourself properly."

The chair tilted to and fro, its legs tapping rapidly against the floor in a kind of dance. More and more violent it became. One of the legs splintered, then snapped off altogether. Someone shrieked. Rebecca was really doing a number on that chair.

In the lamplight, Gillian Shaw's face looked terrified. "My friend, I bid you leave!" she said, her voice breaking.

A cold hand gripped Gabe's and he gave a yelp as his vision iced over. Rebecca crouched beside him.

"That is not me in the chair!" she hissed.

A dentist drill of terror vibrated inside Gabe's skull. He turned his spectral gaze to the end of the table.

What occupied the dancing chair looked more like a squid than a person. Its spindly arms and legs spilled over the sides. Gabe's fear tightened inside his chest and throat, like something squeezing. Atop the bloated mass in the chair was a head. It didn't really have eyes, just holes where they should have been. And yet somehow, Gabe still recognized the face of Nicholas Viker.

"What's he doing here?"

"Tommy Flynn's here too!" said Rebecca. "They must've followed us!"

Gabe saw the blue-lipped ghost step closer to Viker's chair.

"You've got something we'd like, my good lady," Flynn said to Gillian Shaw. "A pretty little amber lens. Some call it a ghostlight. We'd like it back."

"No, I cannot do that!" cried Gillian. Some force had returned to her voice. "Now I bid you depart." She stamped the floor with her shoe. "You are no longer welcome in this room!"

From inside the ragged mouth of Viker came a voice: "You will give it to me. Or I will take it."

"And we won't be tidy about it, neither," said Tommy Flynn. "I haven't raised hell for quite some time and I have a hankering to do so."

"We need to get the ghostlight before they do!" Rebecca whispered to Gabe. "I'll make darkness for you!"

"What about you?" Gabe asked.

He knew his clasp gave her strength and protection. Without it, was Viker now strong enough to consume her? But Rebecca had already released his hand. He could no longer see her, or Tommy Flynn or Viker – just the table of the living, every one of them staring horrified at the thrashing chair.

The lamp nearest Gillian was blown out, then the next, moving on down the table. That was Rebecca, Gabe knew.

But before she could snuff them all, a blast of cold air seeped down the table. The canopy overhead was ripped from its moorings and fell over all the guests, including Gabe, enveloping them.

He smelled burning, heard shouts and screams, then saw fire. Toppled lamps had spilled oil across the table, and the canopy went up in flame. Gabe punched away the fabric and started helping some of the other guests get free.

Fire was now the only light in the room, sending its sharp tendrils high. Black smoke boiled against the darkness of the ceiling. At the end of the table, Gillian Shaw was clawing through tangled strings of beads. She snatched up an amber disk, held it to her eye, discarded it, then tried another. With a cry of relief, she snapped it from its string and returned it to her eye.

Gabe felt a cold clamp on his wrist, and the bright form of Tommy Flynn leered at him with his blue-stained teeth.

"Hello, dear Gabriel," said Tommy. "Thanks for the clasp. You led us right to it. Now let's keep a cool head, shall we? Just let Mr Viker and me finish up here, and you can go."

Gabe pulled free easily. Flynn disappeared. Another cold hand took his, but this time it was Rebecca.

"Quickly!" she said, leading him toward the head of the table. "We need to take the ghostlight!"

Viker seeped past them, aimed straight at Gillian Shaw. At her feet crouched Tommy Flynn, tying her shoelaces together. When she saw Viker through the ghostlight, she whirled in terror, tripped, and fell hard. With a terrible crack her head struck the table's edge.

The ghostlight flew from her hand and spun across floor. One of Viker's long splintered arms zigzagged toward it.

Gabe ran for it – and Rebecca with him – though his whole body recoiled at the idea of getting closer to Viker. The fiendish ghost had already slipped his hand beneath the ghostlight and was trying to lift it. He succeeded. As it hovered a few inches off the floor, Gabe lunged, breaking his clasp with Rebecca and losing his spectral vision. But he snatched the ghostlight from midair.

He had it! In his own grip!

He scrambled up and ran. Just two steps, and icy bands fastened around both his ankles and tugged, just enough to yank him off-balance. As he fell he looked back and saw Viker and Tommy Flynn, each gripping one of his legs.

Gabe hit the floor and kicked free – though there was just the slightest resistance from Viker's hand. But the two ghosts only grabbed him again, higher up his legs.

Towering over him, Viker howled: "Give it to me!"

"You can't have it!" Rebecca snarled, suddenly at Gabe's side.

Gabe wasn't worried about himself; he could break free. But when he saw Viker's jaws start to dislocate, he was worried for Rebecca.

"Run!" he begged her. "Don't let them get you!"

He reached into his pocket and dragged out his bag of iron filings. Ripping it apart, he flung the entire contents at Viker's face. Singed, the ghost recoiled, clawing at his eyes. But the filings didn't seem to hurt him nearly as much as last time. Still, it bought them a few seconds.

"Let's go!" he said to Rebecca, springing to his feet.

The overhead lights came on abruptly, and two firefighters with extinguishers burst into the room.

"You OK?" one asked Gabe.

"Yeah. Someone got knocked out over there," he said, pointing at Gillian Shaw.

"We got her. You get out."

Slipping the ghostlight into his pocket, he bolted into the hallway with Rebecca, down the grand staircase and outside. A fire truck, lights flashing, was parked on the street. On the lawn was a big crowd, and he spotted the grumpy man, his fine clothes a mess, talking to a police officer.

"At least it was more interesting than whale-watching," he said.

But all the chaos around Gabe seemed faint and dim compared to the bright form and brighter eyes of Rebecca Strand beside him. Her hand was refreshingly cool in the humid night.

Smiling in delight, she said, "We got it!"

17

From the lamp over his dining room table, Gabe suspended the ghostlight so it would hang at eye level when everyone was seated. The amber disk was mounted in a brass frame – probably the very same one that Edward Shaw had placed around it all those years ago, to carry on his watch chain. The metal looked tarnished, but the glittering face of the ghostlight was completely unblemished.

Amazing that over all these years, it wasn't even chipped. Maybe it couldn't be destroyed. But even now, in his own house, Gabe worried that some invisible hand – or claw – might snatch it away. All the way home, Rebecca had promised him that Viker and Tommy Flynn were nowhere in sight.

He steadied the ghostlight. His mother was still out on her "little bit of a date," and it was barely nine o'clock. If he heard her key in the lock, he could unhook the ghostlight in a second. She'd be delighted to see Yuri, and meet Callie.

"You guys ready?" he asked them.

During the séance, his two friends had been waiting outside Campbell House – with more and more anxiety when they'd heard sirens and then seen a fire truck and police cruiser pull up. After Gabe and Rebecca had burst out of the smoking building, the four of them had quickly found each other and pelted back to Gabe's place. With the ghostlight heavy in his pocket, he'd felt like a criminal fleeing the scene of the crime.

After all the searching and dead ends, he could barely believe he was touching the ghostlight. Who knew how old this particular one was, how many lamps it had shone from, in what countries and continents of the world. At the table, Yuri and Callie sat side by side before the dangling ghostlight. Standing behind them, Gabe bent to see between their heads.

"You want to sit down now, Rebecca?" he asked.

The room, seen through the ghostlight, was an amber blur. Put your face too close, and you saw a mosaic of a hundred tiny identical images. Sort of like how a fly saw. Lean too far back and the ghostlight became opaque and was nothing more than a pretty Christmas decoration. But with your eye at just the right distance—

He blinked and the room came into focus: the bookshelves, Charlie's birdcage, the furniture, the other side of the dining room table . . .

And then Rebecca Strand stepping into view and sitting down in the chair opposite them.

"Whoa," he heard Callie breathe.

Even though Gabe had seen Rebecca many times before, this was his first time without clasping. It was certainly less startling. No icy grip, no dimming of his vision. The ghostlight showed him the real and the spectral simultaneously. Lift his gaze above the ghostlight, she disappeared; lower it back, and there she was again, smoothing her nightdress and modestly adjusting her shawl. He'd grown very fond of her pale, stern face, the wavy spill of her hair. Her greeny-grey eyes, like a wolf's. They were difficult to look away from.

"I forgot she was in a nightdress," Yuri whispered over his shoulder to Gabe.

"You didn't tell us she was so pretty," Callie whispered over *her* shoulder.

"Guys, she *can* hear you," Gabe reminded them.

"Oh," said Callie. "Right. Sorry."

Very politely, Yuri said, "Hello, Ms. Strand."

"No need to be formal, Yuri. I am so grateful for your help, and I hope your home is in less upheaval today."

Yuri made his ambiguous shrugging noise. "Things are still a mess. But at least no one is crying today. Except Leo, but I think that was because his Lego spaceship broke."

"I love your shawl, Rebecca," said Callie. "Did you make it yourself?"

"My mother started it, and I finished it." Rebecca frowned as if it had been a long time since she'd remembered this. "I think it must be very out of fashion. In my travels around the city, I have not seen anyone wearing one."

"No, shawls are cool," said Callie. "Especially handmade ones."

"Have dresses fallen out of fashion?" Rebecca asked earnestly.

"I don't think so."

"I have seen so few women in skirts."

"Well, leggings are more comfortable. And jeans have pockets. Which is super useful."

"It would be nice to dress in something different," Rebecca admitted. "Alas, I am doomed to go about in a nightdress for the foreseeable future."

"Well, you look *great*," Gabe said, and then thought it was probably a dumb thing to say.

Rebecca smiled. "I'm so pleased we can all see and hear each other at last."

"How is it possible we can *hear* you?" Yuri said. "With the light launcher, Gabe and I heard the other ghosts too. I can understand how the lens can angle the light – but sound . . ."

"Like you, I do not understand how it carries sound. These ghostlights are a mystery. But I am so grateful to have this one returned to me."

Seeing her through the ghostlight felt less personal to Gabe. It wasn't just that she was a little farther away, but her voice sounded like it was being transmitted through a dying radio. When she clasped with Gabe, her voice was crystal clear, and her image, too. He realized he missed her cool fingers meshed with his, and even the pins and needles afterward.

"We actually did it!" Callie said. "Well, you two did it. You were the ones in the burning building!"

"It wasn't like it was an inferno or anything," Gabe said. "And it was a team effort. We should really make a toast or something."

He went to the kitchen and returned with four stacked tumblers and a couple of cans of Brio. He cracked the tabs and poured out the fizzy dark drink.

"What's Brio?" Callie asked.

"An Italian soft drink. Kind of like Coke. I like it better."

"Of course you like Italian beverages," Yuri said, amused.

Gabe carried the fourth glass around the table and set it in front of Rebecca. "I know you can't drink it, but you're part of this."

Returning to Callie and Yuri, he clinked glasses with them.

"To the ghostlight!" This didn't seem quite grand enough so he added, "And to the destruction of the vile fiend Nicholas Viker and the liberation of Keeper William Strand!"

"Nice!" said Callie.

Yuri said, "Hear, hear!" and raised his glass higher.

Across the table Rebecca's tumbler vibrated and lifted for just a second before clunking back down. Through the ghostlight Gabe glimpsed her with her hand around the tumbler, smiling.

"To my brave friends," she said.

"You lifted it quite a bit!" Callie said in surprise.

"Thanks to Gabriel," she replied, "Viker is not the only one getting stronger."

Gabe shrugged to cover up his embarrassment. "I'm like a super battery."

"Do you think Gillian Shaw will go to the police?" Yuri asked. "And report the ghostlight stolen?"

"Nah," said Callie.

"What would she say?" Gabe asked. "'I've lost a piece of magical glass'? 'And by the way I robbed a grave to get it'?"

"Well, she wouldn't say that, obviously," Yuri retorted.

Rebecca said, "Surely she'll assume Viker took it."

"And she's hardly going to report a ghost," Callie pointed out.

"*Two* ghosts," Gabe reminded her. "Tommy Flynn."

Uneasily Yuri asked, "How did they know about the séance?"

"They must be spying on us," said Callie. "I mean, Viker followed us to the library that day."

A troubling thought tumbled into Gabe's head. "Tommy Flynn said something weird to me. He said, 'You led us right to it.' And before that he said, 'Thanks for the clasp.'"

He looked worriedly at Rebecca. "Remember you said, when you were coming back from Quebec, it felt like I was *guiding* you. You think it's because—"

"Because we clasped. And there's some kind of connection between us?"

He swallowed. "I've clasped with Viker and Tommy Flynn, too."

"Hang on!" Callie said. "Rebecca, you can always tell where Gabe is?"

"Not his exact location, no. But I sense the right direction. A star to chart your course by."

Gabe had never thought anyone, especially a girl, would describe him as a star. But his flush of enjoyment was short-lived.

"This would have been good to know earlier," Yuri said.

Defensively, Rebecca said, "I didn't know it had anything to do with the clasp, until now!"

Callie turned her frown on Gabe. "So now Viker can *track* you—"

"*He* grabbed *me!*" Gabe objected. "It's not like I'm going around shaking hands with every ghost I can—"

"How about Tommy Flynn?"

"I had to! To find out where the ghostlight was, remember?"

Callie snorted. "You should've just walked away after he told you!" It was true enough.

"I promised. And I felt kinda sorry for him. His teeth are all blue! And he hardly has any! Anyway, I didn't *know* any of this tracking stuff!"

"No wonder they've been all over us," said Yuri.

Callie's eyes darted around the room. "You're sure they didn't follow us back here?"

"I've been watching and listening," said Rebecca. "And no, there is no sign of them."

"Not yet," said Yuri. "Gabe, you shouldn't be the one to keep the ghostlight. Let me or Callie take it home for safekeeping. We haven't clasped with any ghosts."

Gabe met Rebecca's eye and could sense her violent reluctance. She didn't want to be parted from the ghostlight – any more than he did.

"I've got an idea," he said. "I'll put it in a cast-iron pot. They can't see or move through iron, right? And the pot weighs a ton. I can barely lift it."

Yuri spiked up his hair a bit. "Still, I think it would be safer if—"

"And I'll stand guard all through the night," Rebecca interjected.

Gabe could tell that there was no way she'd be separated from the ghostlight, not when she'd just finally regained it.

"And tomorrow, we must strike!" she said. "We can't allow Viker to get any stronger. We need to restore the ghostlight to the Gibraltar beacon."

"Yuri," Gabe said, "you found a good bulb, right?"

"Yes, the same ones we use for the overhead lamps in the amusement park." For a second Yuri looked wistful. "Not quite as powerful as my light launcher – and I still think mobile is a better way to go—"

"No!" snapped Rebecca, and Gabe was as startled as his friends by the anger on her face. Almost at once she collected herself and said, "I'm very sorry, Yuri, but waiting any longer is too risky."

"Agreed," said Yuri. "But will Viker even come to the lighthouse? He knows we have the ghostlight now. Wouldn't he worry about getting blasted?"

"True," said Callie. "He was a soldier, a really good one. Why would he charge into enemy fire?"

"He wants the ghostlight more than anything," Rebecca said. "It's the only thing that can destroy him, and he needs to destroy it."

"We don't actually need him right *at* the lighthouse," Gabe pointed out. "Just within range."

Yuri scratched his nose. "True. Not *too* far away, though. We want the full force of the beam. So how do we get him where we want him?"

Rebecca said, "I will take care of that."

Gabe wanted to ask how, but he sensed that Rebecca's mood was a little combustible right now.

"So how soon can you get the lamp ready?" he asked Yuri.

"Tomorrow. I have the day off. Give me the key, and I can get an early start."

"We're agreed, then," said Rebecca. "We will put the ghostlight back in the Gibraltar Point Light, and this time I will destroy Viker once and for all."

"We were unlucky tonight, sir," Tommy Flynn said, "just a touch unlucky, but we'll get it yet."

Viker said nothing. Flynn had a habit of speaking when silence was better. He was angry at the blue-lipped ghost, but angrier at himself. He'd been ill prepared for the séance. He'd needed to feed more. His hand ought to have been stronger and his grip unbreakable. What a humiliation to be bested by that living boy, Gabriel.

"Shall we go to his home?" Tommy Flynn asked.

"In time."

They had been ghosting along the city streets, eating a few weak, unsuspecting ghosts. At a busy street corner, Viker paused and looked up at a tall, many-windowed building. Metal ambulances with flashing red lights pulled up to the glass doors of the hospital.

Viker had a pleasant memory of the glorious battlefields of his past. Such wonderful carnage! The stench of blood and death. Even after his death, he had frequented battlefields, waiting hungrily as bewildered ghosts rose from soldiers' mangled bodies.

"Unless I am very much mistaken," Viker said, "we will enjoy a feast inside here."

"Perhaps I'll just wait for you outside, sir."

He saw Flynn's guilty hesitation, but also his craving. "You must be strong if you are to help me, Flynn."

"Well, I'm always happy to oblige, sir. I haven't had a good feed in some time."

"Let us gorge ourselves," Viker said, "and then we will visit the boy and *take* the ghostlight."

18

All that night, Gabe slept with a cast-iron pot cradled in his arms. When he woke, the first thing he did was lift the lid to check that the ghostlight was still there. Raising it to his eye, he made sure Rebecca wasn't in the room, then sprang out of bed and dressed.

Clipping the ghostlight onto a lanyard, he knotted it through one of his belt loops and shoved the amber lens deep into his pocket. When he sauntered into the living room, Charlie greeted him with a perky whistle. "Hello sweetbird-sweetbird!" Through the balcony windows, Gabe saw the island, the lake, and a cloud-streaked sky. On the coffee table was a note from Mom, saying she'd gone out to do a food shop and that she'd get him that coconut milk he'd asked for. It was Saturday, and he didn't need to be at work till one.

"Rebecca, you here?" he asked, heading for the kitchen.

He knew she'd been his sentry while he slept, but he still wasn't exactly sure how she spent the long nights. Reading the books and magazines he left out for her? (She was strong enough to turn pages now.) Pacing the living room? Standing and brooding on the balcony, staring at the island? He felt her presence now – that electrical flutter, more expectant than usual.

"What do you feel like for breakfast?" he joked. "Any requests?"

He was hoping to feel her hand in his. *Ghoulfriend.* It was going to be hard to get that word out of his head.

From his cage, the budgie chirped, "Love-you-plenty-loveyouplenty!"

"Sure you do, Charlie," Gabe said, his head in the fridge.

"Charlie-come-out, out-out-out!"

"Didn't Mom let you out?"

"Hello-Gabriel-you-handsome-devil!"

He glanced into the living room. "Very funny, Rebecca."

"Come-speak-with-me-with-me-with-me!"

"Come in here, I'm making a smoothie!" He spooned yogurt into the blender and added a mix of frozen berries. "Hey, I was thinking about what you said, about giving my dad more of a chance. Do you think we could stop by the intersection on our way to the island? Maybe use the ghostlight to try and talk to him?"

"Yes-I-think-that-is-a-good-idea."

"Give Charlie a rest, OK?" he told her. "Probably freaks him out when you do that. It's freaking *me* out. Just come talk to me!"

"Is-the-ghostlight-somewhere-safe?"

"Chained up in my pocket."

"May-I-look-at-it-please?"

He carried his smoothie across the living room to Charlie's cage. "You think you're strong enough to hold it now?" he asked Rebecca. "You moved that tumbler last night." He set down his smoothie, took the ghostlight from his pocket and held it out.

Charlie made a strange sound he'd never heard before. Then

Gabe realized the budgie wasn't actually standing on his perch but hovering just above it, a slightly squeezed look to him. Heart stuttering, Gabe lifted the ghostlight to his eye.

The cage was filled with darkness. It oozed between the bars, taking the shape of skeletal arms with too many joints and splintered finger bones. Amid all this darkness was a hand that held Charlie so tightly the bird's eyes looked like they might pop out.

Gasping, Gabe stepped back, but another hand darted out and closed icily around the ghostlight. Gabe tugged. The hand tugged back.

"Give it to me!" rasped Viker.

Still peering through the ghostlight, Gabe saw Viker's face assemble itself from the darkness: a ragged crater of a mouth, into which all the light in the room seemed to pour. Gabe leaned back, worried he might be pulled in too.

"Let go of it!" He tried to wrench it free but Viker was much stronger than last night.

Sunlight suddenly angled through the balcony doors and struck the ghostlight. Gabe felt the lens grow warm. A pale amber beam shafted through it and onto Viker's hand. Instantly great sores appeared on his spectral flesh. Viker's grip faltered, and Gabe ripped the ghostlight free.

He backed up, looking desperately around the room.

"Rebecca!"

Had Viker already devoured her? Was she thrashing around inside him even now?

"Gabriel! I'm so sorry! They surprised me!"

She was pinned to the floor, with Tommy Flynn sitting atop her like a bloated gargoyle. He, too, looked bigger than last night. His lower jaw jutted in a most unnatural way.

"Get off her!" Gabe roared, rushing at Flynn.

Flynn's jaws parted, but Gabe was already there, reaching out to Rebecca. They clasped. Gabe shivered as his living energy flowed into her. With a mighty kick she sent Flynn flying halfway across the room. He collided with Viker, who had left the birdcage and stood cradling his injured hand.

"Don't let go of me!" Gabe told Rebecca as Viker came striding toward them.

Pushing the ghostlight deep into his pocket, Gabe planted himself in front of Rebecca.

"Get out of my house!" he roared to conceal his terror.

As if confronted with a force field, Viker came to an abrupt stop. Then with one hand he struck Gabe in the chest. The icy shove made Gabe take a step back and seemed to suck the air from his lungs. Viker shoved him again.

Now Rebecca stepped in front of Gabe. Still holding his hand, she pulled back her fist and slammed it into Viker's shoulder. He stumbled back a bit, but not nearly as much as he had in the Grange House.

Another bright spray of sunlight filled the room. Gabe pulled out the ghostlight, angled it and sent another amber beam at Viker. He roared and staggered back, clutching his head.

"You're no match for us, Viker!" Rebecca told him.

"Not yet," said Viker. "Not yet."

He retreated toward the wall, dragging Flynn with him. Before they disappeared, Viker turned back to Gabe: "I will give your best regards to your father."

And then the ghosts were gone.

Gabe choked down big searing mouthfuls of air as he pedalled furiously. Rebecca had told him "Stop, don't go," but he'd left the condo in such a hurry, he didn't even know if she was with him right now. All he could hear was wind and traffic and his own pounding heart. He needed to be fast. Faster even than a ghost.

Almost there.

He dragged his bike onto the sidewalk and dumped it, no time to lock it up. He sprinted to the intersection and held the ghostlight to his eye.

With relief, he spotted his father in the middle of the crosswalk, staring down at his cell phone, getting run over.

"Dad!" Gabe called out as he waited for the light to change. "Dad! Over here!" He didn't care if he looked like a weirdo, peering through an amber lens like some junior wizard.

His father frowned, like he was trying to remember something. Slowly, slowly he turned his head. His eyes settled on Gabe.

"Gabe?"

Gabe felt a quick, tight ache in his throat.

"Yeah, Dad, it's me! You've got to come with me!" The crosswalk light went white, and Gabe rushed toward his father. "Take my hand and come with me."

If they clasped, he could protect his father, take him somewhere safe.

"I don't understand," his father said, looking around, "how I got here."

"It doesn't matter. Just come with me, OK?"

His father was about to take his hand when he was jerked backward. A shadow had dropped behind him. Viker's crooked limbs clamped themselves around Dad's torso. Towering over Gabe's father, Viker looked like some terrible scarecrow made from straw and animal dung. Gouged holes for eyes, and a long crooked mouth that twitched itself up at the corners.

"No!" Gabe shouted. "Don't!"

In that moment he forgave his father everything. Dad no longer looked confused. He looked terrified. Gabe reached for him. Dimly he heard a car horn blaring and was tugged back. He stumbled onto the sidewalk and looked around furiously at the stranger who held his arm.

"Dude!" the woman said, letting him go. "You nearly got run over!"

Gabe was too stunned to thank her. He looked back through the ghostlight and saw Viker coiled around his father like a python. His jaws opened impossibly wide.

Cars sped through the intersection. In desperation, Gabe looked for a gap and darted out.

"Stop!" he hollered at Viker.

More honking all around him; he didn't care.

Viker turned his sinkhole eyes on him. Gabe broke out in a cold sweat.

"Give me the ghostlight," Viker said. "And I will release him."

Gabe looked at his father's stricken face. "OK, yes, take it!"

The traffic light must have changed again, because there were other people on the crosswalk now. Gabe snapped the ghostlight from his lanyard and thrust it out.

"Hey, weirdo, watch it," said a young man, jostling Gabe and knocking the ghostlight from his hand.

It didn't break. It rolled toward the sidewalk. People stepped over it. Someone kicked it and sent it spinning toward a storm drain grate. Gabe snatched it up before it went through.

From the sidewalk, Gabe shouted to Viker, "Let him go first and it's yours!"

The ghostlight was snatched out of his hand – not by Viker, but by Rebecca Strand, who clasped with him so he could see her bright, furious face.

"Gabriel! What are you doing!"

"It's my father!" He made a grab for the ghostlight, which she held out of reach, clenched tight in her other hand. "Rebecca!"

"There's nothing you can do, Gabriel!"

In horror he turned back to the crosswalk. Viker's mouth became larger still, and the sound that welled up from it made Gabe's knees weaken. It was the howling sound of people who had lost everything: all love, all hope. Gabe's father seemed to stretch as he was pulled toward that mouth, like light toward a black hole. He was inhaled: head, shoulders, chest, arms struggling, then buckling as the rest of his body was slurped inside. Nicholas Viker stood taller now, fed, emboldened.

"No!" Gabe cried out. "No, no!"

"He'll come for me now!" Rebecca said. "We must flee!"

He ran for his bike, and she ran with him, still clasping the ghostlight. Only when they reached the bike did she return it. She also released his hand so he could see the real world properly as he pedalled.

He zigzagged furiously through the city, hoping to throw Viker off his scent. Would that even work? When his legs burned and he could no longer catch his breath, he slowed down and pulled off the street.

Perched on the handlebars, Rebecca clasped with him.

"Why?" he panted. "Why'd you do that?"

Her look was still severe. "Gabriel! You were about to give Viker the ghostlight!"

"To save my father!"

"And then I would never be able to save *mine*!"

She was right, and he didn't know what to say. His chest heaved up and down; his throat was dry and he coughed. He looked away. He knew it wasn't fair, but he blamed her.

"You think Viker would have honoured his word, Gabriel? A *vile* thing like that? He would have seized the ghostlight, *then* eaten your father. We would have lost both our fathers, forever!"

His anger cooled. "What happens to my dad now? Inside?"

"I don't know, Gabriel."

He couldn't imagine it. Swallowed whole. Like a rat by an anaconda, slowly squeezed through the snake's guts. The darkness. The tumult. The panic. Colliding with other confused and despairing souls.

Gabe puts his hands on his hips. He thought he might throw up. "That was the worst thing I've ever seen."

"Truly terrible." Rebecca looked haunted, and Gabe felt suddenly foolish. She'd been living with this terrible fact for over a hundred years. For him it was just a matter of minutes.

"We are still friends, yes?" Rebecca said to him.

"Of course we are."

"We have a common purpose now. So let's go to the island and restore the ghostlight to the lighthouse. And liberate both our fathers."

19

Gabe stumbled through his day, reciting his tour numbly. He couldn't halt the awful images of Viker and his father stuttering through his head. He couldn't forget the howl of those despairing mouths trapped inside.

It was a comfort knowing that Rebecca was beside him, and that Yuri was already up in the lamp room, hard at work preparing the Gibraltar Point Light.

Midafternoon, during a break, he went up and told his friend what had happened. Gabe had to pause a few times to make sure his voice didn't shake too much.

Yuri listened patiently and then, to Gabe's surprise and gratitude, gave him a hug and said, "We will free him."

"I'm worried I led Viker straight to him." Gabe hadn't been able to shake the terrible thought. In his panic, he'd just assumed Viker and Flynn had already known where Dad was. Maybe they hadn't at all. "I'm so stupid!"

Yuri squeezed both his shoulders. "No, anyone would have done the same. Kick that thought out of your head. Look how well work is going here."

Gabe took in all his friend's tools spread out on the floor.

"Thanks, Yuri."

"This is the kind of thing I love. I checked and cleaned the socket, updated the wiring from the fuse box; next I have to install a little frame to hold the ghostlight. Can you leave the lens with me, so I can make sure it's a perfect fit?"

Gabe trusted Yuri more than anyone in the world but still felt himself hesitate.

"I will guard it with my life," Yuri said. "Anyway, I am not the one Viker is looking for."

"I know. I just don't want you getting hurt, in case he comes around." With a sigh Gabe pulled the ghostlight from his pocket and knotted the lanyard around Yuri's belt. "There."

"I will stay here," Rebecca said, clasping with Gabe briefly, "to make sure he's safe."

"And you've got Rebecca on guard duty," Gabe told him.

"Thank you. See you at six, my friend."

Gabe went back to work, feeling a bit lighter. It was a relief not having the ghostlight with him. After his shift finally ended, he biked over to the Island Cafe to pick up a box of sandwiches for everyone. When he returned to the lighthouse, Callie was already there, still in her CN Tower uniform. By the soft way she looked at him, he knew that Yuri must have told her what had happened.

"My goodness, perfect timing," Yuri said. "We are all here now. I have just finished installing the mount and, watch this, the ghostlight should fit like so . . ."

Gently he slid the ghostlight into the snug U-shaped frame he'd made. And finally this amazing amber lens was reunited with the Gibraltar Point Lighthouse after almost two hundred years.

"Rebecca, would you say it's in the right position?"

Gabe glimpsed Rebecca through the ghostlight as she chewed her lip, trying to remember.

"I believe so. I only saw it in place that one night. But yes, I think that's correct."

Beyond the high windows of the lamp room, a plane came in to land at the Island Airport. The sky was starting to lose its colour. The wind picked up, making little ripples in the harbour. The skyscrapers blazed with the low light from the setting sun.

"It's incredible," Callie said now, "that even a little bit of sunlight through the lens could hurt Viker."

"So imagine what we can do with this," said Yuri, taking a very big lightbulb and screwing it into the socket. "Once we flip the breaker downstairs, we have power, and all we need to do is turn on the lamp with this switch here. Now, let's tune up the moving parts."

From his backpack, Yuri produced three cans of spray lubricant and handed one to each of them. "From what I saw last time, every metal joint needs oiling. Callie, can you unlock it, please?"

Callie inserted her lighthouse pendant into the secret keyhole, and the lamp column creakily came to life. The handles sprang out, the platform flipped down with a rusty shriek.

"We need the lamp to be as manouverable as possible," Yuri said.

They set to work. It occurred to Gabe that the lamp hadn't been tended like this in decades. Rebecca took his hand, and he saw her looking on longingly.

"I wanted to be doing this my whole life," she said.

"I know." It didn't seem like nearly enough, so he added, "You're kind of like the keeper now. You're going to light the light, after all this time."

"No. I merely *watch*." Her expression was no longer wistful, but bitter. Her clasp felt colder than usual. "My body may be long dead, but my ambitions and wishes still burn with the same passion. That's the curse of a ghost. To contain this explosion of need and desire, and have no way of achieving it."

She seemed to be grinding her teeth, and there was a restless jut to her lower jaw.

"Have you ever *truly* considered it, Gabriel? What I have lost? What I will never get back? Can you even imagine what it's like?"

"A little, but—"

She sniffed. "You've lost a father, yes. Most people lose parents."

She made it sound like a tiny thing, and he felt anger kindle inside him.

"I just watched my father get eaten by Viker!"

She met his anger with more of her own. "You have no idea of my suffering! You have your whole life ahead of you. I only had sixteen years! Sixteen! Hardly a life at all! How would *you* like that?"

Did she expect him to say he was sorry? Why should he, especially when it sounded like she was blaming him?

"It's not my fault!" he snapped.

"I will never have my dreams, not a single one!"

"What am I supposed to do?"

"Nothing will ever change that! Nothing! Not ever, or ever or ever . . ."

She was in a trance of fury now, stamping her foot. Her mouth opened and snapped shut with animal intensity.

"Do you think," she said through clenched teeth, "that if I ate another ghost I'd feel *something*? A surge of power? And if I had enough power, I could *do* things, couldn't I?"

With her free hand she pushed Gabe in the chest, and he gave a little gasp, not because it hurt – he barely felt it – but because he was so shocked by the rage behind it.

"Knock it off, Rebecca!"

"You think me a monster, don't you? Like Viker?"

She struck him again, and this time he winced like he'd been pelted with a hard snowball. Faintly he heard Callie and Yuri, asking what was going on, and was everything OK?

"If I were strong enough," Rebecca said, gnashing her teeth, "I could do what you're doing right now! Lift things, and push things, and have a little bit of a life! If only I *fed* enough!"

For just a moment, Gabe was afraid of her. He was about to yank his hand free from her clasp, but then her face collapsed and she was weeping, her free hand clamped over her mouth.

"Oh," she moaned. "Oh, I'm sorry."

"You would never do something like that," Gabe said, all his own anger vanquished. "And that's the important thing. That's what counts."

"I struck you. Did I hurt you?"

"I'm fine, really."

"I'm so ashamed."

"Everyone freaks out sometimes. *I'm* freaking out. It's normal. Especially in abnormal times. Like right now. It's OK."

"I'm going to keep watch outside," she said, and broke her clasp with him.

She disappeared and his vision refocused on the world of the living. His friends were looking at him expectantly.

"She's just getting some fresh air," he said. "Outside. On the catwalk."

"That sounded intense," Callie said.

"She's a bit upset."

"You sounded a bit upset too."

"We had a little argument earlier. I think everyone's just a bit stressed out."

He didn't feel like telling them any more. What if they started worrying about some of the violent things she'd said? She didn't mean them. Yuri gave a quick, understanding nod. They worked on together in silence, tending to the lamp. Callie's phone pinged.

"My mom wishing me good night," she said, typing a reply. "What did you guys tell your parents about tonight?"

Gabe looked up from some screws he was tightening. "I told my mom I was sleeping over at Yuri's."

"And I told mine I was at Gabe's. Let us hope our mothers do not call each other." Yuri nodded at Callie. "And you?"

"Sleepover at Jennifer's, who I don't even like that much. We're all doing imaginary sleepovers. I hate lying. But I couldn't see any other way."

Yuri finished repairing the leather foot straps on the gunner platform and slipped his feet inside to check them. "Shall we see how our little beauty is doing?"

Gabe and Callie stood back as Yuri took the beacon through its paces. Murmuring to himself, he raised and lowered the column, swivelled and tilted the beacon. Everything moved smoothly, with hardly a creak.

"Good to go?" Gabe asked.

"We are good to go."

"It should be you at the controls tonight," Gabe told his friend.

Yuri lowered the beacon back to its resting position. "You trust my hand?" he asked. He still wore the compression bandage, but it hadn't stopped him from working hard most of the day with tools.

"Seems good to me," Gabe said. "Anyway, I'd probably just bust it."

"Nooooo," said Yuri, but without conviction.

"You know it's true."

"It's a sturdy machine, but you might find a way to gut it."

"Which is why you should work it!" Gabe said.

"But maybe Callie wants to?"

Callie shook her head with a smile. "Happy for you to do it,

Yuri. You have a special skill with machines. You'll handle it with real panache."

"Panache, I like that," said Yuri, blushing a little. When had Gabe ever seen him blush? "It sounds like a fun dessert, but also powerful."

"Speaking of food—" Gabe began.

"Were we?" asked Callie.

"With Gabe, it is always food," Yuri told her.

"I brought those sandwiches!" Gabe started unpacking the box. "Aren't you guys hungry? I've got a tuna, a caprese baguette here, this one's roasted veg on focaccia . . ."

"We're about to battle with evil ghosts, and you brought a picnic," Callie said.

"There's no occasion that isn't better with food," Gabe insisted. "You're welcome."

"These do actually look very tasty," said Yuri, picking one.

"Can I have the tuna?" Callie asked.

Soon they were all happily chewing on their sandwiches. After a few minutes, Yuri said:

"Rebecca, how do you plan to bring Viker closer to the lighthouse?"

I will lure him.

"Rebecca, that's way too dangerous!" he said. He'd never imagined this was her plan.

I am stronger now.

"Yeah, but so's Viker. We're not using you as bait."

Ferocious as she was, Gabe doubted she'd be able to withstand Viker on her own, especially without his living hand to clasp. He wasn't even sure *he* could withstand Viker any more. He remembered the strength of his grip on the ghostlight; that icy punch in his chest.

"There's no way, Rebecca."

"It's the *only* way." She'd stepped directly behind the ghostlight so Gabe and the others could see and hear her. "You need to know where Viker is before you can annihilate him with the ghostlight."

Callie gave a sigh. "She's right. She's the only one who can see him."

"The ghostlight can see him too," Gabe reminded them.

"Yes," said Yuri, "but once we turn it on, we've lost our element of surprise. Also, we could waste a lot of time splashing light all over the island and maybe attracting the marine police."

Gabe scratched at his neck, thinking. "We need Rebecca. But *I'll* be the bait. What Viker wants most is the ghostlight, so I'll give it to him."

Callie looked at him like he'd proposed taking a swan dive into an empty pool. "You want to explain this, please?"

He explained, and finally saw Yuri look at Callie and nod. "I think this is a good idea."

"You'll still need me with you," Rebecca said. "To be your eyes."

"But we'll be together, at least," Gabe said.

He went to the tall windows of the lamp room. "So where's a good spot to do this? Not too far away, with a clean line of sight . . ."

"Probably best if it's someplace people won't see the beam," Callie said.

"There." Yuri pointed through the south-facing windows. "On the beach. We'd be shining out over the lake, away from the city. And not too many trees or bushes in our way."

"It's good," Gabe said with a nod. "So that's where I'll lead Viker."

"And we'll be right here," Callie promised. "Ready for your signal."

Gabe pretended to miss the last ferry leaving Hanlan's Point. Then he stood dejectedly on the deserted dock, staring as the boat returned to the city. Astride his bike, he made a show of checking his phone, then looking around hopelessly.

Looking nervous didn't take much effort.

He pulled the ghostlight from his pocket and put it to his eye, turning in a slow circle. It changed nothing in what he saw, because it wasn't the real ghostlight but a piece of glass hastily painted in the maintenance shed. He hoped that, from a distance at least, it looked convincing. He returned it to his pocket.

His phone buzzed.

No sign of them yet.

Rebecca had been flitting about, up and down nearby trees, watching out for Viker and Tommy Flynn. And she'd discovered, amazingly, that she didn't actually need to touch the phone to send Gabe texts. As long as she wasn't too far away, she could somehow manage. Which was excellent, because he wanted it to appear like he was alone.

Across the harbour, the skyscrapers glowed; the CN Tower's xenon spotlight lanced the sky. From Ontario Place came the warbled waves of a concert on the outdoor stage. He was grateful for these signs of everyday life, carrying on. It helped calm his churning mind.

"Can you hear me?" he whispered to Rebecca.

I can hear you.

"Make sure you don't get caught in the ghostlight beam."

I'll be careful.

"I don't want you to get hurt."

Don't worry about me.

Gabe's mind cartwheeled ahead through the steps of their plan.

"After we destroy Viker, and free your father, what happens?"

To me, you mean?

"Yes."

I will be free to go.

He remembered how the governess had disappeared in a happy spurt of fireworks.

"So you'll go."

I don't imagine I have any say in the matter.

He suddenly realized he might be saying goodbye to her tonight. He'd known that this moment was coming, but the thought hadn't really settled down and gotten comfortable. He didn't want it to.

"I'm going to miss talking to you. And your texts, too. You use periods and capital letters and everything."

It's simply the way I speak.

"Well, I like it." He took a breath, then added, "I like you, in general."

He looked at his phone, waiting, counting his quickened heartbeats.

I have a confession to make. Our clasp gives me more energy, and lets us speak more easily. But sometimes I touch your hand even when it's not necessary. Just to touch you.

He didn't know what to say; he felt like a balloon filling with happiness. He let her words echo in his head awhile longer. "I'm glad," he said finally, "that you do that."

His phone pinged and a heart emoji appeared on the screen. He laughed. "There's something pretty weird about a ghost using emojis."

They are a great deal of fun! I'm going to miss them. I am going to miss you.

"Look, do you really have to g—"

I see them! Near the fence to the airport.

"Have they seen me?"

They are watching you.

He pocketed his phone. Turning toward the airport, he lifted the fake ghostlight to his eye. He pretended to see something terrifying, dropped the lens on the grass and fumbled to pick it up. The fumbling wasn't fake. Then he hopped onto his bike and pedalled fast in the direction of the lighthouse – and the spot they'd chosen to blast Viker.

He didn't know how quickly he should be going, until his phone vibrated in his pocket and he dragged it out:

Faster!

He sped up, picturing Viker and Flynn chasing after him like crazed dogs. At any moment an icy blow might knock him off his bike. Was Viker that strong yet?

He veered off the road and onto a trail that led to the beach. Not too much farther now. When it got too sandy he dumped his bike and ran. Near a small rise, he stopped, as if he'd run out of breath, and pulled the fake ghostlight from his pocket. He looked around – wishing he really *could* see what was coming. It occurred to him that this might be the very spot where Viker had come ashore, all those years ago, when he murdered the Strands. It wasn't a comforting thought. He fought the urge to look toward the lighthouse, in case Viker and Flynn suspected anything. He just hoped Callie and Yuri were ready and watching. All he could do was wait for Rebecca's signal – and hope the ghostlight did its work.

He didn't need to pretend: he was scared. When the phone vibrated in his pocket he jerked like he'd been shocked with electricity. That was Rebecca's signal. Facing the lighthouse, he waved his arms above his head—

Then turned away, because a light, brighter than any he'd ever witnessed, pounded over him like a tsunami. His shadow was slammed against the sand, so hard he thought it would make a crater. On the fringes of the amber blaze he saw Viker and Flynn closing in on him. He dropped the decoy ghostlight and ran.

Grass and shrubs whipping at his legs, branches raking his chest and face. He burst out onto the road, sprinting. Overhead the amber beam blazed like a searing suspension bridge. He pelted down the gravel path to the lighthouse.

Once inside, he locked the door behind him and charged up the stairs. His feet crunched on the iron filings Callie had sprinkled around as an early-warning system. As he clambered into the lamp room, the heat was intense. Wearing sunglasses, Yuri manned the Gibraltar light, which he'd telescoped off the floor for a better angle. Outside on the balcony, Callie had binoculars to her face and was shouting directions to Yuri.

"Left! A bit more! Lower!"

Expertly, Yuri swivelled and tilted the beacon. Gabe hurried outside. On the beach, the amber light scoured the sand. But he couldn't see Viker or Flynn anywhere.

"Did we get them?" he asked Callie.

"I don't know!"

"You don't know?"

"We got a good shot in, right at the beginning, and then they disappeared. Maybe we obliterated them already?"

"Rebecca, do you see them anywhere?" When no reply came he looked around the catwalk in panic. "Rebecca?"

"She's not here?" Callie asked worriedly.

"No!" She was supposed to come straight back to the lighthouse, ahead of him.

"Maybe it's just taking her a bit longer," Callie said.

"Or Viker has her!"

An object flew past Gabe's head, struck the lamp room window, then clattered to the catwalk. Cautiously he stepped closer. It was the fake ghostlight.

"Check the clearing!" he shouted to Yuri, pointing. "Down there!"

The ghostlight's beam singed the heels of Tommy Flynn disappearing into the trees.

A cold hand gripped Gabe's and gave him a tug. His vision frosted, and Rebecca was there, leading him around the catwalk.

"You're OK!" he said in relief.

"Viker's on the other side of the clearing! Hurry!"

As he pounded around the metal walkway, Gabe rapped on the glass to get Yuri's attention. "I've got Rebecca! Follow me!"

In the clearing Viker stood like a crooked shadow puppet, all angles and limbs. His nostrils and eyes and mouth were sinkholes, drinking in the night.

"Right there, blast him!" Gabe shouted, then pulled Rebecca out of the beam's path.

Before the amber beam struck Viker, the ghost snapped out a very long arm into the trees – and when it snapped back, it clutched Tommy Flynn like a shield.

"No!" screamed Tommy Flynn. "Mr Viker, sir, stop!"

The amber beam made a crater in Flynn's chest.

"No!" he wailed. He clutched at his torso, trying to hold himself together, but his hands melted. In a shower of coloured sparks, something burst from him. In astonishment Gabe caught the outlines of an older man – was it Edward Shaw? It was, and Shaw barely had time to register his delight at his freedom before he evaporated into the night.

There wasn't much left of Tommy Flynn now, and soon Viker would be without a shield.

"Guys!" Callie's voice came from inside the lamp room, where she crouched, peering down the stairs. "Something's inside!"

Confused, Gabe turned back to Viker and Flynn. They were still a good distance from the lighthouse. Was there a third ghost? But then he noticed something. One of Viker's many arms stretched bone-thin along the ground, out and out and out – right to the stout door of the lighthouse.

When he heard Callie's scream he broke his clasp with Rebecca to bolt inside the lamp room. What looked like a huge black spider at the end of a stick was scuttling up the steps with alarming speed. It was Viker's ghostly hand, smoking slightly from the iron filings that coated it.

"Get it!" Callie wailed.

Instantly Yuri swivelled the lamp, but he couldn't tilt the beam down quite enough.

"I can't reach it!"

The hand was clever. It stayed just out of the beam's reach and patted about the floor until it found the lamp's column.

"Aim the light back outside!" Gabe shouted. "At Viker!"

If they blasted his body, surely he would pull back his arm.

Crablike, the terrible hand began to climb the column toward the lamp.

"Just get it off!" Yuri shouted, swiveling back to the clearing.

Callie emptied her entire bag of iron filings on the hand. Acrid fumes rose off it, and it flinched but continued climbing.

Gabe grabbed it. He wasn't expecting it to feel so very solid – and so very, very cold. A paralyzing chill seeped up his arm and through his body. It carried with it a fear so intense he felt he might die.

"Let go, Gabe!"

The voice was Rebecca's and she was beside him, helping him pull his frozen fingers away from Viker's ghostly flesh. When he looked at her to thank her, her teeth were grinding and her eyes had darkened. Gabe felt the iciness of her clasp intensify, and shivered as she greedily pulled his heat and energy into her. Her mouth opened as she lunged at Viker's hand. Caught in a powerful suction, the ghost's fingers tore loose, one by one, from the column, and stretched toward Rebecca's mouth.

Just as they were about to be inhaled, the fingers formed a fist and struck Rebecca in the face. Stumbling back, she fended off Viker's wild punches. Gabe put himself between them. He took a blow to the shoulder and went sprawling, his clasp with Rebecca broken.

"Are you OK?" Callie asked as she helped him to his feet.

"He's *a lot* stronger," Gabe panted. "Rebecca?" Without her clasp, he could no longer see her, or Viker's hand. The iron filings must've fallen off. "Rebecca?"

"Are you still blasting him outside?" Callie yelled at Yuri.

"I can't see him!" Yuri yelled back.

Gabe scooped some iron filings off the floor and hurled them around the lamp. Viker had made his arm so thin it looked like a metal seam – running all the way up the column to the lamp itself.

"He's closed his hand around the ghostlight!" Yuri cried. "He's trying to pull it loose, but his fingers keep melting!"

"Good!" Callie said. "Then he can't take it!"

"He has a lot of fingers!"

"Grab it before he does!" urged Gabe. "Don't let him get it!"

"It's too hot to touch!"

Gabe heard a quick, precise crack.

Viker's skinny arm slithered limply down the lamp column. At the end was the melted stump of his hand. Swiftly it retreated across the floor and down the stairs.

"It's gone!" Callie cried.

"He just gave up!" Yuri exclaimed.

Gabe gave a whoop of triumph and high-fived Callie. Then, with a cold clasp, Rebecca was beside him.

"Viker is still outside!" she told him severely. "We can't let him flee."

"Yuri," Gabe said, "can you see him yet?"

"No!"

"I'll go look," said Rebecca.

"Be careful, please!" She unclasped from him and was gone.

"Hey, guys?" Yuri's voice was pinched with worry. "I think Viker did something to the ghostlight. There's a crack in it. Look."

Yuri lowered the beacon to its resting position and handed Gabe his sunglasses. Putting them on, Gabe squinted at the whisker-thin line that cut diagonally across the inside of the amber lens.

"It's just a little crack," he said worriedly. "It's fine, right?"

But now a bead of colour was spreading along the crack, like a drop of ink, or blood. The light from the lens began to change, from glorious amber to a sickly purple. And there was a sound coming from the ghostlight now too, like wind being sucked down a chimney to extinguish the flames.

"What's happening?" Gabe asked, his skin prickling.

"Viker's on the catwalk!" Rebecca said, clasping his hand.

In an instant Yuri had the ghostlight aimed through the window at the ghost. In this new, bruise-coloured light, Gabe saw Viker as he'd never seen him before. His many-limbed body churned with the bodies of the ghosts he'd consumed, as though they were drowning in quicksand.

Then Gabe made the mistake of looking at Viker's face. The mouth was bigger and wider than any mouth should be, stretching now in a triumphant grimace. And the deep-set eyes drank the purple light into them, like water down a drain. Gabe felt like he was being pulled too.

"Look away, Gabriel!" Rebecca shouted, and he wrenched his gaze free.

"Why isn't the ghostlight hurting him?" Callie cried.

In its full blaze, Viker didn't even flinch. No arms flew up to shield himself. No crater opened in his torso. On the contrary, his chest swelled, as if he were taking a deep and delighted breath. Instead of searing holes in him, the light soaked into him. His head lifted higher, he stood taller – no, he was actually *growing* taller. The hand that had been melted earlier sprouted five new terrible fingers.

"It's making him stronger!" Gabe shouted. "Shut it off, Yuri!"

Before Yuri could reach the power switch, Viker's freakishly long arm shot through the window like a battering ram and knocked him to the floor.

"Get behind me!" Gabe told Rebecca. "Don't let go of me!"

But he wasn't sure how much he could protect her, or himself. From the corner of his eye he saw Callie help Yuri to his feet. Gabe reached for the lamp's power switch. The heat was intense. Something ice-cold clamped around his ankle and dragged him backward. Hitting the floor, he twisted around to see Viker's oversized hand clenched around his ankle. Gabe tried to kick free but felt like all the heat was pouring out of his body through his ankle. He began to shiver. He remembered Tommy Flynn's words about being "drained" by a ghost.

His life draining away.

Callie and Yuri each grabbed an arm and hefted him up.

"He's s-s-still g-g-ot my f-f-foot," Gabe said through chattering teeth.

Yuri dumped some iron filings onto Gabe's ankles. For just a second, Viker's hand unclenched, and Gabe whipped his leg back.

"Rebecca!" He'd lost his clasp with her.

Any chance of turning off the ghostlight was gone. Like an octopus, Viker had poured his entire body over the beacon.

"I'm here," Rebecca said, her hand cool in his. "We need to go!"

Gabe's foot was still so numb he almost tumbled over.

"What about the ghostlight!" said Yuri.

"No way!" said Gabe. "He's all over it!"

With every second Viker was becoming stronger. Soon he'd be able to hurl them from the catwalk. They snatched up as much of their gear as they could, and Callie scrambled first down the stairs.

Yuri followed, and then it was Gabe's turn, still clasping with Rebecca. His last glimpse was of Viker, draped over the beacon, glowing a sickly purple and swelling to fill the entire room.

At the bottom of the stairs, Yuri ripped open the fuse box.

"What're you doing?" Gabe asked.

"This!" Yuri yanked out a breaker and pocketed it.

The overhead lights went out, and the purple glow seeping down the stairs evaporated. An enraged howl echoed within the stone walls, and Gabe heard it even after he'd slammed the heavy door, even as he fled with his friends through the humid night, away from the Gibraltar Point Lighthouse.

Inside the maintenance shed, Yuri turned on a single flex lamp, pushed low so that no one passing outside would notice the light. Callie paced, too worked up to sit. Exhausted, Gabe flopped into the shredded armchair, his forehead slick with sweat.

His hand trembled as he rummaged through his backpack, searching for the bag of almonds he kept in case of snack emergencies. After being clasped by ghosts both good and evil, he felt utterly wrecked. He found the nuts and crammed a fistful into his mouth.

They'd not said a word to each other during their headlong flight. Whenever Gabe had thought of turning back – they couldn't just leave the ghostlight behind! – the impulse died instantly. He couldn't conquer his terror of Viker's bottomless eyes. The icy strength of his grip, draining away his life.

"Gabe, you OK?" Callie asked.

He nodded, guzzling some water. "Better now. Rebecca, you still here?"

His phone buzzed, and he put it on the table for everyone to see.

Here.

Disappointment seemed to emanate from her single word.

Callie clutched her head. "I can't believe we lost it. We just *got* it!"

"It was too hot to take out," said Yuri, looking pained.

"It's no one's fault," Gabe said. "There was nothing we could have done. Viker's too strong. How's your wrist, Yuri? It looks a bit swollen."

"I fell on it, but I'll live."

Gabe rubbed the ankle that Viker had grabbed. It still felt like there was ice trapped inside.

It's no longer a ghostlight. When he cracked it, it became something else.

Yuri asked her, "Did you ever see that purple light before?"

Never.

"What happened to it?" Gabe wanted to know.

"You said Viker's grip was icy, yes?" Yuri said. "Extreme cold meeting extreme heat. Like taking a glass hot from the dishwasher and running it under freezing water."

Gabe remembered the terrible crack, and Viker's ecstatic expression as the purple light struck his face.

With certainty he said, "He did it on purpose. To make himself stronger. He must've *known* it would do that!"

My father said he had a plan. A terrible plan. All these years, I thought Viker wanted the ghostlight only so *we* couldn't use it against him. But I was mistaken.

Gabe slumped. They had failed, magnificently. They'd gone to destroy Viker, to free Rebecca's father and his own, and all they'd done was make Viker more dangerous than ever.

"That was quick thinking, killing the power to the lamp," Callie said to Yuri. "At least he can't get any stronger."

"Until he finds another light source," Yuri answered.

"We need to get it away from him," Gabe said, "even if it's useless to us now."

"You mean going back to the lighthouse?" Yuri said.

He is surely strong enough to move it elsewhere now. I fear he has other plans for it.

20

Over the harbour floated a lantern. With its wick trimmed low, it glowed a sickly purple. No one saw it when it reached the city's shore and glided up Spadina Avenue. Five feet off the ground, it swung slightly to and fro. If anyone at all noticed it, and believed their eyes, they might have imagined it was held aloft by an invisible hand.

"Hold it higher," Viker told Tommy Flynn. "It needs to be seen."

"I am holding it as high as I can, sir," Flynn replied, "considering that I am so very much smaller now."

In disgust Viker glanced down at him. Being blasted by the ghostlight had melted Flynn to a mere candle stub. He had only one frail arm with two fingers and a thumb, scarcely enough to grip the lantern. He barely had a face, which was no great loss.

"Don't sulk, Flynn."

"You might have warned me, sir. It was a nasty shock, getting snatched up and used as a shield. I feared that awful light would end me altogether."

"But it didn't. I saved you. You were nothing more than a waxy little puddle until I bathed you in this new light."

Viker gazed at the purple lens, marvelling not just at its power, but at the simple fact that he finally had it. For decades he had searched for a ghostlight that he could transform. Nearly a century ago, he had been told by another ghost that such a thing was possible. Grip the light long enough and you would crack it. Not only would it cease harming you, but it would spread a new light that would make you stronger than ever before.

"You see how it made you whole again, Flynn."

"I am ever so grateful to you, sir. I hope to have proper arms and legs again soon."

"You understand now what a powerful thing this light is."

"Yes. Thank you for letting me hold the lantern, sir."

Viker wanted the lens back in the Gibraltar lamp, but Rebecca Strand and her accomplices had damaged it somehow. In vain Viker had tried to reignite it, but he did not understand these new sources of power. He'd lived in the age of whale oil and coal and gunpowder. He would need to find a ghost who knew how to repair the lamp.

For now he had a hurricane lantern, stolen from an island marina. He'd placed the ghostlight inside, near the flame. Its purple glow gave Flynn just enough strength to carry the lantern. That was how Viker wanted Flynn. Just strong *enough*.

"They are starting to notice us now," Viker said, as ghosts peeped out from alleyways and walls and storm drains.

"Shall we speak to them?" Flynn asked.

"Keep walking. They will follow."

And they did, trailing after the pair with their hollow eyes locked thirstily on the purple lantern.

Viker strode on, past gleaming towers of steel and glass where, long ago, there had been campsites and warehouses and factories. Hunters and farmers and workers had once toiled and died here. It was never hard to find places where people had perished.

With each crooked step he took, Viker saw more of the dead following in his wake. Some were young, and some were old, and some were very ancient indeed. They came from every era and continent. What they all had in common now was death - and the fact that they still walked the Earth.

While most other ghosts had already moved on.

At this thought, Viker shuddered. He knew that most of the dead went elsewhere. And this *elsewhere* was a place that he meant to avoid eternally. It was here on this Earth where he would remain, in power and glory. Not many things frightened him. But *elsewhere* did.

Here in Toronto, on this night, the dead stumbled after him and his purple light like people who had been deprived of the sun for a thousand years.

As he approached the corner of King and John Streets he saw such a throng of the dead as he'd not seen since the battlefields. But these were not the newly and confused dead. Their clothes dated them from the same era as him. A terrible anger gouged their faces.

"They don't seem terribly pleased to see us," Flynn remarked nervously.

"They will be. Give me the lamp now."

He snatched it from Flynn's feeble grasp and held it higher. All the ghosts lifted their gazes, as if admiring a beautiful star.

Nicholas Viker raised his voice: "My friends, what happened in this fateful place, to bind you here in such numbers?"

From the crowd, a single ghost came forward. She was a wasted thing, her cheeks so sunken they might have met inside her mouth. Every rib could be counted.

These ghosts, Viker thought with disdain, had clearly not learned the trick of *feeding*.

"We perished in the fever sheds," the woman said, waving a skeletal arm to the northwest corner of the intersection. "We came over from Ireland, and before we reached harbour, there was typhus spreading aboard ship, like flame in dry moss. The fever sheds here were already overflowing with our countryfolk, those who'd arrived on earlier ships."

Pushing through the crowd came another whippet-thin ghost, his head crawling with spectral lice. "We crossed the ocean for a new life! What we got was the inside of a stinking shed. We never set foot outside again."

"And so here you died," Viker said, "lesser than the rats that scuttled beneath the floorboards."

"Eight hundred sixty-three of us!" the woman ghost cried, as a rumble of shared outrage moved through the crowd.

"And here you stay!" Viker said. "Prisoners forever! Unable even to stray from these evil sheds!"

The rumble grew to a roar. Viker felt himself swell like a flame fed with pure oxygen.

"You are powerless!" He turned to the ghosts who had been trailing after him through the streets. "And you as well! What dreadful fate befell *you,* that you wander unseen, unheard, uncared for?"

"Murdered!" some of them cried. "Worked to the bone!"

"Our hunting and fishing grounds fouled!"

"Our lands taken from us!" cried yet others.

"Yes," said Viker. "All of you, maltreated—"

Another roar.

"Abused and utterly forgotten!"

The roar intensified to a thunderclap.

"But *I* see you!" Viker shouted from his great height. "I hear you! I will care for you, and never forget you! You are weak but I will make you strong! You are cold and I will warm you! You are starving and I will feed you!"

"How?" they wailed. "How?"

"With *this*!" He trimmed the lantern's wick higher, and the purple light intensified.

The crowd's thunderous noise died abruptly and there was silence until someone cried out:

"What is that light?"

"Oh, bring it closer!"

"I can feel its heat!"

"Bring it closer!"

"It is so beautiful!"

"Bring it closer!"

Turning slowly in a circle, Viker smiled down at them all.

"Join me," he said, "and you will bathe forever in its glow!"

Warily, the gaunt Irish ghost asked, "What do you want of us?"

"The question is what do *you* want?" Viker replied.

Their united answer burst forth like a geyser of lava.

"LIFE!"

"No!" Viker said severely. "You will not regain your old lives. That cannot be. But I can promise you a *new* life. A *better* life."

"Tell us!"

"All of you have been wronged by the living. Yet all around you they go heedlessly about their business. Smug and ungrateful and *alive*. But they needn't be. With a quick, unsuspecting twist of the neck, a pinch of an artery, they, too, might die. Imagine if you had the strength to make it so? To once more make things *move*. To push, to batter, to *feed*!"

"Is such a thing possible?" the lice-ridden ghosts demanded.

"Oh, it is possible, my friends. Behold me. Behold my strength!"

He towered higher still, branching like some monstrous lightning-scarred tree. His limbs lashed out and smashed one window after another. On all sides of the intersection, glass rained down to the sidewalks.

"Give me your rage!" Viker shouted. "And from its furnace we will forge an army so great that we will take the life from all the living. And it will be *you* who rule over *them*. You who will reign over them, from sea to sea, our new, glorious dominion of the dead!"

"Yes!" they cried. "Oh, yes!"

"A glorious thing!"

"A *just* thing!"

"Do you want such a world?" Viker asked them.

"Yes!"

"Will you help me achieve it?"

"For more of that light, I would do anything!"

"Anything!"

"Anything!"

Viker nodded with satisfaction. "Once I ignite a more powerful lamp, I will summon all of you, to be transformed into glorious soldiers. Until then, come a little closer, all of you, and take just a little of its light. Feel its heat. Feel it strengthening you. And then, go forth into the city, among the living, and make mischief upon this dying world!"

21

Gabe woke on the cement floor of the maintenance shed. Wincing, he unfolded his bruised limbs and pushed himself into a sitting position. Yuri was already up, looking through his toolbox, murmuring to himself. Curled in the armchair, Callie skimmed her tablet.

"You guys should've woken me," Gabe said.

Callie looked at him kindly. "You were totally out. You needed it."

It was true; after the battle in the lighthouse he'd never felt so exhausted; his body had been drained by two ghosts: one friendly, one extremely *un*friendly. He looked out the grimy window at the pale morning sky.

"It's just past seven," Callie told him. "The city was a mess last night. Four fires and a big pileup on the Gardiner. Tons of smashed windows at King and John, not just at street level but really high up, which is pretty weird. And," she added more quietly, "hospitals reported a big spike in deaths."

Gabe met her gaze silently. "You think—"

"It seems like too big a coincidence."

"Yeah," Gabe and Yuri said together. Even if he couldn't prove it, even if it wasn't logical, in his gut Gabe suspected Viker was responsible for all these terrible things. "Rebecca, you here?"

His phone buzzed and he dragged it out.

I am here.

"Thanks for standing guard last night."

You're very welcome.

She'd urged them to get some sleep, and promised to stand guard, in case Viker came near. Though why would he now that he had the ghostlight? Still, Gabe was grateful, and touched by the idea of Rebecca watching over them in their sleep.

"Shouldn't we go back to the lighthouse," Callie said, "just in case the ghostlight's still there?"

It's gone. I made a quick trip just before dawn. He's taken it somewhere else.

Gabe realized he was holding his breath, and exhaled. "If Viker can make himself stronger with that light, how about other ghosts?"

"Why would he make them stronger?" asked Callie. "He just wants to eat them! And look what he did to Tommy Flynn!"

"OK, I am going to ask a question that might be unpopular," said Yuri. "But let me ask it, please. Are we sure we want to go on with this?"

"You want to quit?" said Callie.

"*Quit?*" Yuri spluttered. "Callie, this is not *swim team*. This is very dangerous stuff. Viker might be strong enough to kill us."

"And Rebecca, too," Gabe added. He felt weird addressing her like she wasn't here. "I don't know how we can keep you safe any more, Rebecca." He missed her touch, but he was starting to fear how much it tired him. She must have known, too, because she was only texting now.

I can keep myself safe. And I am not giving up. I will not let my father rot inside that fiend.

"I want my father out too," Gabe said, "but—"

"Maybe there is another way," said Yuri. "One that involves adults, I know, I know, I've said this before. . ."

Callie groaned. "It would take so long! They'd want proof and we don't even have a ghostlight anymore."

"We have a *ghost* who can clasp with them!"

"They'd probably still not believe it! Even if they did, they'd want to run tests, and there'd be so many experts and interviews, and probably the police would get involved. And they'd be way more upset that we stole the ghostlight from Gillian Shaw. And broke into a lighthouse. We might end up with criminal charges. And after all that, even if the *grown-ups* did agree to do something, think how strong Viker would be by then!"

No one said anything for a moment. Yuri had a good rummage in his hair. Gabe didn't think he'd ever seen it spikier. After the rummage, his friend loudly drummed his fingers on the workbench, then said:

"That was quite a convincing scenario, Callie."

"Just trying to think ahead."

"So we go it alone?" Gabe said.

"We go it alone," Yuri agreed.

Gabe took a drink from his water bottle and his stomach gave a hungry gulp.

"You guys want some breakfast? The Island Cafe'll be open by now."

Yuri shook his head in fond amazement. "Always your stomach."

"You're not hungry?"

"What I need is coffee."

"The café does a great cappuccino."

Callie said, "Let's have breakfast and talk about what we need to do next."

"Which is?" asked Yuri.

"Getting ourselves another ghostlight."

They washed up in the public bathrooms and biked over to Ward's Island. The café opened early, mostly for locals waiting to catch the ferry to work, but there were a few other early risers relaxing with a newspaper over their big breakfasts and coffees.

Gabe picked a table on the edge of the patio. Across the harbour, he saw smudgy trails of smoke rising from different parts of the city. He imagined Viker's crooked body, cutting an icy path of terror through Toronto. Gabe turned his face gratefully to the sun, wanting it to burn away the deep chill lingering inside him.

When he opened his eyes, Cassie was looking up from her tablet, saying:

"The Burlington Canal Light. It's just an hour from here on the GO bus. After the Gibraltar Point Lighthouse, it's the oldest one on Lake Ontario. Eighteen thirty-three. Really, we should have checked this one out earlier."

"It doesn't sound very important," said Yuri. "It lit a *canal*. It didn't protect a major port or a big city. Why would it have a ghostlight?"

"Did it?" Gabe asked Rebecca.

In the middle of the table, his phone lit up:

I think it unlikely, but I am willing to go and look.

"Worth a try," Callie said.

"And if we find nothing there, then what?" demanded Yuri. "Shall we check every single lighthouse in Canada? Oh, and why not try Amazon, too, they have next-day delivery!"

"So what's your great idea?" Callie asked testily.

"No more chasing after ghostlights. We had our chance at the Gibraltar Point Lighthouse, and we failed. The lamp was too limited. Viker's hand was in the *same room as us,* and we couldn't touch it! There were too many blind spots."

The ghostlight is still essential—

"I disagree, Rebecca," Yuri interrupted. "What we need is more power and more manouverability. And we can have *both* with a light launcher."

Worried their bickering might go off the rails, Gabe said, "OK, guys, we're all a little cranky, and I think we just need some food."

Yuri and Callie both glared at him – and he sensed that Rebecca did too. Fortunately Nate the waiter was coming over.

"This is early for you," he said to Gabe.

"Getting a jump on the day."

Nate started pouring water into their glasses. "You hear about the lighthouse?"

Gabe arranged his face into what he hoped was a normal expression of interest. "No. What happened?"

"Middle of the night, some people saw lights flashing, so a cop came over to check it out."

"And?" Callie asked from inside her water glass.

"All the lights were off by the time he got there. The door was unlocked . . ."

Gabe suppressed a groan. In his panic, he'd forgotten to lock it behind them.

". . . and there were food wrappers and empty bottles. Some kids must've got in there and had their own light show."

"Crazy," said Yuri.

"Sounds like quite a party," Gabe said, remembering the iron filings scattered everywhere. What else might they have left behind?

The waiter asked, "So what can I get you guys?"

Gabe saw that his stunned friends weren't even looking at their menus, so he went into action.

"I think Yuri's going to have the breakfast special with scrambled eggs, hash browns, and can we swap that side of fruit salad for bacon? Sound OK, Yuri?"

Blinking, his friend said, "That is exactly what I want, thank you."

"And for Callie," Gabe went on, "I'm thinking the avocado toast, but easy on the hummus."

"How did you know I'd like that?" she asked in amazement.

"And I'm going for the pumpkin pancakes," Gabe finished. "Oh, and coffees for everyone, please."

"Good call," said Nate, walking off.

"We are going to jail," Yuri whispered.

"No one is going to jail," Gabe said. "You guys didn't leave anything personal behind, right? We all got our backpacks and stuff? Yuri, you got all your tools?"

"I left behind a slot screwdriver."

"OK, well, that's not a big—"

"And a fifteen-millimeter reverse-ratcheting wrench."

Gabe took a calming breath. "Did you leave your wallet and photo ID behind?"

"Of course not."

"Then you're fine. I'm the only one who might be in trouble. Not too many people have keys to that lighthouse. They'll think it was me. And I left the door unlocked."

"But that's good," Callie said. "Tell your boss you forgot to lock up – which is bad, but you'll be super apologetic – and they'll think it was someone else who got inside."

"Hope so."

"You're not the kind of guy who has a wild party in a lighthouse, Gabe," she assured him.

"I guess not," he said, and felt a little disappointed.

Their food arrived. For several minutes everyone was silent, eating eagerly, sipping coffee. His friends had contented looks on their faces; he'd chosen their meals well. His bones felt warmer. They had lost the ghostlight, and left Viker stronger than before, and there was a chance he might get fired, but somehow, thanks to good food, the day seemed a tiny bit more hopeful.

When his phone lit up, Rebecca's message took him by surprise. **Yuri is right.**

"Thank you, Rebecca, I am glad we agree."

We no longer have time to search for another ghostlight. We must strike now, and strike with such a blow that it will destroy Viker. Can your light launcher do that, Yuri?

Yuri dipped his head humbly. "I think so, yes. I will make it as powerful as possible."

"How long will that take?" Callie said cautiously. "You haven't even built another one."

Yuri chimed his fork playfully on his water glass. "Maybe I have been working away in secret these past days."

"You've already got a new one?" Gabe asked excitedly.

"No. But I am close. I still need parts. And they are expensive."

Callie placed her emergency credit card on the table. "Whatever it takes, we can get you."

"Thank you, Callie."

"As long as you make a light launcher for each of us," she added.

"I enjoy the way you think," he said.

"Me too!" added Gabe. The idea of having a light launcher of his own lifted his mood even more. "Tell us how we can help."

As they made plans, Gabe noticed the archaeologist from the

shipwreck dig taking a nearby table. She was with a man who must have been a reporter, because he slid his phone across the table toward her and asked if she minded being recorded.

"So you found out what ship it was?" the reporter asked.

Gabe quietly held up his hand to shush his friends.

"We just uncovered the part of the hull where the name's painted," the archaeologist said excitedly. "It's the *Kingston*."

"And? Was that a special ship?"

"It was a merchant clipper. Three masts. It would've been a common sight in the harbour. It sailed regularly between Montreal and Toronto, sometimes Rochester."

"How'd it sink?"

"We found the shipping records yesterday. It was in harbour, waiting out a storm before setting sail for Montreal. The storm got worse, and the ship slipped its anchor and was capsized near the island. It went down with all hands."

"And what year was that?"

"August 1839," whispered Callie at the same moment the archaeologist did, and Gabe looked back at her in surprise. She was staring at her tablet, her finger skating across its surface.

Yuri caught Gabe's eye and said admiringly, "She really knows how to use her machines."

"Guys," Callie whispered, then choked a little and had to take a sip of water. "The *Kingston* was the ship Serge Delacroix left on! Remember?"

Gabe nodded. "Right after he tried to give the new keeper a ghostlight."

"Are you pulling my leg?" Yuri asked.

"Delacroix went down with the ship," Callie said. "Right here in the harbour. With his ghostlight!"

Gabe shook his head in amazement. "There's been one here this whole freaking time!"

Yuri sat back in his chair with a sigh. "It seems to me," he said, "that we will soon be exploring a shipwreck teeming with ghosts."

22

To Gabe's huge relief, he did not get fired.

When he checked in for work, his manager, Karl, had already spoken with the police and told them there was no way on earth Gabe Vasilakis was responsible for what had happened in the lighthouse. Even when Gabe confessed he'd forgotten to lock the door, Karl just patted him on the shoulder and said, "Well, that explains how they got in. Don't sweat it. You're doing a great job."

But Karl did ask Gabe for the key back, because the parks people needed to clean up the mess inside, and besides, they'd been thinking about updating the lock anyway. For now, the door would be secured with a chain.

So Gabe went off to work, wondering if Karl might think he was a suspect after all.

His phone buzzed in his pocket.

We've lost access to the Gibraltar Point Light.

"It doesn't matter, now that Yuri's making us all light launchers." After breakfast, Callie and Yuri had headed off into the city with a big shopping list and Callie's credit card. They'd agreed to meet back on the island at six o'clock, to figure out how to get inside the shipwreck site.

During Gabe's first tour of the day, the people were pretty

disappointed they couldn't go inside the lighthouse. One little kid actually started crying, so Gabe quickly made up a story about how the front step of the lighthouse was haunted. And if you put something light on it, like a leaf, it would actually move. When the kid tried, Rebecca happily obliged and shifted the leaf. Then everyone wanted to try, and for the rest of the tour, the grown-ups were explaining it to each other: draft from under the door; a light breeze; thermal currents from the hot stone.

Midmorning between tours, Rebecca messaged him:

Let me go to the shipwreck and explore.

Gabe looked around nervously, worried about Viker and Tommy Flynn. He and his friends had agreed not to talk aloud about Serge Delacroix and the shipwreck, in case they were being invisibly spied upon.

"Are you sure we're alone?" he whispered to Rebecca.

Quite sure.

Which meant very sure, but not absolutely sure. Viker had proven himself good at surprises.

"It's risky," Gabe said. "What if you're followed?"

I will be careful.

"You don't want to lead him right to it." Just like he'd led Viker straight to his own father.

It makes sense for me to go on ahead. I can move faster than you. I can pass through barriers. I might not be strong enough to move the ghostlight though dirt or stone, but if I find it, I can lead you right to it tonight.

He couldn't argue with her logic. "It might be dangerous, though, Rebecca. And I won't be there to clasp with you. Isn't it better if we wait and all go—"

I can't wait.

He sensed her mind was already made up. Day by day her impatience and anxiety had compounded, and he knew it was pointless to tell her not to go.

"OK. Please be careful."

She clasped his hand quickly to smile and say goodbye, and then she was off. For the rest of the morning he worried. While his mouth recited the tour script, his brain zigzagged through a series of terrible "what if" scenarios. What if Viker was following her? What if she encountered other ghosts in the wreck who wished her harm?

By lunch she still wasn't back, and he couldn't eat – which basically never happened. Overhead in the trees, cicadas buzzed. A fresh breeze blew off the lake. At a nearby picnic table, a mother used her umbrella as a sun shield, and her little girl solemnly ate a peeled banana.

When Gabe's phone lit up, he made a grab for it and nearly fell off the bench.

I've returned!

"I was getting worried!" He wanted to know everything instantly, but caution held him back. "We're alone, right?"

Yes.

Maybe it was because he'd spent the last couple of hours

imagining the worst, but he asked, "Could you clasp with me for a second? Just so I know it's actually you?"

He held out his hand and felt the hairs on his forearm lift. Something inside him tensed. But when a cool hand enfolded his, it was Rebecca beside him on the bench, looking at him with her green-grey eyes.

"You were worried it might be someone else?"

"I'm just getting a bit paranoid. Tell me everything, but over the phone."

I think I found it!

He struggled to keep his voice soft. "You saw it?"

No. But I overheard two ghosts talking. They were speaking of another ghost who has a small box chained to him. They want the box, but can't touch it because it's made of iron. They're convinced there's treasure inside and they're arguing about the best way to get it.

Gabe felt a bit sad to think they'd probably been having the same argument for over a hundred years.

I tried to get closer, but the ghosts wouldn't move on, and I had the sense that they were wicked. And strong.

"I'm glad you didn't risk it."

Surely that other ghost must be Serge Delacroix. And within the box, the ghostlight.

"I sure hope so. Are they in a place we can reach?"

The workers have not discovered that room yet, and there is still a great deal of dirt, but I think I can guide you down.

"OK, good." He didn't like the idea of crawling down into dirt; and he certainly didn't like the sound of those two other ghosts.

Oh! And one other thing that will be helpful. The entrance gate is secured with a lock and chain, but nearby is a box that contains the key. I watched someone open it by pushing numbered buttons, and memorized the code.

"You're the most useful ghost I know," he said with a smile. "And the bravest."

The shipwreck site was off a quiet stretch of road, halfway between the lighthouse and Hanlan's Point. In the shallows of Blockhouse Bay, the archaeologists had built a circular dam and pumped out all the water so they could do their work on dry ground, digging down into the shipwreck. The walls of the dam were ten feet high, so you couldn't see inside. The only entrance was on the shore, where a caged metal staircase led to the top of the dam.

Gabe and the others waited at a safe distance, while Rebecca took a good look around the site to make sure all the workers had left for the day.

"So you got everything you needed?" Gabe asked Yuri and Callie.

Yuri nodded happily. "We stored all the parts in my work locker before meeting you. But I thought you might like it if I brought this."

He unzipped his bulging backpack and extracted a light launcher. It looked like a bulky flashlight and seemed to be held together with duct tape.

"This is just something I threw together," Yuri explained sheepishly. "It is not finished. Stop looking at it. But I thought, maybe better than nothing? Considering our evening activities."

"Good idea," Gabe said.

"He works so quickly," Callie said. "His fingers are magic."

Embarrassed by the praise, Yuri mumbled, "Let's see if it even works. And here, I brought a few other things that might be useful."

He parted the sides of his backpack to show Gabe more gear than Indiana Jones could ever use. Nylon rope, tools, compact shovels, and other stuff he didn't know the names of but was glad to see. They were *equipped*.

His phone buzzed.

Everyone is gone.

"No security guard?"

No one.

"You guys ready?" he asked his living friends.

Checking the deserted road, they hurried to the entrance. At the lockbox, Rebecca clasped with him and recited the numbers as he punched in the code. With the key in hand, he unlocked the gate quietly.

They hurried up the stairs. At the top of the dam wall was a platform with a second set of steps leading down into the excavation. Gabe felt uneasy being up so high. If anyone was going to spot them, it would be right now.

"Let's be quick," he said, leading them down, where the high walls soon hid them from outside view.

Gabe had hoped to find a three-masted ship, maybe a little rotted and bashed up, but basically *the ship*, resting in the sand, ready to set sail.

What he saw instead was exposed wooden beams that marked the outline of a ship lying on its side. Raised metal walkways formed a grid over the site. Gabe spotted the jagged stump of a mast, some old barrels with rusted hoops, and various crates filled with china shards.

Near the middle of the ship, a metal ladder angled down through an opening in its hull.

"Well, I guess that's our way in."

They made their way out along the walkways toward the ladder.

"There wouldn't be much left of Delacroix by now, would there?" Gabe whispered hopefully. "After a hundred-plus years, under-water, would there even be bones?"

There are bones.

They reached the hole and looked down. There was still some light in the sky, so the hole was by no means completely dark. Still, it made Gabe feel clammy.

He grabbed the rungs. "Light my way?" he asked Yuri.

His friend pulled out his light launcher and sent a bright beam into the ship's guts. Gabe started down. It wasn't too deep. He stepped off onto a dirt-covered floor that wasn't a floor at all, but a wall. The entire ship was on its side. It was very disorienting. To his left and right were doorways (on their sides); and there was a third doorway in the middle of the "floor" shaped like an open grave, with another ladder leading down into it.

"Down?" he asked Rebecca.

Down.

Gabe gulped in some air and went first. Yuri, then Callie, climbed down after him. Little marker flags had been placed around the room, marking rusted remnants of a sink, some cookware, a carving knife.

"This must've been the galley," Gabe said.

"That's a ship's kitchen, right?" asked Callie, who was using her phone as a flashlight.

"Yep. Any mean ghosts hanging around, Rebecca?"

None yet.

"Which way now?"

He was hoping it would be one of the doorways on the left or right, but she said:

Down again.

"Which means we're actually moving sideways across the ship," Yuri pointed out helpfully, "rather than truly going down another level."

"Looks like down to me," said Gabe, grabbing hold of the ladder.

This hole was much darker than the last. As he descended, the air grew clammier. The stink of rotting lake weed rose to meet him. His feet touched down in mud. This room had only been partially cleared. One side was still piled high with dirt. Four metal braces had been set up to prevent the "ceiling" from collapsing. As

Yuri and Callie came down the ladder, an ominous creak eased its way through the ship's ruined ribs.

"I do not like the sound of that," Yuri commented, probing the corners of the room with his light launcher.

Scattered about were a pair of waterlogged boots, a blanket, a broken wooden chest and the remnants of what might have been bunk beds. There were no doorways to be seen.

Callie said, "Rebecca, this room's a dead end."

Gabe's vision frosted as she took his hand.

"Shift that bunk," she said, pointing at some mangled planks half buried in the wall of dirt. "There's a doorway behind there, and I think we will find Serge Delacroix in the next room."

"And those other two ghosts?" Gabe asked.

"Let's hope not. I haven't heard them yet."

"Just wait for us, OK? We go in together."

Gabe broke his clasp with her, because he needed both hands now. With Yuri and Callie, he took turns with the portable shovels, digging out the rotting bunks.

"The archaeologists are going to know someone was down here," Gabe said worriedly.

"It's the only way to get into that room," Callie said.

"We can try to move everything back," Yuri suggested.

"Our footprints are everywhere," said Gabe.

I can smooth them away afterward.

When Gabe had first met her, she was strong enough only to shift dust; now she could lift a tumbler, hold the ghostlight and whisk away footprints in sand. The ship creaked again, and Gabe looked worriedly at the metal braces.

"Come on, let's pull," Callie said, and together they grabbed hold of the bunk and dragged it away from the wall of the dirt.

"Rebecca said the doorway was here." Gabe grabbed a shovel and plunged it into the wall. After a couple of thrusts, the blade punched through into empty space. Callie got in there with her shovel, and Yuri with his bare hands, and they made a hole big enough for them to pass through.

"Rebecca, what's in there?" Gabe asked. "Rebecca?"

No clasp of her hand, no buzz from his phone. Had she impatiently gone on ahead?

Anxiously he looked at Yuri. "Shine a light in there!"

Yuri aimed his light launcher through the ragged hole. His skittering beam revealed a chamber so mounded with dirt it resembled a cave.

Caught suddenly in the light was a whiskered face that was more crayfish than human. Its eyes contracted to pinpricks and it made a terrible rattling sound. At the fringes of the beam, Gabe caught something that made his heart jump.

A familiar woollen shawl.

"Yuri, to the right!" The beam slid over to reveal Rebecca, gripped by the whiskered ghost – and a second ghost, whose limbs were spiky as a sea urchin's.

"Gabe!" she cried, wincing in the light.

"Blast them!" he yelled at Yuri. "Don't hurt Rebecca!"

His friend dialled up the power and struck the ghost with the whiskered head. It gulped as if struggling for air, then flopped around like a landed fish. As it tried to burrow into the dirt, Yuri melted it altogether.

"The other one!" Gabe shouted.

The beam from the light launcher flickered, then died, plunging them into total darkness. Callie switched on her phone flashlight.

"What happened?" she asked, lighting Yuri up so he looked like a ghost himself.

Frantically he examined the light launcher. "It's shorted out!"

Which left Rebecca, alone with that ghost, in the other room.

"I'm going in there," Gabe said, clawing his way through the hole.

He was in total darkness until he scrambled out the other side and wasn't blocking Callie's light. It wasn't enough for him to see Rebecca and the other ghost, but he knew roughly where they were—or had been.

"Rebecca! Clasp with me!" Blindly he thrust out his hand. Finally her cold fingers latched around his, and he saw her, still in the clutches of the spiky ghost, whose spinelike limbs had impaled her in place. Its mouth was now trying to engulf Rebecca's head.

Gabe felt heat and energy pour from his body into Rebecca's. She pulled back her legs and kicked the spiky ghost across the chamber. Its limbs broken, it disappeared through the dirt wall.

"You guys OK?" Callie called worriedly through the hole.

Gabe waited a second to see if the ghost was coming back. "Think so."

"Thank you," Rebecca said, still shaken. "The two of them overpowered me."

"You were supposed to wait for us! Are you OK?" He looked at the places where the spines had pierced her. Maybe it was because of their clasp, but they already seemed healed over. If there had even been wounds in the first place.

The ship's rotted timbers released a long groan. Bits of ceiling pattered down around them.

"They haven't braced that room yet," Yuri told them.

"Where's Serge Delacroix?" Gabe asked Rebecca. "Did you find him?"

"This way!" she commanded.

The tug of her hand was faint but persistent.

"Where are you going?" he heard Yuri call after him. "It could collapse, Gabe!"

"She's found Delacroix!" he called out as Rebecca led him into a webwork of splintered beams and busted crates and soggy bundles. He felt breathless, thinking of all the weight overhead. The ship creaked and grumbled.

Before him was a ghost, twisted into an unusual shape amongst his own skeletal remains. When it looked up, its eyes blazed with fury. "I warned you!" the ghost shouted. "Stay away!"

"That's him?" Gabe whispered to Rebecca.

She gave a nod. "I think he is confused."

The ghost swelled himself up like a puffer fish, his red jacket flashing dangerously. "Do not come any closer!"

Rebecca whispered to Gabe. "Say his name."

"Sir, are you Serge Delacroix?"

The ghost deflated a little. The question seemed to trigger his memory. More forcefully Gabe said, "Your name is Serge Delacroix! Lighthouse Keeper and member of the Order!"

The ghost deflated to his normal size. "Who are you?"

"My name is Gabriel Vasilakis."

"And I am Rebecca Strand. My father was William Strand, Keeper of the Gibraltar Point Light."

"A fine man!" said the ghost.

"You knew him?"

"Of course. We were both members of the Order. A very fine man indeed."

Sheer joy brightened Rebecca's face. She clasped Delacroix's hand gratefully. "Thank you. It is such a comfort, to meet someone who knew him. Even just to hear his name mentioned."

"When I heard of his death," said Delacroix, "I feared something terrible had happened to him."

"He was murdered by a ghost called Nicholas Viker. We both were."

Delacroix's brow furrowed. "Of all the names a Keeper might hear, Viker's was the most feared."

"You knew about him?" Gabe asked.

"Oh, yes. He had been plaguing our cities and ports for many years. And growing stronger. When he started to attack lighthouses, I feared he wanted a ghostlight. So he could create a *ghast*light."

"Ghastlight?" Gabe asked, though, instinctively, he knew what it was.

"You've seen such a thing?" Rebecca asked.

"Mercifully only once. I was an apprentice Keeper at the ancient Cordouan Lighthouse in France. During a fearsome battle, a ghoul breached our lamp room and hurled itself upon our ghostlight. Though the ghoul was instantly destroyed, the ghostlight, too, suffered a fatal blow. A crack opened within it. And somehow that crack changed the nature of the lens. The light that blazed from it no longer destroyed ghosts, but strengthened them."

"Was the light purple?" Gabe asked.

"Indeed it was, a most lurid hue. When it struck the dead, they swelled like corpses left too long on the field of war. Bloated, they became more horrible, and more powerful."

"Viker has made himself a ghastlight," Rebecca told him.

The old ghost looked graver still. "Then you have much to fear. He was a ferocious soldier in his life. We always feared that, with a ghastlight, he might create an army of the dead."

"Sir, do you have a ghostlight?" Gabe asked. "The one that you offered to Keeper Debenham long ago?"

For the first time Gabe noticed the small metal box that Delacroix clutched. He had protected it for so many years, it seemed almost welded to his rib cage.

Rebecca said, "Sir, we need it to fight Viker."

"Yes, yes, of course," Delacroix said. "It is the only thing that can destroy a fiend of his power. You must take it from me."

When Gabe reached for it, he realized with a shock that Delacroix's skeletal hands still clutched the box in a tight death grip. Reluctantly, Gabe pried away the finger bones, one by one.

"Sorry," Gabe said.

Pulling the box free, he noticed it was chained to a metal band around Serge Delacroix's wrist. Truly, the Keeper had taken every precaution to make sure he would never be parted from the ghostlight, in life or death.

"Break my wrist to remove the band," Delacroix told him calmly.

Wincing, and muttering over and over that he was sorry, Gabe did so.

The ghost smiled approvingly. "Your father would be proud of you, Miss Strand. Battling the wakeful and wicked dead."

Rebecca dipped her head. "It was always my most ardent hope to be a Keeper. I will not let death stop me. I will end Viker, and am lucky to have the help of Gabriel and his living friends."

"Will you fight with us?" Gabe asked Delacroix.

"I would, but I feel myself drawn elsewhere."

His gaze drifted, as though to a light only he could see.

"No, please," said Gabe, "don't go yet! We could really use your help!"

"I am sorry. The battle is yours now."

Delacroix's spectral body relaxed as if making a huge exhalation. At the end of this breath, he came apart in a glorious spray of prismatic light.

"Oh, man," said Gabe, dejected. "I was hoping for another ghost ally."

"Guys!" came Yuri's voice behind him, and he turned to see that his two living friends had come after him. "We should get out of here!"

Callie suppressed a yelp as her flashlight illuminated the broken skeleton of Serge Delacroix.

"Is it in there?" she asked, turning her beam on the metal box.

Gabe prized open the lid. Inside, nested in wood shavings, glinted an amber lens. Rebecca ran her fingers over the surface and looked up at him hopefully. Gabe returned her smile.

"Back in business," he said. "Ghostlight versus ghastlight."

23

To find a ghost who was also an electrician should not have been so difficult, but it had taken Nicholas Viker two nights.

As the electrician worked, Viker stood on the catwalk of the Gibraltar Point Lighthouse, gazing hungrily at the twilight city. Its lights were igniting now, creating a constellation more dazzling than the clearest night sky. What a thing, this city! How many souls lived along its wide streets and inside its high towers? Millions. And how many of the *dead* existed invisibly in the same spaces, some slumbering, some wide-awake—and waiting to be summoned?

The past two nights had been most pleasing to Viker. He had roved the rain-spattered streets with his ghastlight lantern, recruiting more followers and urging them to go forth and do terrible things. Two beautiful nights of fires and power failures and streetcar breakdowns and accidents and, oh, yes, deaths.

But all of this was a mere shadow of the great darkness that would engulf the city once his ghastlight blazed from the Gibraltar Point Lighthouse.

He turned and stepped through the window into the lamp room.

"Are the repairs complete, Ms. Kovacic?" he asked the electrician.

"Very nearly," she replied, making the last few turns with her screwdriver.

Viker had noticed that she avoided looking at him; perhaps she found his body disturbing, now that his flesh roiled and bulged with the thrashing ghosts he'd feasted upon. Likely she was frightened of him. This did not displease him.

"It's been nice to use my hands again," she said. "Thank you."

Viker had used the ghastlight to make the electrician just strong enough to lift the small objects and tools necessary to do the work.

"I've replaced the breaker in the main panel downstairs," said Ms. Kovacic, "and reconnected the wiring to the motor and socket. The bulb's in place. All you need to do is flip this switch here to turn the beacon on."

Viker opened his large fist and revealed the ghastlight. Deftly he slipped it into the wire frame before the lamp.

Viker caught Ms. Kovacic licking her lips as she gazed at the lens.

"If you'd make me a bit stronger, I'd be even more useful to you," said the electrician. "I won't disappoint you."

"I know you won't, Ms. Kovacic. Thank you so much for your service." Viker stretched his jaws wide and swallowed the electrician headfirst. Ms. Kovacic's desperate kicks gave him the utmost pleasure and he belched with delight.

"Wasn't that a bit hasty, sir?" squeaked Tommy Flynn, who'd been watching from across the room. "You might've needed her help later."

"There are other electricians," said Viker.

"Took us quite a while to find her," Flynn muttered.

While the glow of the ghastlight provided Viker with all the strength he required, he had no intention of changing his diet. Most of the ghosts he summoned would become his soldiers, but some would become his food. He would have to be more discreet, however. He did not want to alarm his growing army of followers.

The lamp was ready, the ghastlight was in place. All he needed to do was ignite it, and the city of the dead would come to him.

"And when you want to engage the ghostlight," Yuri said, demonstrating to Gabe and Callie, "you just flip it down over the end of the barrel like so. You probably noticed I put a rubber rim around the lens?"

Gabe hadn't, but Callie said, "Because of the heat, right?"

"Precisely," said Yuri, pleased. "The ghostlight gets screaming hot, so if you need to shift it back and forth, you can touch it without getting scalded."

"Great idea," Gabe said.

"The new batteries are also a bit stronger and hold their charge longer. They're still somewhat heavy in my opinion, but what can we do? Overall, I am satisfied. We have more power, and we are completely mobile. All three of us."

Inside the maintenance shed, Gabe looked at the other two finished light launchers on the worktable. For the past couple of days, Yuri had been working around the clock to build them, sometimes with Callie's help when she had time off; sometimes with Gabe's—although Yuri usually only trusted him to pass him tools and get food. They'd worked every spare minute, wherever they could: the maintenance shed, Yuri's bedroom (tricky, since he shared it with Leo) and Gabe's place when his mom was on shift.

"Yuri, these look amazing," Gabe said.

Yuri took a breath, and his forehead creased. "I need to say something. I want to reassure you all—"

"Yuri, you don't need to—" Callie said.

"What happened that night in the shipwreck was unforgivable."

"It wasn't a big deal," said Gabe.

"A complete power failure is a big deal. I was sloppy with the wiring. I was rushing and distracted by everything going on at home . . ."

Yuri trailed off, looking bewildered and possibly on the verge of tears; Gabe was about to give him a hug, but Callie beat him to it.

"It's OK," Gabe told his friend. "I'm sorry this is all happening at once."

Yuri cleared his throat. "It could be worse. My father has not been eaten by a ghost, at least."

It was said seriously, but Gabe couldn't help laughing. "This is true."

"But we will free him!" Yuri said. "And your father too, Rebecca!"

I am sure of it,

she replied over Gabe's phone.

I am so impressed by your inventions.

"Yuri, you're a genius," Callie said.

"Well, not a genius," he said, blushing. "That is too much."

"Brilliant, then."

"OK, that I will accept."

Outside, wind rattled the window and some rain pattered against the glass. It was the second day in a row the amusement park had closed early because of the weather. They said it was Hurricane Jamal rolling up the Atlantic coast. On his way to the island this morning, Gabe had seen a news headline that said: WICKED STORM HEADED FOR TORONTO. The choice of adjective had stuck with him.

"OK, now I know what we are all thinking," Yuri said. "'Who gets to use the light launcher with the ghostlight attached?' Am I right?"

"Oh, yeah," said Gabe.

"Absolutely," Callie said.

"Exactly. So, we draw for it." Yuri turned away from them. With a magician's panache, he swirled back with three nails sticking up between the fingers of his clenched fist. "Longest nail wins."

Callie picked first, then Gabe. When they all revealed their nails, Gabe's was the longest.

"Look," he began, "if you don't think—"

Yuri clapped him on the shoulder. "You will be fine, my friend."

"You're sure?"

Yuri passed him the light launcher. "Just please do not break it."

Gabe flipped the ghostlight up away from the barrel, lifted the light launcher against his cheek and squeezed the trigger. A circle of pale light appeared on the wall.

"That's the lowest setting," Yuri said.

"Rebecca, is it safe for you?" Gabe asked. "I just want to make sure."

From the edge of the light, Rebecca stretched a hand, then an arm, and then stepped in all the way.

"It's cold," she said, "but it doesn't hurt."

"Do you feel weaker or anything?"

She shook her head. "In small doses, I think it's safe enough."

"Maybe just step into it when you need to talk to us."

Yuri said, "Rebecca, you should move back while he engages the ghostlight."

Gabe dialled the power up and, with one hand, flipped the amber lens down over the end of the light launcher.

Instantly it went dark.

"What'd I do?" he cried out in dismay.

"Keep squeezing the trigger," Yuri told him. "It takes a moment. Like water building behind a dam. Count to five."

"One . . . two . . ." Already Gabe felt an impatient vibration through his hands. Heat wafted against his face. Glancing nervously at Yuri, he said, "It feels like a *lot* of power building up in there!"

Amber light exploded from the barrel and branded a circle of light on the wall. It was too bright to look at directly.

"Whoa!"

He released the trigger and passed the light launcher to Callie. "You want to try?"

"Is this more candlepower than the bulb we had at the lighthouse?" she asked as she shouldered the light launcher.

"Much more," Yuri told her.

She released a blast of amber light at the wall, then carefully flipped the ghostlight up and dialled the power back down to its lowest setting, so Rebecca could join their conversation when she wanted.

"So we still need to hammer out a plan of attack," Gabe said.

"Which involves first finding Viker," Yuri pointed out.

From the edge of the light, Rebecca said, "He'll return to the Gibraltar Point Light."

"You sure?" Yuri asked. "There are other lamps he could use."

"This one will make sense to him. He's from another time. And he's lingered so long in this place, it has a pull on him."

"So we've got to surprise him," Gabe said. "Because he's more powerful than ever now."

He remembered how Viker had poured himself over the ghastlight, gorging on it. And who knew how many ghosts he'd consumed in the past two days?

"Look, we've got three light launchers now," Callie said confidently, "and one of them really packs a punch."

"We're also very agile," Yuri added. "We can go anywhere."

"And we'll be smarter this time," Gabe said. "We won't let him sneak up on us again. This time we'll do the sneaking up!"

"And we will have allies," said Rebecca.

"Allies? Really?" Callie asked.

"Last night I made a visit to George Brown," Rebecca told them.

The domed head of the ghostly journalist popped into the light. "Good evening, everyone!"

"Oh, hi!" Gabe said in surprise.

"Very pleased to see you all again. I just dropped by to see if I could be of assistance. What a splendid machine you've created! Miss Strand has apprised me of your current situation. I've brought Joseph Halfday with me—"

Joseph Halfday leaned into the light. "*Aanii.*"

Gabe and his friends returned his traditional greeting.

"Joseph and I have been following the situation in the city," Brown barrelled on, "and the news is not good. A few nights ago I came across Nicholas Viker giving quite an oration at the site of the old fever sheds."

"Fever sheds?" asked Yuri.

"It's where they put the sick during the typhus outbreak," Halfday explained, "in the nineteenth century. A lot of people died, and were angry."

"And Viker has made them angrier still," Brown interjected. "He has spread his gospel of violence far and wide across the city. Fires. Power outages. Subway trains trapped in tunnels. Flickering traffic lights causing crashes."

He rattled it off like the expert reporter he was. Most of it was not a surprise to Gabe; he'd seen it all over the news the past couple of days. His mother had been kept so busy at the hospital she was rarely home – which was just as well, since he'd been out so much at night.

"Now, to the matter at hand," Brown said. "Rebecca has told me what she knows about Nicholas Viker, and it's clear he needs to be stopped. If he comes back to the island, Joseph knows some excellent people here who might be willing to help us."

"I am not their chief," Joseph Halfday said, "but I will speak to them."

Callie said, "That would be great, thank you so much!"

"But we'd feel bad," Gabe said, "putting you and your friends in danger."

"What Viker is doing will only make him more dangerous to all of us," said Brown. "He's using the ghastlight to strengthen other ghosts and make an army that can kill the living. And many of those they kill may end up joining his ranks – as bewildering as that may seem. And so Viker's army will grow. Any ghost who refuses to join may well become food for Viker and his ilk. So you see, Viker is a threat to the living and the dead both."

"So let's see what can be done to strengthen our own ranks," Joseph Halfday said. "You'll hear more from us shortly."

And with that, Brown and Halfday departed.

"Ghost allies," said Yuri, smiling. "Things are looking even better now."

"Guys," Callie said, staring out the window. Gabe didn't see anything, but Callie was already running for the door.

He hurried after her. "What's wrong?"

Outside, he and Yuri followed her up a small hill that offered a view over the amusement park and the harbour. The trees rustled and swayed in the brisk wind. Bruised clouds sagged from the darkening sky. The surface of the harbour was pinched into little crests.

"There!" Callie said, pointing.

From the direction of the Gibraltar Point Lighthouse, a beam of purple light stabbed out over the harbour. "Oh, no," Gabe murmured.

"He's turned the lamp back on!" Yuri said.

The otherworldly light swept across the city. It glinted off the skyscrapers; it painted the old stone buildings a lurid purple. The beam revolved back toward the island. It grazed the Ferris wheel, the roller coaster and a stand of trees. With a dry crinkling sound the leaves turned yellow.

"Did it just kill those leaves?" Gabe asked Yuri in alarm.

Then the ghastlight beam passed right over them. Instantly Gabe broke out in gooseflesh. For a split second Rebecca was illuminated in the purple light, her eyes reflecting its sickly glow.

"It's cold!" said Yuri, rubbing his bare arms.

The beam swept on to the south, over Lake Ontario, and Gabe spotted a plane coming in to land at the Island Airport. Its wings rocked to and fro in the stiff wind. When the ghastlight beam crossed its path, the plane banked sharply and climbed.

"What happened?" Callie asked.

"Light probably blinded the pilot for a second," Yuri answered.

And now the ghastlight made another pass over harbour and city. A ferry was crossing to Ward's Island, and as the beam flashed over its upper deck, Gabe gave a cry. Pressed eagerly against the railings were hundreds of ghosts. And then they disappeared as the purple beam swept past—

And revealed, in the harbour itself, even more ghosts, churning the water with ghostly limbs. They were swimming toward the island, drawn like moths to the glow of the ghastlight.

"Viker's summoning them," Gabe said. "To form his army."

24

Back in the maintenance shed, Gabe's hands trembled as he slung the light launcher over his shoulder.

"I've got an extra battery for each of us," said Yuri, putting one in all of their backpacks. "Heavy to lug around, I know, but we'll be glad of them later."

"Thanks, Yuri," said Callie.

"You paid for them," Yuri reminded her. "The light launchers use a lot of power, so keep them on low until you get a target."

"And let's try not to blind each other," Callie added.

"We've got to watch out for Rebecca, too," Gabe said. "Rebecca, don't get caught in our high beams, OK?"

He stood looking at his friends. He hadn't expected this to happen so soon, and definitely not tonight.

"I don't feel ready for this," he said.

"Do any of us?" asked Yuri.

Callie pulled out her phone. "I have the feeling we're going to be out late. Like, all night. We'd better tell our parents something."

"My mom's doing an overnight at the hospital," Gabe said. "You guys can say you're staying over at my place."

"Works for me," said Yuri, texting.

"But not me," Callie said. She finished typing and sent her message. "There. Another imaginary sleepover with Jennifer."

"Let's go," Gabe said. "We need to shut the ghastlight down before it makes all those ghosts any stronger."

It was raining as they cycled down the deserted main street of the amusement park. A garbage can blew over, and its contents scuttled across the pavement. Crossing the big bridge, they passed only a few people, hurrying for the ferry docks. As soon as he could, Gabe cut onto the grass and angled for Lakeshore Avenue.

The ghastlight continued its dreadful sweeps. Gabe heard leaves curling and fluttering dead to the ground. Every time the beam passed over, it revealed Rebecca, running alongside him. In the purple light she looked anything but sickly. Her stride was strong. She seemed taller than he remembered. And her hands, her fine hands, seemed larger too. Was her jaw a little wider and her teeth somehow sharper? Maybe it was just the shadow chiselling them to points. With a sinking heart, he wondered what the ghastlight would do to her. Make her stronger, certainly – but in what way?

Near the hedge maze, Gabe's bike fishtailed, like someone had kicked his rear wheel. He toppled over onto the grass. As he untangled his legs, the ghastlight swept past and he saw the gleeful face of Malcolm Macbeth MacCready.

"The name's Malcolm Macbeth MacCready!" the ghost crowed.

"Oh, we've met!" said Gabe, unslinging his light launcher.

"Gabe?" Callie shouted, circling back with Yuri. "You OK?"

Though burly, the Scottish ghost was nimble as a leprechaun

and delivered a kick that landed Gabe on his backside. Obviously the ghastlight had already made him a lot stronger.

Gabe scrambled to his feet. Yuri had already jumped off his bike and turned his light launcher to low. His beam swished through the air and revealed the Scottish duellist.

"*This* guy again!" Yuri said. "Gabe, please, let me take him out."

"Oh, no, he's mine!" said Gabe, powering up his own light launcher.

"I'm glad ye've brought yer wee little pistol with ye!" cackled MacCready. "Are ye finally ready for a duel, ye little dandyprat?"

"Oh, I'm ready, ye vomitous bootlicker," said Gabe.

"Vomitous bootlicker?" Malcolm Macbeth MacCready blinked in surprise. "That's rather nice, laddie!" He lifted his pistol. Gabe squeezed the trigger and blasted a hole clean through the ghost's torso. In astonishment Malcolm Macbeth MacCready poked his hand through the hole.

"I'm fair puckled!" he cried, then howled with laughter. "Laddie, that's no regulation pistol ye got there! But look ye, I'm still standing and—" His gaze drifted across the field. "Well, well, what have we here?"

A sweep of the ghastlight revealed a troop of newly arrived ghosts, headed in the direction of the lighthouse. Some trudged, some dragged themselves on splintered wrists, others leapt with terrifying vigour.

"Guys!" Gabe said to his friends. "They've arrived!"

"Do ye think they've come for a duel?" MacCready asked ecstatically.

"Shh!" Gabe said, not wanting to attract their attention.

"Over here!" the Scottish duellist hollered. "I'll send every last one of ye to yer eternal reward!"

In the lurid glow of the ghastlight, Gabe saw the marching ghosts turn in their direction.

"You know what?" Gabe said encouragingly. "I think they'd love a duel with Malcolm Macbeth MacCready!"

"I'm only too happy to oblige!" he said, striding toward the nearest ghost. "Ye there! Ye great hulking barrel of fish guts!"

MacCready fired, and Gabe jolted. Not only did his ghostly pistol make a sound, it blasted the head clean off the other ghost. Like sharks to blood, the parade of ghosts angled instantly toward Gabe and his friends.

"Oh, boy!" said Yuri. "Here they come!"

"I'm ready," said Callie, powering up her light launcher.

The ghosts enveloped them like a thundercloud. Gabe saw Callie's and Yuri's beams flashing like lightning. On all sides gleaming ghosts were shredded. With his own light launcher he melted a ghost wrapped in a tattered wedding gown. He caught glimpses of Rebecca off to his right, fists clenched, punching and kicking. He heard the Scottish duellist bellow, "I'm Malcolm Macbeth MacCready, I'll have ye know!" as his pistol cracked again and again.

Surging toward Gabe now came three more diabolical creatures bloated by ghastlight: a gentleman in a top hat, a woman in a striped jogging suit, and a sly-looking man clutching a briefcase.

"I'll take Top Hat," Yuri said.

"Jogger," said Callie.

"Briefcase," said Gabe.

They unleashed their lights. Jogger, despite being in excellent shape, evaporated easily, but Top Hat was taking a bit more time. Briefcase cursed as Gabe melted one of his legs. The ghost swung his briefcase at Gabe's chest and the blow sent him staggering back, winded.

"Use the ghostlight, Gabe!" Yuri was shouting. "That one's strong!"

Gabe flipped the ghostlight into place. His launcher went dark, and he lost sight of Briefcase.

"Come on!" he shouted, counting down the seconds. Five, four . . . he could feel the heat building behind the amber lens. Three, two . . .

A cold hand clamped over his shoulder. Painfully Gabe's vision frosted and he saw Briefcase's sly face, mere inches from his own. Gabe shuddered. The ghost's eyes were two corkscrew holes, turning like they meant to twist and pull him right inside.

His launcher finally unleashed an amber lightning bolt. But Briefcase was so close that the barrel stuck straight through him and the beam didn't even touch him. Completely unharmed, the ghost clamped harder on Gabe's shoulder, freezing him in place.

Gabe felt Yuri's hand grab him and yank him backward. As he staggered away from the ghost, the light launcher came free, and its amber light blasted Briefcase off his remaining leg. The leg stamped furiously for a moment before melting. "Thanks," Gabe gasped to Yuri, taking aim at more nearby ghosts, cutting through them with the amber beam.

"Let it cool down!" Yuri urged him.

Gabe never wanted to release that trigger.

"Gabriel!" A cool hand held his arm. It took him a moment to recognize Rebecca's voice. "Gabriel, you nearly struck me with the beam!"

"Sorry!"

Instantly he dialled down the power and flipped up the ghost-light. The light launcher steamed in the cooling night air. Across the field the remaining ghosts were keeping their distance now, slogging on toward the lighthouse. Malcolm Macbeth MacCready chased after them, pistol firing, until so many ghosts piled atop him at once that Gabe lost sight of him.

"He turned out to be a very unexpected ally," Yuri said.

"We wasted too much time with these guys," Callie said. "We need to get to the lighthouse!"

She was right. The ghosts would keep coming as long as the ghastlight shone. Shivering, Gabe grabbed his bike and pedalled hard along Lakeshore Road. Normally the Gibraltar Point Lighthouse was hidden away behind trees, but the ghastlight beam must have cleared away all the leaves in its path, because Gabe had a clear view of it even from a distance.

Inside the lamp room, the lamp's purple eye flared bright.

Silhouetted against it was the unmistakably hideous body of Nicholas Viker. He was so swollen that his many limbs jutted out the windows. His massive hand lifted and beckoned to the ghosts marching across the island.

"He's enormous," Callie said on an exhale. "How can we fight that?"

"We've got a clear shot from here," said Gabe. He hopped off his bike and wheeled it behind some bushes. Using them as cover, he crouched and unslung his light launcher. He flipped the ghostlight into position.

"All of us together."

"Make it count, my friend," said Yuri, dropping down beside him with Callie. "We get only one shot before he knows we have another ghostlight."

Heart pounding, Gabe took aim.

"Ready," said Callie, her light launcher against her cheek.

"Me too," Yuri said.

Before Gabe could squeeze the trigger, Viker vanished.

"Crap," Gabe muttered. "Where'd he go?"

Rebecca's cool hand closed around his own. "Wait. Our reinforcements have arrived."

Gabe turned and dialled his light launcher to low. George Brown stepped into the glow. Beside him was a rangy man with a grey moustache and eyes that looked like they'd spent a long time looking at sad things. He leaned upon an oar.

"This is William Ward," Brown said, "not quite so old as you,

Miss Strand, born in 1847, so your paths would not have crossed. They called him the laird of Toronto Island. One of the bravest men I've known. Did a story on him. He captained the island's lifeboat and saved over one hundred and sixty souls."

"None of those make up for the five I lost," Ward said.

Brown gripped his shoulder. "You were just a lad. You must forgive yourself. But take that insatiable hunger to save lives, sir, and turn it to the matter at hand."

Ward's eyes drifted to the lighthouse and its devilish purple eye.

"In all my years, I've never seen such a light."

"It's raising the wakeful and wicked dead," Rebecca told him. "And they will bring death in great numbers if we don't quench its light and destroy the man who controls it."

Ward carefully rolled back his sleeves, lifted his oar and whirled it like a martial arts staff.

"Whoa," Gabe murmured.

"Let's get to it, then," said William Ward.

Gabe guessed the ghastlight had strengthened Ward's ghostly sinew and muscle. Just as it was powering Rebecca and every single ghost it grazed.

"I have also brought some friends," Joseph Halfday said, stepping into the light now. Behind him was a group of Indigenous men and women. Gabe realized he'd glimpsed some of them fishing, that night with Yuri. There were roughly a dozen, and each held a fishing spear in one hand and a long torch in the other. All were unlit at the moment, except for the one held by a woman with a forceful gaze. She wore a simple gown and a fine blanket draped over both shoulders. It was to her that Joseph Halfday spoke now in their own language.

As she listened, the woman gazed at the lighthouse, the purple light reflected in her eyes. Gabe picked out a few words, like *kaa* and *komikaa* and *enh.*

Halfday turned back to Gabe and the others. "Martha Sawyer says that light strengthens what is weakest in us. Our hate, our rage, our greed. These weak ghosts are like a plague of pests that come only to feed and destroy. And our people are familiar with pests."

Gabe got the sense that Halfday wasn't just talking about bugs. Martha Sawyer looked hard at him and Callie and Yuri, then talked to the other Indigenous ghosts before speaking once more with Halfday.

"She says they will fight alongside you," Halfday reported.

"Thank you!" said Gabe.

As one, the ghosts thumped their torches on the ground and the ends sprang into flame. As the ghastlight swept past overhead, the flames flickered but did not go out.

Yuri said, "I'd say we have a pretty good team now."

Gabe noticed that Joseph Halfday now held a spear that one of the other ghosts had given him.

"Do you have any kind of weapon?" he asked George Brown.

For a moment the newspaperman looked crestfallen, then produced a fountain pen from inside his jacket.

"Let's hope it's truly mightier than the sword," remarked Gabe.

"I am dangerous with this, my boy!" Brown made a fake lunge. "No need to worry about me. What's our plan of attack?"

Startled, Gabe realized that everyone was looking at him. When had *he* become the leader? He looked back at the lighthouse. There was still no sign of Viker in the lamp room, which was worrying. The marching ghosts were now converging in the clearing around the lighthouse, as if protecting it. Some clambered up the walls like ants, trying to get even closer to the infernal light.

"Well, if we can get Yuri inside the lighthouse," Gabe began, "he can pull the breaker and cut off the power. After that, we need to destroy Viker—and the ghastlight so no other ghosts can use it." Everyone kept looking at him, waiting for more, so he added, "I am very open to ideas."

Martha Sawyer conferred with the other Indigenous men and women, then spoke to Halfday, who nodded.

"She suggests you lead a charge to the lighthouse door with your friends."

"And what will you guys do?" Gabe asked.

"Watch and see."

With that, Joseph Halfday and the other Mississauga ghosts disappeared.

"I would rather have known their plan up front," Yuri said, spiking up his hair.

"We all ready?" Gabe asked.

Rebecca stepped into view. "Ready!"

Yuri touched his arm. "Remember, Gabe, only use the ghostlight when you're sure you've got Viker."

Gabe had wanted to go in there blasting with everything they had, but he knew Yuri was right. He didn't want to blow his surprise. He didn't want to drive Viker into hiding. Reluctantly he nodded.

With their light launchers dark, they crept down the road to the gravel path that led to the lighthouse. In unison Gabe powered up with Yuri and Callie, and they charged, beams blazing. Beside them, William Ward swung his oar like a club, batting ghosts through the air, shattering their spectral bones.

"Back, you lifeless fiends!" he cried as he plowed a path toward the lighthouse door.

But like blizzard snow, more ghosts pelted down to fill the gap. With ghosts pressing in on all sides, Gabe blasted away. He saw Rebecca kick and punch; he glimpsed George Brown plunging his fountain pen into a ghost so that it deflated like a punctured beach ball. Lancing everywhere were the searing beams of Callie's and Yuri's light launchers, melting ghosts one after another.

Still they came on, endlessly pouring themselves between Gabe and the lighthouse door. The ghosts pushed, they kicked, they clamped their hands around his arms and legs. They tried to wrench the light launcher from his grip.

From above, the ghastlight jabbed directly down, feeding the ghosts. Viker was up there, aiming. A purple glow hung like mist around the entire clearing now. Gabe shivered more violently. His hands began to feel cold, then numb.

"Fight on, my soldiers!" came a terrible voice from overhead.

Gabe glanced up to see Viker standing on the lighthouse roof, robed in purple light like a devilish king.

"Fight on against these tyrants who want to steal your light, your power, your new life! Who want only your oblivion!"

Gabe flipped down his ghostlight and tried to take a shot at Viker, but some ghosts tugged at the barrel of his light launcher, and he lost his chance. Viker had disappeared from view again.

"There's so many of them!" Callie cried in despair.

From the trees, Halfday, Martha Sawyer and the other Indigenous ghosts exploded into the clearing, their torches ablaze. They thrust their spears and fire into Viker's ghosts, who ignited as though soaked in gasoline. They flamed high for a moment before leaving a greasy smear in the night air.

"I like our allies!" Yuri shouted.

They were getting closer to the door. Gabe had lost sight of Rebecca and looked around in panic. When he found her she wasn't fighting at all. She had fallen back, and stood with spread arms, her face bathed in the ghastlight, drinking it in.

"Rebecca, don't!"

"It feels warm, so warm! I feel stronger!"

He rushed back to her and clasped with her. She blinked and settled her eyes on his. Had her pupils always been quite this large and deep? An unsettling current swirled within them.

"I can touch things again!" she said, gripping his hand tighter. "Make things move! For once, I can make things happen!"

How could he blame her? After so many years of sleep and silence and powerlessness, she reveled in this new strength.

"Gabriel, there's only one way to defeat Viker! By making myself as strong as him!"

"I'm not sure that's the best—"

"So I can devour *him*!"

"No—"

She whirled on him with such a fierce expression that he stepped back. "Savagery will only be defeated by savagery!"

And she charged at some ghosts that were coming up behind them, breaking one's legs with a kick; devouring the arm of another as Gabe watched, horrified.

"Gabe, come on!" Callie shouted. "We need you!"

Atop the lighthouse roof, Viker appeared and shouted: "Chill them all!"

Gabe dropped to his knee and took aim. He flipped down the ghostlight, squeezed the trigger and felt the light launcher heating up against his shoulder and cheek.

"Chill them to the bone!" wailed Viker. "To the marrow!"

Amber light torrented from Gabe's light launcher and struck Viker's left shoulder, melting it. A blast of fireworks exploded from the wound. Before Gabe could move the beam closer to his head, Viker tore free and scrambled around to the far side of the lighthouse.

Viker must have shouted orders to his followers, because instantly, a wave of ghosts crashed over Gabe. They clutched at his hands, his arms, his ankles. He whirled, blasting away, but there were too many of them – and they were so very cold.

The light launcher was knocked from his clumsy hands. In the nightmarish haze of the ghastlight, ghosts loomed over him. Their limbs stretched toward him. He was afraid he would break his own teeth, they were chattering so hard.

"Gabe! Gabe!" Knocked to the ground, he struggled to stand. He saw his friends' beams clearing the ghosts away from him. He glimpsed the Mississauga thrusting with their torches and spears. He saw William Ward swing his oar like a scythe, separating a ghostly head from its neck.

The earth shook – at least Gabe *felt* like it shook – as Nicholas Viker hit the ground beside him. Bathed in the full glare of the ghastlight, he was thrice the size of a normal man. His body writhed and gaped with the wailing mouths of his countless victims. His massive hand plunged into Gabe's chest.

Gabe sucked in air, trying to drag himself free.

"I'll drain you!" Viker bellowed, pushing his hand deeper. Gabe felt icy fingers clenching his heart.

"And then I will devour you."

Frost thickened across Gabe's vision. He felt like his heart could barely pump his freezing blood.

"Let him go!" cried Rebecca, thrusting herself between Gabe and Viker.

No, Gabe tried to say with his numb mouth.

She was a fraction of Viker's size, but she blazed with purple light. With a wild cry her jaws parted and she bit through Viker's wrist. Gabe scrambled backward, free of the icy fist. In surprise and rage, Viker reared, his terrible mouth opening like a tunnel-boring machine.

But Rebecca shouted at him from her own set of terrifying jaws:

"I will devour *you*, Nicholas Viker!"

Viker lunged, but she skipped out of the way and bit off another one of his many limbs. She was in a frenzy, and Gabe was desperately afraid for her. He was afraid *of* her. She was reckless, deranged with the ghastlight. Gabe dragged his way toward his light launcher.

With a massive hand Viker swatted Rebecca and, as she lay stunned, snatched her into the air.

On his back, Gabe gripped his light launcher and crooked his finger around the trigger.

"You wish to see your father again, Miss Strand?" Viker's ragged mouth said. "Come, then! Come and join him!"

"No!" Gabe croaked, squeezing the trigger. But the light launcher was still dark, building up pressure behind its amber lens.

Though she struggled, Rebecca couldn't break free from Viker's grip, or the whirlpool suction of his widening mouth.

"Rebecca!" Gabe cried.

She disappeared down Viker's throat.

At last, amber light poured from the barrel and struck Viker dead centre. Gabe's beam was joined by those of Callie and Yuri, impaling Viker against the stone wall of the lighthouse. "We've got him!" shouted Gabe.

But Viker just poured himself through the lighthouse wall and disappeared inside.

"Inside!" Gabe cried, struggling to stand on his numb feet.

Yuri and Callie hoisted him up.

"Go!" Joseph Halfday shouted, as he protected the passage he and his ghost allies had opened to the lighthouse door.

Callie yanked the crowbar out of Yuri's backpack and slid it under the new padlock. Together they snapped the chain. Gabe threw the door wide and shredded the four ghosts waiting inside. Yuri rushed straight to the panel and ripped out the breaker.

Unthinking, Gabe was already charging up the stairs. His amber beam melted any ghost in his path and made the lighthouse look like it was on fire.

When he burst into the lamp room, the beacon was dark.

The ghastlight was gone.

Viker was gone.

And with him, Rebecca.

25

Gabe burst out onto the catwalk, stabbing his amber beam down into the clearing. Amid the churning mass of ghosts, he could not find Viker.

Gone. Viker was gone. Stealing Rebecca away inside him.

But there was no time to search for them, because they were under attack. So Gabe took out his anguish and rage on the remaining ghosts who besieged the lighthouse. Energized and bloated by the ghastlight, they scuttled up the old stone like cockroaches.

"Where is the light?" they shrieked.

"Bring it back!"

"What have you done with it?"

"Bring back the light!"

"Give it back to us!"

Joined by Callie on the catwalk, Gabe scorched the ghouls off the lighthouse walls with his beam. Any that reached the railings were impaled or torched by Joseph Halfday, Mary Sawyer and the others. Gabe glimpsed William Ward inside the lamp room, standing by the stairs with his oar, decapitating any ghost foolish enough to stick its head up. Still others seeped in through the walls and floors, but Yuri was ready with his light launcher to vanquish them.

And George Brown stood by a window with his pen, jotting something down on his starched shirt cuff.

"What're you doing, Brown?" Joseph Halfday hollered in at him.

"Taking notes! What do you think?"

"Make yourself useful!"

"This *is* useful!" Brown retorted, but had to break off to stab a ghoulish policeman in the eye with his pen.

Rain and wind plastered Gabe's hair to his face. Every second he battled these ghosts was a second stolen from saving Rebecca. But something was happening. Fewer ghosts stormed the lighthouse walls, and when he and Callie melted the last of them away, he noticed that the ghosts were actually retreating, marching off toward the city.

"What're they doing?" he murmured.

"I think I found Viker!" Callie said, pointing. Gabe looked across the harbour. From the CN Tower, a blazing beam stabbed straight up, staining the clouds a terrible purple.

"He's using the new spotlight," Callie said in disbelief.

"How powerful did you say it was?" Yuri asked, stepping out onto the catwalk.

In a dazed tour-guide voice, Callie recited: "It's a xenon lamp with over thirteen million lumens. Making it the brightest spotlight in the world. In case you're interested."

And somehow Viker had mounted the ghastlight in front of it.

Gabe braced his light launcher on the railing and took aim. He squeezed his trigger, counted down five seconds and sent a beam of amber light sizzling across the harbour. It struck the top of the observation level, very near the spotlight. But had it struck Viker? Gabe couldn't see any spectral fireworks. The fiend might be hunkered down somewhere out of reach, operating the ghastlight with one of his long arms.

"Save your battery!" Yuri said, putting a hand gently on his shoulder. "It's too far away. He might not even be up there."

Gabe wasn't ready to quit yet. He adjusted his aim and released another blast of amber light. In answer, the ghastlight beam swung down from the churning clouds and lanced across the city.

"It moves?" Gabe asked in horror.

"Normally they keep it aimed straight up," said Callie, "but yeah, it moves."

As the beam struck the skyscrapers, Gabe thought he could see the panes of glass frost over. The purple light kept moving, over the grand copper peaks of the Royal York Hotel, over the Gardiner Expressway. Horns blared and cars swerved.

"He can see the whole city from up there," Callie said.

"He's going to *destroy* the city," said Yuri.

Then the purple beam swept across the harbour. Was it the storm, or the ghastlight itself that gouged deep troughs in the water and sent foam spraying from crests? A tugboat, halfway to the city docks, was caught in the churn, spinning like a toy in a washing machine. Its running lights went out, and it drifted, powerless.

The purple beam seemed to stir the very air, for an icy wind buffeted Gabe. The slanting rain became sharper. Within the clouds lightning flickered. Big bundles of thunder cracked against each other.

And then the ghastlight reached the island. Waves smacked the shoreline, swamping wooden boardwalks. In the marinas, ships slewed in their moorings, wind shrieking through their rigging. Gabe glanced up at the clattering weather vane atop the lighthouse roof, spinning madly. The beam stalked across the island and Gabe glimpsed the long parade of ghosts, marching toward its source. He heard their terrible cheers as the purple light struck them. Before his very eyes, they seemed to swell.

"Are you seeing this?" he asked his friends.

Yuri rummaged in his hair until it looked like porcupine quills. "This is really, really bad."

"They're going to be so strong," said Callie.

Restlessly the beam moved on, crackling icily across treetops, curling leaves and snapping branches.

And heading for the lighthouse.

"Don't look at it!" Callie shouted.

"Get inside!" Gabe urged everyone.

He didn't want to find out how searingly cold this more powerful ghastlight might be. The three of them crouched low as the purple beam stabbed inside. Gabe watched frost crawl across the windows, the glass making a tortured squeal.

"Cover your eyes!" Yuri yelled, seconds before all the windows shattered.

Wind wailed into the room. Gabe shook glass splinters from

his hair and clothing. In the blaze of the ghastlight, he could see all their ghost allies. Near the beacon stood George Brown; at the stairs was William Ward; and outside on the catwalk were Joseph Halfday and Martha Sawyer's group, their torches flickering.

None of them were shaken by the gale-force winds or the debris driven through the air. Indeed, all of them seemed larger than before. And all of them were staring unblinking into the ghastlight as if hypnotized. One by one, their torches flickered out.

Viker was *feeding* them, trying to turn them into the wakeful and wicked dead.

"Mr Brown!" Gabe shouted. "Mr Ward!"

Neither heard him. He scrambled up and put himself right in front of George Brown. The moment the purple beam struck Gabe full on, he began to shiver. George Brown stared through him, his pupils beginning a terrible corkscrew swirl.

"Clasp with me, George Brown!" Gabe's breath plumed in the frigid air. When he grabbed the ghost's hand, it was like the time he'd mistakenly clasped with Nicholas Viker. His teeth jangled with electricity. The taste of blood filled his mouth.

"Gabe!" he heard Yuri saying, as though from a great distance. "If they are going bad, we need to zap them!"

"Wait! Mr Brown, wake up!"

No response. Gabe didn't know how much longer he could hold on.

"Mr Brown," he said through chattering teeth, "if you . . . don't . . . wake up you're . . . going to miss . . . a great story!"

The old journalist blinked, and focused on Gabe. Startled, he looked down at their clasped hands and tightened his grip as if taking strength from it. He *was* growing stronger. Gabe felt more of his own dwindling heat and energy drain away.

"Thank you, my boy," Brown said. "I needed a good kick in the pants. Now let's rouse the others!"

With Yuri and Callie, Gabe moved from one hypnotized ghost to another, blocking their view of the ghastlight and clasping with them briefly. That jolt of living heat and energy was enough to bring them back to themselves.

And perhaps Viker realized he had failed to corrupt them, because the beam abruptly swooped away from the Gibraltar Point Lighthouse.

Winded, Gabe leaned against the railing and watched the retreating ghastlight. It churned the harbour, lighting a path for the dead as they swam toward the city and the CN Tower.

"We need to kill that light!" he shouted above the gale. "Callie, can you get us up there?"

"Yes, but – you sure?"

"We rip out the ghastlight, and put the *ghost*light in its place!"

"You nearly died, my friend," Yuri reminded him.

"We need more power to kill Viker. Even with the ghostlight, the light launcher wasn't enough. This is the only way."

"Gabe, when Viker put his hand inside you, you looked like a wax dummy. You still look a little waxy."

"Viker ate Rebecca! We're not quitting!" In his mind he saw her getting dragged into all that darkness and despair. "She asked for my help. She trusted me. She trusted all of us. If we get our ghost-light in that xenon lamp, we can skewer Viker like a shish kebab!"

"A food metaphor," said Yuri. "Why am I not surprised?"

"How're we going to get back to the city?" Callie asked. "No boats can cross in this!"

He turned his gaze on the heaving harbour. She was right. And the storm was intensifying. On the island trees bowed over. A sea gull nearly slammed into the lighthouse. At the edge of the clearing, a metal sign rattled on its post before ripping loose and slicing through the air. Near the filtration plant, floodwaters steadily crept ashore.

"There's another way," Gabe said. "The tunnel!"

Callie looked bewildered. "What tunnel?"

"From the filtration plant to the city. In 1902 they built a tunnel to pump in clean water!"

"There's a tunnel under the harbour?"

"Yes!" He didn't always mention this on his ghost tour, but was glad he'd studied his script so thoroughly.

"Big enough for us to go through?" Yuri asked.

"If it was big enough for people to dig it, it's big enough for us to get through!"

"But *under* the lake?" Callie said weakly.

Gabe turned his light launcher to low so they could talk to their ghost allies. "Mr Brown, Mr Halfday, everyone else, you don't need to come with us."

Joseph Halfday stepped into the circle of light. "We will come with you."

"You sure?" Gabe felt like he'd asked too much already.

"And I," said William Ward. "You'll need me."

"I never miss a good story," added George Brown.

Downstairs, Gabe needed Yuri's help to open the door, the wind was so strong. Head bowed, he crossed the clearing in slow motion. When he and his friends reached Lakeshore Road, what he saw staggered him. Over the lake, waterspouts whirled into the air like reverse tornadoes. Breakers crashed against the beach, seven feet high. Planks from the boardwalk flipped up like xylophone keys torn free by a devilishly musical hand.

The floodwater was already at Gabe's ankles; seconds later, halfway up his calf. The water had a hard pull, like a cold skeletal grip that wanted to drag you into the deeps.

Gabe fought his way toward the filtration plant. Yuri lost his balance and fell. The current pulled him a good ten feet before Callie caught and grabbed him. "You OK?" she asked, but he was more worried about his light launcher, hurriedly drying it off with his shirt.

They pressed on, fighting with every step. Every time Gabe lifted a foot, he was nearly pushed off-balance. Branches and debris swept past. The gate to the filtration plant was only a few hundred metres away, but it seemed an impossible distance.

A canoe swirled out of the darkness and nearly bowled Gabe over. He made a grab for it and missed, then saw it stop, impossibly, in the midst of the current. When he played his light launcher on it he saw Joseph Halfday and the Mississauga fishermen holding it steady. The sight of their lit torches cheered him more than he could say. As did the presence of George Brown, already sitting in the canoe and not looking remotely wet or ruffled.

"Get in," William Ward said from the stern. His ghostly oar was dug into the water, eager to paddle.

The boat rocked as Gabe scrambled inside with Yuri and Callie. Amazingly, there were two real oars, sliding around the bottom. Gabe snatched up one and Callie the other. Crouched in the middle, Yuri held on to the gunwales, his hair standing on end without any help from his hands.

"Aim for the gate!" Gabe said.

He wasn't sure if his desperate paddling was doing any good, or whether they were being guided entirely by their ghost allies. They swerved around a concrete planter, ricocheted off a park bench.

"How're we going to get through the gate?" Callie shouted.

"Bus!" Yuri bellowed.

"What?" Gabe worried his friend had cracked.

"Bus!" Yuri wailed again, pointing.

The yellow school bus that had been parked forever by the Artscape studios was on the move, driven by the surging water. It angled toward them on a collision course.

"Whoa whoa whoa!" cried Yuri.

Gabe and Callie dug in with their paddles, and Yuri plunged both hands into the water, scooping backward furiously.

The bus missed them by a hair, then flattened the chain link gate. They surged straight through after it, onto the grounds of the filtration plant. The bus careened ahead and smashed a large opening in the main building.

"No need to break in, at least," said Yuri cheerfully.

Their canoe was washed right inside the building and beached itself in an office that was, happily, unoccupied. The three of them splashed out onto the wet floor. Gabe was grateful to be out of the howling wind and lashing rain. Hurrying to the door, he opened it a crack and looked up and down the empty corridor. He hadn't planned on bashing through the wall of the filtration plant, and could only hope the staff had already left the island.

"What now?" Callie asked. "How do we find the tunnel?"

Gabe hadn't the slightest idea. "Yuri, help me out here."

"Any staircase going down, we take," his friend said simply.

They crept out into the corridor. The whole place seemed eerily deserted. Callie whispered, "I always thought this place looked like a secret government facility where they experiment on mutant children."

"Seriously?" asked Yuri.

"Hah!" Gabe said to his friend. "Not just me."

"There," Callie said, pointing down the hallway to a serious-looking door with huge hinges. The sign said: TUNNEL ACCESS: AUTHORIZED PERSONNEL ONLY.

When they drew closer, Gabe saw that the door was secured with a daunting electronic keypad. He looked at Yuri hopefully, but his friend shook his head.

"We need a code or security card for this."

"Maybe not," Gabe said. "If ghosts can fritz up amusement park rides, maybe they can frizzle this. Mr Brown? Can you just, I don't know, touch it a lot?"

George Brown obliged, and Gabe watched the console flash and honk. From within the door came a series of clicks and thumps.

"That sounds promising," said Callie, pulling at the door. It didn't budge.

"What now?" Gabe said, flustered. The floor was under an inch of water now. The entire lake seemed intent on sinking the island.

Yuri looked at him. "Touch the console!"

"What?"

"Just go ahead and put your fingers all over it! You'll break it for sure!"

"That's not true!" To prove it, Gabe pushed random buttons, then slapped the control panel a few times.

With a single *thunk*, the door swung open.

"That was a fluke!" he said.

Overhead lights flickered on automatically as Gabe hurried down the stairs, probing ahead of him with his light launcher. The dank smells of water, earth and rust rose to meet him. He heard a heavy thud behind him and turned to see Yuri closing the door.

"We don't want water getting down here and flooding the tunnel."

"Good point." Gabe swallowed; he hadn't thought of that possibility.

"This is a lousy time to bring it up," Callie said, "but I'm a bit claustrophobic. I mean, a lot claustrophobic."

With each step down it got hotter and clammier. At the bottom of the stairs a low-ceilinged tunnel stretched into darkness. Strapped to the walls were thick pipes, some old-looking, some newer, humming as they pushed clean water underneath the lake bed to the city.

Callie had stopped and was breathing heavily.

"Short walk," Gabe promised her.

"Under the lake, yeah."

"It's OK," Yuri said. "This tunnel has been around over a century."

"That worries me too, but thanks."

"Just a quick stroll. Like walking from Front Street to College."

"That's not a short walk!"

Very gently Yuri said, "You can do it, Callie."

"Are we all here?" Gabe asked the air around him. "Our allies?"

"Still with you," Joseph Halfday said, stepping into the glow of his light launcher.

"We'll keep watch behind you," George Brown added.

Gabe started out at a slow jog, trying not to think of all that weight overhead, the millions of tons of lake pressing against the ceiling. Overhead lights flickered on slowly as they approached, then flickered out after they passed. Their three light launcher beams let them see much farther ahead.

"We're probably halfway now, right?" Callie puffed beside him.

"Yep," Gabe said, not knowing if he was lying.

"Oh my goodness." Yuri pointed his beam at the ground. A shallow gap in the concrete floor, about five by five feet, revealed the clay underneath. In it were footprints of naked human feet. "Those are very big toes."

"I read about this!" Gabe said. "When they dug the tunnel, they found these fossilized footprints in the lake bed. They might be ten thousand years old."

"I hope we don't meet whoever owned these feet," Callie said. "Come on!"

Unease prickled along Gabe's neck. Running into ancient ghosts seemed all too likely down here. His eyes pushed into the darkness, willing the tunnel to end.

Up ahead, glimmering in his beam suddenly, were five girls in summer dresses. Gabe was no expert on clothes, but these looked old-fashioned.

"William?" one of the girls cried. "William, is that you?"

William Ward rushed past Gabe, dropping his oar as he cried out: "Rose! And Jane! Cecilia and Phoebe, I see you! And Mary Ann!"

It was a joyful tangle as they threw their arms around each other, pulling each other close.

"Those," said George Brown quietly, leaning into Gabe's beam, "are his younger sisters. When he was just fifteen, he took them sailing on the bay. A gale sprang up, and the boat capsized. All his sisters drowned. Only William survived. And he never forgave himself."

And now here they were, the ghosts of William Ward's sisters. As if they'd sifted slowly through the layers of sand and clay and rock to arrive inside this tunnel. As if they'd been waiting for him all these years, to give him what he most needed.

As Gabe stood watching their reunion, he wasn't sure he'd ever seen such overwhelming happiness. When he heard William Ward's voice again it was hoarse.

"I'm sorry!" Ward said. "Oh, I'm so sorry. Can you forgive me!"

"Yes," said one of his sisters, and another said, "Yes, of course," and yet another said, "It was an accident. You tried your best," and all of them said, "We always forgave you, William. Forgive yourself now. Please, do."

They spoke quietly together, too low for Gabe to hear. He felt he should turn his light off and give them privacy. But he couldn't. He wanted to witness this beautiful thing.

When William Ward turned back to them, he looked quite different. The deep lines had disappeared from his face, like there was less gravity tugging at him.

"I must go, I'm afraid. I feel myself leaving."

Gabe nodded. "Yes, of course."

"Thank you!" Callie cried out.

The tunnel was suddenly lit like a meteor shower. In sprays of colourful light, William's ghostly body came apart, along with those of his sisters. Reunited and released at last, to finish their journey elsewhere.

"We'll miss that oar," Yuri said as it, too, evaporated.

Gabe tried to laugh, but it sounded choked and he realized his own eyes were wet.

They marched on through the tunnel, the hum of the pipes, the whirring of ventilation fans. He wondered about the world overhead, the raging storm and water, the ghastlight churning the city into mayhem – all of it temporarily hidden.

Overhead, the lamps flickered off; their beams were suddenly the only source of light.

"Why'd they do that?" Callie asked nervously.

"Broken sensor most likely," Yuri replied. "Keep moving, they'll come on again."

But they didn't. An urgent hand closed coldly around Gabe's.

"Behind us!" George Brown cried out.

Gabe whirled and aimed his beam down the tunnel. Ghosts surged toward them, scuttling along the walls and ceiling like insects. He flipped the ghostlight into place and counted down seconds as the light launcher powered up. Yuri's and Callie's beams came first; then his amber light joined theirs.

Ghosts toppled and melted, yet some eluded their barrage and charged on. In relief, he saw Joseph Halfday and the other Indigenous ghosts rush to confront them with their spears and torches. But when Gabe's light launcher, then Callie's, began to flicker he caught Yuri's eye worriedly.

"Better throttle back!" Yuri shouted. "We're almost out! We need to change batteries!"

No time now! Reluctantly, Gabe dialled down the power until his light stopped flickering.

Bursting through the knot of ghosts came Tommy Flynn, thrice his usual size, though he still had a ghastly hole in his middle. Judging by his expression, he was still very ticked off about it. His blue teeth were bared and his eyes were scribbled black holes.

"As you can see, my boy," he cried out to Gabe, "it's a losing battle you're fighting!"

He was not only bigger, but quicker, cartwheeling and dodging and leaping from one wall to another like some insane parkour expert – and making it almost impossible for Gabe to get a clean shot.

The next thing Gabe knew, his light launcher had been struck from his hands, and its dimming light played over Tommy Flynn as the ghost knocked him over and sat upon his chest. When Gabe struggled to throw him off, Flynn gripped either side of his face with his icy hands. Gabe felt like he'd been welded to the floor.

"Ah, all that life and heat!" Tommy Flynn cried. "I'm going to have it! All of it!"

In a blur, Malcolm Macbeth MacCready dropped down on Flynn, put a pistol to his head and blew it off his shoulders.

"That'll teach ye," shouted the Scottish ghost, kicking Flynn's astonished head like a football down the tunnel, "to refuse a duel with me!" He turned to Gabe. "Y'all right there, laddie?"

"Thank you!" Gabe gasped, scrambling up and grabbing his light launcher.

"Don't mention it! I canna remember when I last had such a *crackin'* good time! Now, git goin', and I'll hold 'em off for ye!"

The last he saw of Malcolm Macbeth MacCready, the Scottish duellist was standing tall in the middle of the tunnel, his spectral pistol – with its endless supply of bullets – blasting away.

Gabe ran with Callie and Yuri, their Indigenous ghost allies bringing up the rear, fighting with torches and spears while George Brown jotted some more notes on his cuffs.

Gabe's light launcher flickered dimly now, but up ahead he caught sight of the tunnel's end. With all his friends and allies, he charged up the stairs. They burst out through a fire door onto the street. It took Gabe only a moment to get his bearings. Two blocks away, the CN Tower towered up, and from its summit blazed the ghastlight.

Worse than any nightmare.

More desperate than a fever dream.

It was a dark vortex of wailed words from voices too numerous and anguished to untangle.

Inside Viker's body, Rebecca Strand did not know if her eyes were open or closed – or even if she had any eyes at all. There was nothing to see, but always a sense of sickening motion.

Lurching, spinning, tilting, without cease.

She was aware of her body – did she have one anymore? – being shunted and squeezed, tugged and nipped, beyond her control. She was a limp little bit of nothing, being puppeted about by a terrible force.

Things grazed her, and were gone.

She tried to speak.

Did she make any sound?

It was so noisy here.

She did not know if there was anything left of her.

She struggled to remember her name, to picture her face, to net something from the whirlpool of her memory.

What was she? Anything?

Or nothing at all, now and forever?

26

In the glow of the roving ghastlight, Gabe glimpsed ghosts converging on the CN Tower. From the south they dragged themselves out of the harbour. From all other points of the compass, they trudged down the blustery streets, or leapt like gargoyles across rooftops, chasing after the purple beam.

"Come on," Gabe said, "let's get to the tower before they do."

They ran. He saw yet other ghosts, shrinking back into alleyways and walls, looking fearful and confused, like they'd just woken into a nightmare. Car alarms bleated, overhead electrical lines sparked, shrill police sirens threaded themselves through the wailing wind.

Outside the tower, two police cruisers were pulled up in the deserted plaza, their red and blue lights flashing silently. Three officers stared up at the purple ghastlight. Another talked on a walkie-talkie as she made her way to the doors.

Gabe crouched behind a cement planter and waved Yuri and Callie down beside him. With their light launchers, the three of them definitely looked weird, if not downright suspicious. It was close to two in the morning.

"How do we get inside?" he asked Callie.

"There's a service entrance," she said, pointing down a ramp.

Gabe heard a shout and peeked over the planter. The officer was chasing after her walkie-talkie, which scudded across the ground. When she tried to pick it up, it veered off in a new direction. A gun flew out of another officer's holster and twirled. Driverless, a cruiser jerked forward, its siren burping and tooting.

"Look," said George Brown, clasping Gabe's shoulder so he could see the ghosts' mischief, and how many more were entering the plaza.

"They're everywhere," Gabe said to his friends. Callie led them down the ramp to a metal door and tapped her pass on the lock. It opened with a beep.

"We need to switch batteries," Yuri said.

"This way." Callie took them down a nondescript corridor and into a staff room. Yuri got right to work on the three light launchers. He unscrewed hatches and slid back housings, removed old batteries and replaced them with the new ones.

"It's not ideal," he said as he worked. "These new ones don't have as much power. But at least we have full charges."

Less power; a more powerful ghost. Gabe checked the ghostlight's amber lens for any evil cracks. It had taken a beating on the island – like him. Bruises ached across his body, and his insides still felt shivery.

Yuri came over with a roll of duct tape and wound two loops around the barrel of his light launcher. "The coupling was a little loose. Should be good now."

"Thanks, Yuri." He took a breath. "This next part—"

"We can do it," Yuri said.

He didn't even have a plan. He looked at his two friends and felt overwhelmed with gratitude. It wasn't *their* father trapped inside Viker, but they'd stuck with him all the way, even as it got more and more dangerous.

He turned his light launcher to its lowest setting so their ghostly allies could be seen and heard.

"Callie, can you show us a map of the observation level?" he asked.

"You've really never been up?"

Both he and Yuri shook their heads. "I should've given you guys a tour. OK." She pulled her tablet out of her backpack and within seconds had a floor plan on-screen. "The elevators run through the centre of the tower and come out in the middle of the LookOut Level. It actually has three decks. The main deck is pretty straight-forward. Floor-to-ceiling windows all around. Stairs, here, down to the glass floor. And stairs, here, go up to the revolving restaurant. And from there it's another flight up for the EdgeWalk. There's a hatch to the outside."

Gabe swallowed. "And that's where the spotlight is, right?"

"It's mounted on the sloped roof and sticks out over the catwalk."

"This catwalk," Yuri asked weakly, "how wide is it?"

"Five feet maybe."

"Railing?"

"No railing."

"Have you ever gone out there?" Gabe asked her.

"Are you crazy?"

Yuri's hands were clenched, frozen, in his hair. "It will be very windy up there tonight. We'll get blown off!"

Callie said, "There's safety harnesses that clip onto a rail. It goes all the way around the outside of the tower."

"The wind is of no concern to us," said Joseph Halfday from the edges of the light. "All storms pass through us. Let *us* go outside. I believe we're strong enough to remove the ghastlight from the lamp."

To prove it, he lifted one of Yuri's screwdrivers off the table.

"The lens will be extremely hot," Yuri warned him.

"That won't bother us either," Halfday replied. "If you trust us, we can put the ghostlight into the lamp and train it upon Viker."

Gabe looked at his living friends. Tempting as it was, it didn't seem right. Even if the ghosts *were* already dead, they could still be harmed by Viker. *Devoured* by him.

"We trust you absolutely," Gabe said. "But we're not letting you go out there alone. Once we take the ghastlight, Viker will be all over us. You'll need us and our light launchers. We need each other for this. Everything we've got."

"Let me slip outside first, unnoticed," said Joseph Halfday. "I will see where Viker is. I'll remove the ghastlight, and make the lamp ready for your ghostlight."

Yuri turned to Callie. "Can you find us a detailed picture of this spotlight?"

"I'll try." She tapped and swiped on her tablet. "This is as good as I can find."

"OK," said Yuri, peering at the grainy photo. "It has insulated handles, good. We already know it's on a swivel mount, because Viker is moving it. So . . . the lamp itself is totally enclosed . . . but look, this is good news: there is a metal frame outside at the front, to hold different coloured filters, I guess. The frame must be adjustable: if it's holding the ghastlight, it will hold the ghostlight."

"We need to destroy the ghastlight," Callie said. "In case they take it back."

"Very good point," said Yuri. "Get it inside and we can smash it." He pulled a hammer from his backpack.

"How much stuff do you *have* in there?" Gabe asked.

"Everything."

"And after that," said Callie, "we put the ghostlight in the spotlight."

"I'll do that," Gabe said.

"Why you?"

"Rebecca saved me from Viker; I need to save her now."

The others nodded and seemed to accept this. Very quietly, Yuri said, "Please do not break the lamp."

"I'll be very careful, believe me."

"We'll have the most powerful ghostlight in human history," Callie said.

"And we will be with you," said Joseph Halfday, "with torch and spear."

"And pen," added George Brown.

"OK, I think we've got a plan," said Gabe. When he picked up his backpack he heard crinkling. "Oh, anyone want a snack bar?"

"Now?" Callie exclaimed.

Gabe took out a handful. "I've got dark chocolate; this one has shredded coconut; almonds in this one – no nut allergies, right?"

"Unbelievable," said Yuri.

But he smiled as he took a snack bar. Callie gratefully accepted one as well, and they wolfed them down.

"Ready?" Gabe asked after they'd all taken long drinks from their water bottles.

Callie guided them down a corridor to the freight elevator, which was waiting with doors open. Just to make sure there were no uninvited passengers, Gabe checked it out first with his light launcher. On the long ride up, he adjusted and readjusted his strap. He wiped his sweaty hands on his pants. He couldn't keep still. He wished he'd gone to the bathroom beforehand. Callie and Yuri looked as fidgety as him. It was a long ride. His ears popped.

"We'll need to sneak past the security guard," Callie said.

"There's a security guard?" Gabe asked.

"Of course there's a security guard!"

Yuri rummaged in his hair. "This would have been useful to know earlier."

"Don't worry, they usually just sit around near the café. We just need to make it to the stairs. No one goes up to the top level."

The elevator slowed, and the doors opened more loudly than

Gabe liked. Cautiously they stepped out. Before them was a wall of angled windows. Beyond them, the purple beam of the ghastlight lanced down over the city. Gabe heard someone talking out of sight.

"... I didn't turn it on! I wouldn't know how ... no, I don't know why it's purple ..."

Callie peeped around the corner, then waved for them to follow. Off to the right, a security guard had his back to them, talking into a walkie-talkie.

"OK. I'll send the elevator down for the police, yes, right away ..."

Gabe looked at Yuri in alarm. If the police came up here, they'd never get to do what they needed to.

"Sameer!" Callie hissed to the security guard.

Gabe was just as surprised as the guard, who snapped around so quickly that he dropped his walkie-talkie.

"Callie?" he said. "You shouldn't be up here." Sameer tried to sound stern, but wasn't doing a great job. He couldn't have been more than a couple of years older than them. He looked swamped inside his uniform.

Callie said, "Please don't send the elevator down to the police, OK?"

"What're you talking about?" He noticed their light launchers for the first time, and frowned. "What're you guys? Ghostbuster interns?"

"Listen, Sameer, we don't have much time, but I'm going to tell you something ..."

He sighed. "Does this have anything to do with your ghost blog?"

"Oh," she said, looking pleased. "You've actually read it?"

He made a face as if he'd been scalded. "No, I don't dabble in the occult."

"Well, that's unfortunate, Sameer, because a giant cannibal ghost is taking over the city and we have to stop him."

"Um . . . ," said the security guard.

"But we have a special lens" – she pointed at the ghostlight on Gabe's light launcher – "that will destroy him. But we need to get it into the spotlight."

Sameer nodded. "Yeah . . ." On the floor his walkie-talkie squawked impatiently.

"Don't pick that up," said Callie.

"I have to pick that up."

"Luckily," Callie persisted, "we also have some nice ghosts helping us. Would you like to see them?"

Before Sameer could reply, she panned her light launcher beam so it revealed Joseph Halfday, his Mississauga allies and George Brown.

"This is a projection," Sameer said, but he seemed unsure.

"My friend." Joseph Halfday walked up to him and offered his hand. "Clasp with me, and you will see even more clearly."

Reluctantly the security guard took Joseph's hand. Gabe felt a pang of sympathy for Sameer as his eyes widened; he shuddered, then yanked his hand free and cradled it like a baby against his chest.

Gabe gave him a reassuring smile. "I know how you feel."

Sameer swallowed. "So, thanks for showing me the ghosts," he said meekly, his eyes straying to the pile of textbooks on a café table, "but I just really wanted to study for my exam, so . . ."

"Please help us," Joseph Halfday said.

Helplessly, Sameer looked at Callie. "So, tell me this again?"

"Big ghost," she replied. "Makes King Kong look like Curious George."

"And you're—"

"Going to zap him," said Yuri.

"But why can't the police—"

"They can't help us," said Callie. "And that's why you need to go and lock the elevators up here, right now. Please."

Sameer's walkie-talkie squawked and he looked tortured but turned it off.

"You can say your battery died," Yuri suggested. "And the elevators broke down. It's a crazy night out there."

Beyond the windows a bolt of lightning unzipped the sky and Gabe felt the instantaneous crack of thunder in his molars.

"That was right overhead!"

"The tower gets hit by lightning hundreds of times a year," said Callie. "The antenna's a lightning rod. It's all very safe."

With Sameer trailing after them, they took the stairs toward the Edgewalk. Gabe swept his light ahead to make sure there were no waiting ghosts. The uppermost level was windowless, with a sloped roof. Rain and wind pummelled the outside. Unless he was very much mistaken, the tower was swaying.

"It was made to bend," Callie said.

"This much?"

"Pretty sure." She sounded less confident. "There's the hatch."

A ramp led up to twin doors in the sloped roof. They looked bank-vault thick; they looked like something that protected you from a thousand feet of empty air – and murderous ghosts.

"It'd be good to know exactly where Viker is," said Yuri.

Joseph Halfday stepped into the light. "He's higher up. I just went out and saw him standing on a structure even closer to the summit."

"The SkyPod," said Callie.

"He's making some very fiery speeches," added George Brown, "to the dead of the city."

"So he's not actually near the spotlight?" Gabe asked hopefully.

"No," Brown replied, "but he's got a very long arm that reaches down to move it."

Gabe shuddered to think how many freakish limbs Viker's body had now acquired.

"I think I can steal away the ghastlight without him noticing," said Joseph Halfday.

George Brown's forehead creased in distress. "Let me do it, my friend."

"You take notes," Halfday told him. "And write the story. With me as a hero."

"That is a promise," said Brown as they clasped hands.

Halfday looked at Gabe. "Once I take out the ghastlight, you must be ready with the ghostlight. Viker will strike quickly."

"We should get ready to go outside," said Callie.

Gabe's stomach gave an unpleasant lurch when he looked at the safety rail bolted to the room's ceiling. He followed it with his eyes to the metal hatch, where it went through a gap to the catwalk encircling the tower.

"So how does all this work?" He nodded at the thick black cables dangling from the rail.

Callie snatched down one of the red jumpsuits hanging from the wall. She measured it against Gabe, then handed it to Yuri instead because he was a little taller.

"I've watched people get rigged up a few times," she said, selecting another suit for Gabe, then herself. "Saw a wedding here once."

"Hey, you guys aren't serious," said Sameer, who'd been watching everything. "You're not really going out there!"

"Believe me, I am not happy about this either," said Yuri.

"If I open these doors for you, I am going to lose my job!"

"No one will ever know," Callie said. "Sameer, can you give us a hand?"

There was a lot of zipping and buckling and cinching of straps. Sameer took one of the dangling safety cables and hooked it to the back of Gabe's harness.

"Yuri, that look solid to you?" Gabe asked his best friend.

"I am no mountaineer," Yuri said as his own cable was snapped on, "but it looks sound. Here, let me help you with this."

Yuri picked up Gabe's light launcher and carefully removed the ghostlight from the end. He zipped the amber lens into a pocket in Gabe's jumpsuit and gave it a pat. "Right here."

"Thanks," Gabe said, looking on wistfully as Yuri leaned his light launcher against the wall. "Guess I won't be needing it now."

He blinked as it floated into the air and turned itself on. In the beam's low light, he saw George Brown's grinning face.

"Don't mind if I have a go with it, do you?"

"Be my guest!" said Gabe.

"My pen is impressive, but it would be a shame to let this fine machine go to waste."

Not for the first time, Gabe was grateful for how the ghastlight had supercharged his ghost allies.

"Are we ready?" he asked, regarding Callie and Yuri in their red jumpsuits, gripping their light launchers.

His living friends nodded. George Brown winked. He heard Joseph Halfday say something in Anishinaabemowin to Martha Sawyer and the other Indigenous ghosts, and they thumped their torches on the ground, making the flames leap higher.

"You wait in the doorway," Halfday told them, "until you see me coming back with the ghastlight."

Yuri patted the hammer jutting from one of his pockets. "I will gladly smash it into a million pieces."

"Sameer, can you open the doors?" Callie asked as they walked up the ramp, their safety cables trailing after them on the rail.

"Lights off," Gabe reminded the others.

Sameer needed two different keys to unlock the heavy doors.

Gabe braced himself. As the doors swung open, the storm burst inside like a symphony gone mad. Pelting rain, howling wind and a clash of thunder. Framed in the open hatchway was the glittering night city, smeared by mist and rain. The ghastlight beam stabbed down from somewhere to the left of the hatch.

Very carefully Gabe stuck his head out into the wild night. The catwalk curved around the tower, jutting from the base of the sloped metal roof. To the left, ten metres along, was a fixed ladder that slanted up the roof to a platform. On this platform was the spotlight.

It was too bright to look at directly, but in the purple haze that hung about it, Gabe made out the splintered fingers of a massive hand – at the end of a very, very long arm – clenched around one of the lamp's handles. Viker was moving the beam to and fro from high above.

His hand, however, seemed unaware of Joseph Halfday creeping stealthily closer. Gabe prayed that Viker's eyes stayed focused on the city.

The wind raged around Joseph Halfday but did not buffet his body or shift even a hair on his head. Indeed, the ghastlight was making him bigger and taller before Gabe's eyes.

The ghost didn't need the ladder to reach the platform or the spotlight. He merely stretched out his arm, put his hand caressingly into the beam, then turned to look back at Gabe. Joseph Halfday's eyes were swirling pools of purple light – and Gabe realized they had made a terrible mistake.

"What's he waiting for?" Callie hissed beside him. "Why doesn't he just yank out the lens?"

Gabe should have realized how tempting it would be for a ghost to come so close to this new ghastlight. All that power! He saw the dreadful yearning in Joseph's face. Was he thinking about what he might become? All that he might *make happen*?

"We've lost him," Gabe breathed.

"Do you want me to blast him?" said Yuri, taking aim.

But then Joseph Halfday shook his head, as if clearing away unwholesome thoughts. His hand seized the ghastlight and pulled it from its mount. In the blink of an eye, the spotlight lost its fiendish colour. Joseph rushed back toward the hatch with his prize.

He only made it halfway.

Viker's massive hand seized his ankle. Thrashing, Joseph was plucked into the air. A blast from Yuri severed Viker's wrist, and Joseph fell back to the catwalk. In a heartbeat three more long limbs darted down and snatched him up again.

"Gabe, get the ghostlight in!" Callie was shouting.

Fighting his terror, Gabe plunged onto the catwalk. The entire city swelled before him. Car alarms and sirens welled up from the streets; he saw fires. The wind plastered his suit against his body, drove his hair into his eyes, deafened him. The width of a city sidewalk was all that lay between him and the edge of the universe.

He fought his way toward the untended spotlight. The beams

of three light launchers lanced overhead, striking at the arms that lifted Joseph Halfday higher and higher. Each time one of Viker's limbs was melted, a new one sprouted in its place.

In a flash of lightning, Nicholas Viker was suddenly illuminated. Standing astride the tower's SkyPod, he was already so much bigger than he'd been on the island. He was a colossus of the dead, built from countless devoured souls and strengthened by the ghastlight. His head looked helmeted with horns – and Gabe's stomach churned queasily when he realized the horns were actually the twisted and sharpened bodies of other ghosts, their outstretched arms frozen in torment.

In the volley of light launcher beams, Gabe saw Joseph Halfday being lifted toward Viker's vast mouth. Before he was devoured, Joseph hurled the ghastlight with all his might. It flashed purple as it disappeared out over the lake. Then Joseph was gone.

Sick with guilt and fear, Gabe reached the ladder to the spotlight. As he grabbed for the rungs, an icy blow knocked him off his feet. He sailed off the catwalk. It was all too fast to feel any fear. His safety line held fast, and he went flying along the rail, his feet swinging over empty air.

He hurtled away from Callie and Yuri, losing sight of them around the tower's curve. At last he slowed, got his feet back down on the catwalk and staggered to a stop.

Battered by the storm, he stood unsteady and alone. He patted his pocket and was relieved to feel the outline of the ghostlight. He didn't dare take it out, even though he was blind to ghosts without it.

His skin crawled. If there was anything worse than seeing Viker, it was *not* seeing Viker.

Clumsily he began to run, skidding on the slick metal, dragging his safety line after him. He needed to get back to his friends, to the spotlight. He was defenceless out here. With every step his terror grew. His breath was ragged as he waited for another invisible smack – or worse, the cold plunge of Viker's hand into his heart.

Another flash of lightning, and through the grilled catwalk he saw what no one should ever see: hundreds of enraged ghosts scaling the sheer walls of the CN Tower.

He sped up. He could see Yuri and Callie now, fighting their way toward the unmanned spotlight. Their beams scorched Viker's spectral flesh again and again but did nothing to slow his attacks. Gabe ran with all his speed, arms churning to keep balance on the slippery catwalk.

"They're coming up the tower!" he shouted to his friends.

He reached the ladder and hauled himself up the slanted roof to the platform. There were railings around it, at least. Raindrops hissed on the spotlight's hot surface. He unzipped his pocket and pulled out the ghostlight.

"Cover Gabe!" he heard Yuri shout from below, and a protective mesh of light launcher beams closed around him.

His hand trembled with the wind, with pure terror.

He slotted the ghostlight into the metal frame and immediately the beam disappeared. Gabe knew that within the lamp, the light was building behind the lens. The heat coming off the metal was so intense he worried it would melt.

"Come on, go!" he shouted. "Go!"

In flashes of lightning, and the blaze of light launchers, Gabe saw countless ghosts seep up over the edges of the catwalk. He saw Mary Sawyer and her Mississauga allies fight them back. He saw Viker swat Yuri against the sloped roof, the light launcher jolted from his grip. And he saw Callie lifted into the air like a rag doll, screaming and kicking. Only her safety tether kept her from being carried higher.

At last an amber beam exploded from the ghostlight.

The storm-shredded sky glittered gold; the skyscrapers glowed as if burnished with a sunrise.

In all its centuries, the ghostlight had never burned brighter.

Gabe seized the spotlight's handles and trained it on Viker. The beam sliced through the arm that clutched Callie. Like a rotted branch, the spectral limb fell away in a torrent of fireworks.

Callie landed hard on the catwalk but didn't miss a beat. She snatched up Yuri's fallen light launcher just before the wind blew it over the edge, and tossed it back to him. Together, she and Yuri turned their beams on the ghosts flooding up from below, helping George Brown and their Mississauga allies.

"Where is the light?" the fiends wailed.

"Bring back that beautiful light!"

"*Give it back!*"

Gabe angled the ghostlight higher, toward the summit of the CN Tower and the vast body of Nicholas Viker. With the searing amber light, he blasted at the clawed limbs that surged toward him and his friends. From every wound, liberated ghosts rocketed free like Roman candles. They disappeared into the night so quickly that Gabe couldn't see who they were. Was his father among them? Rebecca? What if he never saw her again?

But Gabe also knew that every ghost he set free made Viker weaker. And without the ghastlight to feed and strengthen him, Viker slowly began to wither.

Hope surged through Gabe's veins. When Viker tried to move out of range around the tower, Gabe aimed at his chest, and impaled him. In vain Viker tried to pull free, but this new amber light was too powerful. With his long limbs, he wildly began to snatch up the ghosts scaling the tower. These ghosts, who'd come to serve him, he now crammed into his mouth by the fistful. In dismay Gabe saw Viker swell again – and start to pull free from his beam.

"Gabe!" he heard Yuri shout.

From the corner of his eye he saw Viker's dark fist plunging toward him. He blasted it, saving himself and the spotlight, but a second limb sprouted from the severed hand. It pounded the platform and gave it such a twist that Gabe tumbled right off.

Away from the ghostlight.

He hit the catwalk, the breath knocked out of him. Before he could stand, Viker battered the catwalk until a segment ripped loose and went spinning down.

Gabe fell with it. His safety line caught him, and he dangled from the rail, a thousand feet over nothingness.

"Listen to me!" Rebecca cried into the whirlpool of darkness and wailing. "Listen, all who can hear me! You still exist; you still have energy, you are still very much *here*! We are prisoners inside the fiend who ate us! But we are still *ourselves*! And was there ever a prison that could not be escaped?"

She knew she didn't have much time. With every moment she would become more like the other poor souls trapped here, confused and despairing. Nothing but an endless echo of pain. What strength she had, she had to use now.

"Rebecca Strand?"

Where this faint voice came from, she couldn't tell. But it was familiar.

"Yes! Yes, it's me, Rebecca! Who are you?"

"Joseph Halfday!"

"Oh!" Her ember of hope was quick to sputter. If Joseph Halfday had been devoured by Viker, had all the others, too? Including Gabriel?

"We are fighting Nicholas Viker!" Joseph Halfday said. "As we speak we are in battle! I took the ghastlight away from him, but that is the last thing I know."

"Everyone, please listen!" Rebecca cried. "There are brave ghosts fighting to free us. We must help them!"

She felt as though the wailing storm abated somewhat. Was this expectation she felt? Were some ghosts actually listening to her?

"There are so many of us here," Joseph Halfday said. "Shall we work together?"

"Yes," came one faint, faraway voice.

Then a second: "Yes!"

More loudly: *"Yes, let us work together!"*

"I still have some strength in me!" Rebecca cried. "All of you do. So let's strain and push and fight, *as one,* to escape! Viker is using us for our energy. To move himself and strike and hit. I feel my body pushed and pulled in directions against my will. *Resist!* If you feel pushed one way, push the other! Push back! *Fight!*"

The dark, howling symphony calmed altogether, and spoke as one. "Fight!"

"Push back!"

"Resist!"

"Escape!"

"Escape! Escape! Escape!"

"Swing over to us, Gabe!" Callie shouted from her intact section of the catwalk.

"Pump like you're on a swing!" Yuri hollered.

"Protect the ghostlight!" Gabe shouted back.

He knew what Viker could do to it. Close a cold fist around it and squeeze. Crack it, and the ghostlight would become another *ghast*light.

Immediately, Yuri and Callie trained their light launchers on the spotlight, trying to fend off any spectral limbs that neared it. Gabe began to swing, but not for the safety of the catwalk. He strained for the sloping roof and the ladder that would take him back to the twisted platform – and the spotlight.

In a flash of lightning, he saw Viker's massive claw-shaped hand hanging directly above him. It stretched itself into long nimble fingers. It reached for the metal clasp that held him to the safety rail.

"He's going to unclip me!" Gabe shouted.

Inside the dreadful void, Rebecca felt herself being stretched, and she imagined herself straining to grab hold of something precise. This action, she knew, was the will of Viker.

So she fought it.

With all her might and fury she pulled in the opposite direction.

Helplessly Gabe watched as his friends' light launchers struck Viker's hand. Though the infernal flesh smoked and shredded, the nimble fingers still worked away, unfastening his safety clasp.

Suddenly the fingers went limp. Viker's hand dangled at the wrist, shook uncontrollably for a second, then rapidly withdrew.

Gabe had no idea what had happened, and he didn't care. He pumped toward the roof and grabbed hold of the ladder. He hauled himself up the rungs to the platform. It slanted at a crazy angle now, but he wrapped his legs around the metal column that supported the spotlight and grabbed hold of the handles.

The ghostlight was his once more. He angled it high, searching for Viker's head. Within the monstrous body, Gabe noticed a weird churning. Deep inside this fiend, things were pushing against him more than usual. Limbs jutted and retracted and flailed as if in rebellion.

"It's like he can't control himself!" Callie cried.

And Gabe thought: Rebecca.

He thought of all her power and anger, charged by the ghast-light, and trapped inside Viker. She would not stand for captivity. He imagined her ferocious face and grinned.

"There must be some part of him that's weakest!" Yuri shouted. "A heart?"

"What heart?" Callie yelled.

"The head, then!" said Gabe, because he'd finally found it, and it was somehow pouring itself down the slope of his body, like a T. rex head on an escalator, jaws wide, ready to feed.

"Aim at the head!" Gabe shouted. "You too, George Brown. Join your beams with mine!"

Four beams became one and blasted away Viker's mouth. *There*, thought Gabe, *he can't feed any more!* But a new mouth opened raggedly in another part of his head as it surged toward them. They sheared off the top of his horned skull. Still the head plunged closer.

Gabe felt a cold grip on his shoulder and looked into the urgent face of Martha Sawyer.

"*Inaabiwin!*" she shouted.

Gabe shook his head, not understanding.

"Inaabiwin!" She pointed up to the flickering sky, then pushed Gabe hard toward the ladder.

He clung to the rungs, bewildered—

Until, a second later, lightning struck the spotlight. It poured out through the amber lens in two jagged forks. Each struck Viker in one of his terrible whirlpool eyes. Amber light poured from his ears, his nostrils, his ragged mouth – and his head swelled, then exploded. What remained of his skull fell like spectral meteorites, disintegrating long before they reached the ground.

Vents and craters opened now in his headless body, spewing not blood but prismatic eruptions of light. The freed ghosts arched high over the city, more glorious than any fireworks Gabe had ever seen.

27

The storm lost its breath. The rain eased to a drizzle. The harbour stilled. The battering lake pulled back from the shores. Between the scudding clouds a moon appeared.

"The other ghosts are fleeing!" Yuri cried out happily.

"No wonder!" Gabe said. "After Viker started eating them!"

Back at the ghostlight, he helped clear away the very last of them as Yuri and Callie and their ghost allies made a full circuit of the catwalk.

"Did we lose anyone?" Callie asked when they'd finished.

George Brown appeared in the pale glow of his own light launcher.

"Only Joseph Halfday. Everyone else is still with us."

"Good, that's good," said Gabe in relief. "And Viker, do you think we got all of him? Every last bit?"

"The way he exploded, we must've!" said Yuri.

"Mr Brown," Gabe said, "do you see any sign of him?"

"We've been looking," George Brown replied. "And see nothing! I believe, my boy, that we've truly and finally done it!"

Gabe allowed himself a deep breath; what felt like his first in a very long time. He'd never quite forgotten that he was perched on a crooked piece of metal, a thousand feet above the ground, but now it struck him with full force. He tried not to look down. Thank heavens he was still attached to the safety rail at least.

"Come back over here, Gabe," Yuri urged him from their safe section of the catwalk.

"We need to take out the ghostlight," Gabe said, "but it's too hot to touch."

"Allow me," said George Brown, and he joined Gabe on the platform and slid the amber lens from the spotlight. It glowed as if it had just come from a furnace. "I'll hold it till it cools down."

Gabe aimed the spotlight back up at the sky, where its white beam reflected off the underbelly of the thinning clouds and brightened the entire city.

He climbed down the ladder, but there was no catwalk underneath anymore, so he needed to swing himself over to Yuri and Callie. They waited at the edge with outstretched arms, grabbed him and hauled him into a tight hug. They were all drenched and bruised and utterly exhausted.

Gabe looked over Callie's shoulder to watch the last of the spectral fireworks fade from the sky.

"Is that it?" he asked. "Did they all just disappear? All the ghosts inside him?"

Joseph Halfday. Keeper Strand. His own father. Rebecca.

"I don't know," Yuri said. "But let's get inside."

Sameer was waiting for them at the hatchway, staring like they'd stepped from the pages of a comic book. "That. Was. *Insane*."

"Glad you enjoyed it, Sameer," Callie said. "Could you unhook us, please?"

Inside, Gabe angled one of the light launchers so its palest beam lit the area around the hatchway. As he unbuckled and unzipped himself from his suit, he kept his eye on the light and saw the Mississauga fishermen returning from the catwalk. He thanked each one as he'd heard Rebecca do, *chi-miigwech*, especially Martha Sawyer, who had saved him from being struck by lightning.

When the last fisherman entered the tower, he was speaking excitedly in Anishinaabemowin to his friends, pointing outside. His excitement seemed happy rather than fearful.

"Mr Brown," asked Gabe, "do you know what he's saying?"

George Brown hurried into the light at the same moment as Joseph Halfday. The two ghosts embraced and burst into tears.

"My dear friend," said George Brown. "I feared I would not see you again."

Joseph Halfday gave Brown's domed forehead an affectionate rub. "Thank you for freeing me!"

"I was a small part of that effort," Brown said, nodding to everyone in the room, visible and invisible.

"Being trapped inside that monster was not something I would wish on my worst enemy," Halfday remarked.

"Did you see Rebecca?" Gabe asked him.

"See her? No. But I *heard* her. She called us all to arms, every ghost locked inside. Told us to resist! To fight back!"

"I knew it!" Gabe said to Callie and Yuri. "When Viker was about to unclip me, remember, his body went all weird."

"Like it was at war with itself," added Yuri.

"So you helped free yourselves," Brown told Joseph Halfday. "Whenever that fiend faltered, we were all able to strike with twice the speed!" He held the ghostlight out to Gabe. "And without this, we certainly would have been lost. I believe it's cooled down now."

"Thanks," Gabe said, grateful to have the amber lens back in his own hands.

The other ghosts crowded into view to embrace Joseph Halfday. Gabe wondered if they were welcoming him back – or bidding him farewell.

"Is he moving on to a new place?" he asked George Brown.

Joseph Halfday must have heard his question, because he turned and said, "I will stay here." He nodded at his people. "We have been here a long time, and we have been patient, but I want to stay until we are seen and heard better than before."

Gabe caught Sameer watching everything with astonishment, and then the security guard pointed to the open hatchway.

"Who the heck's this?" he asked.

A girl in a nightgown, woollen shawl and boots stepped inside.

Gabe rushed to her. Their hands reached for each other and clasped. His vision frosted over and she shone before him as the real world dimmed. The clasp used to be alarming, but now he welcomed it, this feeling that it was just the two of them. No matter how many other people might be in the room.

"Thank you," she said.

"I think you saved my life," he said, and told her what had happened outside.

She smiled. "I might have done that, yes."

Gone was the furious, frightening energy that had animated her face when the ghastlight struck it.

"Was it terrible, inside?" he asked.

She nodded gravely. "My stay was short, at least."

"Unlike some others," said a voice behind her.

In the lighted hatchway stood a tall man with a craggy face and thick eyebrows. His wracked body looked like someone who had endured unimaginable suffering, and yet his face beheld Rebecca with utmost joy.

"Father!"

Gabe felt their clasp break so she could run to Keeper Strand and throw herself into his waiting arms.

"Did you hear me?" she asked him. "Inside?"

"I did. At first I thought it must be another hallucination to torment me. Your voice was the sweetest thing I'd ever heard."

Gabe watched as they talked and told their stories.

"It was my fault that you died that night with me," he said mournfully, and all his years showed themselves in his lined face. "I am so sorry, Rebecca. I should not have brought you with me to the lighthouse."

"No," she said with force. "It was the greatest moment of my life. I would not have it otherwise. Not for anything in the world. It was the night you agreed to let me be Keeper. My eternal regret is that it will never come to pass."

Keeper Strand smiled – perhaps the first smile he'd made in almost two hundred years.

"Not so, my dear," he said. "Look at what you've achieved. You've served the light. With your friends, you have destroyed one of the greatest enemies of the Order, the most powerful of the wakeful and wicked dead." He gripped his daughter's hands tightly in his own. "Keeper Rebecca Strand."

She did not speak, only pushed her face harder into her father's chest, her tears shining in the light.

Gabe watched the two of them with a forlorn ache in his throat. He'd freed his own father, at least. That was some comfort, even if he'd never have a proper chance to say goodbye. He hadn't the first time, either. Gabe could only hope that wherever his father was now, it would be better than the insides of Nicholas Viker.

"Thank you, all of you," Keeper Strand said to everyone in the room. "I feel a strange, but welcome, pull on me."

"Yes," Rebecca said. "Viker delayed you from your longer journey. You have no reason to stay here, Papa."

"I must go, but I have a feeling you will follow."

"I will. Soon, I promise."

Keeper Strand stroked the cheek of his daughter one last time, and then every particle of his body became coloured light and streamed through the hatchway into the night sky.

Rebecca watched until her father's light could no longer be

seen, then turned back to Gabe. He was glad when she clasped his hand again.

"Will you really go?" he asked her.

"I'm not sure I have a choice."

"Maybe you don't have to go right away?" he suggested.

"I was only ever here so I could free my father."

Gabe nodded. "I'm glad you got to see him again."

"And you yours," she said.

He looked at her in confusion, then saw someone standing just behind her in the hatchway.

His father's head was still bent over his phone, which he held clutched against his chest like it was the most important thing in the universe. Gabe felt a deep stab of disappointment. After everything, Dad was still locked in the same faraway state.

He felt Rebecca's hand on his back, giving him a gentle shove. Slowly he approached his dad. He was close enough, finally, to read the phone's screen. This message that had consumed all his father's attention just before death, and forever after. It turned out it wasn't a text message.

"You died making a restaurant reservation?" Gabe said sadly. "It makes sense, I guess. Food and Pauline: that's what you cared about most."

His father looked up. For the first time his gaze was firmly and lucidly on his son.

"It was for you and me."

Gabe glanced back at the screen and noticed the name of the

restaurant; it was the one they'd often visited as a family, when he was younger.

"I thought we could have lunch, just the two of us," his father said.

"That would've been nice, maybe," Gabe said warily. He felt like he was being nudged toward an emotion he wasn't ready for yet, and he dug in his heels. He reminded himself of all those awful, empty conversations he'd had most recently with his father. "You really think that would've fixed everything?"

"Fixed? What needs fixing?" Dad looked genuinely confused. "I went away for a while – is that what you mean? – but now I'm back and we can see a lot more of each other. I love you plenty, Gabe."

Those familiar words from his father might have unlocked him, but they were just words that even a budgie could repeat endlessly.

"*Did* you, though, Dad, really?"

Gabe's use of the past tense struck his father like a blow – as if only now did he fully realize he was dead. That all his chances were behind him, and there could be no more.

"Of course I did! You can't have doubted that. Please tell me you didn't."

There was true despair in his voice. Within Gabe, a fault line opened in the bedrock of his anger.

"I hated you. So much."

His father's face filled with such unfathomable sorrow that Gabe instinctively took his hand. Their grip was icy and seemed to carry a current of all Dad's confusion and regret. And finally Gabe told him everything he'd felt in those days after he left, all his loneliness and sadness and rejection. Silently his father listened.

"I'm so sorry, Gabe," he said afterward. "You're right, I was a lousy father – but I wasn't always, was I?"

His pleading tone made Gabe ashamed. In that moment he realized how unfair he'd been.

"No," he said, "you weren't. You were a good father. I have so many good memories."

Some of the anguish left his father's face. But Gabe sensed there was something more that his father needed from him. He recognized the look from William Ward, from some of the people at the séance.

"I forgive you, Dad." Gabe hugged him as best he could. His father's head and neck were only empty air, yet Gabe was sure he caught the scent of his shaving cream.

"Thank you, Gabe."

"I want you to go somewhere good, Dad."

"Me too."

"Somewhere with a really great kitchen."

His father smiled back. For the last time, they told each other "I love you." Then his father lifted a hand in farewell and, like a comet, he sped from the room. Gabe's heart shared some of that same weightlessness. He felt Yuri's arm around his shoulder, giving him a squeeze.

"So, this is very emotional stuff," Sameer said, "but there's cops downstairs and they want to come up."

"Not yet," said Callie.

"Probably we're going to jail," said Yuri, quite cheerfully. "If I am in jail, my family will not be able to return to Russia."

"No one is going to jail," said Sameer, standing tall in his baggy uniform. "Not if I have anything to do with it. This was my watch, and I'm responsible for letting you guys up here. If anyone takes the fall, it's me."

Gabe looked at the security guard, astonished at this new boldness.

"Anyway, you guys are freaking heroes. I saw it! You nuked that humongous ghost dude. You deserve a parade! I'm telling this story, even if they think I'm a lunatic!"

"Actually, Sameer," said Callie, "it's my story to tell. Ghost blogger, remember?"

"Oh. Yeah. OK. But what am I going to tell the cops?"

"Tell them the spotlight went crazy in the storm. Hurricane winds ripped off part of the catwalk. You were all alone up here. We were never here."

"How're you going to get out?" the security guard asked.

"We'll take the stairs."

Once more, Gabe felt Rebecca's cool clasp. He knew what she was about to say.

"Does it have to be now?" he asked. He tried desperately to think of something else to make her stay. "If you go, who's going to be Keeper?"

"You'll be here."

"Me?"

"And Yuri and Callie. There will be others like Viker."

"Hey, that's not fair. Why can't you help us?"

"Gabriel, I am tired. I am almost two hundred years old!"

"But we're not Keepers!"

"After all you've done? Of course you are."

Haltingly Gabe said, "I guess I would just rather you *didn't* go. Don't go."

She placed her palms gently against his chest and tilted her face up to kiss him. It was the most astonishing thing Gabe had ever experienced. All that tingling energy that had often coursed between their hands now electrified the surface of his lips and spread across his flushed face, down his shoulders and arms, his torso, to every bit of his body. When their mouths parted he had no idea how much time had passed. All he knew was that he wanted more.

"Goodbye, Gabriel," she said.

He knew it was pointless to argue. "Bye."

She came apart in brilliant specks of light and blazed a path across the night sky. He stared after her a long time. When he turned, Yuri and Callie were watching him sympathetically. He realized they were holding hands.

He gave a surprised laugh and said to Yuri, "Who was it who said, 'We are not the kind of boys who have girlfriends'?"

"A-ha," said Yuri. "I was wrong, it seems. What was it like, kissing a dead person?"

"Yuri!" Callie said, smacking him on the arm.

"It was great," said Gabe. "Wish we'd done it sooner."

Sameer said, "Guys, the police are sounding pretty ticked off. Can I send down the elevator?"

"Just let us grab all our gear," Callie said, "and give us a head start. Thanks, Sameer!"

They made their goodbyes to George Brown, Joseph Halfday and their other ghost allies; then Callie led them to the stairwell.

As they started down, she asked, "Do you guys want to know how many steps the CN Tower has?"

"Oh my goodness, let me guess, please," said Yuri. He mumbled some quick calculations to himself. "Sixteen hundred!"

"So close! One thousand seven hundred and seventy-six."

Gabe smiled and asked, "How do you guys feel about what Rebecca said? About us being Keepers?"

Yuri spiked up his hair. "I am in *high school*! I do not have any more time for extracurriculars."

Callie snorted. "My parents don't even want me to be a *journalist*. A member of a secret order of lighthouse keepers? That's going to be a hard sell. Still." She swayed her head side to side. "It would be a super-cool job."

"This is not a job," said Yuri. "No salary, no union, no benefits. Anyway, how can we be Keepers without a lighthouse?"

"You solved that problem," Gabe said. "Who needs a lighthouse when you have a light launcher? You always wanted to make a genius invention, and you did."

Yuri grinned, pleased. "You think so?"

"Absolutely, my friend."

"Well, maybe we could be Keepers part-time, in secret," Yuri suggested. "But only if all three of us are going to do it."

Gabe looked from Yuri to Callie, then nodded. "I think we're all in agreement."

He patted his pocket to make sure the ghostlight was still there. Then, out of habit, he pulled out his phone, even though it hadn't buzzed. He felt a stab of loss, knowing that he would never again receive messages from Rebecca Strand.

But when he glanced at the screen, he saw that she'd left one behind for him.

It was a heart emoji.

28

"My family always overdoes it," Callie said to Gabe.

There was so much food they'd needed two picnic tables to spread it all out.

"Are you kidding?" Gabe said. "This looks amazing."

His father would have approved of the cosmopolitan buffet. Gabe and his mom had brought a big moussaka (he hoped they'd salted the eggplant enough) and a Greek salad; Yuri's parents had brought pelmeni dumplings, an Olivier salad, and a plov with rice, carrots and raisins. And Callie's family had provided the rest: there were all sorts of curries, and bhaji fritters, and spicy sausages, and croquettes (from the Ferreira side of the family), and lots of very tidy crustless sandwiches (from the Strand side).

"We'll never eat all this," Callie said.

"There are a lot of us," Yuri pointed out, looking at the crowd of guests, most of whom were Callie's siblings and aunts and uncles and cousins.

She sighed. "I'm embarrassed by how many dentists there are here."

"Not to mention the orthodontists and periodontists," Gabe added.

"Oh, shut up," she said with a laugh.

A week ago, Gabe had asked his mom if they could have Callie and Yuri over for dinner. And Mom had said, "Why not their parents, too? I'd love to meet them." And when Callie had invited *her* mom and dad, *they'd* said, "Yes, how lovely, but why doesn't everyone just come to our end-of-summer picnic?" And so it was finally agreed that all three families would meet on the island. The location had been Gabe's idea.

It had been two weeks since the battle at the CN Tower. Amazingly, they'd made it down all those stairs and outside without being noticed by the police. At Gabe's place, they'd had enough time to get a couple of hours' sleep, wash up, grab a quick breakfast and make sure Callie left before Gabe's mom returned from her hospital shift.

The light launchers were safely hidden in the back of his closet, wrapped in old clothes, ready when they were needed. And the ghostlight rested inside a cast-iron pot that no ghost could see through, or touch.

All the damage to the Gibraltar Point Lighthouse, to the CN Tower, to the island and the entire city, was explained away by the freak storm.

None of them went to jail.

And so life had gone back to . . . normal*ish*. Callie kept giving tours of the CN Tower, and working on her blog, and her entry for the writing contest. And Yuri and Gabe kept working at the amusement park. Once, while he was giving his tour beside the lighthouse, his phone had vibrated, and he'd yanked it from his pocket, hoping it was Rebecca. It wasn't. Just like all the other times it had pinged.

Gabe looked around at the happy chaos of the picnic. People were starting to crowd around the buffet with paper plates. A big splotch of curry had already fallen onto the grass. A small person was crying because she'd spilled an entire bottle of ginger ale down her front. Gabe spotted Yuri's little brother, Leo, tearing around with some of Callie's cousins. A grown-up was telling them to get some food. Callie's father talked to Yuri's father; and there was his mom, talking with Yuri's mom, who was smoking and gesturing animatedly and laughing, all at the same time.

He could tell Mom had been a little confused when she'd seen Callie holding hands with Yuri – she'd been so convinced Callie was *his* girlfriend. But she didn't say anything.

And Gabe was also relieved she hadn't brought her new boyfriend with her – even though Gabe had said it was OK. "Far too early for that," Mom had replied. But she'd seemed happier lately, and that made Gabe happy too. He wished his brother Andrew had been able to make it, because he definitely felt a bit out-familied here.

"So you guys ready to meet my parents?" Callie asked.

"Yes, of course," said Yuri. He did a quick rummage of his hair, and Callie patted it back down.

"It'll be fine," she told him.

"I am a bit of an oddball," he said.

"Yes, but you're *my* kind of oddball. Relax, they already like you."

When the three of them walked over, they got a very warm

greeting from Callie's parents. There was praise for the food they'd brought, some questions about their summer jobs, starting school again, and – from Mr Ferreira – an inquiry about their future goals.

"Dentistry for me," Gabe told him.

"For me as well," Yuri said.

"Serves you right for asking, Dad!" Callie said as everyone laughed, including her father.

"Nicely done," Mr Ferreira said, and then to Yuri: "But I happen to know your passion is engineering, like your father here."

"This is true," Yuri admitted.

"And he was just telling me the wonderful news about his certification."

"The English lessons, they helped!" Mr Baranov said jovially. "But the best teacher was my Yuri."

Gabe smiled. When Yuri had called to tell him, a few days ago, he'd sounded so happy and relaxed – even as Leo had wailed "Legos!" in the background. Gabe had felt a weight of his own lifted too: he wouldn't be losing his best friend.

"Engineering is a very fine profession," Mr Ferreira was saying now, and Gabe caught Callie's eye roll.

"I agree," said Yuri. "But there are many fine professions. Being a journalist or writer, for instance."

Gabe said, "Did you see how many followers Callie has for her blog now?"

"Ten thousand and forty-three," said Callie's mother, giving Gabe a smile that somehow seemed familiar.

He realized that she had the same eyes as Rebecca Strand, the same shape and colouring. Which wasn't so extraordinary, since Callie's mother was a Strand herself – in fact, she was Rebecca's niece, with a lot of *greats* in front of it. It made him feel immediately fond of her.

"Summer goal achieved," Callie said, clearly pleased. "It was all because of my last post."

"An extraordinary story," her mother said.

Gabe wondered if she'd ever realize the story *wasn't* made up. He'd read it himself several times. It was their story – his and Callie's and Yuri's, and Rebecca's of course – or the very beginning of it, at least. (It was too long for one short story.) Callie had changed the names and written it like fiction. She'd told him it was the piece she'd decided to enter in the contest. Even if she didn't win a prize, Gabe had an inkling that her mother, at least, might be coming around to the idea of letting Callie go to journalism school.

After a while he excused himself to get some food, and walked off a little way, to see if he could catch a glimpse of the lighthouse. As usual, it was elusive, hidden away by trees.

He was thinking about Rebecca Strand's eyes.

When he felt a cold clasp on his shoulder, he choked back a yelp. His vision frosted at the edges. Beside him stood George Brown with his sideburns and ink-stained cuffs.

"What a fascinating gathering!" said Brown. "Many families from many places brought together for the first time. And so many strong personalities! It seems everything's working out splendidly."

"Thanks for doing those favours for me," Gabe said.

"Oh, it was nothing. I was glad to do it. It turned out Mr Baranov's certification papers were misfiled – it happens all too often, believe me – so I merely floated them over to the proper desk and put them at the very top of the right pile. And now, justly, he is an engineer again."

"You've made his family so happy."

"As for Callie's blog – that's the right word, isn't it, *blog*; such an ugly word – as for her number of followers, well, I hardly needed to do anything at all. She already had almost ten thousand! I gave her a few extra clicks to put her over the top. A tremendous story, by the way. That girl has talent."

"I'll tell her you said so."

"Please do. Well, I should be off. I'm a busy man. Goodbye for now, Gabriel. I know we'll be talking again before long."

And the ghostly journalist disappeared.

"What are you doing alone over here?" Yuri asked, walking over with his plate. "Are you brooding over Rebecca?"

"Nah," said Gabe, smiling at his friend's old-fashioned choice of words.

"You are lying. She was a wonderful person. But she was also dead. You will have to make better choices next time."

"Shut up, Yuri!"

"You will see. This year at school you will meet a living girl and things will go much better for you."

They were both laughing now. Yuri clapped him on the shoulder and said, "Well, brood a little more, but come back soon, there are a lot of people who want to compliment your moussaka."

Gabe didn't wait long. The afternoon sun was casting its long light across the harbour and the city; the breeze had a wistful freshness that signalled the end of the summer. But as he walked back to the noisy picnic, toward all the families, toward his excellent friends, he felt like there were a lot of things, just beginning.

What remained of Nicholas Viker was next to nothing.

Just a tiny, greasy stain in the shadows at the base of the CN Tower. It might have been mistaken for a bit of graffiti.

The truth was, however, that there was still a bit of life left in Nicholas Viker. Or a bit of *death*. He had seeped into the pores of the concrete and was incapable of moving. He had no eyes, so couldn't see. But he could somehow hear the voice that spoke to him now.

"You're looking quite poorly, sir, if you don't mind me saying."

It was without a doubt the voice of Tommy Flynn.

Viker had no mouth, so he couldn't reply. He could not curse Flynn for his insolence. He could not beg for help.

"Goodness me, there's not much left of you, is there?" said Tommy Flynn. "But I'd recognize you anywhere! It *is* remarkable, isn't it, how things do come around. Why, not so long ago, things were very bad for me. Do you remember? I had a great *hole* through my middle! Ho ho! What *fun*! And then, a talkative Scottish fellow blew my head off with a pistol! But here's something wonderful, sir. I'm not boring you, am I? You'd tell me if I was. Just make a sign."

Viker could not see or speak, but he could still feel fury. A little bit of his stained self - was it a hand? - twitched on the concrete.

"Oh, I did see that, sir, that little *spasm*! I'll take that as a no and carry on! Well, after I lost my head in that tunnel, I floated up and out and there I was at the bottom of the harbour! I was resting, quite peaceful, having a nice long think, and then suddenly *plop*, your ghastlight sank down right beside me. How it got there, I couldn't tell you. Do you know, sir?"

Tommy Flynn cocked his head and waited politely.

"You seem to be having trouble speaking, sir. It's all right. So there I was at the bottom of the lake and the ghastlight was angled just so. And a bit of moonlight passed through it and warmed me. You probably know the feeling, sir. Wasn't long before I was right as rain! Strong as ever! I took the ghastlight with me on my way to the surface and had a nice little wander. And here we are, sir! Reunited! It really is wonderful to see you, sir."

Viker couldn't see what happened next, but Tommy Flynn opened his mouth and inhaled him.

"That was very satisfying. Yum. Very satisfying indeed."

And Tommy Flynn carried on, invisible, through the twilight streets of the city, the ghastlight snug in his jacket pocket.

Acknowledgements

I would like to thank my earliest readers: Philippa Sheppard, Nathaniel Oppel, Kevin Sylvester, and Steven Malk. Many thanks also to: Christine Fischer-Guy for telling me about the verbal skills of budgies; Vera Brosgol for sharing her childhood experiences as a Russian immigrant; Bernadette Coren for sharing details of her mother's childhood Anglo Indian experience; and Darin P. Wybenga, Traditional Knowledge and Land Use Coordinator for the Mississaugas of the Credit First Nation, for being an authenticity reader for *Ghostlight*. Finally, I am very grateful to my editors Lynne Missen, Nancy Siscoe, and Bella Pearson, whose great suggestions have haunted many of my novels.

Kenneth Oppel is the bestselling author of numerous books, including *Airborn*, which won the Governor General's Award for children's literature and a Michael L Printz Honor Book Award, and the *Silverwing* trilogy, which has sold over a million copies worldwide. Some of his other books include *The Boundless, Every Hidden Thing*, and *Inkling. The Nest* and *Half Brother* both won the Canadian Library Association's Book of the Year for Children Award. His latest novels are *Bloom* and its sequels *Hatch* and *Thrive*. Kenneth lives in Toronto with his family. Visit him online at www.kennethoppel.ca or twitter @kennethoppel

GUPPY
BOOKS

Guppy Books is an independent children's publisher based in Oxford in the UK, publishing exceptional fiction for children of all ages. Small and responsive, inclusive and communicative, Guppy Books was set up in 2019 and publishes only the very best authors and illustrators from around the world.

From brilliantly funny illustrated tales for five-year-olds to inspiring and thought-provoking novels for young adults, Guppy Books promises to publish something for everyone. If you'd like to know more about our authors and books, go to the Guppy Aquarium on YouTube where you'll find interviews, drawalongs and all sorts of fun.

We hope that our books bring pleasure to young people of all ages, and also to the adults sharing these books with them. Children's literature plays a part in giving both young and old the resources and reflection needed to grow up in today's ever-changing world, and we hope that you enjoy this small piece of magic!

Bella Pearson
Publisher

www.guppybooks.co.uk